"Let's practice some more." Chance offered Caro his hand.

She nodded, her blond hair falling over one shoulder as she took his hand. He pulled her to her feet. In a moment she was up against him again.

Damn.

If she had any idea how it tortured him to have her pressing against him like she was, well, suffice it to say, she'd probably call off the rest of their self-defense lesson.

"Remember," he said into her ear. "Step, wedge, thrust."

He didn't give her time to comment, just wrapped an arm around her. She didn't hesitate this time, shoving her leg between his own, thrusting back, using such force that he didn't have to fake falling down.

He loved the way her eyes lit up with triumph.

"That was easy." She grinned.

"Let's do it again."

It was all he could do not to lean down and plant his lips on hers.

Her Cowboy Protector

**Pamela Britton &
Cathy Gillen Thacker**

Previously published as *The Ranger's Rodeo Rebel*
and *The Texas Lawman's Woman*

ISBN-13: 978-1-335-04183-8

Recycling programs for this product may not exist in your area.

Her Cowboy Protector

Copyright © 2019 by Harlequin Books S.A.

The Ranger's Rodeo Rebel
First published in 2016. This edition published in 2019.
Copyright © 2016 by Pamela Britton

The Texas Lawman's Woman
First published in 2013. This edition published in 2019.
Copyright © 2013 by Cathy Gillen Thacker

This edition published by arrangement with Harlequin Books S.A.

For questions and comments about the quality of this book, please contact us at CustomerService@Harlequin.com.

® and TM are trademarks of Harlequin Enterprises Limited or its corporate affiliates. Trademarks indicated with ® are registered in the United States Patent and Trademark Office, the Canadian Intellectual Property Office and in other countries.

Printed in U.S.A.

www.Harlequin.com

CONTENTS

THE RANGER'S RODEO REBEL   7
Pamela Britton

THE TEXAS LAWMAN'S WOMAN   223
Cathy Gillen Thacker

With more than a million books in print, **Pamela Britton** likes to call herself the best-known author nobody's ever heard of. Of course, that changed thanks to a certain licensing agreement with that little racing organization known as NASCAR. She's won numerous awards, including a National Readers' Choice Award and a nomination for the Romance Writers of America Golden Heart® Award.

When not writing books, Pamela is a reporter for a local newspaper. She's also a columnist for the *American Quarter Horse Journal*.

Books by Pamela Britton

Harlequin Western Romance

Cowboys in Uniform

Her Rodeo Hero
His Rodeo Sweetheart
The Ranger's Rodeo Rebel
Her Cowboy Lawman

Harlequin American Romance

Rancher and Protector
The Rancher's Bride
A Cowboy's Pride
A Cowboy's Christmas Wedding
A Cowboy's Angel
The Texan's Twins
Kissed by a Cowboy

Visit the Author Profile page at Harlequin.com for more titles.

THE RANGER'S
RODEO REBEL

Pamela Britton

For Josey Lynn and Bobbie Stone,
two of the most amazing trick riders in the rodeo
business, and women I'm proud to call my friends.

Chapter 1

It had turned into the day from hell.

"Come on." Carolina Cruthers patted the pockets of her jeans one last time. "Please tell me I didn't do what I think I did."

But her denim pants didn't hold the keys to her truck any more than her hands did, which meant she'd either lost them in the barn or they were somewhere inside her truck.

Dang it. She peered quickly around the parking area of Misfit Farms, her blond braids nearly slapping her in the face. The bright afternoon sun turned the farm's newly installed fence the same color as the new cars on Via Del Caballo's main drag: pristine white.

In truth, Carolina had no idea why she bothered to look around. She knew she'd dropped her keys somewhere in her truck. She'd done it enough times the past month it was a sure bet. Nobody would come to her rescue, either. Today was Monday. Misfit Farms was closed to clients and visitors. This was the day when she and her boss, Colt Reynolds, reviewed rodeo business. They had talked about their specialty act this morning, the upcoming schedule and any changes they needed to make after their weekend performance. Her boss had left earlier along with his wife, Natalie. There was nobody walking around the state-of-the-art horse facility.

Now what? She cupped her hands and peered through the truck's window. Her keys weren't in the ignition, so they were most likely—

On the floor.

Yep. Just beneath the edge of the driver's seat, glinting in the sun, sat the horseshoe charm Colt and Natalie had gotten her for Christmas. The charm lay on the black mat of her truck as if making fun of her dilemma. Lucky. Yeah, right.

She'd done it again. She'd locked her stupid keys in her dang truck. This was…what? The third time in the past month? And all because of…

James.

The reason for her absentmindedness settled into the pit of her stomach like a load of cement. She probably had a million texts on her phone right now, the same cell phone tucked inside her purse, the one resting on the bench seat in the rear of her vehicle.

Think.

She picked up a braid and absently started chewing—a habit of hers. Colt and Natalie wouldn't be back for at least an hour. That meant it was just her with no cell phone and no access to a landline unless the barn office was open or she broke into her boss's house. If that was the case, there was a phone upstairs in the abandoned apartment above the barn. Abandoned... but not for long.

That had been the other piece of news that had rattled her. Her boss had decided to stay home the rest of the season. Colt was putting his brother in charge of their rodeo specialty act. Chance Reynolds was the guy's name. A man who'd been out of the business for years. And yet Colt thought he'd be better suited to take over. Not fair. She'd been around longer. She'd put in years of blood, sweat and tears, not with Colt and the Galloping Girlz, but with another team. She'd even taken over when her friend Samantha had decided to run off with her movie-star boyfriend. Why Colt had decided to put some former Army Ranger in charge was beyond her, but it had seriously bummed her out.

Keys, she reminded herself. She wouldn't be able to go home and sulk unless she found her keys.

The walk to the main barn was a short one. The horses in the stalls hung their heads out to greet her. Hanoverians, Trakehners and other imported warm bloods mixed with the occasional Thoroughbred. They peeked at her curiously, ears pricked forward as if asking, "Food?"

"Not yet, guys," she said.

Carolina kind of understood why Colt had decided to sit out the rest of the rodeo season. His wife, Natalie, a famous hunter/jumper rider, with a waiting list of people wanting to train with her, was about to have a baby. The doctor had recently grounded her. Colt wanted to be around to help with the baby when it came. Someone needed to keep riding all the horses, and that was Colt. Carolina didn't blame him. She just couldn't stand the idea of some flatlander telling her what to do. It made no sense.

At the far end of the barn, near a patch of sunlight that nearly blinded her, was the office, its fancy French doors closed. She said a silent prayer heavenward and turned the handle.

It didn't move.

She rattled it some more, just in case, jiggling the door so hard dust fell from the sill above. The door wouldn't budge. Okay, fine. Up to the apartment she would go. No big deal. When she got home she'd pour herself a big glass of wine. Maybe even take a bath. It'd been forever since she'd had one of those.

The stairs to the apartment were outside at the back of the barn. It was a steep climb that had her heart thumping from the exertion of taking the steps two at a time, but her reward was a door handle that slid down easily. Carolina released a breath of relief and all but dived for the phone.

A man stood in front of her.

A tall man with black hair and green eyes and a face that resembled her boss so much she knew in an instant who he was.

Chance Reynolds.

And he was naked.

He should move, Chance thought, standing in the living area of his new home. He should, but he couldn't seem to make himself, because there was something so incredibly priceless about the look on the woman's face.

"Oh, my goodness, I'm so—"

The rest of what she'd been about to say was lost in her mad scramble to run away.

You would have thought he was naked. As he glanced down at himself he admitted she probably thought exactly that. He wore military-issue underwear that happened to be the same color as desert sand. In other words: nude.

"Hey, wait," he shouted. He grabbed the jeans he'd thrown over the back of the small couch.

"Really." He ran and tugged, ran and tugged, hopping and skipping as he headed for the door. The woman was already at the bottom of the steps by the time he poked his head outside, his pants still open at the zipper. "Stop."

She paused with her hand still on the rail. "I'd like to borrow your phone," she said without making eye contact.

"Hold on." He zipped up his jeans and glanced back inside his apartment for a shirt. He'd been extremely sleep deprived when his brother had dropped him off at three this morning, and he wasn't sure where anything was. His bag sat by the door, but he saw no sign of his shirt, not even on the floor of the tiny kitchen to the left of the door.

"Seriously," he called. "Come back up. I'm dressed."

She slowly faced him, her eyes looking anywhere but at him. When she peeked up and noticed he was shirtless, she immediately glanced away, her face turning red.

He laughed. "All right, I'm half-dressed."

"I just need to use the phone," she repeated.

"Feel free." The woman with twin blond braids took a deep breath, apparently weighing her options. Chance didn't mind. It gave him the opportunity to study her. She was slight of build and wearing jeans and a black shirt that hugged her curves and displayed the narrow width of her waist. He had a pretty good idea who she was. Carolina Cruthers. He'd seen her picture on his brother's website. Trick rider. His new employee.

She must have made up her mind, because she slowly climbed the stairs, her boots clunking up the wooden steps, the sound echoing off the roof of the covered arena a few dozen feet away.

"Need to call a tow company," she muttered on her way by.

He swung the door closed behind her. "If you're having car problems, I can take a look."

"No, thanks." She'd clearly been to the apartment before, because she walked straight to the phone in the kitchen.

"Thanks." She turned away from him, dialed a number. "Hi," he heard her all but whisper into the white handset. Curious, he followed her. Her gaze met his and she half turned away. "This is Carolina Cruthers. I—" She slapped her mouth closed and, judging by the way her full lips pressed together, she wasn't happy about what someone said on the other end. "Actually, yes, I did." She lowered her voice even more. "I'm at work." She gave an address, one he instantly recognized as his own. Well, it'd been his when he was a kid, growing up on Reynolds Ranch. He still owned fifty-plus acres to the east, part of his inheritance when his dad died. One day he would build there, but for now, he was ensconced in his brother's fancy barn.

"I'll be waiting." She hung up, lifted a hand in apology. "Sorry to bug you."

"How long before they get here?"

Her eyes dipped down, but not before he spotted the way they lingered on his chest. He supposed he should feel self-conscious standing in front of her half-naked, but he hadn't spent the last eight years of his life in the military, four of them as an Army Ranger, without learning how to be comfortable in his own skin.

"Half hour, they said. Maybe more."

"Locked your keys in your truck again?"

Her eyes widened in surprise, and he caught his first good look at their color. Light blue. The color of the sky first thing in the morning. The ring around the pupils so dark it made the lightness stand out. Some men might find her twin braids, worn jeans and dirty boots attractive, but he liked his women far more feminine.

"I guess Colt told you about me."

He'd been told the woman had been through a lot. He scanned her arms and her face. No sign of the bruises his brother had mentioned. He *did* notice, though, that for someone who tried to project toughness, she had a very fragile-looking face. Tiny chin. Small nose. High cheekbones, and skin as pale as the fresh snow that sometimes fell in the desert.

"He told me you were in a spot of trouble."

"That's one way of putting it," she said before tipping her chin up. "Thanks for letting me use your phone. I'll wait outside."

"No need." He spotted his shirt on the floor near the couch, up next to the wall. He must have shed his clothes on his way to bed. "Sit down and relax."

The words brought to mind a different image, one that had no business slipping into his thoughts, especially given what she'd just been through. *Especially* given where he'd just come from. Behind enemy lines. Fighting insurgents. Trying to survive. He still couldn't quite grasp he was home again.

Home to babysit the woman in front of him.

Because that's what it boiled down to. Truth was, his brother had been worried about his rodeo trick rider. Really worried. Concerned enough that he'd put Chance in charge of the rodeo act. Carolina had been acting funny, too, Colt had told him. Like locking her keys in her truck and forgetting portions of her routine. His brother had a feeling there was more to the breakup with her ex than she let on. He was pretty sure she was being stalked, not that she'd tell anyone anything. Typical cowgirl. They thought they could handle anything without a man's help.

"Thanks, but that's okay." She took a deep breath, and though she was tiny, she tried to make herself look ten feet tall by standing up straight. "I can wait outside." She turned to leave.

He cleared his throat. "I bet I can open the door of your truck long before a tow service gets here."

She paused with her hand on the door. "No, you can't."

"Yes, I can." Breaking into vehicles had been part of his military training. That, and a few other things she didn't need to know about. "Sixty seconds, maybe less."

"You think?"

"Just give me a knife."

"A knife?"

"That's all I need."

She didn't look convinced. "There's some utensils

in the kitchen drawers, I think, if you really want to give it a try."

Try? Army Rangers didn't just try. They *did*.

He moved forward. "Chance Reynolds."

She wiped her palms on the front of her jeans before saying, "Carolina Cruthers." She shook his hand.

She couldn't take her eyes off his chest, and the sight of her blushing, embarrassed and so clearly uncomfortable, gave him an odd sort of pleasure. It shouldn't. He wasn't back in the States to get involved with anyone. In a short time, he'd be back over there—the Middle East again—as a private contractor. Besides, relationships with cowgirls weren't his thing. He'd gone that route before, during his high school rodeoing days, but they were too independent for their own good. Drove him nuts.

"I'll meet you downstairs." She backed away, spun and exited the door like a horse bolting for the barn, which he supposed in a way she was.

Carolina Cruthers.

He tasted the name on his lips. She wasn't what he'd expected at all. The Carolina from the website had looked pretty enough, but he'd figured she'd be loud and crass and obnoxious. A cowgirl in overalls, a cowboy hat and with a piece of straw hanging out of her mouth. This Carolina was shy and innocent and, yes, *pretty*.

And as he listened to her feet fly down the steps, he couldn't decide if that was a good thing…or bad.

Chapter 2

Please let him find a shirt. Please let him find a shirt. Pleasepleasepleaseplease.

"You ready?"

She jumped.

He stared at her with concern. "Easy there, sparky." He smiled, his big strong jaw with its ridge of muscle along the bottom jutting out. "You'll give yourself a heart attack."

He wore a shirt. Thank God he wore a shirt. But for some reason, the sight of him with clothes on wasn't any better than the sight of him half-naked. Damn that Colt Reynolds. Why hadn't he told her he'd come home? Then again, maybe he had. Maybe she'd been so distracted by James's latest text she'd missed that tiny tidbit of information. It wouldn't surprise her. Not that it mattered. Nothing could have prepared her for the sight of Chance Reynolds in the flesh. Something about the man made her want to melt into the ground. Maybe it was his eyes. Or maybe it was his height and the way his bearing and short hair had the stamp of a military man. He was taller than Colt. His face was shaped differently, too. Chance was one of those guys who could easily be in films, with his sweeping brows and thick lower lip. He had scruff on his chin, too, and along the ridge of his jaw, a stain of color that turned his tan skin a darker brown. She'd taken one look at him and turned as stupidly speechless as a starstruck teen.

"Sorry." She forced a smile. "I'm a little jumpy today."

He gave her a look that she didn't quite understand, maybe because she had turned away too quickly. It had almost seemed like sympathy, although he had no reason to feel sorry for her…unless. Goodness, he didn't know about James, did he?

"Here." He headed toward her truck, holding what looked like a butter knife in his right hand. "Let's get you squared away."

He did know. Of course Colt had told him. Why wouldn't he? One of his employees had come to him battered, bruised and scared. The cops had been called. James had been arrested. Any responsible employer would share that news with a new employee.

Not an employee. His brother.

Whatever. But Colt didn't know about the threats that had been coming more and more steadily in recent weeks. She'd told no one about those except for law enforcement and her social worker. Having a boyfriend beat her within an inch of her life was enough. No wonder Chance looked at her so sadly.

She *was* sad.

Click.

The sound startled her. Chance had opened her truck door, and she had no clue how he'd done it.

"That's incredible," she said.

Movie-star man simply smiled. "You should see what I can do with a spoon." He grinned, tossed the knife into the air and caught it by the handle like a ninja warrior. That's what he looked like, his arms huge, muscled and toned. His chest had been pretty spectacular, too. He had a deep ridge between his two pectoral muscles, and beneath that, square-shaped mounds, each one smaller than the other. His skin had looked as soft as lambskin, and so toned and hard she'd flushed like a piece of fruit in the summer sun when she'd spotted him standing at the top of those stairs. She'd never had a reaction like that to a man before. Never.

Movie-star man stared at her oddly.

"Th-thank you so much," she stammered. And now she couldn't even talk right.

"You're welcome."

She hated that she found him attractive. She would be working with him. That should have made her feel depressed, not…titillated.

"I should call the tow company," she said, shuffling past him, pulling her truck door open and reaching for her purse. Sad that she had the tow company's phone number memorized. She grabbed her phone… and saw it.

Twenty missed calls. Thirty text messages.

Oh, dear Lord.

"What's wrong?"

"Nothing."

She couldn't tell him what was wrong. This man was her new boss. The last thing she needed was to give him a bad impression by admitting how messed-up her life was.

"Is he stalking you?"

So he *did* know about James.

His eyes said it all. *I know enough.*

"Is he?"

She wanted to crumble. It made her so angry she fought back tears. She was *not* that woman, the one from some reality TV show who allowed a man to beat her and terrorize her and then crumbled at another man's feet. She was strong. She could handle this. She could.

She was *not* her mom.

"Let me see your phone."

She didn't want him to look, and that killed her all over again, so much so when he reached for the phone she didn't try to keep it away from him. It fell limply into his grasp.

"Wow." He looked up from the screen. "Have you read these?"

She shook her head. What could she say? That she'd been too scared, and that had upset her all over again. How had it happened? How had she turned into such a complete loser? How had she followed in her mother's footsteps?

James, she admitted. He'd beaten the confidence out of her.

"We're calling the cops."

"I called them already. Yesterday." At least she'd found her voice again.

"And what did they say?"

"That they'd done everything they could. They talked to him. Warned him. I've filed for an emergency restraining order, but it's not doing any good. He…" She swallowed. Why was this so hard to admit? "Follows me."

He might even be outside the gates of Misfit Farms right now. He had been before.

"I'm taking you home."

She straightened. "No. I can handle my ex."

His expression was firm and implacable. "You don't have a choice."

"And you don't have a vehicle." She hadn't seen one other than Colt's big pickup truck.

"Colt said I could use his."

"But then I'd have to leave my truck here."

"I'll take you wherever you need to go from here on out."

"That's too much." She took a deep breath and repeated, "I can handle this."

She could handle a fifteen-hundred-pound horse. Do tricks on them nobody in their right mind wanted to try. James was a scrawny human who liked to terrorize little women. She would deal.

"Look," he said. "I wanted Colt to tell you this, but he was afraid you'd think he'd overstepped his bounds. Plus, I think he wanted to spare you the embarrassment."

She tensed.

"The truth is, I'm not just your boss."

She couldn't move. She had a feeling she wouldn't like what came next.

"I'm your bodyguard."

She blinked. "Excuse me?"

"You're the reason why Colt put me in charge of his specialty act. Well, that and the fact my sister-in-law is pregnant and Colt plans to stay home with her soon. But while I learn the ropes, he's asked me to keep an eye on you, and if you don't mind, I'm going to do exactly that. Stay here. I'll be right back with my brother's truck."

She shook her head, attempted to catch his sleeve, but he was already gone.

I'm your bodyguard.

Dear Lord in heaven.

Her humiliation was now complete.

"You really don't have to do this," Carolina said, smoothing down her blond pigtails.

"Actually, I do."

His brother had filled him in on the situation last night. Told him about his idea, too, to put him in charge. It'd seemed stupid at first. He hadn't ridden a horse in years, but Colt had insisted. The act didn't involve riding, at least not on his part. It was all tricks from the ground, done by sleight of hand and verbal commands. The Galloping Girlz did the actual riding. All he'd have to do was learn the routine and keep an eye on the woman standing in front of him. A little woman. Someone easy to terrorize, by the looks of things.

"Where to?" he asked.

She didn't seem happy, but when he opened the passenger-side door, she climbed in. "Do you know where the rodeo grounds are?"

"I think I do." It'd been eight years, but he was pretty sure he could still find his way around.

"I live about a mile from them."

Clear across town. Well, so be it. Those hadn't been mild threats on her phone. They'd been a stream of vitriol so nasty he didn't blame her for being distressed. If he'd had someone threatening to do those things, he'd be a little distracted, too.

"How long did you date this guy?"

She'd settled into her seat. "About a year."

"Long time," he observed, backing out of Colt's parking spot next to a massive six-horse trailer with the name *Rodeo Misfits* on the side.

"Too long," she added.

He cocked an eyebrow at her in question.

"I wanted to break up months ago, but I was…" She licked her lips.

"Scared," he finished for her.

She nodded. "Turns out, I'm not the only woman he's done this to. I felt like such an idiot when I heard that."

He was about to put the truck in Drive, but something in her eyes stopped him. She had the air of a woman who'd seen something terrible, something she didn't want to see again but that still haunted her soul.

He drummed his fingers on the steering wheel. "You know, maybe you should move into the apartment above the barn. Just temporarily. Colt said I could have it, but I can bunk down with Colt or at my sister's place down the road."

She sat up in her seat. "No. I can't do that."

But the more he thought about it, the more he liked the idea. He didn't know the woman next to him, not really. His brother had told him a lot. City girl who'd grown up with a love for horses. She'd found trick riding relatively late in life: sixteen. She was twenty-six now, and his brother said she was good, doing tricks he'd never seen before.

Brave.

But not at this moment. He felt a keen sense of protectiveness. The same kind of urge he'd felt when he'd stumbled into a village of Afghans, scared, dragged into a war they didn't want, kids crying, women terrified. Tore him apart. The urge to shield them and keep them from harm was one he had never ignored.

"Ready?" She met his gaze, peering up at him with an unblinking stare. "You can take me home. Nothing will happen, I promise. I can handle this on my own. Don't make this a bigger deal than it already is."

Because then you'll give my ex the power. He read the words in her eyes. He understood that look, too. When he'd been fighting over there, he'd seen the same expression of resolve. They didn't want the US military's help. They wanted to be left alone to deal with things on their own. They wanted independence.

He couldn't blame her for that.

"As long as you think you have it handled," he said.

"I do."

He nodded, and she faced forward again, so clearly relieved he couldn't help but feel a twinge of admiration for her as he put his brother's truck in gear and drove toward her home.

"Colt told me you'll only be Stateside for a short time?"

He appreciated her attempt at conversation. For some reason, sitting next to her made him antsy. "Going to work for DTS—Darkhorse Tactical Solutions. Just taking a sabbatical while my sister-in-law finishes cooking her baby."

She smiled. That was better. He liked that smile. It tipped the end of her nose up and made the corners of her eyes wrinkle. Pretty eyes. Blue as the desert sky on a winter morning.

"What will you be doing for them?" she asked.

"Typical contract work." He glanced at her as he passed between the white fencing his sister-in-law insisted was de rigueur for the ranch. He had to admit, the place looked spectacular. When he'd first driven up, he'd been blown away by the changes made since his brother's wedding. Huge barn. Covered arena. Irrigated pasture. Turned out, they'd been sitting on a gold mine and never known it—a natural aquifer supplied water to the ranch, as well as a few neighbors, for a price.

"I've always wondered what a military contractor does." She smiled again. "I assume you're not building houses."

He shook his head. "We're a security service. Mostly corporate executives, although we do escort the occasional civvy. Our job is to keep someone safe while they do business in war-torn towns."

A blond brow arched. "Business? When there's a war going on?"

"Yup. Sometimes it's military business, sometimes it's civilian business. The need for oil never stops, and billion-dollar corporations need protection for the people who work to bring the product to market. Plus there's road reconstruction companies and real estate investors—"

"You're kidding."

"Nope. War or no, life goes on."

She lapsed into silence, and he let her contemplate his words. A lot of people had no idea what it was really like in the Middle East. All they saw were the bits on TV. Five minutes of chaos followed by days, sometimes weeks, of normalcy. Well, as normal as life in a war-torn country could be. In those moments, people tried to get on with their lives, businesses tried to regroup and recoup. It wasn't as if life stopped. The corporate machine kept moving.

"This is it," she said, interrupting his thoughts. "Turn here."

He followed her directions, turning down a street with two-story apartment complexes on both sides.

"Thank you," she said as he pulled up in front of her building.

"Not so fast." He shut off the engine. "I'm walking you to your door."

She shook her head, the twin braids sliding behind her shoulders. "There's no need. He's not there. If he was, we'd see his truck parked down the road."

"Has he done that before?"

He saw her eyes flicker. "Not lately."

He had a feeling that "not lately" meant not within the last few days. She might be putting on a brave face, but her eyes conveyed the pictures in her mind.

"I'm still walking you to your door," he said, slipping out of the truck. "And I'll be by tomorrow to pick you up around ten."

Her forehead wrinkled as though she wanted to argue, but she nodded just the same and then slid out of the vehicle. She walked ahead of him as she crossed the tiny grass hill separating the road from the apartment complex.

"I'm the second one on the left," she explained. "Bottom floor."

Which was why they didn't see it at first.

BITCH.

She stopped in her tracks. He did, too. Her front door had been shielded from their view by her neighbor's tiny porch, the word that'd been spray painted in red only visible from a certain angle.

"Son of a—" She didn't finish what she wanted to say, but there was no need. She froze, eyes wide, hands clenching and unclenching in…what emotion did he see on her face? Dismay? Disgust? Rage? Maybe a combination of it all.

"You're staying with me," he said firmly.

"Yes." She turned to face him, and to his surprise, tears glinted in her eyes. The sight kicked him in the gut. "And I'll stay at the ranch, too, if you don't mind."

Chapter 3

There was something completely mortifying about having to accept the help of a near stranger. Worse, she'd had to call her boss and tell him what had happened. Colt Reynolds had been completely kind, but then again, he always was. She'd never met someone with such a huge capacity to help people in need. In hindsight, it should be no surprise that his little brother was the same way.

Well, there was nothing *little* about him.

"You really don't have to move in with your brother, though," Carolina said, glancing behind them to make sure no silver 4x4 followed. So far, so good. No sign of James. "I can stay in my horse trailer. I do it all the time."

"Does it have living quarters?"

"Well, no." Not technically. She'd never been able to

afford one of those big fancy trailers. Her own humble stock trailer was all she had in the world. That and her truck. "I converted the tack room into a space where I could sleep. It has a bed over the hitch and electricity for a portable stove. It works fine."

"Does it have a bathroom?"

"Well, no—"

"A heater or air-conditioning?"

"No, but maybe I could live in the Galloping Girlz trailer? It has living quarters." She paused. "Or maybe I can stay in Colt's trailer?" Her boss had her dream trailer. Shower. Kitchen. Living area.

One day.

"Maybe, but we'll need to use it on the weekends for rodeos." He stared at her. "What are you doing to do? Move in and out every weekend? And before you suggest it, the trick-riding rig is out, too. There's a perfectly good apartment at the ranch. You're going to stay there and I'll move in with my sister or brother. Capisce?"

She didn't want to, but she nodded just the same. Carolina glanced at the neighborhoods they passed, her mind settling on one word: rodeo. James would follow her to one of them. She would stake her life on it, and there would be no way to avoid the man—not in a public place. Her stomach curdled thinking about it.

They passed the burger joint outside town, and she caught sight of a young couple facing each other in the gravel parking lot. The girl sat on the tailgate, a look of love on her face as she gazed into the eyes of the captain of the high school football team.

Okay, she had no way of knowing if that were true. Carolina looked away from the scene because it made her think of her own childhood. Had she ever really had one? There'd never been time to date anybody, much less a football player. She'd been too busy working two jobs and trying to graduate. She'd refused to flunk out like her mother. Carolina had been determined to do things differently, but look what it'd gotten her. The first man she ever dated had ended up being a complete psycho—just like the men her mom used to bring home. It was enough to put her off men for the rest of her life.

"I'll move back into my old room at Colt's," Chance said, drawing her attention. "I don't think they've completely babied it out. And they won't mind, not once we explain the situation."

Oh, yeah, sure. Explain that Carolina's ex-boyfriend was even crazier than she'd thought. Great.

Do not start crying.

She inhaled sharply. Tears were for babies. She wasn't one and she wouldn't act like one, either. So what if she was in a spot of trouble with her ex? She'd deal with it. And she had help, she thought, glancing at her companion in the truck. Chance was much younger than her boss, at least five years, but clearly older than her. And while her boss was a handsome older man, Chance Reynolds wasn't handsome. The former Army Ranger was drop-dead gorgeous. Like Tatum Channing, only with a way better body. She should know. She'd seen the whole enchilada.

Carolina!

"Have you lived here long?" he asked.

"My whole life." She'd known who the Reynoldses were long before they'd known her. Their father was legendary in rodeo circles. A member of the Hall of

Fame, a world-renowned horse trainer. She'd heard about the dark side of Zeke Reynolds, too. His infamous temper. His ghastly horse-training techniques. Even that he might have beaten the boys and their sister. She'd seen no evidence of it, though. Her boss never spoke ill of his dad, and when she'd brought Zeke Reynolds up one day, all Colt had done was shrug and repeat what Carolina thought—the man had been a legend.

"You go to the local high school?" Chance asked.

The only high school. "Via Del Caballo High."

"Go, Chargers," Colt sang.

She smiled. A rearing horse was the school's mascot, and it was the reason why she'd gotten into horses, much to her mother's dismay. Carolina had always been fascinated by them, but when one of the local cowboys had brought his horse to the football game her freshman year—in a foil and cardboard costume made to look like armor, of course—she'd been able to touch one for the first time. It'd been over for her ever since. Once she'd looked into those liquid brown eyes, her life had changed.

"You graduated a few years ahead of me," she said. "I remember your sister, Claire. She graduated my freshman year. She always seemed nice."

"My sister is the best," Chance said. "Kills me what she's been through."

Cancer. Not Claire, her son. Leukemia. But they had it on the run, she'd heard.

"You'd never know there was anything amiss from meeting her."

Claire Reynolds was her hero. A woman she could look up to, and she did. Natalie Reynolds, too. Natalie had been in a horrible riding accident before she'd met Colt. They'd told her she'd never walk again, and now look. By comparison, Carolina's problems seemed small.

"Everyone has a cross to bear," he said softly.

She gulped at the kindness and understanding in his eyes. She forced her gaze away and out the window. They were out in what Carolina used to call the boondocks back when she was growing up. The town of Via Del Caballo had faded into tiny ranches—or wannabe ranches, as Carolina called them—single-story houses surrounded by white fences and small arenas. She glanced behind them again. Still no 4x4 in sight.

"We're not being followed," Chance said.

She jerked around so fast her braids nearly hit her in the face. "How do you know?"

"Simple." He glanced at her quickly, the line of his jaw so strong and masculine she swallowed. "I doubled back when we were in town."

He had? Good heavens. She hadn't even noticed.

"You should get in the habit of that, too," he said in a matter-of-fact tone of voice. "Pick a street you know isn't a dead end, one that will allow you to double back. If someone's following you, they'll take the same route, and you'll know it's a bad guy, because nobody's going to do circles for no reason."

She nodded.

"And don't assume he'll be in his truck, either."

She glanced at him sharply, because that's exactly what she'd been looking for.

"He could change vehicles." He rested his wrist on the top of the steering wheel in a manner of complete ease. She supposed compared to driving in a war zone, her situation must seem like Disneyland to him. "And if you are being followed, don't let on that you know. The worst thing you can do is speed up and try and outrun him."

"What do I do?"

"Call 911. Or me. Head to the police station. The man's not going to follow you there. Not unless he's stupid."

She hadn't really thought about that. Yipes.

"If you aren't paying attention," Chance continued, "and you notice he's followed you to the ranch, don't worry too much. Just come on inside. He's not going to come down our road, and if he does, I'll take care of him."

"What about Natalie's clients? Or Claire's? What if he somehow sneaks in thanks to them? What if he hides out or waits until I'm alone?"

Claire ran a canine rescue not far from where Colt lived. Natalie ran a successful horse-jumping business. There was no telling who might accidentally let James in—if it came to that. Carolina doubted he'd come after her like that, though. He was simply mad she'd turned him in. It made him feel like a big man to terrorize her. He was succeeding, and that made her angry all over again. No man should ever have that kind of power over a woman.

"I'll have Claire call her clients tonight and explain what's going on."

Oh, great.

"I'll ask Natalie to take precautions with her clients, too."

So the whole family would now know what an idiot ex-boyfriend she had. Terrific.

BITCH.

Her skin prickled as she recalled the red color. She never would have thought he'd go that far. Now that some of the shock had faded, it made her furious. How dare he deface her property? Granted, it was just a tiny apartment, but she'd worked hard to get the place, and now her landlord would likely throw a fit—and she'd have to pay to fix it, too.

"It'll be okay," Chance said, patting her leg, which made her madder, because she wasn't some little girl who needed a pat on the head—or the leg, as the case might be. She was a full-on adult who could take care of herself.

Then why are you glad a former Army Ranger is sitting next to you? And why are you grateful he'll be with you tonight? And why does the sight of his hand on your leg make you all squirmy inside?

They were questions she refused to answer.

Prickly.

That was the word he would use to describe her. Chance pulled his brother's black truck into its parking space and added the word to his list of *stubborn, fiercely independent* and *dogged.*

"Looks like your brother's back," Carolina said.

Colt and Natalie had matching trucks, except for their different colors, and they'd clearly returned from running errands. Chance hadn't heard them leave this morning, which just went to show how completely wiped he'd been from his long journey home. It'd been an eight-hour hitch to Europe, then another eight across the pond. A quick stop on the East Coast, where he'd managed to snatch a nap in an empty hangar only to be headed out again less than an hour later. All told, he'd traveled for twenty-four hours. He'd gone straight to bed once he'd arrived home. Not that it'd helped. He was still bone tired.

"I'll go in and talk to him," he said.

"No. That's okay. I can explain the situation."

Yup. Independent.

He shook his head. "We'll go in together."

It was strange walking up to the house he'd grown up in. Strange and unsettling, in a way. Saying he'd had a bad childhood was like saying Abraham Lincoln had a bad night at the theater. His father had terrified all three of his kids, but he'd taken out his temper on Colt the most. His brother used to say their dad tried out his evil tricks on him first, then used them on Chance or Claire. As they'd gotten older, they'd gotten wiser, especially Colt. He'd taken to preempting their dad, but not always. There'd been times when none of them had been able to avoid the drunken fits.

And so as Chance turned the handle to the front door, he braced himself. He hadn't been inside since his brother's wedding, not even when he'd returned home last night, and he really wasn't sure what to expect.

"Anyone home?" he called, though he knew there was. He took two steps and then stopped.

Where before there'd been a small sitting room and a room beyond, there was now open space. The wall he'd been thrown against as a twelve-year-old—after he'd dared to tell his dad he was too sick to walk to school—had been removed. The kitchen was still to his right, but the wall separating it from the sitting room had been removed. The whole first floor was open, and it felt so different that he instantly relaxed.

"We're up here," a female voice called. His sister-in-law, Natalie. "In your old room."

He caught Carolina's eye. She couldn't seem to stop her gaze from moving around the room, as if she were in awe of the scope of the place, and maybe even a little intimidated.

"I'll stay down here," she said.

"No. Come up. I'm sure they won't mind."

He glanced around again. It was like a whole new home.

Maybe that was the point.

He glanced at Carolina. She clearly didn't want to go, but he touched her shoulder and urged her forward. He could feel the tension beneath his hand as they headed toward the stairs on the left. The staircase was the one thing that hadn't changed. The oak banister he'd tried to slide down still existed. His father used to make them march up those stairs when they'd been bad. Chance remembered looking up at the top landing, heart pounding...

Enough.

That was in the past. He was a different person. Not the frightened child who'd grown up with an abusive father. And this was a different house. Pictures of Natalie jumping the most amazing horses hung on the stairwell wall. Pictures of his brother, too, at rodeos and reining competitions. Pictures of Natalie's protégée, Laney, in the winner's circle. And in the middle of it all, a picture of the three of them, Colt, Claire and Chance, blown up big, and smiling. He was young. His mom held him in her lap, which meant his dad must have taken the picture.

"Is that you?" Carolina asked.

He jerked his gaze away from the image. "Yup." He tapped the picture. "And Claire and Colt." Not that anyone would need to be told. They all had dark hair. Only the eyes were different. Colt's were hazel, Claire's and his own eyes were green.

"You were so young," she observed.

"Yes, we were."

There had been good times, he reminded himself, heading the rest of the way up the stairs before she could ask any more questions. His trip down memory lane had started to sink his mood, and he refused to let his father have that kind of power over him. Not ever again.

"Hey, guys," he said, stopping before his old room, first door on the left, a smile instantly lifting his lips. It looked as though a box factory had exploded.

"Hey, you two," Natalie said, returning his grin somewhat sheepishly as she, too, peered around the room, her hands on her pregnant belly.

"How'd you sleep?" Colt asked with an equally wide smile, getting up from the floor and dodging some boxes. After Colt had finished thumping him on the back, he leaned back and clutched his shoulders. It was good to look into his brother's eyes.

Chance chuckled. "I never made it off the couch."

"You didn't?"

He shook his head. "Just stripped down to my Skivvies and passed out."

He glanced at Carolina. She had the same look on her face as someone who'd just discovered their zipper was down. He almost felt bad for her. Almost. He'd never been one to resist teasing a person.

"Lucky I wasn't naked when Carolina here came bursting through the door this afternoon."

"I didn't burst," she said, tipping her chin up before looking at his brother and his wife. "I thought the place was empty."

"She knew I was half-naked and wanted a glimpse of my hot stud flesh."

Carolina gasped.

"Chance!" his sister-in-law said. "Quit teasing her. You're making her uncomfortable."

He almost said that was the point, but held his tongue. The blush staining Carolina's cheeks was adorable.

Adorable?

Best not to dwell on that too long.

"I'm glad he was able to help you out," Colt said to Carolina. "Although I think you should start leaving a spare set of keys here."

"I think you're right," she grumbled.

It was then that Chance noticed what his brother and sister-in-law were doing. "Wow."

"Baby equipment," Colt explained, going back to his position on the floor and picking up a screwdriver. "Changing table, crib, a new dresser that should have taken me ten minutes to put together." He rubbed his jaw. "But it's been a little longer than that."

"Because he won't listen." Natalie's blue eyes were clearly teasing.

"Why should I follow the directions?" Colt asked. "Obviously, they're for dummies. We're not dummies. I can figure it out on my own."

Natalie tsked. "Said the man who built the chicken coop that fell down two days later."

Colt shook his head, his eyes seeming to ask the question, *can you believe her?* But he smiled, and Chance had to admit, it was good to see. Colt had waited to join the army until Chance was old enough to get out of the house, too. Claire had already fled, married to Marcus, and so both he and Colt had left for the military together. The difference was that Colt had done only one tour, then returned home to nurse their ailing father—Lord only knew why—while Chance had stayed. Truthfully, the military suited him better. He loved how everything was black-and-white. He relished the camaraderie. The simplicity of being told what to do—and then doing it. His brother hadn't had a good experience in the military, whereas Chance fit in like a foot in a boot. He couldn't wait to go back, this time as a private contractor. More money for doing basically the same job, and a career he loved.

"So what can we do you for?" Colt asked, picking up a small square of wood.

Carolina had been quiet beside him, which struck him as odd. He doubted she was quiet very often, but she seemed to be waiting for him to explain.

"Carolina was wondering if she could sleep in the apartment instead of me."

That stopped Colt. Natalie looked up from reading the directions. They both stared at Carolina with concern.

"Is he back?" Natalie asked.

Carolina nodded, and Chance watched as Carolina's lids caught and held tears. Only she wouldn't let them drop. She straightened her shoulders, clearly getting control of herself. Chance had to admire her for that.

"He left a message on my door," she explained.

That was one way of putting it.

"Well, sure, you can stay anywhere you want," Colt said, glancing at his wife, who nodded. "But where will you sleep?" he asked Chance.

"I was thinking at Claire's place."

"That's too far away," Colt said.

"You can stay here," Natalie interjected. "I mean, if you don't mind pieces of baby equipment and the smell of baby powder and new diapers."

"I told you," Colt said, "I'll have it together in ten minutes."

"That's what you said ten minutes ago."

"I hadn't even started ten minutes ago."

Another long-suffering sigh from Natalie. She caught Chance's eye and smiled.

"I don't mind sleeping in here," Chance said. "I'll bunk down on the floor, like we used to do when we were kids."

Colt's smile froze. So did Natalie's when she glanced at her husband's face.

They would hide from their dad under the bed, but before that, before their mom died, they'd played games. "You remember the time you couldn't find Henry?"

A smile slipped onto his brother's face. "I do." His gaze encompassed his wife and Carolina. "My pet squirrel. I caught it out back. Stupidest creature that ever walked the earth. Afraid of everything. It must have figured out how to get out of the cage, because one day it was gone."

"We never told Mom," Chance said.

"Nope. Then one day, Chance hears something under his bed."

"Only at night," Chance added. "Thought it was a mouse."

"But it was Henry, and it took us days to catch that damn squirrel again."

That was back before their mom died, back before they'd found her—

Okay, enough. This was part of the reason why he'd come back. He needed to put the ghosts of Christmas past to rest, just as Colt had done.

"We never did tell Mom," Colt said, smiling at Carolina. "She used to get so mad at us for bringing whatever creature we found outside into the house. Remember the lizard?"

Chance grinned. "You mean the one I left in my pocket and that crawled up Mom's arm when she went to do the laundry?"

They both laughed, and Chance caught Natalie staring at them wistfully, a smile on her face, too. "It's good to hear you two reminisce."

"You should have heard our mom shriek," Chance said.

"But she laughed about it," Colt added.

One of the rare times she'd laughed.

"Anyway," Chance said, forcing the memories away. "I already took Carolina home to get some of her things, so I'll just help her settle. Grab my stuff, too. Move in here." Not that he had a whole lot. Just a bag.

"Have at it," Colt said. "But when you're done, I'll expect some help assembling this mess."

"Hey, wait." Natalie frowned. "What is this? *He* can help you, but I'm not allowed?"

Colt scooted toward his wife and rested a hand on

her belly. "Because you're pregnant and you should be resting while I do the manly work."

Natalie smiled, the look of love on her face prompting Chance to back out of the room and call out, "Have fun."

He couldn't get out of there fast enough, and he realized he'd forgotten to talk to Natalie about her clients. Oh, well, he'd do it later. Gushy, mushy love always made him uncomfortable. That kind of stuff wasn't for him. He had more important things to do.

"Ready?" he asked Carolina.

She sighed, her pretty blue eyes filling with determination. "As I'll ever be."

Attagirl.

Earlier, when she'd been about to cry, he'd had the damnedest urge to pull her into his arms and hold her tight. He'd wanted to console her and let her know he would protect her.

No chance of that ever happening, he told himself. No chance at all. He wasn't stupid. Touching Carolina might be a little different than touching other women. He had no idea why that was, but he always listened to his instincts. His instincts told him to keep clear of Carolina Cruthers.

And he planned to heed them.

Chapter 4

It was ridiculously easy to settle into Colt and Natalie's apartment, given that Carolina's tiny two-bedroom apartment had been her home for the past year and a half. Easy, and if she were honest with herself, a relief. No sign of James and no more worries about surprise visits in the middle of the night. Not unless James broke through the iron gate blocking the driveway of Reynolds Ranch and then walked more than two miles to the riding facility. She doubted he'd ever do that, and if he did, they'd see him coming. The only fly in her ointment was her new boss.

Chance Reynolds.

It was as if her thoughts had summoned him.

"Knock, knock?" he called from the other side of her apartment door, adding a rap from his knuckles while she stood in the kitchen, frozen.

Crud.

She was still in her pj's, a gray pair of sweats that hung loose around her waist and had a big hole in the knee. And the T-shirt she wore doubled as a nightie. No bra, either.

"I'll be right there," she called out, making a beeline to the bedroom. Someone had recently decorated the room in a horse motif. She dived beneath a brown-and-black bedspread with a Western star in the middle to find her bra, which she'd apparently ditched atop the bed last night. She felt every second tick as she slipped the thing on, then ran a hand through her loose hair, hoping she looked presentable as she headed to the door.

Presentable? Why? asked a little voice.

She wasn't going to think about that and pasted a smile on her face as she opened the door. "Chance. Hey."

He seemed amused as he eyed her up and down, although what it could be she didn't know. The baggy sweats? Or the messed-up hair? Crud. She hoped her makeup didn't look as if it belonged on *The Walking Dead.* She hadn't even thought about last night's mascara leaving streaks beneath her eyes.

"Took you long enough," he said.

Chance slipped past her, and she ducked back to avoid him touching her.

And there it was.

Attraction. She might as well admit it. Chance Reynolds was more handsome than her boss's good friend Rand Jefferson, a man who played Hawkman in the movies. Whereas Rand had the muscular build of a Greek statue, Chance was more athletic. More Captain America than Hawkman. She much preferred that.

"What's up?" She followed him to the kitchen, where he set down a brown duffel bag, clearly a relic from his past.

"I brought you some presents," he said. "The kind that might save your life."

She caught a glimpse of what was in his bag, something wicked looking and clearly meant for self-defense. "What kind of weapons do you have in there? I really don't like guns."

"No guns." He held up what looked like an electric razor.

She crossed her arms in front of her. "What am I going to do with that? Shave him to death?"

"Huh?" He glanced at the device in his hand. "Oh. No. It's not a razor." He pressed something on the front. An electronic charge crackled through the air. "It's a Taser."

She straightened in surprise. She'd been thinking about getting one of those.

His smile should be obnoxious this early in the morning. What was it? Seven? But it wasn't obnoxious. It was adorable. He was clearly proud of himself.

"Where did you get it?"

"That's not all I got." He set the Taser down on the table. "There's this, too." He held up a can with a bright red lid. "Pepper spray. There's two kinds. The industrial size." He reached into the bag again. "And the key-chain size. Easier to hold when you're walking alone at night."

Not that she planned on walking anywhere alone.

Her curiosity got the better of her, though, and she moved up next to him, fingering the Taser.

"I got it from a friend of mine," Chance said. "Owns a karate studio, but he sells these on the side. Speaking of that, we should teach you some moves. Basic self-defense stuff. You never know when you might need it."

"Brass knuckles?" she said, holding up a feminine version. They'd been painted pink.

He shrugged. "Hey, sometimes simple is best, but I'd have to teach you how to punch in order for them to be effective."

No, thanks. The thought of him touching her in any way, shape or form was…disturbing.

"What's this?" She held up a nasty-looking object with prongs.

"That's the big daddy." His smile was pure, childish delight. "You see these? You can shoot them at your assailant. It's a Taser, too, but it's the kind the police use. Really high voltage. Knock your guy to the ground. The other one is more of a deterrent. It'll hurt like hell, but it won't knock someone to the ground." He took Big Daddy from her. "This one will do some damage."

She didn't know whether to be amused or repulsed by his enthusiasm, although she wished she'd had some of these items before. Some of her amusement faded.

"How about this one?" she asked, spying another small can of something.

"Horn. Blow it if you feel threatened. Usually that's enough to scare away most assailants."

She pursed her lips and moved on. "And this?"

He seemed disappointed. "That's just a flashlight."

Her smile returned. He set Big Daddy on the table,

eyeing the smorgasbord of self-defense with a self-satisfied expression.

"What do you think of this?" He held up a key chain in the shape of a cat. "Isn't it cute?"

"Yeah." She studied it. "What does it do? Unfold into a ninja star or something?"

He shook his head. "You hold it like this." He placed the cat in his hand, the points of the ears sliding in between his fingers so that they stuck out from between his knuckles. "Instant shish kebab."

"Nice."

Clearly, it was one of his favorites, at least judging by his small chuckle. "Which one do you like?" he asked.

She followed his gaze, studying the things he'd brought. She should be pleased he hadn't brought her a gun, although she wouldn't be surprised if that weren't in her future, too.

Carolina fingered the big can. "How badly does the pepper spray sting?"

"It's nasty. He'll be blind for hours."

She jerked her hand back. "Blind?"

He dismissed her concerns with a wave. "Unable to open his eyes," he added quickly, "but that's only if you point it at his face. Which you should, but if you don't, it burns the skin, too."

"I see."

"What smells so good?" he asked with a sniff of the air and a mercurial change of subject.

She smiled. "Coffee. Freshly made. Would you like a cup? It's hazelnut flavor."

"Got any food?"

Food? "I, uh. Well, yeah. I have eggs and bacon."

"Perfect. I'll whip us something up while you look things over."

"Wait." *What?* "You don't have to cook."

"I don't mind. I'm used to fending for myself, remember. You should really pick up and handle the items I brought over. Get a feel for them."

And that was how she found herself staring after him in surprise as he opened up her fridge. She huffed in resignation.

While Chance cooked breakfast, Carolina touched each self-defense mechanism. She sighed quietly. Maybe it was *his* kitchen. He was the one that should have been living in the apartment. But as she picked up each of the items, she remembered how Colt's sister had told her about the time her fiancé had made her breakfast while her son was really sick. They hadn't been together back then. It'd just been a kind gesture. Carolina remembered thinking she'd never find a man to do something so nice. Despite women's so-called liberation, the men she'd been dating reverted right back to the Stone Age. Women did the cooking, cleaning and laundry. And yet here she was, watching the most gorgeous male she'd ever seen flip eggs in a pan like some kind of master chef.

She wanted to kiss him.

Not because she hoped to start something, but because she was so very thankful for his concern. She might have been annoyed and humiliated yesterday to learn her boss wanted him to be her bodyguard, but she'd thank Colt later when she saw him. The worry and fear that James would come back were gone. And now she would have some form of protection. All in all, things were looking up—thanks to Chance.

"So, what did you decide?" he asked, setting down a plate of heavenly smelling eggs and bacon in front of her. "Which one do you want?"

"Well, it's a toss-up between Hello Kitty the weapon and the pepper spray."

"Take both."

She didn't know why she felt self-conscious as she touched the cat-shaped weapon, but she did. She set it down, unable to resist digging into her breakfast. But as she lifted her fork, she suddenly took great care not to get any on her lips because for some reason she felt terribly exposed.

"I can't afford both, I'm sure," she said, making sure she didn't chew with her mouth open or something.

"You don't have to pay for them. They're gifts. From me."

"I can't accept them."

He was busy gobbling down his own breakfast. "Sure you can," he said between swallows. "I get all this stuff at cost. Part of my new job. I'll be outfitting my clients with these types of weapons."

She lifted the bacon to her lips, spotted him watching her again, and her cheeks heated up. Why was he staring at her? She took a bite and then set the bacon down, even though she just about groaned at how good it tasted. Golly, the man could heat up a room with the look in his eyes.

"Still," she said. "I don't want to take advantage. Even at cost, I doubt I could afford any of it."

He didn't say anything, and when she finally got the nerve to look up at him, she noticed the most bizarre expression on his face.

"What?" she asked.

He rubbed his chin. "Ah. Yeah. Like I said. I'll take care of it. You can pay me back slowly if you want."

"Chance—"

"No arguments," he interrupted. "This is your safety we're talking about. You need to be prepared."

She couldn't argue that point, so she continued eating her breakfast, feeling his gaze upon her all over again. Man, she wished he'd stop watching her.

"Thank you," she said once she finished.

"You're welcome," he said, shooting up suddenly with his plate in hand.

"I'll wash that."

"No. That's okay. I've got it. Here. Give me yours."

She handed him the empty plate. He hurried to the sink and, sure enough, washed her dishes for her. As she sat in her chair, she stared at the weapons and wondered why she'd never been able to find a man like Chance. Just her luck he was leaving for the Middle East in a short while. And that he was her boss's brother. And that he knew about James and so probably had a low opinion of her life choices. So if that was a spark of attraction in his eyes, she knew he'd never act on it.

"Thanks," she said, standing.

He grabbed a rag and dried his hands, but when he met her gaze, he seemed to freeze.

"I mean it, Chance. You've really taken a load off my mind. I'd been thinking about getting some pepper spray. Now I don't have to worry. And if I get in a bind, I have Ninja Kitty to poke James's eyes out with."

He didn't say anything, but then seemed to nudge himself back to life, tossing the towel he held to the counter. "Protecting people is my job."

Something about the way he said the words made her tilt her head. He seemed upset, as if he were disappointed in something…maybe her?

"I should get going," he said, moving past her.

"Chance, wait."

It was one of those moments when you call someone back and you don't know why. When you know you want to say something, but you don't know what. When words form, only to be immediately discarded. She'd already thanked him.

"I'll ask Colt to take what I owe you out of my next paycheck."

He nodded. "Whatever." He slipped out the door.

What had she done? Something had definitely soured his mood. He couldn't get away from her fast enough. Only after he left did she realize he'd left all his weapons behind.

Chapter 5

Three days later she was no closer to solving the riddle of Chance. They were slated to work together, and she was a little nervous. She watched him from a distance as he and Colt gave direction from the side of his trailer, which was parked in the middle of the arena. Colt had just taught Chance the part of the skit where Teddy stole the handkerchief out of Chance's back pocket. Usually, the next part of the act was Teddy jumping in the trailer by himself. Only the horse had refused to load.

"I swear he's like a petulant kid," she heard Colt say as he gave the signal for Teddy to load up for the fourth time. A signal that was ignored. Teddy stood, handkerchief in his mouth, and any time one of the men approached him, he ran away. This, too, was part of the act, and when Colt told the horse to stop and to come to him—the last part of their act together—Teddy usually obeyed. Not today.

"He gets in these moods," Colt said. "But he always performs when it's for real. I've never had him duck out on me or nothin'. I swear he likes the applause."

They were out of doors on a day so calm and clear it looked like a masterfully painted backdrop of a movie set: bright blue sky, puffy clouds that dotted the ground with their shadows, mountains in the distance. Carolina had once visited her friend Sam on location. They'd been filming a scene with her husband against a fake background so similar it felt eerie. The only difference today was they were surrounded by a carpet of green, not asphalt, and the emerald-colored grass was thanks to the irrigation system that was the envy of their neighbors—and made the ranch worth a small fortune. Colt had been offered a sweet deal to sell the place but had flatly refused. It was a family homestead, and he planned to keep it that way, or so she'd been told by Sam.

"He's a character, all right," Chance said.

"Teddy, knock it off."

Carolina could hear the exasperation in Colt's voice. Apparently, Teddy could, too, because he dropped the handkerchief and trotted over to Colt as if that had been his plan all along. "You nut," Colt said, but he patted the horse's neck and smiled.

Chance crossed his arms. "Okay, so normally the act ends with Teddy jumping in the trailer while the Galloping Girlz enter the arena, but you want to change all that, so what does it matter if he loads up or not?"

Colt nodded. "You're right. It doesn't matter. I'm

looking forward to jazzing up the routine. People have seen the old act a million times."

Chance tipped his cowboy hat back, hands on his hips. It didn't seem fair that a man who'd been off the ranch for almost a decade could look so good in a cowboy hat and jeans. But Chance did. Carolina wondered if the boots he wore had been his before he'd joined the army.

"You'll get the hang of it. And Teddy will behave when you're out on the road."

"I'm sure I will."

Colt waved for Carolina to come closer. "You ready to learn the new part?"

"As ready as I'll ever be," she said because she really didn't want to work with Chance. After their breakfast together, things had changed. Sure, it was one-sided. She doubted he felt anything other than mild annoyance that he had to babysit her. But she had developed a full-blown crush. And they'd be working side by side—for hours.

Carolina slipped between the rails of the wooden fence, glancing at the covered arena on the other side of the barn. Lessons were in full swing. Carolina heard Natalie calling to one of her clients as she schooled her horse over a jump. Something about weight in the heels and keeping her hips open—whatever that meant. The smell of dust and a water-soaked pasture filled the air.

"All right," Colt said. "Chance, you're up first. I need you to try and swing up on old Teddy here without a saddle."

Chance eyed the animal skeptically. "He doesn't have a bridle on."

"I'm aware of that, Chance," Colt said, deadpan.

"Perhaps that's why I want you to climb aboard, so you can practice riding him without a bridle."

The skin between his brows wrinkled. "Won't he run off?"

"Just do as I ask, please."

Chance studied the horse as if contemplating the odds of his brother's request being a prank. Satisfied with what he saw, he moved forward. "You know, the last time you told me to do as you asked, you blew the toilet seat off with me on it."

Colt chuckled. "This is different."

Chance grabbed a hank of mane. He shifted around a bit, as if trying to recall the position he needed to be in to complete his task. With a deep breath and a giant heave, he threw his leg over the horse, slipped, and almost fell to his knees. He shot them both a grimace before trying again. To Carolina's complete shock, he swung up the next time as if he'd been doing it his whole life, and maybe he had.

"Wow," his brother said. "Impressive."

All week long, Carolina had told herself there was no way Colt's idea for a new routine would work, not when his brother hadn't ridden in years. And yet there Chance sat, staring down at her triumphantly, looking as if he belonged on an old Western movie poster with his black hat and denim shirt. All he'd need was a black eye mask to be a Western hero like the Lone Ranger.

"Okay, that was easy," Chance said. "What's next?"

"Bill the Barrel Man. He's going to play the part of bad guy."

"Yeah, but he's not here."

"You'll have to use your imagination."

"I didn't know that man was still around," Chance said.

"Still going strong after all these years. We follow the same rodeo schedule, which is why this'll work out great. He actually seemed a little excited about joining in on our routine. Said we can practice it when we're at the rodeo this next weekend." Colt turned toward the middle of the arena and pointed. "Bill's going to be off on the sidelines dressed as Dastardly Dan."

"Who?"

Colt waved away his brother's question. "You'll be just finishing up your act with Teddy. The Galloping Girlz will be announced. Carolina will ride in as if all is well. She'll stand up on Rio's back, only Bill will jump out of his barrel and grab her horse's bridle or something. We'll have to work out the details of that. I want it to look kind of like Pitiful Pearl."

"Pitiful Pearl?" Chance asked.

His brother released a long-suffering sigh of impatience. "You know, like those old black-and-white movies without the sound. Overacted skit. Lots of arm waving and facial expressions. Caro will be perfect."

"Caro?" Chance asked, eyeing her anew.

She had a hard time meeting his gaze. "It's what my friends call me."

He smiled wickedly. "I could be your friend."

Oh, dear Lord in heaven.

He was teasing, she knew that, just as she knew his words shouldn't affect her, not after everything she'd been through. Yet they did. The man was too gorgeous for his own good.

"Anyway," Colt said, eyeing the two of them askance. "Caro will be pulled from her horse…somehow. I want you to swing up on Teddy and rescue her."

"Rescue her how?"

"You know, ride up to her at breakneck speed, clasp her hand, then swing her up behind you. Like in the movies. Then you'll ride back to the trailer and Caro will grab a rope. She'll stand up on the back of Teddy and the two of you will set off, and she'll rope Bill and drag him back to his barrel, or maybe out of the arena. I haven't decided yet. And not really drag. He can sort of be walking, but pretending to fight you the whole time. We'll have to see what looks best." He turned toward his brother. "My biggest concern is your riding skills. We'll need to work on them. It might take a while before you're in the proper shape to lift Caro up from a run."

"Nah. I'm in the best shape of my life." He patted his abs.

Carolina realized she chewed on the end of her hair again and flicked the strands away, thinking Chance was right. She remembered what he'd looked like without his shirt on, and it still gave her hot flashes.

Colt didn't seem as convinced. "I don't doubt for a minute you can run a mile, but riding a horse is different."

"Oh, yeah?"

"Don't get your knickers in a twist—"

Chance dug his heels in Teddy's sides. It was like a scene straight out of an old Western. Teddy shot off, though quite frankly, the horse probably bolted more out of shock than anything else. The biggest surprise was how well Chance rode. Well, for about five seconds. Teddy turned right. Quickly. Chance listed to the left.

"Oh, no!"

He landed with an *oomph*.

Colt's laughter filled the air. Carolina almost ran toward Chance, but Colt stopped her, the sideways look he shot her full of amusement. "This is going to be fun."

If he landed on his butt one more time, he would shoot himself. God bless it. And in front of Caro, too.

Caro. He liked the nickname. Just as he enjoyed watching her eat bacon.

Ump. Stop it.

He'd told himself he would keep his mind out of the gutter today. Had convinced himself it was just his long hitch in the army that had him practically combusting on the spot when he'd watched her slide that damn piece of pork in her mouth.

"Just let go of the mane," his brother ordered.

Focus. You'll fall on your ass again if you keep thinking about Caro's mouth.

"You'll never get better if you use your hands to hang on and not your legs."

Chance released an oath of frustration, although if he were honest, it wasn't simply because of his trouble riding. "I told you. I can't hold on unless I'm grabbing the mane."

They'd been at it for over an hour, and Chance had lost count of how many times he'd fallen off. Everything was fine at a walk and a trot. There was just something about Teddy's lope that threw him off balance, especially in the corners.

"Maybe we should work through things at a walk," Carolina suggested, looking like a pink candy cane in her curve-hugging spandex suit, which reminded

Chance there was other things she could stick in her mouth.

STOP!

He needed to get control of his wayward thoughts.

"Yeah, you're right," his brother said. "At this rate, you and I will be old and gray before he learns how to ride again."

"I know how to ride."

His brother turned to Carolina, so Chance couldn't see his face, but he must have made a derogatory expression, because Carolina bit her lip, then looked at the ground—as if she didn't want him to see the amusement in her eyes.

"Fine."

Okay, so yeah, it was humiliating to keep falling off in front of the oh-so-gorgeous Caro, but at least he got back up and tried it again.

Colt turned back around to face him. "Let's do a run-through of the act."

Carolina still wouldn't look up at him, not even when he rode up next to her and Colt.

Colt patted Teddy's neck. "Let's take it from the part where Caro swings up behind you."

"Good. Fine. Whatever." What did it matter if she was privately laughing at him? It wasn't as if he was trying to impress her or anything.

His brother turned toward Carolina. "When you get on, stand up. Chance will do a big circle around me. If you're feeling brave, Chance, try it at a trot. Maybe Caro can help keep you balanced."

Chance held out his hand. Carolina played peeka-boo with her eyes, glancing at him once, then twice, but never holding his gaze. She slapped her palm into his, and as Chance wrapped his fingers around hers and pulled her toward him, he experienced the strangest sensation. He froze for a moment—something that seemed to keep happening around her—and it made him wonder if the jet lag had affected him worse than he'd thought.

Or maybe he'd simply bumped his head one too many times during today's rehearsal.

"Ready?" he asked Caro.

She nodded. He pulled, and with an ease that left him in awe, she slid on behind him. Seriously. It was as if she had a magnet on her butt. The feel of her warm body up against his own, the suit she wore so thin it was like having her naked…

STOP.

He needed to take a deep breath. Big mistake. She smelled like Downy fabric softener. He'd always loved the smell of that stuff.

"Are you okay?" she asked.

"Fine."

One. Two. Three.

He did the same thing when he was out on the gun range. Counted down to calm his mind and get his brain focused.

"You're just really good," he added. Good to feel up against him, he privately added.

"She's a professional," Colt said, staring up at them both. "Caro, go ahead and stand."

Chance felt hands on his shoulders. There was a moment when he caught a whiff of her perfume or body cream or whatever it was she wore, and it blended with the smell of her hair. It had been a long, long time since he'd smelled something that smelled like, well, a woman.

Honeysuckle.

That was it. The kind that used to grow alongside what was now the hay barn. His mom had loved that honeysuckle. Chance had loved it, too. His dad had ripped it down in a fit of anger.

"Okay, good," Colt said. "Chance, go ahead and walk."

He was so deep in his thought, it took him a moment to hear Colt's words. Caro was all business, already standing up behind him.

"Let's trot instead." Chance dug his heels into Teddy's side.

"No," Caro said. "Wait. Maybe we should—"

Whatever she'd been about to say was cut off by the fact that he'd started to slip off to the side again. He pulled himself toward the middle. Carolina clearly thought he was in trouble, though, because her hands gripped his denim shirt, as if she planned to physically hold him in place.

"I'm all right," he told her.

She let go. He somehow managed to stay put, because he'd be damned if he fell off while she stood up—actually stood up on two feet—behind him. Talk about humiliation. He wondered if she knew how often he got up in the middle of the night to check on her, just in case that crazy ex of hers showed up. He might suck at riding, but nobody better mess around with him when it came to protecting what was his. Well, not *his*, but his responsibility. That's for sure.

"That's good," Colt said. "Caro, quit worrying about him. He's not going to fall off. Chance, use your body weight to guide Teddy toward me. See if Caro can grab the rope."

Rope? What rope? Somewhere in the middle of all this Colt had snatched a rope from the horse trailer. He held it out. Chance shifted his weight to the left, relieved when Teddy obeyed the silent instructions and headed for his owner. Chance's legs were growing weak, and though he hated to do it, he grabbed Teddy's mane. Maybe the horse sensed Chance's growing desperation to prove himself in front of Carolina, or maybe he was hanging on so hard Teddy became confused, but one minute they were trotting and the next Teddy was in a lope.

"Whoa, whoa, whoa," he told the horse, pulling back on the animal's mane as if it were the reins.

"Lean back," Colt yelled.

He couldn't lean back. Carolina was there. "Teddy, whoa!" he heard her order.

But it was no use. Worse, he could feel himself slipping. Carolina clutched the fabric at his shoulders, and damned if she didn't hold him in place for a stride or two, but he was too much deadweight.

"Caro, let go!" Colt shouted.

The stubborn woman refused to listen, and Chance knew they were both going down.

"Shit."

It was the last word he said before he fell. Caro said something, too, but he didn't catch it because he hit the ground hard, and he'd somehow managed to land on his back, and then, in that strange way that time seemed to slow down when something bad happened, he saw Carolina fall toward him. He reached for her, used his arms to absorb the impact, but she still landed on top of him with an *oomph*.

They both lay there, trying to catch their breath. She lifted her head, and the world did that freezing, dizzy thing. She peered into his eyes, inches away, and it didn't matter she had a crazy ex-boyfriend and Chance had no intention of sticking around. Nothing mattered except the color of her eyes, the way the sunlight touched her skin, turning it as translucent as a pearl. Nothing mattered except how her body felt in that skintight costume and the way his body responded.

"Sorry." He abruptly thrust her away.

"You guys okay?" Colt asked, running up to them.

"I'm done," Chance said, hopping to his feet. He held out a hand for Caro. He didn't want to, but he did it anyway. She took it, and he actually felt relief.

Relief!

It was in that instant Chance realized he might have a problem. A big problem—and her name was Carolina Cruthers.

Chapter 6

Clearly, the man didn't like her, or maybe he was just embarrassed by his lackluster performance. Carolina didn't know, but a week later, as they set to depart for a rodeo, she realized she missed the Chance who had teased her in the kitchen.

"You ready?" he asked, slamming the door of Colt's truck. She glanced back at the Rodeo Misfits trailer hooked up behind them. The competition didn't start until tomorrow. She and Chance were to go ahead and set up camp and settle the horses. The other girls would make their own way north later in the afternoon.

Colt's plan was to perform with Carolina this weekend, then for Chance to take over next weekend, but she feared that wouldn't happen. Every time they'd practiced, Chance had fallen off. Not as much as he had that first day, since he'd been practicing with his old rope horse, Frosty, to get himself in better shape. But he wasn't quite ready. If Chance fell off just once during the performance, it would ruin the act. Her boss knew it. Chance knew it, too, and Carolina wondered if that was what had soured his mood.

"Let's hit it," she said with a smile.

He didn't respond, and she tried not to feel offended again. No matter what bothered the man, she still owed him a huge debt of gratitude. She hadn't seen James in over a week, and she felt reassured by the can of pepper spray in her purse and the Hello Kitty on her key chain. He hadn't been by the ranch, either, and she'd taken matters into her own hands and changed her cell phone number, which had stopped the texts. With any luck, he'd given up on his scare tactics, too. She could go back to her own place on Monday and quit having to depend on others for help.

Quit having to be around Chance. Well, except on weekends. And during their practice sessions. And when they traveled to rodeos together.

Okay, maybe she wouldn't be able to avoid him.

"Listen," she said as they pulled out of the driveway, light dots of water sprinkling the windshield. Coastal fog—common in the fall—had pushed its misty fingers inland and covered the land like a kid hiding his eyes. It would be like this every morning until spring came along. "I don't think I ever really said thank you."

He glanced at her quickly. She kept her gaze off him, too. They were leaving Misfit Farms behind them, the white fences on both sides of the road a muted gray.

She sighed. "I'm sure this wasn't how you hoped to spend your time Stateside, babysitting me."

He shook his head. "I'll tell you how I didn't plan to

spend my time." His expression was wry as he glanced at her again. "Falling on my ass every five minutes."

Was that what bothered him? Wounded male pride?

"It's not every five minutes," she said, smiling again. "It's every ten."

His expression said it all. *Great. Thanks.*

"But you're doing good considering it's been nearly ten years since you've ridden."

"It's not the riding that's the problem," he said. "It's when you climb onboard that I get into trouble."

It was true. He'd been able to lope Teddy around on his own for the past two days, but when she jumped up behind him, it threw him off.

"You'll figure it out."

"Better be soon. Colt doesn't want to have to leave the ranch again, what with Wes and Jillian's upcoming wedding and Natalie about to pop. Colt's the best man and has too much to do. They should have done a shotgun wedding in someone's backyard like Colt and Natalie did." Carolina had heard about the infamous wedding. They'd surprised everyone after a charity event held at the ranch. They'd been married in front of every A-list celebrity in Hollywood, many of whom still popped by, including Rand Jefferson. But that was to be expected, Caro reminded herself. Rand had married her friend Sam, one of the former Galloping Girlz, and Sam couldn't resist coming out and riding with the girls from time to time. Carolina had gotten used to having a world-famous actor as a friend.

"How long have you known Wes and Jillian?" she asked.

It was because of Jillian that Natalie had met Colt. From what she'd heard, Colt had been happy living a life secluded on the ranch, his sister less than a mile away, and only leaving on the weekends to perform. Natalie had been in a bad horse accident, and Wes and Jillian had suggested Colt could help her learn to ride again. They'd fallen in love along the way. And the rest was history.

"I've known Wes my whole life," Chance said. "His mom was friends with our mom, but he's mostly my brother's friend."

"Wes seems nice," Carolina observed. "And Jillian is amazing with animals. Once one of Natalie's jumping horses was limping and they couldn't figure out why. Jillian came over and told her it was a torn muscle. They took the horse to the vet clinic, and Mariah used some kind of infrared device to confirm the diagnosis. It was unreal."

"I've heard it's crazy how good Jillian is reading animals."

It was the first conversation—their first real conversation—since their practice session in the arena. She smiled. She liked talking to him. It was easy. Not awkward and uncomfortable. "I think she does more than simply read them. It's almost like she can talk to them or something."

"Dr. Doolittle," Chance said. "That's what Colt calls her."

"Exactly like—"

She bolted upright in her seat. Chance slowed down as quickly as he could with horses in the back of the trailer. They'd reached the end of the drive and the iron gates that guarded the entrance of Reynolds Ranch. In the distance was James's truck.

Son of a—

Chance must have realized who it was, too, as she'd given him a detailed description of James's truck, as well as a picture of the man himself. It might still be early enough that the headlights painted the pavement gray, but James's big silver truck was hard to miss. Her ex must have realized they'd spotted him, because suddenly his lights flicked on. He peeled out so fast his tires kicked up a stream of dust and rubber.

"Damn," Chance said.

Yes, damn. She'd truly hoped he'd leave her alone now. That he'd had his fun. But being faced with the reality of James's presence was like discovering a gaping hole in her arm, one so big and ghastly she didn't know how it could ever be fixed.

"I don't understand," she whispered.

They both watched as James sped off, his taillights fading to small points of light before disappearing altogether.

She clenched her fists. "Why won't he leave me alone?"

The side of Chance's jaw ticked, his eyes slits as he stared at the spot where James had been parked.

"Bastard's gonna be sorry."

She hardly said a word the rest of the ride. That was okay. Chance was busy checking his six, even doubling back once, not that she seemed to notice. Carolina seemed too lost in her own thoughts, fiddling with a strand of her hair, probably wondering what she could do to keep James away.

Nothing.

The simple truth was, there were some men who didn't want to take no for an answer. Who were crazy.

Who did things no sane man would ever do. Over there, in the Middle East, Chance had seen things. He shook his head, not wanting to think about it. Suffice to say, he'd probably taken James a hell of a lot more seriously than she had, knowing what he knew about certain individuals.

He gripped the steering wheel. "I won't let him hurt you."

"He knows where the rodeo is," she said in a small voice.

He glanced at her, about to ask how that was possible, when he realized she was right. Of course he knew. Colt's rodeo schedule was posted online. It was no big secret where they would be. And even if it hadn't been online, rodeos had their own websites, and they listed who their performers would be. He was an idiot for not thinking of that sooner. Of course, he'd been hoping the guy had given up. The sight of him sitting in front of the gate had changed all that. It'd been nearly two weeks since Carolina had moved to the ranch, and James clearly still had it out for her. That meant he was capable of anything. Maybe even scary things. Like the stuff Chance had seen while serving.

"If he shows up, I'll take care of him."

She nodded, her gaze firmly fixed ahead.

"In the meantime, maybe you should call the lieutenant in charge of your case."

"I will once we get there."

"Not that it'll do any good," he said, checking his six once again as he merged onto a new road. "James's gonna do whatever he wants. His type of man always does. He's mad at you for breaking up with him, and he's trying to make you pay."

She stared out the front windshield, clearly oblivious to what was around her. "I never should have started seeing him."

"Hindsight is always twenty-twenty."

"Yeah, but I wasn't even looking to get involved with someone. From day one, my whole focus has been the Galloping Girlz. When he asked me out on a date, I actually said no."

"Sometimes you can have a gut feeling about someone."

They were headed into the Sierra foothills, to a town whose claim to fame was the rodeo they held every fall. It was getting to the end of rodeo season. Any cowboy that found himself behind in earnings would be at the Tres Rios grounds in the hopes of a last-minute score of cash that might nudge them toward the top of the standings, and the National Finals Rodeo.

Carolina hugged herself. "When we first started dating, he was really charming."

Chance simply nodded, keeping quiet. He sensed she wanted to talk to someone. He would listen.

"We had so much fun. He was so attentive, and I liked that. I'd never met a man who so clearly wanted to spend time with me, but then it got to be a little annoying. One day, I decided to go out to a bar with everyone in our group. I wasn't planning on picking up anybody or dancing. It was just a night of fun for us girls to relax, you know, away from a rodeo or practicing out at Colt's place."

She shook her head, her lips pressing together for a moment. Her hands clenched.

"James told me I couldn't go." She looked at him then. "I laughed."

She shook her head again, her gaze shifting to the scenery in front of them once more—the mountains in the distance capped with snow, the hills nearest them scorched brown by the California sun—her face as cold as the stone in the hillside.

"He hit me. *Bam*." She mimicked the motion of being struck in the head. "One minute, I was standing, and the next, I was on the ground. I remember thinking, *did he really just do that*? Only he had, and then he was holding me and telling me how sorry he was, and I wanted to believe him…"

So she'd forgiven him. She didn't need to say the words. Chance knew she'd let him back into her life, as many women did with their partners.

"He was good to me after that, and I started to think he'd just had a bad day. You know, that I must have pushed him too hard. That it was somehow my fault." She pinned him with a stare, her gaze so intense it was as if she tried to turn back time with her mind. "It's amazing how easy it was to believe it was a onetime thing. Two months later, he hit me again, and that was the time I told him to go to hell, only he didn't take the news well."

She touched the side of her face this time, as if touching invisible scars. "Thank God one of my neighbors came along when he did. He said he'd heard my screams. I honestly don't know if James would have stopped. I ended up in the hospital. I don't remember much about how I got there. The police came. I filed charges. I thought James would leave me alone after that, especially since he'd be in jail, but the bastard posted bail the next day and then he was out and the phone calls started."

"He's angry."

"I'm the one who should be angry." She inhaled, a sigh of resignation and possibly disgust. "But I'm scared."

"Don't be." He'd said the word so sharply she had immediately turned to look at him. "Don't be afraid. I haven't served eight years protecting this country to let some lowlife scumbag push you around. He has no idea who he's messing with."

He was driving, which made it hard to maintain eye contact, but he did his best, and he hoped she saw how serious he was.

Carolina swiped at her eyes. "He's going to make an appearance at the rodeo. How much do you want to bet?"

"I'm not going to take that bet. Not when I think you're right."

She pulled her legs up onto the bench seat and hugged her knees. "Maybe I shouldn't perform."

"Don't," he said again, just as sharply. "You've changed your life around enough already. Don't let him take this away from you, too."

He didn't realize what he was doing until he did it. He pulled over to the side of the two-lane county road.

"What's the matter?" she asked.

"First of all," he said, stopping the truck, "I'm checking to make sure he's not following us. With the hill behind us the way it is, he'll crest the top before he realizes we've pulled over."

She glanced behind them, trying to see through the horse trailer and the road beyond. "I noticed you doubled back earlier, but he's not following, is he?"

"Not yet. But he might have been smart. Might have

left ahead of us, but I think you're right. He knows exactly where we're going. Sitting outside the gate this morning was his way of telling you he knows your schedule, and man, I'd like to beat his face into a pulp because of it."

She looked ahead again, still hugging her knees.

"But I won't, because there's more than one way to skin a cat."

He rested a hand on her knee, and she jumped. He hated that she jumped. This week, he'd done his best to keep his distance from her. Easier to do that, considering his inconvenient attraction to her. However, trying to maintain space hadn't helped his concentration riding Teddy. He'd fallen off more times than a drunk on a bar stool. Still, his need to comfort Carolina in that moment outweighed his common sense, and he squeezed her leg. She looked up at him, and those blue, blue eyes drew him down and down and down, and it wasn't until he was inches away from her face that he realized he'd dropped his head toward her own. And that she hadn't moved away while he did so.

He shot back so fast he nearly clocked his head on the driver-side window.

"Sorry." If he hadn't been wearing a cowboy hat, he would have run his fingers through his hair. "I was just going to say everything will be okay."

She nodded in agitation, and it was then that Chance got his second shock where Carolina Cruthers was concerned.

She was attracted to him, too.

Chapter 7

He'd almost kissed her.

Carolina was certain of it.

Thank God he'd stopped himself. But *why* had he stopped? It was driving her nuts. It shouldn't. She should be grateful. It was too soon. Way too soon to be thinking about kissing another guy. What was she? Crazy? And he was leaving in a couple of months. She couldn't have picked a worse possible man to have a crush on.

But crush on him she did, and she was beginning to think he might have noticed.

He had hardly said two words since he'd started the truck and pulled back onto the highway. Had he seen her cheeks fill with color? Had he noticed the way her breathing had quickened? Did he know she'd become frozen with anticipation as his head had lowered toward her own? It wasn't right. They'd been talking about her twisted ex-boyfriend, for goodness' sake. She should have sworn off men for the rest of her life, not been practically panting the first time someone new tried to kiss her.

"I'll unload the horses." He put the truck in Park again, this time out back behind the rodeo grounds.

"I'll check in with the rodeo manager. Find out where it's okay to set up."

He nodded. She waited for him to look her in the eyes, and when he didn't, tried not to let her disappointment show as she inhaled a deep breath of pine-scented air. What a messed-up piece of work she'd turned out to be.

But he doesn't know about that other thing.

And he wouldn't, either. She would make sure of it, she vowed, heading for the rodeo office.

"Well, lookee here," said Hank Havens, a person who characterized the epitome of a rodeo man. Big hat, wide girth, cheesy smile. "If it isn't Spider Woman in the flesh."

Spider Woman. The nickname he'd given her when she'd nearly had a wreck with her horse, somehow managing to hang on to the underside of her horse's neck during the middle of a performance. That was when she'd first started out with the Galloping Girlz. She thanked the Lord it hadn't ended badly.

"Hey, Hank." She forced a smile. "Just checking in."

The man had the eyes of a laser scanner, and they beamed up and down, the wrinkles beneath his oversize cowboy hat deepening. "Why, you look as miserable as a herd of wet cattle."

She tried to muster a smile. She truly did. "Been a long drive."

His gray eyes narrowed, and she knew he didn't believe her. She toyed with telling him all about James, but she hated to drag him into the whole mess. She didn't want anyone to know how stupid she'd been.

"Okay if we toss the horses in one of the stock contractor pens?" she asked.

Hank's big jowls quivered for a moment, as if he were about to say something. Then he smiled. "Why, sure. 'Course, honey. You don't even have to ask."

She slipped outside before he could probe deeper and took a calming breath when she paused outside the portable trailer that served as the rodeo office. They were only an hour off the main highway, but it felt as if they were hours away from anywhere.

The rodeo grounds were in a clearing ringed by tall pine trees. A massive arena was in the middle of it all. Grandstands stair-stepped their way toward the sky. It seemed like such an arbitrary location, as if God had plopped down a tiny toy rodeo play set in the middle of nowhere. Truth was, they were surrounded by a small logging town. There were homes in the hills around them, and one of the nation's biggest sawmills was not far away. The townspeople loved their rodeo, too. They would celebrate tonight by hosting a big rodeo dance, an event Carolina always avoided like the plague.

James stood in front of her.

She almost screamed, realizing too late that it was actually Chance.

"Did I scare you?"

He knew he had, but she still said, "No."

He'd removed his hat. A red ring from the hat indented his forehead. He'd fluffed up his hair, too, and she realized he'd tried to look like her ex on purpose.

"Where's your cat key chain?"

"In my purse. In the truck."

"Good place for it."

"I was just walking to the rodeo office."

"You could be walking to an outhouse and be attacked, which is why you need to carry it around with you at all times," he said sternly. "Don't go around with your head down. Look up and survey your surroundings, and most of all, be prepared."

He was still angry, although not at her, she realized. At James. Something about that anger stirred feelings in her own heart.

"I'm sorry."

"Don't apologize." He tipped her chin up with his hand. Her breath caught. "This is *not* your fault. None of this is the result of something *you* did. He's a lowlife piece of scum, and if he comes near you, he'll be sorry."

How was it possible to be so afraid of one man and yet so incredibly attracted to another at the same time?

Crazy.

"He won't come here." The words were more of an affirmation, one she'd been repeating to herself the whole way there.

"If he does, I'll take care of it."

Chance never looked away, and she took this time to examine his face. He looked more like his sister, Claire, than his brother, with his green eyes and dark hair. But it was the expression on his face that held her attention. She'd never seen such a look of fierce determination—and it was all aimed at protecting her.

Frankly, it turned her on.

* * *

Sleeping arrangements.

He'd been thinking about it the whole damn way to the rodeo. It hadn't been a problem before he'd damn near kissed her. But now he'd be a fool to share a room with her, not when he clearly couldn't be trusted to keep his distance. No. It'd be better if he found her a hotel room or another place to stay, or a place for him to stay. There was just one problem.

James.

What if he showed up in the middle of the night? What if he watched her bunk down in someone else's trailer? What if he sneaked up on her? Chance couldn't allow that to happen, which meant sticking to Carolina like glue, which meant sharing the trailer with her.

Yippee-ki-yay!

So when she showed up at the trailer after a quick practice session with the girls, he needed to tell her his plan. She wore that skintight bodysuit he was growing to hate, or maybe love, and he tried not to notice the way it showed off her every curve. "Look, I was thinking you might be uncomfortable with me sleeping inside. You know, gossip and all that, so I was going to grab a blanket and set up camp outside."

"What?" She appeared genuinely surprised, the evening sun shining into her blue eyes. "I don't care what people think."

"Well, I do. I'll keep watch out here."

"Not going to happen." She crossed her arms over her chest, apparently digging in her heels over the issue. "People can gossip all they want. I already owe you so much. I'm not going to be responsible for booting you from your bed."

He didn't like the images the word *bed* provoked. "I thought with everything that had happened between you and James, you might be uncomfortable sleeping with a strange man. I mean, sleeping near a man you don't know all that well."

Why did he feel like a bumbling fool all of a sudden? Was it the fact she stood, blue eyes wide, blond hair streaming down her back, her body silhouetted by the sun?

"You're my boss's brother." She forced a smile. He could tell by the way it didn't quite wrinkle the corners of her eyes. "It'll be fine."

Somehow he doubted that.

"I promise not to bite," she added.

Yeah, but would he be able to keep from biting her? That was the question.

She'd been lying. It would not be fine. She recognized that fact within two minutes of stepping inside the trailer.

"I need to take a shower," she announced.

He'd followed her inside, but her words made him freeze. "Oh, yeah. Sure. I'll wait outside while you do that."

For a fraction of a second, she wondered what he would do if she invited him into the shower with her, but as quickly as the thought came, she chased it away. She did not need that type of complication in her life, not matter how tempting.

"Thanks," she said instead, forcing another smile.

The moment he closed the trailer door, she leaned her head against a nearby cabinet and groaned. This weekend was not going how she'd planned. She'd meant to keep her cool, to treat him like a big brother, to shove her damn physical attraction to the furthest reaches of her mind, where she'd slap a giant iron bolt across it and never think about it again.

Ha.

Carolina took a cold shower. When she finished, she pulled clothes out of her duffel bag. She layered on item after item, partly because she was freezing and partly because it would act as barricade against her own desires. She hoped.

"Your turn," she said, stepping outside, hair still wet from the shower. She shivered in the cool night air. "I'll wait out here while you do your thing."

Chance frowned. He obviously didn't like the idea of leaving her alone.

"And look," she said, holding up her Hello Kitty key chain. "I brought protection." She patted the pocket of her sweats. Well, the first layer of sweats. "And pepper spray. I promise to scream if James makes an appearance."

"Just the same, I would feel better if you were inside with me."

While he took a shower? No, thanks. That was all she needed, to imagine water sluicing over his arms and belly and...other things. While she wondered what it would be like to glide her fingers down—

She swallowed. "I'll wait here."

He must have realized she wasn't going to heed his wishes, because he glanced around them once—as if searching the bushes for James—before turning toward the trailer.

"Stay by the door," he ordered.

"Yes, sir!" She saluted.

"I'll be quick." She waited a full minute before patting her other pocket and then pulling her cell phone out. With a deep breath and a silent prayer, she dialed the familiar number, grateful her number was blocked from caller ID. James answered after the second ring.

"Leave me alone," was all she said.

He didn't say anything, and for a moment she wondered if the call had been dropped, but then she heard James's quiet laughter, the kind that sent goose bumps up her arms and fear deep into her soul.

"I mean it, James. Leave me alone."

"Who's the guy?"

It took her a moment to figure out what he meant. "My new boss."

"Oh, yeah?"

"It doesn't matter who he is. You're out of my life, remember? Gone. And if you don't leave me alone, I'm going to call every news station in town and have them do a story about ex-boyfriends who stalk their ex-girlfriends after they beat the crap out of them."

Silence.

She'd never threatened to go public before. She hadn't even told Colt and Natalie about the abuse until she'd gotten out of the hospital. And she'd downplayed the seriousness of the matter. It wasn't until James had shown up at the ranch one day that she'd come clean to Colt. In hindsight, it must have been shortly after James's visit that Colt had thought of the idea of putting his brother in charge.

James laughed. "If you do that, I'll sue you for defamation of character."

"You could try," she said. "But your mug shot is online. Kinda hard to call me a liar when the proof of your guilt is on the internet for all to see." He didn't respond, and his silence gave her courage. "So unless you want to be this week's special feature, I suggest you give me a wide berth from here on out, got it?"

"My, my, my. Someone's grown some claws. Wonder if it has anything to do with the new man in your life."

"You're right. I do have claws. Hello Kitty claws. And I'll use them on you if you don't leave me alone."

"Are you seeing him?"

"I'm not dating anyone. Not now. Not ever. I'm done with men. Most of all, I'm done with you. Now leave me alone, or I swear to the good Lord, you'll be sorry."

She hung up before he could ignite her temper any more.

"I take it that was James?"

Chance leaned against the trailer door. Wow. That must have been the world's shortest shower. "I called him," she said. "Told him to leave me alone."

"And you think he'll listen?"

"If he has any sense he will. I threatened to out him on television if he didn't."

He nodded, his hair still wet, as was hers, but she'd bet he looked ten times better than she did. He looked as though he'd come from a photo shoot, one of those sexy-men-out-of-the-shower shoots, complete with white T-shirt clinging to his damp skin and skintight jeans.

"We should probably turn in." He stood back so she could enter the trailer. "Long day tomorrow."

And she would have to sleep by him. This would be a long night.

Chapter 8

When Chance woke up the next morning, he'd have been the first one to admit his bad mood. Sleep deprivation did that to a man, especially when the lack of sleep involved a woman.

Who wasn't in the trailer.

He checked the bathroom. And the bed where she'd slept, the same damn bed he'd thought about crawling into last night, even though he knew she'd kick him out if he did.

I'm not dating anyone. Not now. Not ever.

Her words should have served as a stern reminder why he should steer clear. Instead they were like a call to arms, at least as far as his body was concerned. He couldn't stop thinking about her.

Where was she?

The trailer wasn't that big, and since she wasn't inside, she must be outside, after he'd specifically told her not to leave without him.

Damn it.

He burst outside so fast he knocked the trailer door open all the way, its boom no doubt startling their neighbor.

"There you are," he said, grimacing slightly at the accusatory sound of his words. "Where were you?"

"Sorry," she said, somehow looking five years younger in her bulky sweatshirt and ponytail. "I thought I would feed the horses."

"And I thought I told you to stay put."

"You did, but I made sure the coast was clear. And just in case, I brought my kitty claws and my pepper spray." She held both up, then put them back in her pockets. "Even if James had shown up, I would have been okay."

"Famous last words."

"No. Really."

How could he make her see things through his eyes? It was the most frustrating part of this whole situation.

"Carolina, I'm serious. Once, when I was over there, in the Middle East, we found a woman huddling behind some bushes. Strangest thing we'd ever come across way out in the middle of nowhere. At first we thought she might be some kind of radical Islamist—you never know these days—but we took one look at her face and knew she was no terrorist."

He stepped toward her, hoping she'd see the utter seriousness in his eyes.

"She'd been beaten by her husband. Guess he took offense to some other man trying to talk to her. Blamed it on her, and so she ran."

Her face paled. "You don't have to tell me any more."

"Yes, I do. I need you to understand something about the opposite sex, something that not a lot of women know, but that I saw firsthand. There are men out there who think they own their wives or girlfriends—I mean, *own* own. They look upon women as a commodity. As a thing. It was bad over there. Worse than you can possibly imagine. This poor woman was married to such a man. We tried to get her some help. Tried to take her to our embassy. Asylum. Whatever you want to call it. Didn't do a damn bit of good. The sons of bitches wouldn't let us help her. We had to turn her over to her own people. We heard later that she'd been beaten to death the next day."

"Oh, Chance. I'm sorry."

He shook his head. "Don't be sorry for me. Be sorry for that woman. You have a choice, Caro. You can either stick with me and be safe, or you can go trotting off on your own and put yourself at risk. After what I saw over there, I don't trust any man that puts his hands on a woman. James is no exception."

She nodded. "Okay. I get it."

"I hope you do."

"I was coming back to change. I want to put Rio through his paces. He's still pretty green, and I'm not sure what he'll be like in this arena."

Rio. Her new stunt horse. He'd watched her practice this past week, marveling at her ability. She was by far and away the best trick rider of the Galloping Girlz, doing things no sane woman should do, like standing on the shoulders of one of the other girls, a stunt he'd never seen before. But no matter how brave she was, she'd be no match for James.

"I'll watch," he offered because there was no way he wanted her walking to the arena without him. It was bad enough he'd somehow missed her getting up to feed the horses. If he were honest, he wasn't angry at her so much as at himself.

"You don't have to do that."

"Go change," he offered by way of response. "I'll wait outside."

Damn lack of sleep. It made him edgy. And impatient. And cranky.

But she didn't leave right away. She held eye contact, her eyes seeming to be as blue as the wild lilac that bloomed in the spring. It was still too early for direct sunlight, but she didn't need light to shine. A piece of hay stuck in her hair. He told himself to ignore it, but instead he reached for it, slowly, so as not to scare her.

"Thank you," she said softly, but he didn't know if she thanked him for wanting to keep her safe or for removing the piece of hay.

"You're welcome."

She entered the trailer and closed the door softly. Chance backed up a step and collapsed into a camp chair he'd set up outside. This attraction thing needed to stop. In a couple months, three at most, he'd be overseas again. Plus, he'd heard her earlier. *I'm done with men*, she'd said. *Never again.*

Bad timing. Bad idea. Bad choice.

He was a combat veteran, one who took his career seriously, and he needed to stick to the mission—protecting her.

The trailer door opened, and she paused for a moment. She'd changed into a skintight leotard, one with a silver swath of fabric that ran up her leg, intersected her middle and ended at her shoulder. It left nothing to the imagination. Again.

Damn.

He stood up quickly. "Let's go."

She didn't say a word, simply fell into step beside him. It took her only a moment to tack up Rio—the horse's special saddle so light it looked as if it required hardly any effort to lift onto Rio's back. Off-white in color, the saddle was smaller and flatter in the back and, yes, had a saddle horn, but it was tiny compared to a normal saddle.

"Arena could be crowded," he observed as she slipped on Rio's bridle.

"That's okay. There's always people around."

It was early morning, and a crispness hung in the air, typical of mountain rodeos. But the time and temperature didn't stop people from wandering about. Slack—a section of the rodeo not attended by the general public—would start in an hour or so. Most competitors currently tended to their horses, though a few were already riding.

Chance scanned the perimeter and sidelines for anyone who might look suspicious, but there was nobody. Everyone was on horseback, which helped eliminate potential threats, unless...

"Does James ride?" he asked.

Carolina huffed in laughter as she opened the arena gate. "Hardly."

He nodded and then peered up at the grandstand. Nobody there, either. He wished he had his scope. The pine trees surrounding them would make a great hiding place.

You're being paranoid.

Maybe he was, but her conversation with James had put Chance on edge. It hadn't sounded very friendly, and it made him think this thing between them was far from over.

"I won't take long," she said, swinging up on Rio's back with the ease of a ballerina. "Colt will be here later, and he'll want to go through the whole routine with me and the girls."

And Chance would get to watch. That was fine. He liked to be in the background, keeping an eye on things. Like now. If James showed up, the man would be in for a surprise. And it wouldn't be just him jumping the man. He would bet a half a dozen cowboys would come to Carolina's rescue if anything were to happen. You didn't mess with women at rodeos—not if you valued your life. More importantly, you didn't mess with his woman.

His?

Well, not like that, he reassured himself. Not *ever* like that.

Caro set off on Rio, nodding and waving to the cowboys she passed, blond ponytail bouncing up and down in rhythm to her horse. Everyone knew her. That removed some of the tension from his shoulders. More friendlies meant fewer potential hostiles to keep an eye on. Chance scanned every face in the arena, all the while watching as Caro brought Rio up to speed. It was hard to keep his eyes off her once she began her tricks.

She amazed him.

He couldn't watch her hang upside down without feeling his stomach drop somewhere near his toes— the same feeling he got when he jumped out of a plane. And yet, he marveled. If he saw the move a million times, he'd never grow tired of it. Her hair whipped around as furiously as her horse's tail while she performed her repertoire of tricks. When she stood up on Rio's back, it was almost anticlimactic. Easy. Not much of a challenge compared to galloping upside down with nothing more than a single leg hooked around the breast collar.

POP.

Chance flinched. Caro's horse bolted.

"Caro." He jumped over the fence so fast he damn near tripped on the top rail. Caro had somehow managed to clutch the back of the saddle, but her legs hung down, her lower body flopping about. She might have been okay except Rio wasn't a seasoned trick horse. Spooked, he started to buck. Hard.

Dear God.

Caro's grip slipped. He could hear her yelling, "Whoa, Rio, whoa," but it did little good. One of the cowboys in the arena turned his horse and galloped toward her, but it was too little too late. Like a rag doll tossed by a petulant kid, Caro flew through the air, arms splayed, legs akimbo. She landed with an audible thud that twisted his gut.

"Caro!"

She didn't move, and it sent him into a panic he'd never felt before. Not when he'd been caught in a firefight. Not when he'd spotted that IED six inches from his left foot. Not when that shell blast had knocked him back on his keister.

"Caro." He all but threw himself down. "Can you hear me?"

She groaned.

"Caro."

She muttered something, and he leaned in close to hear it.

"I'm going to kill that horse."

He drew back quickly. Blue eyes met his own.

"Don't worry. I'll do it for you."

She nodded, winced and clutched her head.

"Are you hurt?"

"Just banged up, I think."

"Stay still while we wait for the EMTs to arrive."

"EMTs? I don't need an EMT." She slowly sat up, a clod of dirt falling off the front of her shirt.

"I said don't move."

"I'm fine." She waved him back.

Dirt covered her leotard and her face and was in her hair. "You are not fine."

"I've survived worse." She started to stand.

"Carolina Cruthers, you are not to move another inch until an EMT has checked you out!"

He'd never yelled at a woman before, but there was a first for everything. His words had the desired effect. She froze in place and stared up at him.

"Jeez," she said, eyes wide. "I got bucked off my horse. No big deal."

He shook his head, trying to convey the seriousness of his words. "You weren't just bucked off. You were shot."

Chapter 9

Caro thought she'd misheard him.

"Excuse me?"

"I heard a gunshot just as Rio started to buck."

Shot.

She jumped to her feet.

"Hey!"

She ignored him. *Rio.*

She didn't know the man who had come up alongside of the gelding, leaned over and caught the reins. She ran toward him and Rio, searching the horse for blood, for a limp, for some sign of injury.

"Caro!"

She didn't stop, despite her aching foot and shoulders. Plus, she was pretty certain she'd have a massive bruise on her hip tomorrow. She ignored it all because if Rio had been shot…

"You okay?" the cowboy who held Rio's reins asked. The man, who seemed vaguely familiar, stared down at her with a look of concern and kindness.

"Fine." Her words came out in a rush, as if she could slow down time by speeding up her words. "Easy, Rio."

She placed her hands against his brown coat. He'd begun to sweat, his bay color stained a darker shade. His veins were distended. His sides expanded and contracted quickly. *Shock?* A quick scan didn't reveal any noticeable injuries. Maybe Chance had been wrong—

There.

On the point of his butt, right next to his tail, a small swelling.

"Do you see anything?"

She glanced at Chance, who had come up behind her. She saw the worry in his eyes. She pointed to Rio's injury in response, moving in for a closer look. It had started to swell, but there was no blood. No hole, either, where the bullet might have gone in. In fact, the wound looked more like a bee sting than a bullet wound.

"Are you sure he was shot?"

"Shot?" said the man who still held Rio's reins. "Are you serious?"

"I thought I heard something, too," said another cowboy. "A *crack* right as her horse started to bolt."

"Must have startled him," surmised the first man, tipping the brim of his straw hat. "That's why he started to buck."

"No," Chance said. "He was shot *at.*"

"Shot at?" the cowboy said in disbelief. "As in someone fired a bullet at him?" He shook his head. "No one's going to shoot at a horse, not at a rodeo."

Carolina tried to remain calm. A person would do

that if he were angry because she'd broken up with him. If he wanted to hurt her because she'd dared to go to the police. If he were enraged because she'd threatened to publicize what he'd done to her.

"There's no bullet hole," said one of the men.

"No, there's not," she mused, turning toward Chance in question.

"Because he wasn't shot with a rifle." Chance's gaze encompassed them all. "It was an air gun. I could hear the hiss of the cartridge when it discharged."

"You some kind of gun expert, then?" the man in the straw hat asked.

Chance nodded. "I was an Army Ranger. Combat active. Discharged two weeks ago."

That shut the man up, and it explained a lot to Caro, too. That's why Rio was swollen and not bleeding. The bump was a welt. She straightened suddenly as a new thought penetrated.

Did James watch them?

"He's gone," Chance said, placing a hand on her shoulder. "There's no way he'd stick around, not after watching you get back up. He knows you're okay."

"Which means he might be back."

"I don't think he wants you dead." He shook his head. "It's like I said. Some men can't take rejection. But James is not stupid. He just wants to see you scared."

"Someone trying to hurt you?" asked the cowboy.

James had already hurt her. And now he'd hurt her again. And almost her horse. She wanted to cry, except she didn't. She took a deep breath and said, "My ex."

The answer seemed to satisfy the man, because he pulled the brim of his hat down low, as if preparing to face someone on a most-wanted poster. "If someone's trying to hurt you, Carolina, I'll tell a few of the boys. Nobody will get near this arena again. Not without us checking them out."

"What about tonight?" she asked. "What about when Slack starts in an hour or so? What about when I perform?" And as she said the words, emotion built inside her. "He's not going to stop just because people are around. He's insane. Crazy." Just like Chance had said he was.

And he'd tried to hurt her horse.

Funny how you could go around blaming yourself. How you could deal with someone doling out punches. Live with it, even, but when that same someone tried to injure an animal you loved…

She looked at Chance. "I'll be right back."

"Where are you going?"

Pain shot up her leg as she turned away, but she didn't care. Rio could have been hurt from that shot, no matter that it was a rubber bullet, a pellet or whatever kind of projectile James had used. If it'd hit Rio in the wrong spot—the eye, maybe.

"I'm calling the police." She paused, turned back to face the men. "And then I'm going to call the local media. And then I'm going to hire a hit man to kill that son of a bitch."

Chance's brow lifted. It brought the edge of his cowboy hat up, so she could perfectly see the play of emotion in his eyes. Surprise. Dismay. Mostly though, she spotted approval.

"Attagirl."

Chance smiled. She was true to her word, not that any of her calls amounted to much of anything.

"We'll have an extra patrol run by the rodeo grounds tonight," said a black-clad officer who didn't look old enough to shave, much less own a gun. "In the meantime, I'll call VDC PD and see what they can do on their end."

Carolina nodded at the young officer. "Anything you can do to help."

Help? This kid didn't know how to help. He'd probably never discharged his weapon anywhere other than the firing range, much less in the line of duty. Yet Caro appeared to be strangely reassured by the man's words.

It irritated the heck out of Chance.

"What's going on here?"

They both turned, and Chance was relieved to see his brother. "Something wrong?" Colt asked.

Chance had tried to call him earlier, but he'd only gotten Colt's voice mail, and he refused to leave messages when someone was driving.

"James shot my horse," Carolina stated.

"What?" Colt glanced between them. "Is Rio okay?"

"He's fine," Chance answered. "It was an Airsoft rifle, probably. Rubber pellet. We found it after searching for an hour. Rio has a welt the size of a grapefruit on his rear. He'll be fine. When we get back to the ranch tomorrow, I'll have Ethan take a look at it to be certain, but I'm pretty sure it's just bruised."

His future brother-in-law, Ethan, was a veterinarian. He'd know what to do, and that made her feel a little bit better.

"That does it," Colt said, looking as angry as a stepped-on rooster. He jerked his hat off his head. "That son of a bitch is going down."

"We've got things handled, sir," said the kid cop.

Colt ignored him. "Carolina, on Monday I'm taking you straight down to the courthouse and you're filing suit against him. I don't know what you can charge him with, but something's got to be better than nothing."

"Don't worry. I plan to do more than that," Caro said, hands on her hips.

Chance suspected James had crossed an invisible line with her. Good. She needed to realize this was a serious matter. He hadn't been kidding when he'd said men could do horrible things to women they professed to love.

"In the meantime, Chance, you're not to leave her side." His brother's gaze fell on him.

Chance cocked a thumb at Carolina. "Tell her that."

"I know," she said, her face grim. "I'm sorry. Chance has been trying to keep an eye on me, but I didn't want to be a bother. Believe me, I'll be more careful now."

"And I'll be more alert."

Chance was mad at himself for taking his eyes off their surroundings. For watching Caro as she practiced. He should have scouted the perimeter before she rode. Should have insisted she forgo practicing. It wasn't as though she didn't know the routine. She could have sat out one practice session, but he never would have thought James…

"She could have been killed falling off her horse," Colt said the same thing he'd been thinking.

And if Caro had been seriously injured, he would never have forgiven himself. As it was, he felt a deep, rolling rage. James had clearly wanted her to be bucked off, and something else, too.

Chance stroked his jaw. Something about the whole situation was off. He couldn't quite put his finger on it, but it was the same kind of feeling he got when a group of insurgents showed up at a strange and obscure location. There was always a method to a crazy man's madness.

"I think it's safe to say your assailant won't be back," said the baby boy in blue—an Officer Walker. "Men like him usually run scared after they've made a move."

Chance tried not to laugh. As if Officer Walker had been on the force long enough to make that assumption. However, Chance would bet the cop was right. There were enough cowboys and cowgirls pissed off about the whole thing that James would be stupid to try something again. Too many people on alert now.

"Here's the plan," Chance said to the group, splaying his hand in Caro's direction. "You're not performing tonight. Delilah can take your place."

"What?" Caro's mouth dropped open. She looked toward his brother as if he could help change Chance's mind, and that irritated Chance all the more.

"She doesn't know the new routine," Chance added, "but she can figure it out. She's watched you enough times."

"My brother's right," Colt said. "We can't take any chances. You're grounded until further notice, and you—" he turned to Chance "—you're going to stick to her like glue. I'll sleep in Bill's trailer tonight. I don't want any gossip starting about a single girl sharing a trailer with two men. You and Caro can take mine again."

It quickly became clear that Caro wasn't just mad, she was livid. Two hours later, as the crowd cheered in the distance for the Galloping Girlz and their new routine, Caro prowled around the interior of the trailer like one of the military dogs his sister cared for.

"This is ridiculous," she said after pacing across the length of the trailer for the tenth time. "There's a million people out there. James wouldn't dare try and pull something tonight."

"Just the same, you're staying in here."

"What about tomorrow?" She shook her head in aggravation, her blond hair flying over her shoulders. "Am I supposed to sit around all day?"

"Think of it as a vacation."

"I should go home."

"And be at the ranch all by yourself? I don't think so."

She released an oath of frustration. "Natalie would be there."

Her eyes implored him to see reason. Wasn't going to work.

"And your sister's not far away," she added.

He shook his head, emphatically so she got the point. "I'm not willing to jeopardize their safety because you're bored."

She drew up short. Clearly, she hadn't thought that far ahead. A second later, she flounced down on the couch opposite him.

"I can't stand being pent up like this."

He reached behind him and stretched his arms. "Then do something productive with all that energy."

"Like what?"

It was one of those things—a suggestion he hadn't known he was going to propose, and something he probably shouldn't mention. "Training."

She cocked a brow at him, and with her hair down and loose around her shoulders and her black T-shirt clinging to her every curve, he began to doubt the soundness of his suggestion. He should be keeping away from her, not planting ideas in her head.

"What do you mean?" she asked when he failed to explain.

Don't do it. Do not do it. You know how uncomfortable she makes you feel. Touching her will only complicate matters. He'd had enough fantasies about her last night.

"Self-defense."

The voice inside his head groaned, but he couldn't ignore the fact that she needed training. Pepper spray only went so far. If that bastard ex of hers was crazy enough to shoot at her horse, no telling what else he would do. And if he ever caught her off guard, if he managed to surprise her one night at the ranch, she wouldn't have time to get out her spray or arm herself with a weapon. Today was proof of that. So if Chance taught her a few of the moves he'd learned in the army, she might have a fighting chance.

"You should learn to protect yourself."

Oh, yeah? asked the voice. *Who's going to protect you?*

"You mean learn karate or something?"

"You don't need karate. There's a lot you can do with just your hands."

And if he needed proof of what a bad idea this whole thing was, those words sure did seal the deal, because there was a lot she could do with her hands…and he wished she'd do it all to him.

Chapter 10

She should have said no.

Later that evening, Carolina wondered what the hell she'd gotten herself into. At least, she'd been granted a momentary reprieve. She had been downright embarrassed earlier. When the girls had returned, Lori had banged on the door, shouting, "Whadda ya guys doing in there?"

Carolina had wanted to die. Despite telling Chance she didn't care what everyone thought, she didn't want to be thought of as a floozy – shacking up with the boss's brother. Although word would spread quickly that she had an issue with an ex, so she probably had nothing to worry about.

"Now, remember, you're never going to win if you're facing a man with a gun."

They stood between the two trailers, in an area

shielded from people passing by, the grass in between them trampled from their feet.

"I know," she said, nervously tucking her hands into her pockets.

"The best thing to do if that happens is run. But not straight. Zigzag. Do the unexpected. And dive behind something if you can."

She nodded. It was late. The rodeo had ended long ago. Colt had gone off to tend to the horses. The girls had fled somewhere else…probably to the local bar. That left her and Chance alone, the sun at an angle that lit the tops of the trees on fire, the sky a yellow orange that would have taken her breath away if she wasn't already breathing hard in anticipation of what they were about to do. It was ridiculous. It wasn't as though Chance would hurt her. He was going to teach her to keep from being hurt.

"The first thing I'm going to teach you is how to deflect a punch."

Whoo boy. That was training she could have used a while ago. And it was crazy, because merely thinking about that night made the lip James had split in two hurt. The memory was so powerful it was all she could do not to run away. Her heart ran away instead.

Despite her feelings, Carolina held her ground. Damn that James. Damn any man that would try and hurt her.

"Do I use my arms?" It was what she'd done the night James attacked her. She had lifted her arms and used them to cover her face…

"No. Not quite. But first things first. If someone comes at you this way—" Chance stepped in her direction, and she flinched slightly, which was ridiculous, because she didn't have anything to fear from Chance. His eyes narrowed.

"I'm not going to hurt you," he said quietly.

"I know."

He stared at her in concern, and it made her breath catch just as it had yesterday. How could a man be such a warrior on the outside and so warm and tender on the inside?

Chance tilted his head. "If this brings back too many memories, we can stop."

"No. I need to learn this."

"Good," he said. "Because if you listen to me closely, from here on out, you'll be the one in control. No one will ever hit you again, I promise."

She looked down at the ground to hide her eyes. Despite her earlier anger, she wanted to cry again, and she hated that. She was not the crying type. Never had been. Never would be. And yet somehow, she'd become Pitiful Pearl—in the flesh—and damned if she knew how she'd gotten that way.

She sucked in a deep breath. "Okay. Show me again."

For the longest time, his eyes roved over her face, as if trying to decide if he should trust her words.

"Bend your arms up like this," he said at last. "Like a crossing guard holding a sign."

She followed his instructions.

"Good. Now. When I come at you—" he stepped even closer "—you move your arm like I showed you. Are you ready?"

Another deep breath, one that seemed to stoke the fires of determination in her heart. She could do this. She was not the sniveling ninny James had reduced her to. She could trust this man.

"Ready?"

He swung a fist in her direction. She deflected it. Easily. Quickly.

"Good job."

And the victory she felt, the euphoria at deflecting his swing, made her feel—well, she couldn't help but smile. It felt good to take charge.

"Do it again," she told him.

He swung once more, faster. She moved quicker this time, and the maneuver worked the same way. So easy. So simple. With practice she probably wouldn't have to think about it.

"That was great," she said. Never again would she find herself cowering before a man, letting him hit her, being afraid for her life.

Chance smiled his approval, and she thought it was a crying shame no woman had caught his interest. With his masculine skills and easy smile, half her teammates wanted to go after him. Half of Natalie's clients seemed enamored with him, too. She didn't blame them.

"Now," he continued, "sometimes people will try and grab you when they realize you can deflect a punch. I'm going to teach you some pressure points that will help deter anyone who tries to grab you. The first one is here." He pointed to his wrist. "Right above the bone. If you dig your thumb in, you'll bring a man down. Trust me." He offered her his arm, motioning for her to try it.

"I don't want to hurt you."

"It's okay. I'm going to swing again, only this time when you deflect, I'll grab you, too. You clutch my wrist and press as hard as you can where I showed you."

For some reason, she crouched. He grinned, and she

had the inexplicable urge to do something crazy—like laugh. Instead she waited.

He came at her fast. She deflected. He grabbed. She pressed. *Hard.*

"Ow, ow, ow." He dropped to the ground. She released immediately. He sucked in a breath.

Carolina gulped. "Oh, my goodness. Did I hurt you?" She closed the distance between them. When he stood and bent his head to examine his wrist, they were only inches away.

"No, I'm good. You just surprised me, is all."

He looked up at the same time she did, and they were face-to-face, his breath on hers and her breath on him. His eyes peered down at her so softly, she couldn't believe how it felt to have him there, next to her. Exciting. Reassuring. Peaceful.

"Well, good," she mumbled. "I'm glad." She looked away, because her heart had begun to beat so hard she was sure he could see it. Or maybe he heard it thundering in her ears.

"Okay. Yeah. Well." He stepped back. "There's one more maneuver I'd like to show you."

He clenched his hands, and she wondered if he'd felt it, too, that moment when the ground beneath her feet seemed to slide off the side of the earth and it was all she could do not to hang on.

To him.

She wanted to hold him.

"Turn around," he said.

Did he still feel it, she hoped, as she blindly followed his instructions. And then he was there, right there, up behind her, and she could feel the heat of him and she almost groaned.

Oh, holy hell.

She bolted. Spun. Faced him.

"What?" His expression was bewildered.

She didn't know *what*. Something crazy was going on, because she was never going to let a man get close to her again, not even one as nice as Chance.

"I heard a bee," she lied.

He chuckled. "No bees. Just me."

It was no use getting attached to Chance. He was leaving soon. Colt had told her a half-dozen times that Chance would only be Stateside long enough to witness the birth of another nephew or niece. Then he was gone. So even if she did like his smile and the kindness in his eyes and the way he made her feel safe and protected, it was temporary.

"Go on," he urged. "Turn around."

She didn't want to. She didn't, but she had no choice. He came up behind her again, and everything around them retreated. The two trailers side by side. The people walking by on the road. The horses and dogs that wandered the rodeo grounds. Everything.

"You don't need to be afraid," he whispered into her ear.

She wasn't afraid. Not even a little.

"I promise not to hurt you."

No. He would never do that. She knew that with every fiber of her being.

"This is what you do if someone grabs you from behind."

She tensed because she knew he would touch her, and a second later, his hands were on her shoulders and she almost gasped.

"They'll probably wrap their arms around you." His

hands slid down. She smelled his clean scent—a combination of talc and citrus—and it caused her to close her eyes.

"You'll never break free by trying to use your hands."

No. She'd learned that lesson the hard way. The thought was a sobering one, and it caused her to sharpen her focus.

"The first thing you do is insert your foot between my legs."

She did as instructed, which meant their legs touched. Her sharpness faded again at the feel of his rock-hard limbs. *Oh, dear goodness.*

"Now, take your elbow and jab it into my ribs."

"But I—"

"Do it."

She jabbed. Hard.

The breath gushed out of him. The scent of him faded as he moved away slightly.

"Good," he wheezed. "Now, this next time, take a step back. So it's leg between, jab and step back. All in one move. Then as he's falling backward, slip down and out of my arms." He closed the distance again, wrapped an arm around her neck. "Quickly. Do it."

She hesitated.

"Now."

She jabbed. He grunted again. She thrust herself back. They both went down.

"Whoa," he cried, somehow shifting so she landed on top of him. "You forgot the leg."

They lay belly to belly, breath to breath, and his eyes were full of amusement and something else. Something that made her whole world tilt and her heart soften.

"I'm sorry."

"Don't be." He tucked a stray piece of hair behind her ear. "You're doing great."

Everything warmed. Her face. Her skin where they touched. Even...

She rolled away. "I'm no good at this."

"You will be." He sat up. "It just takes practice."

She wasn't talking about self-defense. She was talking about *her*. About her disastrous past. About how she seemed to pick the wrong man or the right man at the wrong time. She met his gaze, and she knew he was the latter. Any woman could see that, even someone as messed up as her.

"Hey," he said, clearly reading her distress. "It's okay. You'll catch on."

"I don't think I'm cut out for this. My mom—"

She stopped herself, but he'd caught the words.

"What about your mom?"

She shook her head.

He scooted closer, using a single finger to turn her chin so she faced him.

"What about your mom?"

Carolina hated the fact she'd brought her up. That she was somehow blaming her for her troubles. She'd never been one to point the finger at anyone but herself, and she wasn't about to start now. Still, Carolina couldn't escape the need for the truth in his eyes, and she needed to tell him, if only so he would understand how messed up she was.

"She wasn't the best role model in the world."

"No?"

"Apparently, I've learned a lot from her."

That was an understatement. Different men all the time. Some were nice. Some were kind. Some were old and wanted things no man twice her age should want, not from her.

"Don't blame yourself for James."

"He's exactly the kind of man my mom would bring home."

"And he's gone from your life."

"Not yet."

"But he will be."

Would he? These days it seemed as though the bad guys were in and out of jail faster than someone could change a tire. And if that happened, if James was arrested for assault and he went to jail and then got out on bail the next day, presuming he would even make it to jail, what then? Who would protect her then? Chance would be long gone. The district attorney had told her it'd be months before James went to trial. Suddenly, Carolina wished with all her might that Chance wasn't going to leave.

"Hey." He must have read the fear in her eyes because his eyes softened. "It'll be okay."

It would not. Nothing would ever be okay again. She had only to look into his eyes to know that.

Carolina had fallen for the wrong guy. Again.

Chapter 11

He wanted to kiss her.

With her eyes searching his, imploring, it was all he could do not to lean down and plant his lips on hers. He couldn't. Wouldn't. Shouldn't.

She blinked. He did, too, and the momentary break in eye contact was enough. He stood, held out a hand.

"Let's practice some more," he said.

She nodded, blond hair falling over one shoulder. She was so tiny. Too small to defend herself against a man like James, at least not without any self-defense training. That James had struck her, that he still taunted her—well, it started a fire inside Chance's heart, one that he focused on instead of how appealing she looked at that moment.

She took his outstretched hand. He pulled her to her feet, and she landed against him.

God.

If she had any idea how aroused he was with her against him, well, she'd probably call off the rest of their lesson.

"Remember," he said into her ear. "Step, wedge, thrust."

He didn't give her time to comment, simply wrapped an arm around her. She didn't hesitate this time, planting her leg between his own, thrusting back and using such force he didn't need to fake falling down.

Damn, he loved the way her eyes lit up with triumph. "That was easy," she said.

"Let's do it again."

It was a form of physical torture. He came up behind her, his body buzzing and warming in places he wouldn't acknowledge. She thrust her leg through his own—bringing to mind other things she could do with her legs—then shifted back up against him, her rear end coming into contact with his midsection, which made him groan.

She froze. "Did I hurt you?"

Not in the way she thought. "I'm fine. Just keep going."

She thrust back. He dropped to the ground, and he couldn't take any more. It wasn't like him to quit, but there was no shame in knowing your own weak spots. Caro Cruthers was definitely a weak spot.

"I think we should call it a night."

It was a good time to do exactly that. The sun had dropped low, and they were quickly losing daylight. Soon the shadows would deepen, and he'd rather be inside when that happened.

Inside. With Caro.

It was a thought that repeated itself as they readied for the night. He managed to distract himself for a bit by cooking dinner, but all too soon it was time to turn in.

"Thanks," she said, standing by the bedroom doorway. "Really, Chance. I appreciate all you're doing to help me."

"Think nothing of it," he said, turning away, having to turn away, because if she stared across at him with her big blue eyes one more time he'd…

What?

He didn't know, but he didn't want to find out.

"Good night," she said, closing the bedroom door.

Son of a—

Don't think about it. Don't think about the fact that right now she's on the other side of that door, stripping out of her clothes, tugging tiny little panties down over her hips.

You don't even know if she wears panties.

That was the problem, he told himself. He had no business wanting to find out.

He gazed out the trailer window. As he had so many times before, he told himself to focus on the job at hand. He doubted that bastard James would try anything. Not tonight. He knew they were on to him. After he'd shot Rio, the putz had probably headed back to Via Del Caballo, which was where they should be tonight.

Chance sighed. He should have used Colt's truck and taken her home. But no. She'd insisted on sticking around, wanting to be there for the team despite not performing.

He busied himself with work. He had a new job, and DTS had forms for him to fill out. Fortunately, he could do much of it through his smartphone. There were emails to answer, too, notes from his former combat buddies. Messages on social media from people he'd met over the years. He had no idea how long he'd been on the couch when he heard a noise. It came from the other side of the door.

Carolina.

She groaned, a groan of fear, pain and anguish.

Ignore her.

She cried out again, and against his better judgment, he crossed to the door and opened it slightly. A light outside the trailer perfectly illuminated her face. Her blond hair contrasted with the dark brown pillows.

Nothing would have convinced him to take the bed. The bed was for her, he'd insisted, especially since her body still ached from being bucked from Rio. Chance had been grateful when she hadn't argued. He needed a door between them.

"No!" Carolina flinched. His stomach sank to his toes. She was probably dreaming of James.

How could someone hit a woman? He'd never understood the need to beat someone who couldn't defend herself.

Carolina's head swung left, then right, as if she fought off blows in her dreams.

Damn it.

He didn't want to. He really didn't, but he couldn't stop from entering her room. The bed was above the hitch of the trailer, which meant there was no way for him to walk along the side of the bed. All he could do was use his voice.

But, man, did he want to touch her.

He couldn't believe how badly he fought the urge. He wanted to crawl up beside her, brush the fear from her face with his fingers, ease the pain of her cries and tell her everything was all right. Nothing would happen to her.

She flung an arm up, but then she quieted and he continued to watch.

He needed to leave. He turned before he could convince himself to do otherwise, but he didn't stop at the couch. No. He burst into the cool night air before he could think better of it. There were chairs out in front. He settled into one of them. Wouldn't be the first time he'd kept watch outside. And sitting in a canvas director's chair sure beat propping himself up against a rock. He tipped his cowboy hat down and closed his eyes.

It was the last thing he remembered.

When he opened his eyes, Caro stood in front of him, holding out a mug. He shot up in surprise, but not even scrubbing a hand over his face helped to clear his mind. *Son of a—*

He must have conked out. That wasn't like him. Not when he was on watch.

"Here." She waved the mug in front of her. "You look like you need this."

He took the steaming cup from her, knowing a big sip of caffeine wouldn't shake the cobwebs from his mind. "Sorry," he said. "I had meant to keep watch, maybe get a little shut-eye, but not sleep until dawn."

She smiled. "Busy day yesterday."

"That's for sure." He took a sip of the coffee, wincing at its strength.

"What's wrong?" Her blue eyes widened with concern, and he marveled that she could read him so easily.

"Strong."

"Sorry. I usually get the dark roast."

"I'll go get some sugar."

"No, no. I'll get it. I think there's some inside."

"Stay," he said, standing. "I saw it last night when I was cooking."

He didn't give her an opportunity to respond. He needed to get up and stretch his legs. Inside the trailer, Chance headed to a cabinet to the left of the sink. The sugar was right where he remembered.

He heard a noise outside.

The hairs stood up on the back of his neck. He didn't usually get such strong premonitions, but when he did...

He set the mug down on the counter, turned and ran for the door.

"Let me go!"

Chance froze, but only for a split second because his instincts had proved right. James. He jumped off the steps at the same time Caro used one of the maneuvers he'd taught her yesterday, the one that allowed you to twist away from someone who'd grabbed your arm. James, a big hulk of a guy, tried for her again.

"Hey!"

James glanced at him, and Chance plowed into him with everything he had.

Oomph.

James might be big, but he didn't have years of combat experience. He didn't know there was a pressure point on the side of the neck that would send spasms through your whole body and make you cry out in pain.

"Don't move," Chance said, easing the pressure, but only a bit.

"My neck." Big paws tried to swipe him away.

"I *said*, don't move." More pressure, more cries of pain, but the hands dropped.

"Caro, call the police."

She ran into the trailer to get her cell phone.

Enraged gray eyes met his own. James might be big, but his eyes were tiny. His lips were thin, though that could be because he grimaced in pain. Still, Chance didn't know what Caro had seen in the man. She could do so much better.

"I'm going to let you up." He released the pressure again. "Slowly."

James didn't move. Not when Chance slipped off him and not when someone—Chance didn't know who—appeared and asked, "Need any help?" Chance wasn't sure who the man meant—him or James. Chance glanced around. Other people were coming out of their trailers.

"You broke my neck," James said.

"I didn't." Chance stood.

James groaned. "My whole body feels numb."

"It's just a nerve. It'll come back."

Silver eyes snarled at him.

Chance ignored him. He wasn't going to get into an argument with the man. Instead he said, "Don't get up. If you do, I'll put you back down again."

"Piss off, ass wipe." James tried to move. Chance grabbed an arm and twisted it. James yelled. He tried to get away, but Chance flipped him over onto his belly and then jabbed a knee into his kidneys.

"Aaaah."

"I *said. Don't. Move.*" Dumb-ass bullies. They always did the opposite of what they were told.

"Chance, they're on their way."

He looked up and spotted Caro standing above them, face pale, eyes wide as she gaped at James.

"Caro," James pleaded. "I just wanted to talk to you."

Chance grunted. "You had your chance when she called you."

"Face-to-face," he added.

"Oh, yeah?" Chance said, leaning in to him. "And shooting her horse was a way to start a conversation."

"I didn't shoot her horse."

"Not with a gun, no, but you shot at her horse with a pellet gun."

James bent back, trying to make eye contact with Caro. "I didn't shoot at you. Honestly."

"Yeah, right," she said.

"What's going on?"

His brother. Word spread fast among the rodeo community when trouble was afoot.

Colt touched Caro's arm briefly. "Did he hurt you?"

"I'm fine," she said, lightly patting his hand. "I didn't let him get close enough to hurt me."

"James!" Colt shouted. "I told you to leave her alone."

"He won't come near her again," Chance said, pressing a little harder on James's wrist. "Right, big boy?"

"Piss off."

"What did he do?" Chance heard someone ask.

"He tried to assault Caro."

"Is this the guy that's been harassing her?"

"He's the one that shot her horse."

"I say we drag him *behind* a horse."

Clearly word had spread about Caro's problem. People were mad. Not surprising. When someone took pot-shots at livestock, it was kind of a big deal.

"Here, I'll hold him," said one of the wide-shoul-dered steer wrestlers.

"You can piss off, too," James said.

"Thanks." Chance stood, ignoring the man on the ground and handing over control. The steer wrestler knew exactly where to press, and when Chance was satisfied he had James under control, he sought out Caro. She stared at the man who'd made her life hell. She lifted her head, and their gazes connected. In her eyes, he saw fear, sadness and self-reproach. Before he could think better of it, he crossed to her side and pulled her into his arms.

This.

This was what he'd wanted to do since yesterday. This right here. Hold her. Comfort her. Tell her everything would be all right. She resisted at first, but of course she would. Then she buried her head in his shoulder and it felt good, as if this was where she was supposed to be. Chance met his brother's gaze. Colt was smiling. Or was it smirking? Either way, his small nod seemed to signify approval.

Someone else watched him, too. James.

Yeah, that's right. I'm here to protect her now. Former Army Ranger. Combat ready. And if you touch her again, look out.

The fierceness of his emotions startled him. He'd never felt anything like them in his life. And they were all for Carolina.

She couldn't get away from the rodeo grounds fast enough.

Caro tried to let the breeze from the passenger-side window cool her face and her emotions, but it wasn't working.

"They're going to let him go," she said.

"You don't know that," Chance said. "Small-town police departments tend to take a harsher view of people who violate restraining orders, especially when they might have shot a horse twenty-four hours before."

"Yeah, but you know what it's like these days. Nobody ever stays in jail long."

He didn't disagree, and the knot in Caro's stomach pulled tighter. They were less than a half hour away from home, crossing the San Marcos foothills, the mountains brown from lack of rain, but the scenery no less spectacular. Valley oaks dotted the hillsides, the tips so full of foliage they hung to the ground, providing much-needed shade for wildlife. On any other day, she might have enjoyed the bright blue sky and the fluffy clouds staining the mountains with their shadows. Not today. She had shadows of her own to deal with.

Chanced glanced at her. "When you get back, you should call the officer in charge of your case."

"His name is Officer Connelly, and I already left him a message."

"And I think you need to keep staying at the ranch."

She didn't want to. She wanted life to return to normal. She sighed. "Yeah, I probably should."

That meant more one-on-one time with Chance. A double-edged sword. Last night, she'd woken up from a nightmare only to sense him staring at her. She'd wanted to open her eyes, but she hadn't. If she had, she might have done something stupid like hold out her hand to him. He might have seen what she couldn't hide.

Instead he had slipped away, and she'd tossed and turned, wondering if she should have opened her eyes.

No. She'd done the right thing. She knew that.

Carolina tipped her head back, letting the sunshine soak her face, enjoying the peace it brought her. All too soon, the peace ended when they crossed through the double gates to Reynolds Ranch. She should feel better about coming home—although it wasn't her home. That was the problem. She would be forced to live there for however much longer it would take to get James out of her life.

Chance cleared his throat. "Looks like my sister is here."

She snapped awake. Claire?

Sure enough, Chance's sister stood by the entrance to the barn, one of her rescue dogs sitting at her feet, a smile on her face as they pulled up. Caro couldn't get out of the truck fast enough. She adored Claire Reynolds, soon to be Claire McCall. The woman had been incredibly kind to her the past year.

"I was just leaving you a note," she said, her long black hair so dark and her green eyes so light she always reminded Caro of one of those dolls sold in dime stores with eyes as big as nickels. "Natalie told me you should be home soon."

The front door slammed as Natalie came outside, too. Her baby bump was barely noticeable despite the fact she was due to deliver soon.

"I thought that might be you," she said, her blue eyes echoing the smile on her face. "How was your drive?"

"Long," Carolina muttered before she could stop herself. She cringed. Some of her own self-loathing must have leaked out.

"Colt filled me in," Natalie said kindly. "You going to the police station today?"

She shook her head. "I already called. Officer Connelly isn't on duty today. I have to call first thing in the morning."

"Natalie told me what happened," Claire said, smoothing her black hair, which was clipped up atop her head. The style suited her heart-shaped face. "That's why I brought you Inga." She patted the dog's head.

"Inga?"

Carolina didn't understand. She glanced at Chance as if he might be in on the secret, but he simply nodded knowingly.

Claire's smile was a wide as a sunrise. "I brought you a Belgian Malinois, and she's yours."

"Mine?" Her gaze slipped over them all, settling on Chance.

He had clearly caught on right away, because he said, "She's perfect."

She still didn't get it, not really. "You mean she's mine to keep?"

Claire nodded again.

"You can keep her up in the apartment," Natalie said. "We don't mind. She's house-trained, too. And they're great dogs. I have one, but she's over at Claire's house nursing puppies."

"I don't know what to say."

Claire lifted a hand. "Say yes, but I'll understand if you want to think about it. Trust me, though. Inga needs a job, and you need protecting. It's a match made in heaven."

Inga whined. Caro's gaze fell on the mostly black dog. The animal stared straight at her, bouncing from one paw to another.

"Come on," Claire said, motioning her over. "Make her acquaintance."

Caro walked over slowly, hesitant. "I've never owned a dog before."

"This isn't a dog. This is a military war dog, and they're the closest thing to a human canine you'll ever find. They're a little more high-strung than a normal dog, but with your active life, you won't have any problem with her, and if you do, I'll take her back. Like I said, the main thing is to make sure you're protected."

Caro squatted, showing the dog her hand. Inga immediately licked it. That gave her enough confidence to touch the dog's majestic head. Black eyes that matched her black fur peered back at her. They were specked with brown, just like her coat. She was soft and she smelled like coconut oil. When the dog pushed her head into her, as if to say, "It's okay," a lump formed in her throat.

She looked down at the ground, overwhelmed with gratitude. Her eyes burned, though there was no reason to cry.

No one had ever done anything so nice for her. Everything she'd had, it'd all taken hard work. People didn't give her things, not even temporarily. She sucked in a breath. These people—Claire, Natalie, Colt, Chance—they not only gave from the heart, they cared.

Inga moved. Carolina felt a wet nose against her cheek, then a warm tongue. She closed her eyes, opened her arms and the dog walked into them.

"Thank you," she said, burying her face in the dog's scruff and having to work hard to get the words out over the lump in her throat. "I don't know if I'll be able to keep her. I mean, it would mean moving from my apartment."

"Something you may want to do, anyway," Natalie counseled.

"But I couldn't possibly say no to such an adorable animal." She met Claire's gaze. "This is the kindest thing anyone has ever done for me."

"You're welcome," Claire said with a smile.

"I'll go grab some tea," Natalie said. "We can sit outside and watch you work with her."

When Caro looked up, she spotted Chance gazing down at her, the smile still on his face, his military stance still present despite having been out of the armed services for weeks. She would never forget the way he'd jumped in to help her. The way he'd taken down James. And as he smiled, as he watched her pet her new dog, she admitted how much she liked him and how much she wished he were sticking around. She wanted to be a part of his family. She wanted to know what it was like to have the support of loved ones. To know she would always have a place to come home to.

It broke her heart because she'd never have that.

Chapter 12

Chance woke up in the middle of the night, his stomach churning.

The police had released James.

Caro had shared the news yesterday after she'd insisted on going to the police alone. Apparently, it was no big deal when someone violated a restraining order. A felony, yes, but as a police officer had explained to Caro, James wasn't considered armed and dangerous, not without proof. It was his word against hers that he'd shot at her horse, so they'd had to let him go. A slap on the wrist.

Chance hadn't had a solid night's sleep since.

Officer Connelly had tried to reassure her. Told her the police would do what they could. Step up patrols. Yadda, yadda, yadda. Chance knew none of it would work. James was out there. Obsessed. Angry. Insane. Chance had seen it before. He'd probably see it again.

He got out of bed and slipped on clothes without making a noise—he owed this talent to his years in the military. If you disturbed the barrack, something might be thrown at your head. He pulled on his cowboy boots and then headed out into the night.

Carolina's apartment was dark. She was probably sound asleep, unlike him. Moonlight cast a silvery sheen over the metal roof, the reflection of its face a bright smudge in the middle. It wouldn't be light for hours, but that was okay. His internal clock still wanted him to believe it was midafternoon, Kazakhstan time.

He paused on the front stoop, listening. Nothing but the sound of crickets, and in the far distance, a rooster that appeared to be messed up about the time of day. All was as it should be. Carolina slept, Inga stood guard and the world continued to turn.

It'd been his idea to give her the dog. Claire hadn't balked. She, more than anyone, understood what it was like to be a single woman, alone, with no one to share her life. That would change soon. She would marry Ethan in December. Her Christmas present, she claimed, and Chance couldn't be happier for her.

The barn was dark, too, but he wasn't headed that way. Teddy was kept in a pasture. No fancy stall for him. The old cow horse didn't like being cooped up. It was a simple matter to halter the horse and lead him to the tie rack. Chance didn't know how the animal would take to being ridden, but he needed the practice. Yesterday, while Caro had gone to the police station, he'd pulled one of the Galloping Girlz up behind him from a full-on run. Not once, but several times, and everyone who'd been out there had hooted and hollered. He'd never been so relieved in his life.

"You want to run again?" he asked Teddy, patting the animal on the neck. It'd been years since Chance had taken a midnight ride. Years since he'd knotted the lead rope through the halter and beneath the horse's chin and then swung up without a saddle. When he'd been a kid, riding at night was the only time his dad could be counted on to leave him alone. Zeke had been passed out by then. Too drunk to beat the crap out of him for sneaking a ride on one of his horses. Small miracle Chance and his siblings had turned out normal. He grinned wryly. Well, somewhat normal.

The moon lit the ground a light gray. There was a light over the main barn, which helped to illuminate the outdoor arena. He headed toward it without a second thought, giving old Teddy a warm-up, the midnight air cool against his face. The moisture in the air clung to his face as he broke Teddy into a lope. The horse behaved like the perfect gentleman he was, and that gave Chance time to think.

About *her*.

The look on her face when Claire had given her Inga… It'd been one of such startled gratitude. It was as if no one had ever given her anything before. He realized then he didn't know much about her, and even more startling, that he wanted to know more. Why didn't she talk about her family? What did she like to eat in the morning? Did she prefer ice cream or cupcakes? Country music or pop? *Why?* he asked himself. Why did he want to know? It shouldn't matter. And yet, strangely, it did.

"You going to practice until your legs fall off?"

He damn near fell off Teddy, and it was a sign of how distracted he was that he hadn't seen her approach.

Son of a— His men would have never let him live such a thing down.

He pulled Teddy up. Carolina peeled herself away from the shadows alongside the barn. That was why he hadn't seen her. She'd purposely stayed hidden.

"I saw you from your window." She pointed over her shoulder at the apartment. Except it wasn't his window. It was only ever supposed to be a temporary stop. Natalie was thinking about hiring an assistant to live there once he was gone and this thing with Caro passed.

"Just thought I'd get in a little more practice."

Her hair caught the moonlight, the blond strands backlit by the light above the barn. She'd left it hanging down, and he wondered if that was because she'd just come from bed. *That* particular thought prompted images he didn't need.

"Wanna try and pull me up?"

Did he want to touch her? No. He had a feeling that a barrier of jeans and a long-sleeved shirt wouldn't be enough to keep him from feeling it again—the sense of possessiveness, the need to protect, the desire to hold her and…do what? Love her and leave her?

"Sure," he answered. Experience had taught him to face his problems, and Carolina had definitely become a problem.

She strolled to the arena gate, slipping through on nearly silent feet, and his heart thumped the way it did the morning of an op. His mouth had gone dry, too. All because of *her*.

"You want to me stand in the middle?" she asked.

On the rail or off to the side, he didn't care. It would all lead to the same thing: touching her. "Wherever you want."

She nodded and stopped in the middle. He took a deep breath, and though he'd practiced the maneuver what felt like a million times, he was nervous. This weekend would be the first time he would need to actually perform Colt's routine, but he'd yet to practice it with Caro. He'd been putting it off.

Teddy seemed to know what they were about to do. The horse had been through the routine enough times Chance didn't doubt the animal had it memorized. Sure enough, when he lightly tapped the animal on the sides, Teddy lurched into a canter. There was no need to guide him with his makeshift reins. If Chance hadn't been afraid of them slipping over his neck, he would have let them go. Instead he clutched them with one hand, gathering speed as he rounded a corner, the dew so heavy now it stung his face.

Carolina held out a hand. He reached for her, tensing, because things had to be timed perfectly. Teddy would need to slow down and Chance would need to lock his hand with hers. A hand that shook, he admitted, clutching the reins tighter.

Three. Two. One.

They touched. He lost focus, but only for a split second, and then he was pulling and she was swinging and suddenly she was up behind him.

"Good job!"

He'd done it. There would be no need to humiliate himself in front of a huge crowd—

Her hands slipped under his arms, her fingers touching his belly and his stomach contracted from the heat. He tilted left. She corrected right. He clutched Teddy's mane, and somehow they both managed to stay on.

"Sorry," he heard her say, her warm body pressed up against his own. "I didn't mean to startle you."

"You didn't."

It had happened again when they'd touched. Electricity. Fire. Desire.

Son of a—

"Do you want to try it again?"

He grimaced inwardly. "Sure." He pulled Teddy up.

She slipped off and oh, thank God, stopped touching him. It was like stepping from a hot shower and into cool evening air. He could breathe again.

"I'll go to the other side of the arena then."

Teddy knew the drill. There was hardly any need to prompt the horse into a run. The wind felt good against Chance's face. He wished he could still keep running instead of leaning left, holding out a hand then pulling her up behind him.

There it went again.

His pulse. His breathing. His very sanity. The moment she touched him it was all he could do not to lean away from her.

"I think we're good," he said, pulling Teddy up.

"I should probably try to stand."

She smelled like honeysuckle. And that damn fabric softener. "Maybe we should try that when it's daylight."

"Just put him back into a run. It'll take a sec."

If he protested again he'd look like a wimp, and a wimp he definitely was not. So he clucked Teddy forward, the horse completely at ease carrying them around in the dead of night with nothing but bats and owls for an audience. He felt her shirt, the press of her palms against his shoulder. It was a new form of torture, but only because out of nowhere came the image of her touching him elsewhere, and it caused him to stiffen and her to cry out. Before he could help steady her, she'd begun to fall. He couldn't believe it. He'd practiced the move a hundred times with the other girls.

"Caro—"

He was so discombobulated he couldn't quite catch her, and this time she fell on her side, her gasp of pain enough to make him jerk on the rope and stop Teddy.

His heart thundered as he slid off Teddy. "Caro! Are you okay?"

She clutched her ankle. "I'm still sore from falling off the other day."

When James had tried to kill her. Well, maybe not kill her, but certainly ruin her practice session. "Where does it hurt?"

"My ankle."

"Let me see," he said. "Lean back."

"I'll be okay." She tried to push his hands away.

"Just relax. I'm trained for this."

He was also trained to keep his cool while under fire, not fall apart when a woman touched him. He wouldn't dwell on that, though. He needed to remove her boot, a tricky task. He looked into her eyes, and he could tell she tried to hide how much pain she was in.

"Can you take it off?"

He watched her eyes, big and blue, in the moonlight. Her blond hair was mussed, and her lips strained to keep from quivering. He hated seeing her in pain, just as he'd hated seeing the fear in her eyes when James had confronted her.

"I'll be gentle."

He slipped off her boot. She grimaced, but didn't

move. He chuckled when he saw her socks. They were black. With smiley faces.

"Happy socks," she explained.

Happy socks. Because she needed something to smile about.

"I like them," he said. "And your ankle doesn't feel swollen."

"I think it's just sprained."

"Let's get you up." He would have to touch her again. "Here." He bent down and slipped an arm behind her.

Shampoo.

He tried not to breathe too deeply as he helped her to her feet. She leaned against him, and his body reacted to how good she felt. It'd been so long…

"I'll help you to your apartment," he said.

"I can walk by myself."

"And hurt your ankle even more? No. I'll wrap it for you once we get to your place. And you should probably stay off it for the rest of the week. Here. Let me turn Teddy loose. Can you stand for a second?"

"Yes."

Sweet relief. That's what he experienced when he stepped away.

Teddy seemed only too happy to be set free in the arena. Chance tossed the halter toward the rail. He'd come back for the horse later. With a deep breath, he headed back to Caro, silently reciting the list of reasons for nipping this damn physical attraction in the bud.

"Ready?" he asked, not wanting to touch her, yet knowing he'd have to slip an arm around her again.

"Ready." She didn't like being a burden. He could see it in her eyes. He spotted something else, too. A shyness that seemed to make it hard for her to look at him. She couldn't hold his gaze for more than a second.

She felt it, too.

It was like discovering the monster under your bed was really a soft, fuzzy toy. A cute little unicorn. Something that could be taken out and played with. He looked away, at the ground.

She wanted him. He wanted her, too.

Life just got a whole helluva lot more complicated.

Chapter 13

He knew.

The thought repeated in her head, the words keeping time with every painful step.

He knew...he knew...he knew.

She'd tried to hide her stupid teenage-like crush from him all week. She knew how dumb it was that she had feelings for him, had been hoping they would fade. And now look at her. Her experiment to prove to herself that touching Chance wouldn't be a problem had completely backfired and nearly broken both of their necks.

Dumb, dumb, dumb.

Those were the next words to keep time with her hops. She felt every hard, sinewy muscle as he helped support her steps. He smelled good. Like talc and pine trees with a hint of cedar.

"Almost there," he said.

Thank God.

They entered the barn, their path barely lit by the light that illuminated the parking area. Horses stirred. Heads popped up. One of them even nickered softly.

"I hope we don't wake up Natalie and Colt."

"We won't," he said, his arm snug around her. "I know for a fact my brother sleeps like the dead."

Why couldn't James have been more like Chance? Chance was the type of man who would do everything in his power to help the weak and infirm. And to protect those he loved. He had integrity, strength and kindness, and she doubted she'd ever meet another man like him.

And he would be gone in a short time.

She knew that. Accepted that. And yet...

Chance paused at the base of the stairway that led to the apartment.

"I can make it from here," she said.

"Up those stairs?" She couldn't see his face all that well, but she could hear the determination in his voice. "Not a chance."

He urged her forward, and together they took the steps one at a time. Caro was relieved once she stood in front of her door. "Okay, thanks. I'm good." She tried to disengage from his arms.

"No. I'm going to take a look at your ankle in the light, get you some ice. Wrap it for you."

Of course he would. He was a man who would take care of a woman, see to her needs. Not abuse her and give her bruises.

When she opened the door, Inga barked. Loudly.

"It's okay, Inga," Carolina said, flipping on the light.

Inga wagged her tail, a canine grin on her face. Caro wondered if the dog sensed the kindness of the man at her door.

"Kitchen," Chance said. She hobbled over to the small table and chairs...and it was over. He no longer touched her. She no longer had to smell him and marvel at his strength and otherwise react like a sixteen-year-old girl.

"Ice first," he said. "Set your foot on this chair." He pulled one out for her, and she did as he suggested. "Let me see."

His fingers brushed her ankle and she gasped, but not because of pain. A bolt of pleasure had zipped through her.

"Sorry," he said.

She slumped in her chair. Her crush on him had gotten *worse*. She couldn't look him in the eyes. With his dark brows and five o'clock shadow, he was too handsome for his own good.

"It doesn't look too bad." He gently turned her ankle. "Definitely swollen, though. You did something to it. Best to stay off it for now."

He carefully set down her foot and headed for the fridge. This was worse. With his back to her, all she could think about was how wide his shoulders were beneath his black shirt. And when he bent to retrieve the tray of ice from the freezer, she noticed how tight his jeans were. By the time he'd finished making her an ice pack, she was as red as the bottle of ketchup in the fridge.

"Here."

"Thanks."

Just leave. She couldn't take humiliating herself

anymore. He obviously knew how he affected her, and yet he simply stood over her, staring.

"You going to be okay by yourself?"

No. She didn't want to be alone. She wanted him to be with her, but that was crazy and stupid and ridiculous. Not to mention, never going to happen. Men like him weren't attracted to women like her. They dated smart, beautiful women who ran triathlons and held down six-figure jobs. She was a lowly rodeo trick rider with a messed-up personal life and no family to speak of. Definitely not his type.

"I'll be fine." She forced herself to look into his green eyes. "Thanks."

He frowned, and she wondered if he knew how hard she fought not to grab his hand and pull him down toward her. She tried to hide her thoughts behind an impersonal smile.

"If you need anything," he said, "let me know."

"I will."

He backed away, slowly at first, and then quickly, slipping through the door as if he could read every thought in her mind and as a result couldn't get out of there fast enough. He left her with Inga and her thoughts and a nearly overwhelming ache of pent-up frustration that had her leaning forward and covering her face with her hands.

She moaned.

This sucked.

He sent Natalie to check on her the next day. Why? Because he was a chicken. A big lily-livered, ridiculous chicken who didn't want to face the soft plea in her eyes.

"She's okay," Natalie said, a big smile on her face as she waddled into the kitchen. "A little sore, she said, but she's walking on it this morning. She told me to tell you she'll be good for this weekend's rodeo."

The rodeo.

Never before had he dreaded something as much as he did his solo performance at the Jacksonville rodeo. Another long drive and a longer night spent keeping an eye on Caro.

"You okay?" Natalie asked, settling down behind the table, no mean feat given her size. Up until a few weeks ago, she'd hid her baby bump well. But she'd suddenly sprouted, the doctor grounding her from all riding activity, which was why she was in the house on a weekday morning, when normally she'd be outside getting the horses ready for a day's worth of riding lessons. His brother and Laney had taken over that task. His sister-in-law was officially on maternity leave.

"I'm fine." He scrubbed a face over his hand. "Long night."

She cocked a bright blond brow, and it occurred to him that she kind of looked like Carolina with her light hair and blue eyes. Carolina was smaller, though, which was good, given her profession.

"Riding at midnight," Natalie huffed. "What were you thinking?"

He was thinking about privacy. About making an ass of himself without anyone watching. About being able to steer clear of Caro, but that hadn't worked out too well.

"It's easier to practice when no one is around."

"You mean when nobody can watch you fall off."

He nodded.

She might have teased him further, but Claire sailed through the front door. She carried a wiggling mass of black fur in her arms. Adam, his sister's son, was right behind her.

"You guys!" Adam yelled. "Youwon'tbelievewhat Ethanwantstodo."

"Adam, slow down," said Claire, smiling at them both. "They can't understand you."

Adam slid to a halt. And Chance nearly laughed as his nephew slowly straightened, took a deep breath, then said slowly, "You won't believe what Ethan wants to do."

"Better," his sister said, her eyes twinkling.

"What does Ethan want to do?" Chance asked.

"Just a second. I need to set this four-legged maniac down on the ground." The tiny Belgian Malinois made a beeline for Natalie.

"Bella!"

Natalie squatted and opened her arms. It wasn't easy for her to bend, but somehow she managed to scoop up the puppy. The excited pup made little snuffling sounds, licking her face and hands and any other available body part.

"I swear that puppy came out of the womb loving you." Claire pulled out a chair next to Chance. "What's up, bro?" she asked, the smile on her face stirring emotions in Chance's heart. He'd never seen her so happy. Not when she'd been married to Marcus, and not before, when she'd been younger. Of course, they'd all had a rough start, but Claire had pulled through. His sister was blissfully in love with Ethan, and it showed.

"Chance is tired," Natalie answered for him. "He was up at midnight practicing the routine."

"Midnight?" Claire said, incredulous.

"Carolina fell off. Hurt her ankle."

"Caro was with you?" Claire asked.

Chance didn't respond. He didn't need to, because he said to Adam, "Go on. Tell me your news. I can tell you're about to burst."

"They were out there together," Natalie said in a stage whisper.

"Ethan wants to start a wounded-warrior therapy program," Adam said, glaring at his aunt, clearly wanting everyone's undivided attention. The look was so much like his sister's, right down to the black hair and green eyes, that Chance almost laughed.

Claire ignored her son. "Chance Reynolds. You could have killed that girl practicing in the dark."

"She's fine." He brushed off her concerns with a wave of his hand. "What do you mean, a wounded-warrior therapy program?"

His sister sat up straighter, and it was clear she didn't want to drop the subject of Carolina, but pride for her husband had won out. She ruffled Adam's full head of hair. A year ago, during his cancer treatment, he'd been as bald as a baby chicken. These days, it was hard to imagine his six-year-old nephew in the battle of his life.

"Ethan wants to open an equine therapy program for veterans," Claire said.

"That's great." Natalie beamed her approval.

"That *is* a great idea," Chance said. He'd heard a lot of positive things about horses and their ability to help PTSD.

"And he said *I* could help," his nephew all but sang, green eyes full of pride.

"Which is a good thing, since we all know how I feel about horses." Claire's eyes were full of amusement.

Yes, he did know. Their dad had ruined riding for Claire, but at least she'd been mounting up more and more lately thanks to Ethan, who loved riding as much as the rest of family.

"I'll make some calls," Chance said. "See if I can't help him out with funding and whatnot."

"That'd be wonderful," Claire said with a wide smile. "If you're not too busy with Carolina, that is."

Claire and Natalie exchanged glances, and Chance found himself suddenly uncomfortable. So much so he stood to leave.

"Oh, no, you don't." His sister pulled him back down. "We all know you have a thing for her."

He blushed. Actually blushed. "I don't have a thing for Carolina."

"Baloney," Natalie said. She ruffled the fur on her puppy's head, smiling at that animal for a second before pinning Chance with a gaze. "We can see it in your eyes."

"You like Carolina?" said Adam, tipping his head sideways, clearly curious in a you-like-pumpkin-pie kind of way.

"Not like that," Chance lied, and then, as a way of changing the subject, asked, "How's Lady?"

"She's doing great," Claire said. "Gonna wean the puppies next week, including that one." She pointed to Bella. "Now tell us how long you've had a thing for Carolina."

"So you *do* like Carolina?" his nephew asked, clearly confused.

He backed away. "I'm going to go see if Colt needs help saddling up the horses."

"He likes her, all right," Natalie said.

He ignored her, which clearly amused them all, especially when Adam asked, "Do you think he wants to kiss her?" The two of them laughed harder. Damn women.

But as he stepped out on the stoop, he knew he would miss them. He would miss all of this. Miss the mornings when the sun stained the grass the color of lemons. When that same sun lit the tree leaves a bright green. And when the earth smelled of sage, hay and horses. It would be hard to leave.

The realization struck him with the force of a runaway horse.

He'd never wanted to come back to this place. But his brother's insistence had changed his mind. As he looked around him, he understood that his brother had created something from nothing. The only thing recognizable about Reynolds Ranch these days was the old house behind him and the big red hay barn. Everything else—the arena, the new barn, the pastures—it was all different. Better. New.

A home.

He gulped, his stomach churning. Thankfully, the sound of a car coming up the drive distracted him from his thoughts. One of Natalie's clients, no doubt. First lesson of the day. She'd probably wander out soon. Her version of maternity leave was sitting in a lawn chair in the center of the arena schooling her clients. But the car didn't park out in front of the barn. No. It headed straight for the house. Unmarked police car.

His stomach dropped.

He could make out the image of a man inside. He wore a cowboy hat, which made Chance wonder if he were wrong. When the car door popped open and he caught a glimpse of the broad-shouldered man, he knew he'd been right. The man could be a spokesperson for the police officers' association.

"Is Carolina Cruthers here?" he asked. Late thirties. Brown hair and light-colored eyes. He wore a black polo shirt with a gold star on the front, jeans and cowboy boots.

"I'm right here."

They both turned. Caro had appeared at the entrance of the barn, and Chance could tell by the way she played with a strand of her hair that she was nervous. Cops didn't make house calls, not normally, and that this one had could only mean bad news.

Chapter 14

Caro's stomach muscles were stretched so tight someone could strum them like a guitar.

"Sorry," she said, stepping aside to allow Officer Connelly inside her temporary apartment. Chance was right behind him. She'd insisted he join them for whatever news they were about to hear, especially since he'd taken on the task of bodyguard.

"Don't worry about the dog." She motioned for Inga to stay. "She won't hurt you unless I tell her to."

Officer Connelly didn't look convinced as he stared at Inga. Her new dog had the eyes of a predator, and they fixed on the new arrival, gauging whether he was friend or foe.

To give the officer credit, the dog's appearance didn't appear to intimidate the man. "Nice dog."

"Gift from my sister," Chance said. "Former military dog."

"Yeah, I heard there was a rescue out here." The tall man with the dark hair and light eyes looked around. She tried not to let her embarrassment show. She didn't plan on staying long, and so there was still just the couch, the bed, and the rickety old kitchen table and chairs.

"Inga, *sit*," she told the dog when it appeared she would get up and investigate the new arrival. The dog instantly sat. "Let's go to the kitchen."

The same place she'd sat last night when Chance…
Don't think about that.

"I'm sure you know I've come out here to talk about James." Officer Connelly glanced between the two of them as he took a seat. He was a big man. Taller than Chance, and…thicker. Not fat. Just bigger through the shoulders, arms and legs. Like a prizefighter without the boxing gloves. "Your report to me on Monday made me curious."

Caro's pulse pounded at her neck. She glanced at Chance, who seemed equally on edge.

"Men like your ex don't usually go to such lengths to get back at a woman. I'm not saying it doesn't happen," he said with a quick look at Chance, almost as if he sensed Chance knew differently. "It's just not normal for them to follow someone out of town."

Chance nodded. "That struck me as strange, too."

Caro spread her hands on the table. "Do you believe me now? About him shooting at me?"

Officer Connelly had seemed a bit taken aback she'd reported the incident at the rodeo grounds. It'd almost been as if he'd been defending James, telling her he doubted someone would actually shoot at a horse and that she had to be mistaken. She'd left the police station disillusioned and depressed, especially when she'd learned the other police department had released James once he'd posted bail. But now here was Officer Connelly, and she wondered if she'd had it all wrong. Maybe he'd been playing devil's advocate.

"The fact that Mr. Edwards followed you out of town seemed a little extreme, but I never doubted it was possible. He's clearly stalking you. I started checking around. Went out and spoke to a few people."

He pulled out his cell phone and scrolled until he found what he was looking for. When he did, he read drily, "April, two years ago, charged with assault, never convicted. And a year before that, different town, different assault, but same MO. Charges filed, never convicted. Why?" Officer Connelly stared at the two of them for a long moment. "That's what got me curious. Files said nothing. Just charges dismissed."

"He scares them," Chance speculated.

Officer Connelly's eyes flew up to meet Chance's. He seemed surprised, then impressed. "That's exactly what he does. Terrorizes his victims until they agree to drop the charges."

Caro leaned back in her chair. "But he hasn't made any demands."

"Not yet," Chance said.

Her stomach twisted. This wasn't over, then. Not by a long shot.

"How bad did it get for those other women?"

"Bad enough they refused to testify against him."

James would keep going. Scaring her. Terrorizing her. Driving her crazy.

"What should we do?" Chance asked.

"Be vigilant," Officer Connelly said. "Keep your eyes and ears open."

"That won't be a problem." Chance dropped his words like a grenade—harsh, quick, angry. His face hardened, too. "Son of a bitch will have another think coming if he goes near Caro again."

"Good," Officer Connelly said. "But we have to do things by the book."

"Do we?" Chance lifted a brow, and it was clear by his expression he had his own ideas of how to get James to leave her alone.

Officer Connelly nodded. "He needs to be put away. Legally. With a public record."

Chance leaned forward. "My way won't clog up the judiciary system."

What Chance talked about was wrong, but it still made her feel protected, safe and, yes, relieved he would go to such lengths.

She touched his arm briefly. "Chance, it's okay. We'll figure out a way to lock him behind bars."

Connelly's eyes had never left Chance's. "Caro tells me you're ex-military."

"Army Ranger."

"Shame to mess up a future career in law enforcement out of a need for revenge."

"Who said I was going into law enforcement?"

She watched as Officer Connelly sized Chance up. He frowned, apparently disappointed by what he saw. "Private contracting then?"

Chance nodded. "When the time comes."

Another long stare. "There are other ways to serve your country, you know."

Caro didn't understand what was going on between

the two of them. Chance suddenly gripped the edge of the table, appearing capable of injecting venom into someone's veins. She leaned forward to get their attention. "Can we get back on topic?"

Chance had the grace to look abashed. Officer Connelly seemed amused, but he shot her a look of apology.

"Did you confront James about what happened at the rodeo grounds?" she asked. "His shooting at me, I mean."

"He denied it. No surprise." Officer Connelly shook his head. "But reading his files, I have no doubt he's capable of doing that and much more."

"Maybe you should stay home this weekend," Chance said.

"No." She looked between the two men. "I won't let him ruin my life. Trick riding is my job. I get paid to do it. No work, no money and I'm broke enough as it is."

She hated admitting that in front of Chance. She already felt like a failure, but she needed him to understand he couldn't ground her. She had to work, especially if she wanted to switch apartments. She'd need a security deposit, and she had Inga to take care of now. She glanced at the dog.

"She goes where you go," Chance said, clearly following her gaze. "Even to the rodeos."

"Good idea," Officer Connelly said.

Chance shot him a look that obviously indicated he didn't need his approval, and then he shifted his attention back to her. "This weekend, you'll stay in the trailer with me again. I'll tell the girls they should stay with friends. It occurred to me last weekend he might think you're in there with them and do something aimed at hurting you, but injuring all of them instead."

She hadn't thought of that, and the idea sickened her. She'd never forgive herself if someone got hurt because of her poor choice of a boyfriend.

"Let me know if anything else happens." Officer Connelly stood. "I've put my cell phone on my card. Call me, even if it's on a weekend." He slid the card across the table. She caught his full name then. Brennan Connelly.

"Thank you," she said.

Officer Connelly turned when he reached the door. "I know it might be tough, but don't let James bully you. That's what he's used to doing—and getting away with it. I would hate to see that happen again."

She nodded. "I don't plan on letting him get close to me."

"Good."

The moment the door closed behind the officer, Chance said, "I still think you should stay home this weekend."

"No."

"If it's money you need, I'm sure Colt could put you to work around the ranch, especially with Natalie out of commission."

"No," she said more firmly, meeting his gaze, though doing so caused her stomach to flip. "I'm going to keep on doing what I do no matter what James throws in my direction."

She thought he might argue the point, but instead he smiled—a small one, but it was enough to make her look away, her cheeks filling with color.

"He's not going to hurt you."

She nodded, still refusing to look at him.

"I won't let him."

It was torture, him sitting across from her. Caro was aware of his smell and his heat, and, yes, damn it all, the primordial desire to be with him. He was a man who would do anything to protect her from harm. That was the attraction. It was stupid and cave woman–ish, but she couldn't help herself.

"Caro?"

Could he see her breath quickening? Did he spot the pulse at the base of her neck? Had he taken note of how she clenched her hands into fists?

"I should call the other girls." She stood, too quickly, and pain shot up her leg. She tilted to the left.

And he caught her.

The world turned topsy-turvy. Her whole body ignited. Her gasp wasn't because her ankle hurt. It was because her body lit up like she had fireworks inside of her, all booms and wooshes and zaps, and now she tingled in places she didn't want to think about.

"Sorry," she said, her face heating. "I forgot about my ankle."

He seemed puzzled by her reaction. Or maybe it was concern she read in his eyes. And surprise. "You shouldn't be walking on it."

"I'm fine." She hopped for the couch, where she'd left her phone, and though she tried to hide it, she would bet he could see her grimacing. "I'll see you later on for practice."

"No," he said sharply. "You need to stay off that ankle for at least a couple days."

They needed to practice, to nail down the fine points of their new routine, yet she couldn't find the courage to argue the point.

"Yeah, maybe you're right."

His eyes lit up. With relief?

"I'll send Natalie up here to check on you later."

"Thanks."

And he was gone. She grabbed one of the couch pillows, covered her face with it and screamed.

Chapter 15

The Jacksonville rodeo grounds were nestled in the Diablo mountain range, halfway between the Bay Area and the Central Valley. It was pretty country, Chance thought. Different from the Sierra foothills, with more oaks and fewer pine trees. Warmer, too.

Caro had caught a ride to the rodeo grounds with one of the girls. He shouldn't have felt grateful that she wanted to ride with her friends. He should have insisted she go with him, but he didn't. When she'd collapsed against him the night before, he'd nearly gasped from the reaction her touch had ignited. The thought of sitting next to her for the six-hour drive to the Jacksonville rodeo grounds was unbearable.

"So you're flying solo this weekend, huh?"

Chance turned to see who'd spoken, smiling when he caught sight of Bill walking toward him. They'd been reintroduced at the last rodeo, but it was as if Chance had never stopped competing on the high school rodeo circuit where they'd both started out. Bill was still the wisecracking funny man he'd always been.

"Yup. Gonna be performing on my own. Hope I don't run you down."

"Nah," the little man said, shaking his hand. Tonight his face would be covered with black makeup and the cowboy hat he currently wore would be replaced with a backward baseball cap. He'd be wearing clothes three times too big, too. Bill was one of the best barrel men in the industry, someone who wasn't afraid to throw himself in front of a fifteen-hundred-pound animal and who would do whatever it took to keep someone safe. Chance respected that more than Bill probably knew.

"Cutting things kind of close, aren't you?" he said with a wide smile. "Rodeo starts in a couple hours."

"We decided to leave this morning." He frowned. "For security reasons."

Bill's face darkened. "You really think that guy will come after Caro again?"

"*That guy* needs his ass kicked," Chance muttered. "He sent her a text this week." Just thinking about it sent his blood pressure soaring. "Told her he couldn't wait to see her perform this weekend."

Bill stroked his face. "Hasn't she got a restraining order against him or something?"

"Restraining orders only do so much." Chance tipped his cowboy hat back. "So, yes, we think there's a good chance he'll be here. It's a public event, and as long as he stays at least a thousand feet away, technically, he can do whatever he wants." He looked around, taking in the barren hills, the flat terrain and the aluminum grandstands that seemed to jut up out of nowhere. An elementary school sat in the distance, and beyond that, the only residential area of town. Jacksonville was truly a single-stoplight town with one grocery store, a tiny strip mall and not much else. "At least we should be able to see him coming."

"And everyone knows what he looks like," Bill said with a nod.

Chance had asked Caro for a picture of James. They'd distributed it to every person they could think of via social media, asking everyone to share. They hoped it would keep people on the alert.

"Extra eyes on the ground should help," he said, turning back to the trailer. "My plan is to set up a corral by our rig. The other girls are going to stay with friends. Caro's staying with me. That's why I pulled in next to you. I was hoping I could use one side of your trailer as a wall. I can make a bigger corral that way."

"Sure," Bill said.

They set to work, but it didn't take them long to erect the portable panels Chance had brought. Having to use only three sides helped. He'd be able to pull the work trailer in and out when he performed. Caro and the other girls arrived shortly thereafter, and Chance did his best to ignore her while keeping an eye out for James. They filled hay bags and water buckets. Finally, they unloaded the horses.

"Guess we should probably get ready," Caro said, gazing up at him with trepidation in her eyes. It killed him every time. He hated seeing her worried. Hated that some lowlife putz of a man could wreak such havoc with her nerves. She had enough on her plate as it was.

"Don't think about it," he said. "He sent you that

text to mess with your mind, that's all. I doubt he'll be here this weekend."

She tried to put on a brave face, and damn it, he admired her for it. "I'm going to head over to Lori's trailer and get ready."

He needed to get ready, too. The trailer was part of the act, which meant he'd need to pull it closer to the arena.

His first solo performance.

Okay, yes, that had him a little on edge, too. He'd been practicing for weeks, all of it leading up to this moment, and as his brother had said, there was no dress rehearsal in this business. You had to dive in and do it, and while Chance hadn't fallen off the horse once this week, there was always the possibility something could go wrong during a live performance.

It didn't take him long to dress, and he wouldn't need to move the trailer until it was time for his act, but that didn't stop his hands from shaking as if he was back on the front lines. He tried to keep himself busy, checking in with the rodeo manager, making sure the pen they'd erected wouldn't fall down, double-and even triple-checking buckets and feed bags. When Chance heard the first roar of the crowd, he nearly jumped, which irritated him to the point he almost bit the head off a little girl who stuck her hand between the metal rails to pet Rio. Her look of terror and distress made him realize he needed to calm down. He wasn't facing a firing squad. Compared to running for his life, this was small potatoes.

From that point forward, he kept himself firmly in hand. They were surrounded by trailers, with cowboys and cowgirls riding by. Chance scanned each person. Ever vigilant. Always on the alert.

"You ready?"

He turned to see Caro standing behind him, looking as sexy as ever in her stop sign—red trick-riding outfit. She'd pulled her long blond hair into a ponytail and applied extra makeup Not that she needed it. Her blue eyes always looked bright, but with eyeliner and mascara, they glowed like the stars in the sky. A ridiculously poetic thing to think, but it was true.

"As ready as I'll ever be."

She smiled. "See you over there."

He watched her grab Rio from the pen. She'd already saddled him earlier, so it was a simple thing to slip on his bridle. She mounted up shortly after, beautiful, confident and completely at ease. It made him feel like an idiot for being nervous.

You've faced men with rifles pointed at your head. This is just a little rodeo. And a small-town one at that.

It didn't feel small-town.

Concentrate on the routine.

He did a mental run-through: Teddy in the trailer. Pull into the arena. Let Teddy out. First trick is circle Teddy. Right circle. Left circle. Stop. Rear. Dance on hind legs. Dance on all four legs. Stop. Teddy bares his teeth and smiles at the crowd. Bow. Climb aboard. Stand again. Circle without reins and wave. The girls come in then. They perform. Bill jumps at Caro. He rescues Caro. Caro ropes Bill. Done.

Simple.

With a deep breath and a calm resolve, he untied Teddy and loaded him up. He checked his reflection in the driver-side window to make sure his black cowboy hat wasn't crooked and then climbed into the truck and started the engine.

Ready or not, here I come.

It took a bit to make his way to the arena, but once he was close, rodeo officials cleared a path. He hung back from the rear gate, watching as the last of the saddle bronc riders tried to cover their mounts, all the while keeping an eye on the grandstands, the people milling around, even the people on horseback. This rodeo was a security nightmare, but he had no choice except to roll with it.

His teammates arrived. They lined up next to Caro and Rio outside the arena. Over the previous month, he'd learned their names: Judy, Lori, Ann, Delilah. All of them young, lithe and amazing, but none of them as pretty as Caro. He spotted more than one cowboy eyeing the pretty blonde as she sat atop her horse, waiting. With her hair pulled back and her regal posture, she looked like a vision an artist would sculpt.

Someone tapped his window.

"You ready?" asked one of the rodeo producers.

He gave the thumbs-up.

Through the exterior of the truck, he heard the words, "Ladies and gentlemen, we've got a special treat for you this weekend."

The surge of adrenaline shooting through him made it hard to breathe. He told himself to relax as someone opened the gate, but he still needed to clutch the steering wheel to steady his hands. The truck's engine strained once the tires sank into the deeper footing. Chance tried to ignore the hundreds of faces staring down at him. His hands gripped the wheel so tight his knuckles started to hurt.

"The Jacksonville rodeo welcomes Chance Reynolds and his amazing rodeo misfit, Teddy!"

That was his cue. He slipped out of the truck and the roar of the crowd nearly made him stumble backward. He could feel their presence, like an invisible force field that touched him and stirred something inside him. He waved as he headed for the back of the trailer.

"Ladies and gentlemen, Chance Reynolds comes from a long line of rodeo performers. The horse he's performing with today is a second-generation trick horse, and you won't believe what he can do."

Looking into the horse's soulful eyes helped calm his nerves. Teddy had done this act hundreds of times. He'd probably do all the moves without commands, so it was simple for Chance to step back and let the horse out. The crowd cheered when Teddy paused and nodded his head, his long mane flying, one of his front legs pawing the ground. Colt said that happened sometimes, that Teddy loved to perform, and he would ham it up in front of certain crowds. Clearly, today was one of those days.

"Okay, kid, let's do it."

He motioned for the horse to circle. It was like being at home. Teddy set off with a flick of his head, and when he finished one circle, he changed directions. The crowd roared its approval. Chance gave the command to stop. The audience seemed to hold its breath. Chance lifted his arm. Teddy reared. There were gasps and cries of delight and then more applause, the cheers growing louder as Teddy began to hop, or dance, one hop, two, three. Chance began to relax. It was so easy, his brother's constant schooling coming to his aid. He didn't need to think about the next move. He simply gave the signal for Teddy to stop, and then without him asking, the horse pranced in place. Beautiful to watch. Perfect performance.

Chance blinked. Out of nowhere, he thought of another black horse, a beautiful black mare that his dad had beaten into submission. The image made him wince. She'd been a heck of a performer, too, but Teddy performed out of love, not fear. His brother had done a remarkable job with the rescue, using a kind touch and a gentle heart. And it showed. The horse seemed to read Chance's thoughts, smiling at the crowd all on his own.

"Teddy, bow," he told the horse, and the animal stretched his front legs apart, his head sinking between his knees.

"How about that, ladies and gentlemen? But it's not over yet. Welcome to the Jacksonville rodeo arena the Galloping Girlz!"

And that was Chance's cue to hop aboard. Trick riders used a line of people holding paper streamers to keep their horses from ducking off the rail. He would join those people, albeit aboard Teddy, and hold out his hand so the girls could slap it on their way by. Carolina circled around behind him, and Chance turned just in time to see Bill the Barrel Man jump out of his can. Chance laughed. Bill wore a black scarf over the bottom half of his face and a hat big enough to cover the state of Wyoming.

"How in the hell…" He had no idea how he'd fit the damn hat into the barrel.

"Here goes," Chance whispered to himself.

He'd never practiced the routine with Bill, but no one would have known it. It went exactly as it had the previous weekend when Colt had played the part of hero. Caro was perfect, too, screaming when Bill seemed to snatch her off her horse. And sore ankle or not, she landed perfectly. Bill wagged his eyebrows at the crowd, and the audience laughed, booed and happily played along.

It was time.

Chance nudged Teddy forward in Caro and Bill's direction. The horse needed next to no instruction. Caro threw her hand out. Chance leaned down, reached for her, and she flung herself up behind him. Somehow it all worked. Just as they'd practiced.

The crowd thundered their approval.

Chance was acutely aware of Caro's presence, but it was okay this time. He didn't falter. Didn't mess it all up like he had so many times before. Today they were on fire. A team. And it felt…perfect.

They galloped toward the truck and trailer. Caro reached for the rope. She scooped it up smoothly and then stood. This, too, the audience loved, because they'd figured out what she meant to do. Bill made a big production of trying to run away, big hat flopping, pants slipping down, and suddenly Chance wanted to laugh, too. He'd never felt so free before. So at home. So perfectly at ease.

Caro's rope slid around Bill's waist, and the barrel man's arms became pinned to his side. The audience laughed, hooted and cheered. Caro somehow managed to tug Bill off his feet while standing up on Teddy and holding on to Chance. That wasn't supposed to happen. Bill was supposed to fight the rope on his feet, but the barrel man rolled with it. The coup de grâce came as they dragged Bill out the arena. The man had layered his clothes, and they began to slide off him. Bill left behind first his black pants and then what looked like a pair of sweats and then another layer of…something. Boxer shorts, maybe. Chance struggled to keep a straight face as Caro jumped down, and he turned Teddy back toward the arena.

"Ladies and gentlemen, give a hand for Chance Reynolds, will you? And the Galloping Girlz and the wonder horse Teddy!"

The roar of the crowd was something to behold, and as Chance stood in the middle of the arena, waving, smiling and drinking in their applause, he realized he could get used to this. His gaze snagged on Caro standing outside the arena. Even from a distance, he could see the glint of her blue eyes. She grinned at him, and he couldn't help but grin back.

He could get used to a lot of things if he weren't careful.

Chapter 16

He seemed distracted, Caro thought, as they sat outside the trailer later that night. It was so unlike Chance
that Caro wondered if there was something wrong.

"Were you unhappy with our performance?" she
asked.

His green eyes shot to hers, and his handsome face
flinched.

"God, no."

And that was all he said. Two words. She supposed
she should be grateful for that.

They'd stowed all the horse tack away in silence. Of
course, her teammates had been around then and she
hadn't been put off by his lack of talking. But then the
girls had left—gone to a rodeo dance or something.
Caro had changed into a gray T-shirt and jeans and
joined Chance outside. Still nothing. They sat beneath

the trailer's awning, watching the horses eat their dinner in the makeshift corral. The sun set slowly behind them.

"You're so quiet," she ventured to say.

"Just tired." He took a sip of his beer.

Maybe she should have gone with the girls. However, fending off the advances of drunken cowboys had never been her thing. And with the threat of James looming, she would have been a fool to step out of Chance's protective custody.

She grimaced. It would probably beat sitting next to him in silence, wondering what it would be like to be with him, to be his in every sense of the word.

"I'm going inside," she said.

Ridiculous. It wasn't dark yet—not all the way. Dusk had dimmed the lights, but she could still see his face beneath his cowboy hat. He acknowledged her words with a tip of his beer bottle.

That hurt.

She had no idea why. She didn't want him to fawn all over her. She was too independent for that. A little conversation would be nice, though. So it would be far easier to be out of sight, where he'd be out of mind, and she would stop thinking about what might have happened if she'd met Chance before James. Things might have been different. She might not have felt so nervous, on edge and confused when he was near. Handsome cowboys had always been a weakness, but they were usually more trouble than they were worth and that was a lesson she should have learned by now.

"'Night." She started to turn away, but then quickly added, "Thanks for dinner."

"Welcome."

And that was that.

"Crap," she muttered, slipping inside the trailer. "Crap, crap, crap, crap."

She missed Inga. Maybe she should have brought the dog like Chance had said, but the thought of leaving her locked up in the trailer all day didn't seem right, not yet, at least. Not until she learned what it meant to travel. And so she'd left her behind. Now she wished she could hold her tight. Dogs loved people no matter how undeserving they were.

At least you're not afraid of Chance anymore.

She almost laughed. That was an understatement. Working together had changed that. Actually, last weekend, when he'd jumped to her defense, had changed that. The man would never hurt her. He would die trying to protect her. Actually *die*. *Some* men were worthy of love. James wasn't.

She sat down on the couch, and just like she had back at home, picked up a pillow and covered her face with it, screaming. She wanted to let loose some more. To deafen her own ears with her frustration, but she couldn't, not if she didn't want Chance charging in, coming to her rescue.

"What's wrong?"

She damn near dropped the pillow.

Chance.

"I heard you scream."

"I, uh." What to say? "Stubbed my toe."

Lame.

"You stubbed your toe?" he repeated, glancing at her boot-clad feet.

He had to know she was lying. She'd never been very good at it.

"It was the bad leg. Jarred my ankle."

His gaze narrowed. "Let me have a look."

"No, no." Because there he went again. Sir Galahad. The man could make her feel like a princess in need of rescuing. "I'm all right."

Except her nipples were erect.

She caught a glimpse of them as she glanced down at her foot. She planted the pillow over her midsection so fast he glanced at her askance.

She could see the spark in his eyes. He knew she felt the current of electricity between them. That she'd had fantasies about him. That when they'd performed together it was all she could do not to kiss him after his so-called rescue.

He knew.

"I think maybe I should leave," she said softly. She meant sleep somewhere else. Somewhere far from her thoughts and desires.

"Maybe you should."

It was all the proof she needed to know she'd read him correctly. She stood, her humiliation so acute her cheeks burned with a nearly physical pain. He must think her one of those women, the kind that couldn't keep her hands off men and went from one man to the next. She wasn't that type at all. She'd spent weeks warning herself away from him, and look where it'd gotten her—more attracted to him than ever before.

"I'm sorry."

She tried to rush past him, but he stepped in front of her. "Don't."

She didn't want to look at him. She really didn't. "Don't what?"

He inhaled deeply before he said, "Don't leave. It's not safe out there."

And it was then, at that precise moment, that Caro realized he fought it, too. That everything she felt, he did, too. That the desire coiling in her belly, teasing and taunting her, also teased and taunted him. Made his hands shake like hers. For some crazy, insane reason the realization made her want to cry.

Lord help her. Lord help them both.

"Maybe I could sleep with the girls—"

"No," he said sharply. He lifted his hands, gently touched her cheeks. "Stop saying that." He peered intently at her with eyes the color of jade. "You can stay right here, where you'll be safe."

Her eyes filled with tears. She had never felt so cherished and cared for in her life. "Thank you," she said softly. But now it was time to be brave. To be bold and do something she would never have done before James.

She stood on tiptoes and lightly kissed him.

He froze. She didn't move, either, just stared into his kind green eyes. And then she did another brave thing. She walked away. Outside. Into the cold night air. Where they wouldn't be tempted to do something crazy.

And that was the point.

She left him standing there, and Chance wanted to follow. Lord, how he wanted to grab her hand, to jerk her to him. Instead he went to the fridge and grabbed another beer.

What the hell?

He removed his cowboy hat and tossed it onto the couch. He swiped a hand through his hair. What the hell was he thinking? She wasn't the one who should be leaving. He was.

"Caro, wait."

He flung open the trailer door. She sat outside, and his relief she hadn't gone far made him clutch the door handle tighter. That's what happened when you became distracted. When you lost your focus. You lost sight of the objective. Keeping her safe was the objective.

"Come inside." He took a deep breath, trying not to focus on how pretty she looked sitting in the half-light of dusk. His lips tingled where hers had brushed his own.

She looked up at him, and the gratitude in her eyes caused him to feel things he probably shouldn't.

"I'll sit outside and keep watch."

"Like you did last weekend?"

Did she know he'd spent the whole night outside? True, she'd found him in the morning, but she couldn't know he'd been out there all night.

She knew.

"You don't have to do that," she said, clasping her hands in her lap. "James wouldn't dare come after me with you around, not after what happened last time."

No. He wouldn't. "Things are just easier if you come inside."

She sighed and gazed at the horses. Her blond hair caught the fiery dusk light.

"What a pair we are," she said. "Two grown adults. One of us who seems to be genetically programmed to pick the wrong man. Another one of us with a long history of keeping himself unattached, or so I've heard."

Her words drew him out of the trailer. What was the point of trying to fight it anymore?

"I stay out of relationships for a reason," he said.

She held out her hand. It took him a moment to realize she wanted a sip of his beer, a beer he'd forgotten he was holding. Watching her take a sip, seeing the way her lips wrapped around the opening of the bottle... Well, he needed to look away.

"I know," she said. "Your sister told me."

"Oh, yeah? What else did she tell you?" he asked, sitting next to her. This was a mistake. He should have stayed in the trailer. Or one of them should have.

"That you never let yourself get too close. You keep your distance as a way of protecting yourself. You stayed away all these years because you can't face the truth."

"And what truth is that?"

She pinned him with a stare. "That you're afraid." She took another sip of his beer. "All the places you've been. All the gunfire you've faced, but the thing you most fear? Caring about something too much."

"What?"

She nodded. "That's what Claire said."

"She's wrong."

She handed his beer back to him and shrugged. "Maybe."

He stared at the opening of the bottle. He wasn't afraid of caring. He loved his family so much he fought for their freedom.

"But you know what I just realized?" She met his gaze again. "So what? You're a damn fine man, Chance Reynolds. Any girl would be lucky to spend just one night with you."

"Excuse me?"

"I don't need commitment, or want it," she said,

leaning toward him. "I just want one night. And before you say it, I know you plan to leave soon and never come back. I understand."

What was she saying?

"I'm going back inside the trailer." She stood slowly. "I'll be waiting there for you. If you don't follow, that's okay. But if you do, I think it'll be a night neither of us will ever forget."

She walked by, touching him on her way past, just a brief caress, but enough to convince him she was right.

Something awaited him. Something that might be remarkable and spectacular. Something he should maybe avoid at all cost.

Something he was helpless to resist.

Chapter 17

Would he follow?

Lord, Carolina didn't know.

All she knew was she had to try. What if he was the man of her dreams? What if tonight was her one chance to hold him? What if she could convince him to stay?

She knew it likely wouldn't happen. Men like him didn't give up entire careers for women like her. But what if there was a chance he might?

He wasn't coming.

She stood in the middle of the trailer, waiting, her pulse speeding up with each passing second. If she couldn't convince him to stay, so what? Chance was the most virile, attractive, sexy man she'd ever met. Unbelievably good-looking and thoroughly masculine. Was it wrong of her to want to spend a night with him? What red-blooded female wouldn't want that?

The trailer door opened.

She couldn't breathe. Her heart seemed to stop beating because the look in his eyes…

The air gushed from her lungs. Her knees grew weak, *literally* weak. She swooned like a heroine in an old Western movie. "You can't tell my family about this," he said, his voice rough. "My brother would never approve."

"No," she said, her skin tingling and igniting like a live wire because there it was again—a surge that hit her whenever he was near. A singe of heat seemed to sear her to the soul, telling her he would do things to her no man had ever had done before.

"And it'll only be this one time."

"I know."

Just quit talking.

"Caro—"

She made the decision for him, going to him, brushing her body up against his, nearly gasping at how good it felt to finally drop the barriers and set the attraction free.

His eyes flared. She waited, hoping he would reciprocate. His head slowly lowered to her own.

Bliss.

The touch of his lips was like trick riding in front of an audience. Addictive. Electrifying. Crazy.

Yes.

The word sang through her brain as she tipped her head sideways and opened her mouth. *Yes*, she thought again, feeling his tongue slip between her lips and caress her own. *Yes*, she sang as he swirled his tongue around her own, stroking her, teasing her, taunting her.

She pressed her hand against his chest. He was so

physically fit. It turned her on. Everything about the man aroused her. She wanted to be with him. To touch him. To please him in a way he'd never been pleased before.

"Chance," she murmured, pressing herself against him, sliding up the length of him.

"Jesus."

It was all he said, but it was enough. She grew bold, touching him there, feeling his pulse beneath her fingers as his whole body stilled. Everything inside her reveled at the fact she'd done that. She'd made him react.

He pushed her up against the trailer wall. It should have scared her. It should have reminded her of James. But it didn't. It turned her on because she wanted him against her.

"What are you doing to me?" he mumbled.

He lifted her up. She wrapped her legs around his waist, the center of him against her own core. Her whole body contracted and pulsed in response. He kissed her again, hard, and he was so strong he could have easily used brute force, but he didn't. She loved that about him.

She lifted her hips. He grunted, kissed her harder, and she knew that all he need do was continue holding her like he was and she would lose it. She would shatter into a million pieces. And only his arms would hold her together.

Chance's hand slid up her side toward her breast, and she almost shattered right then because the feel of him cupping her, squeezing her, melding her...

She drew back, gasped, "Bed."

His eyes were a smoky black. "Yeah," he said. "Bed."

* * *

Just one night.

The words repeated in Chance's head as he carried Carolina toward the trailer's bedroom.

God, he wouldn't last, not if she kept kissing him like she did. And touching him and moving against him. Almost in self-defense he tossed her onto the bed, but if her body had set him on fire, the look in her eyes nearly drove him to the edge.

Her hands tugged at the edge of her shirt, lifting it, teasing him with a glimpse of her flesh first, then all of it.

He simply stood, watching.

A part of him marveled, took a snapshot of the moment, fixing in his mind how she looked: tousled hair, glittering eyes, pouty mouth. She could have tempted a holy man to give up his vows, and he was no holy man.

Chance didn't want to move. He feared spooking her and inadvertently stopping her sexy striptease. She took the choice away from him, shooting forward, her gaze scanning him, her hand slowly reaching for him. Her palm landed on his chest, and he closed his eyes. Her hand slipped lower, and he knew what she would do. Still, he gasped when she touched him. She tipped her head sideways, pressed up against him, her tongue hot and warm slipping between his lips. Dear Lord. Sweet…so sweet. Like molasses and brown sugar and hot sauce. He couldn't get enough of her.

He slipped a palm beneath her bra. He felt bare flesh and heat, and he suddenly wanted more. He leaned her back against the bed and slid his lips against her bare flesh.

"Chance," she said softly, his name both a groan and a verbal caress. Her hips lifted upward.

His hands found the waistband of her jeans, and he popped the button, slid the zipper free. He tugged them down, and the sight of her tiny pink underwear shot a fresh spurt of heat through him. They matched her bra, which her breasts spilled out of, nipples still hard.

"You're going to be the death of me," he groaned.

"What a sweet death," she answered with a crooked smile.

Something inside him flipped. He pulled her boots and her jeans off in one motion and then simply gazed. She had the body of an athlete and the beauty of a swan. He couldn't wait to taste her. All of her.

His head lowered. She arched upward again. His mouth found her thighs. His hands found her center, and she let out a groan that drove him almost over the edge. He tasted the salty sweetness of her flesh. He held her down because she writhed beneath him. The ache in his groin turned into a burn.

"Chance," she said, sitting up, her hands finding his. She pulled him up and he couldn't resist.

Their lips found each other's again, but this time her hands were between them. She unbuckled his belt and then unbuttoned his pants. She slid his boxers down. He kicked off his boots, and a second later, his jeans and everything else. He was right where he wanted to be. With Caro. He opened his eyes and gazed into twin blue pools. He slid his fingers into the thick depths of hair, testing its weight and its silkiness.

"Are you sure?" he asked.

She nodded. "I've never been more certain of anything in my life."

Her eyes sparkled like stars. She slowly unbuttoned his shirt and slipped it down his shoulders. Her heat called to him, filling him with a feeling he didn't know. It made him feel awkward, clumsy and inept. She challenged him to be his best, and he worried he would disappoint. "My turn," she said, slipping her bra straps down one at a time.

He helped her slide the garment off. She was the prettiest thing he'd ever seen with her hair fanned out beneath her. She never took her eyes off him, and he didn't want her to. It made their act all the more erotic to have her begging him with her eyes.

What are you doing to me? he silently asked.

Almost as if she heard the question, she lifted a hand and touched the side of his face. His nipples grazed her chest and she gasped. He lowered his head, his lips finding her hardened nubs. Her hips thrust upward and it was almost his undoing, but somehow he held on to control as he nipped and suckled her. She groaned in pleasure.

She pulled him up. He knew what she wanted. He wanted it, too, anticipating their kiss as he'd never anticipated anything before. Her lips were like butterfly wings. He nuzzled them apart, and when they kissed once more, he knew he'd never taste anything so perfect again. He gently nudged her legs apart. She opened for him, welcoming his length. Chance closed his eyes because slipping into her was like coming home.

She wrapped her legs around him. Hard. She moved her hips. Fast. She clutched him to her. Tight.

Lord…

He wouldn't last. She moved beneath him as though she knew his every desire. He lost all sense of time, space and himself. They were joined not just physically, but emotionally, mentally and through a tenuous connection he couldn't quite explain.

"Chance."

He heard the same need for release he felt, and so he kept the rhythm going faster and faster and faster until her cry echoed his own. He spiraled down a well of pleasure he'd never experienced before.

His breaths matched hers.

That was his first coherent thought, which was amazing given she held him so tightly it was a wonder he could breathe. Slowly, her hold loosened until he was able to shift back and look into her eyes.

She smiled.

He couldn't breathe. It was the smile of an angel, and it called to his heart.

Chance knew nothing would ever be the same again.

Carolina awoke with sadness clinging to her heart.

For a long moment, she simply lay in his arms, absorbing the heat of his body, listening to the steady drone of his pulse, admiring the taut smoothness of his skin. The sun had just started to rise. It cast a pale glow over them both.

Sad.

She'd known it was only for a night. She'd gone into this with her eyes wide-open. But as he'd held her, as he'd brought her to pleasure over and over again last night, each time had been a little more bittersweet, a little more heartbreaking.

"What are you thinking about?"

His words startled her. She looked up and realized his gaze was upon her. She lifted up on her elbows.

"Long day," she improvised. "We won't get home until midnight."

His hands found her shoulders, his thumb brushing her bare skin in a comforting way. "We could always stay another night."

Everything inside her stilled.

"I could call Colt and tell him the truck won't start. We could hang out here until morning."

But as quickly as the rush of pleasure warmed her, it faded, leaving coldness in its wake. And then what? Delay the inevitable? She almost said those exact words, but she didn't want him to know how much his suggestion tempted her. She'd made it clear last night that she understood their being together was a onetime thing. He needed to know she meant it.

"Nah," she said as dismissively as possible. "We should probably get back."

He would never know how hard it was for her to pull away from him, to get dressed as if nothing out of the ordinary had happened, to slip on her clothes. Or how difficult she found it not to race back and kiss him once she was done. But she knew this man. She knew if she pushed him and gushed over him, he would run. She didn't know how she knew that. She just did. So Carolina kept her cool as she headed out the front door, pausing and giving him what she hoped was an impersonal wave goodbye.

He never saw her collapse against the door. Never saw her close her eyes, nor the way her lips silently formed the word *damn*.

Chapter 18

She was true to her word.

Chance didn't know what to think. Carolina had ignored him for the rest of the day, simply going about her business and acting as if nothing had happened between them, and that left him...

He tried to think of the word.

Confused.

When they performed later that afternoon, she did not give away their intimacy. She treated him like a prop—which he supposed, in a way, he was—completing her portion of the act and then dashing out afterward. By the time he drove back to their spot, she was already waving goodbye.

"Gonna catch a ride back with the girls," she said, barely giving him a smile before ducking her head into the truck and taking off.

He almost called after her, wanting to tell her it was a bad idea, that she should stay with him and help him load up the panels because they never knew if James was around, but that was an excuse and she would know it. She'd be fine on the road with the girls. He'd made sure each of them carried pepper spray and at least one other had a Taser, the kind with ejectable prongs. Yeah. They'd be okay. And so he let her go.

Just one night, but God help him, he'd begun to want two.

Colt's smiling face was the first thing to greet him as he pulled in to the ranch, something that surprised him. It was close to midnight. The Galloping Girlz trailer was parked alongside the hay barn, which made Chance feel moderately better. Carolina had made it home safely. The apartment above the barn was dark, however. She must have returned home well ahead of him and already gone to bed. He didn't want to think about what she might look like in that bed. It would do crazy things to his insides.

"Welcome back," his brother said.

"What are you doing up?"

Sage and fresh-cut grass. That's what it smelled like when he stepped out of the truck.

Home.

"Couldn't sleep," his brother answered.

Colt headed straight for the back of the trailer. Teddy needed to be unloaded. Chance would take the panels off the trailer tomorrow. Too tired and too dark tonight.

"Word on the street is your first solo performance went off without a hitch."

Chance smiled. "Went as well as could be expected." Strangely, he didn't want to let his brother know how much he had enjoyed it. "Still wish you could have been there."

"Nah. I needed to stay here, just in case. I knew you'd be fine."

Hard to believe B day was right around the corner, as he'd been calling it. Birth of his brother's baby. "Natalie okay?"

"She's fine. Now tell me what you thought. Did you like it? Bill called, said you nailed it both times."

"It was good." He flipped the trailer latch up, and the bar slid free on a nearly soundless hinge. Teddy lifted his head to peer over the divider as if asking, "Who's there?"

"That's all you have to say?" his brother asked. "'It was good'?"

No. It'd been great. The most intense surge of adrenaline he'd ever had outside of jumping out of a plane, only this type of rush didn't nearly kill him. But as great as it'd been, nothing compared to his night with Caro. Nothing.

"Just tired." He stepped inside the trailer, unlatching the divider. Teddy rode untied, the horse immediately turning and unloading himself. Colt caught him by the halter.

"You mind telling me what's going on?" His brother glanced at the Galloping Girlz trailer. "Caro came home, and I had to practically pry things out of her. She headed straight to the apartment, and I haven't seen her since. And you don't seem like a man who'd just nailed his first solo performance. You miss shooting people or something?"

No. He didn't miss that at all. He missed his military family. Dusty, his best friend. Mark, his commander. He still stayed in touch with them. Still saw them when he had time to video conference, but they weren't going to be there when he went back. It was his first time thinking about that, and it put a new perspective on things. It wasn't that he needed their camaraderie. He'd make new friends. It was just that things wouldn't be the same.

"I'm out of sorts," Chance admitted.

He and Colt had always been close. They'd looked out for each other when they were younger. When they were old enough, they'd turned their attention to Claire, protecting her, making sure she was okay when their dad fell into one of his drunken rages. They might be older now, but they were still close despite Chance's longer stint in the army.

"You know," Colt said, "you don't have to leave."

They'd reached Teddy's corral, Chance pausing for a moment outside the horse's pen to glance back at his brother. He rested a hand on the top rail.

"I know," he said, unbuckling Teddy's halter. One would think the horse would be tired after the long ride, but the gelding shot off, bucking, running and shaking his head until he hit the middle of his pen, where he stopped and sniffed the ground. Chance knew what would come next. Sure enough, the horse carefully lowered himself down, then rolled with joyful grunts and flailing legs. Chance couldn't help but smile.

"You could take over Rodeo Misfits, you know," his brother added. "Permanently."

Chance immediately shook his head. "Nah. Not for me."

"No, wait," Colt said. "Hear me out."

They both leaned against the fence. Chance could

barely make out his brother's face, but he could tell by his voice that this was one of those serious moments in life. They'd had a few of them over the years. When their dad was sick. When they'd signed up for the army. The day Claire turned three and Colt had pulled Chance aside and sworn to protect her. He'd been five years old at the time, and he still remembered it like yesterday.

"Natalie would never want me to give up Rodeo Misfits," Colt said. "It's part of her life. But we're crazy busy right now. It's all I can do to keep up with the work around here. We have Laney to help, but it's not enough. There are horse shows and clinics and big international competitions coming up. Rodeo Misfits needs to take a backseat, but I hate to do that. It's a family business, one that was started by our grandfather."

"I know."

Colt continued as if he hadn't spoken. "Our dad nearly ruined its reputation. It's taken me years to get it back. I hate to let it all go while I go on hiatus, so why don't you take it over for me?"

"Colt—"

"Ah, ah. Don't talk." His brother lifted a hand. "You can go back to private contracting at any point in your life. And I don't want to give up the rodeo business if I don't have to. I just need a little bit of time. You can give me that, right? Stick around for a while. Live in the apartment if you want. Or build your own place. I know you've always wanted to do that out by the pond. Go for it. This land is as much yours as it is mine and Claire's."

"Can I talk now?"

His brother nodded. "Sure."

"I'm not going to lie. I really liked performing in front of a crowd."

Colt lifted up on his heels. "I *knew* it."

"And I could see how it might get addicting."

"The best high in the world."

"But I have a plan. Back to the Middle East. Make a ton of money. Save up for the house I want to build."

"You could make a ton of money performing."

"That's your money."

Colt shook his head. "No, it's not. It's our money. Our family. Our life. Don't turn your back on it."

"I'm not."

"And you're good at performing. And you won't get killed doing it. I hate the thought of you leaving and going back."

"Colt—" He sighed.

"No, let me finish. Things are good here. Claire is happy. Adam is getting better. You should be a part of that happiness."

"I am."

Colt grunted. "Vicariously."

"I keep tabs on all of you."

"Through the internet."

Chance smiled. "It works."

"It's a cop-out."

He winced. "Ouch."

"You're running away. Again. Even Caro agrees."

"What?"

"I talked to her about it earlier. Asked what she thought of you sticking around. She said you were a natural. That once you got in front of the audience you came to life." Colt shook his head. "She said it was cool to watch."

She thought he was good? During all their time together last night, she'd never once brought it up.

"You two okay?" Colt asked. "She seemed a little strange when I asked about you."

He almost laughed. *I'll bet.*

"We're fine." And that's all he would say about that. "Look, I'll think about it," Chance said before Colt asked any more probing questions. "It's been a long day. Honestly, I'm too tired to think."

But he wouldn't take over the Rodeo Misfits. He'd made a commitment to his new employer, Jax Stone. He would honor it. He always did.

"I guess that's all I can hope for." Colt frowned, and Chance suspected his brother knew the truth. "We want you here, bro. All of us do."

Chance's gaze snagged on the apartment window above the barn.

All?

Caro shot back from the glass. Had he seen her? What had they been talking about? Had Chance told Colt about their night together? Was Chance even thinking about her?

He'd looked up.

So, yes, she'd been on his mind. Or maybe he'd sensed her gaze. She'd gone from being stalked to the one doing the stalking. Stupid woman.

Inga's nails clicked against the hardwood floors as she made her way back to her couch. There was a bed in the apartment, but she refused to sleep in it. It wasn't hers and never would be. Two people had lived there—she would make it three—but none of them permanently, so there was a hodgepodge of old furniture, mostly rejects from the old house, but the furniture all worked together somehow. She would love to find someplace just like it…eventually. When life settled back to normal.

Normal. Hah. "I knew what I was getting into, didn't I, Inga?"

The Belgian Malinois rested her head against the edge of the couch while Caro buried herself under the blankets. She'd watched Chance pull in, hadn't known Colt was in the barn until she'd watched him walk up to his brother. A part of her had been disappointed—she'd been hoping Chance would come up to the apartment, but she knew that wouldn't happen with his brother watching.

He still could come up, though. Later.

Her heart began to pound just as it had when he first pulled in. He hadn't said a word to her when she'd left, but she'd seen the look in his eyes. He'd watched her walk away with an unmistakable glint. The heat of a man who'd had the time of his life and wanted more. His look had buoyed her spirits for the rest of the day. She'd been hoping it'd meant something. That he wouldn't simply let her end it.

The silence of the night was almost unbearable.

Carolina waited, breathless, for him to arrive. Colt had to have gone back to bed. Chance could easily sneak out. A horse banged against a stall, and she about came off the couch. Inga whined. She glanced at her cell phone. An hour had gone by.

Chance wasn't coming.

How long she waited for him she had no idea, but

eventually she drifted off to sleep, waking only when her alarm sounded early the next morning.

He hadn't come.

She sat up in bed, Inga catching her eye. Caro mustered a smile for the dog.

"I'm a fool, aren't I?"

She tried to keep her disappointment at bay. It wasn't as if they were a couple. She'd made it clear she understood the rules. She'd just hoped he might break them.

Maybe he'd be up, too. She'd set her alarm for 5 a.m. so she could help out with feeding the animals— her way of helping to pay the rent, so to speak. The thought that Chance might be below her in the barn prompted her to dress quickly. Sweatshirt and jeans, her typical morning attire. Hardly glamorous, but she did brush her hair and apply a layer of lip gloss before heading downstairs.

BITCH.

Caro froze.

It was one of those moments when your eyes see something in front of them, but your brain can't process the information.

SLUT.

WHORE.

The words were sprayed everywhere. Stall fronts. The office door. The wall of the tack room.

"Son of a—"

The Reynolds's beautiful barn. Ruined. Because of her.

The horses.

She raced to the first stall. The animal seemed fine. So did the next one. And the next. But the barn. Caro's eyes filled with tears, humiliating, shameful, saddened tears. This was *her* fault. *Her* problem with James. *Her* mess to clean up.

"What the—"

Caro jumped, but it was Colt, not Chance, who stood near the barn's entrance. When she spotted the horrified expression on her boss's face, she couldn't hold back the tears.

She inhaled deeply and forced out the words, "I'm so sorry," before losing it completely and covering her face with her hands.

Damn him, she thought. *Damn that James Edwards.* This was the final straw. Somehow, she'd make him pay. She needed to figure out how.

Chapter 19

"What a mess."

"Shh," Natalie hissed, glancing in Caro's direction. "She'll hear you." She shook her head, scrubbing the paint off the front of a stall as best she could given her ever-expanding girth. "She feels bad enough as it is."

The stall fronts were wood. They'd been stained a natural gold, and fortunately for Natalie and Colt, they were waterproof. The paint didn't stick to the surface well, which meant a rag and solvent would wipe away the paint. Unfortunately, the solvent smelled horrible, and the paint made a mess of the rags and their hands.

"What did Chance say?" Claire asked, working on getting rid of the letter *W*. Adam had insisted on helping, though she wasn't certain he should be reading the offensive words. Fortunately, he didn't know what any of them meant.

"He would kill him," Natalie said.

"You mean James." Claire rubbed a little harder. Right now she wanted to kill him, too.

"Yes, James. I also think Colt wants to kill him." Natalie worked on an *H*, but she made slow progress because she couldn't put her back into it.

Claire wouldn't be surprised if she had the baby a little early. She'd dropped in the past week, an observation she kept to herself. She had a feeling her sister-in-law was a bit nervous. Not that she blamed her. First children were always a little terrifying.

"Mommy, what's a whore?"

Natalie gaped. Claire almost laughed. She glanced at Caro, who clearly hadn't heard the question—she was too busy working on the word *SLUT*.

"It's someone who likes men," she improvised.

"A lot of men," Natalie muttered.

"Are you a whore then, Mommy?"

Natalie and Claire exchanged glances. They both burst out laughing.

"No, honey," she chortled. "I'm not a whore."

"But you like men?" There was such a look of wide-eyed innocence on Adam's face that it somehow made it all the funnier.

"I do, but I'll explain it to you later."

"Okay," said her son, the curiosity in his green eyes fading before he went back to work.

Please, God, don't let him ask his teacher what the word meant. That would be just her luck. Although she wouldn't complain. Adam had recently gone back to normal school, as he liked to call it, and she was beyond pleased. He was thriving.

Only a few weeks until Christmas. They were marking each day on the calendar. Only a few weeks until he was deemed cancer free.

"He's going to get an education helping us clean up," Natalie said with a glance at the word *BITCH*.

"We're in luck. He knows that's a female dog."

Natalie smiled. "Thank God for that." She continued scrubbing. "And thank God all the words are short."

"Yeah, it's too bad the men aren't here to help." She smiled at her sister-in-law before rolling her eyes. "I'd like to see my brother come up with a PC explanation for what a whore is."

"Me, too," Natalie said.

They'd gone to town to talk to Officer Connelly. All of the men. There was no proof it was James they'd caught on videotape spray painting the walls, but they all knew it was. The man had worn a ski mask and baggy pants. Chance and Colt were trying to see what they could do about it, but Claire had a feeling she knew the answer. Nothing.

"Okay, that word's gone," Caro said, coming up behind them.

"Good. You can get started on *BITCH*," Natalie said.

Caro didn't immediately move off. "I'm sorry about this, Natalie. I really am."

Natalie paused, rested a hand on her giant belly. "I told you it's okay."

"I know, but I still feel bad."

Claire could tell her sister-in-law empathized. Claire felt bad for her, too.

"Not to worry," Natalie said, going back to scrubbing, her free hand resting on her belly. "We'll be done in a flash with all of us working together."

Caro turned away, clearly with the intention of helping Adam next, but she stopped. "What did you say?"

Claire paused, too, wondering what was up.

"I said it'll go fast since we're such a big group," Natalie repeated. "Fortunately, the paint is not staining the wood. Thank God for a good water sealant."

Caro had a blank stare on her face. She half turned toward the entrance of the barn. "I wonder if that would work?"

"How what would work?" Claire asked, because clearly her sister-in-law hadn't noticed the expression on Caro's face. She wasn't talking about the paint.

"A group of us," Caro said.

"Doing what?"

"Confronting James."

Natalie understood at last. "You're going to confront him?" She glanced at Claire.

Caro nodded. "Those women. They dropped the charges against him. They were too afraid. But there's safety in numbers."

Claire nodded, supporting the idea. It could work.

"I need to call Officer Connelly," Caro said, smiling for the first time today. "I'm going to see if he'll work with me to contact the other women. Maybe if I can convince them to reopen their cases, James will leave me alone."

"You want to *what*?"

It was the first time she'd spoken to Chance all day, and it wasn't to talk about what had happened between them. Instead she'd come to him with a harebrained idea of confronting James.

"I already talked to Officer Connelly," Caro said. "He couldn't tell me who the other women were, but he promised to talk to them to see if they'd go along with my plan. If they do, Officer Connelly will break the news to James. Leave me alone or he'll have two other women pressing charges. That would be three strikes. That should scare the you-know-what out of him."

They were outside, Chance having just come from town, the sun so bright it turned Caro's eyes a neon blue. He admired the effect for a moment before focusing on her words.

"So you're hoping to threaten him? Is that it?"

She nodded. "More or less. Leave me alone or more troubles will come your way."

"And if the other women don't play along?"

For the first time, she lost some of her enthusiasm. "Then I'll try it without their knowing. Lie if I have to, though I'd really hate that."

He'd rather drag the man out behind their barn and cut the rope right when they got near a cliff. It was bad enough James terrorized Caro, but now he'd targeted his family. The man needed to pay.

"No way, Caro. I say you keep a low profile until your first court appearance. No more rodeos. No more going out unless you absolutely have to. I've already talked to my sister about using one of her dogs for protection. You already have Inga, so I know James won't get too close. A few canine razor blades ought to put the fear of God into the man. Frankly, I'd like to stand by and watch."

"Stay home?" Her face paled. "And give up rodeos?"

"Temporarily," Chance said, hating the look on her face. He hated all of this. Nobody was allowed to mess with the people he loved.

Loved?

The people he cared for, he quickly amended.

"But trick riding is my job."

"I know that, and I already talked to Colt about it. He's going to hire you to work on the ranch with him. You'll be earning money and staying out of James's reach at the same time."

And staying away from him. He couldn't help but think that might be for the better. When he'd spied James's handiwork this morning, he'd experienced such a huge surge of rage it'd scared the hell out of him. He'd wanted to track James down—a skill he possessed and one he could use to his advantage if need be—but he hadn't trusted what he might do to the man. Compounding Chance's rage was the knowledge it'd been partly his fault James had gotten so close. He'd been exhausted from his night with Caro and the long drive home. He'd been off his game. He should have heard James outside—should have seen him. Chance hadn't, and it enraged him all the more. Colt had talked him down, but the whole thing had been a slap in the face.

"They've already been so kind to me," Caro said softly. "First with the apartment, and now this." Her blue eyes were troubled. She fingered the strands of her ponytail absently. "I don't think I can accept their offer."

"You can, because we'd all rather you be safe than sorry."

"Yeah, but there's a fine line between being a victim and a mooch."

"You're not a mooch."

"I'm still going to wait until I hear back from Officer Connelly."

She tipped her chin up, and he almost smiled. Bully for her. Instead of moping about her situation or getting angry, she'd devised a plan. The urge to kiss her right then was so surprising and so unexpected he took a step back.

"Keep me posted."

Her blue eyes lost their luster. "I will."

He couldn't get away from her fast enough, and that should have been his first clue their one night wasn't enough. His second clue came that night when she texted him.

Heard from Officer Connelly. The other two women won't do it.

And he finally understood what it meant to feel sympathy pangs. His stomach twisted in a knot at her words. She might not be in front of him, but he could practically hear her disappointment, sadness and regret.

I'm sorry, he texted back.

I guess I'm grounded.

He hated James more in that moment. It wasn't right he could affect her like this. He shouldn't be able to terrorize women and get away with it.

Especially when one of those women was his.

Chance might as well admit it. He would always despise the man for what he'd done to Caro, but something had changed.

Nobody was allowed to hurt someone who was his. Not now. Not when he'd been a kid. Not when he'd been in the army.

The man was going down. Chance simply needed to figure out how he was going to do it.

Chapter 20

She stayed home the next weekend, and she hated it.

It'd been one of the hardest things in her life to watch Chance leave without her. Her teammates had waved goodbye, too.

"Not easy, is it?" Colt said, turning to her as they stood in front of the barn.

"No."

He patted her back. "You'll get back to it soon enough."

Maybe.

The rodeo season would end soon. Chance would be gone. Nothing would be the same again.

"Come on." He gave her a wry grin. "Let's muck stalls."

So she kept herself busy. Inga kept her company. That helped, but only so much. Officer Connelly had called to say they'd moved up James's court date. It was the best he could do, he'd told her. He'd also said to be extra careful. There was no telling what James was capable of. His scare tactics hadn't worked, and that might make him desperate enough to try something else.

Carolina didn't see Chance when he returned from the rodeo. He had a meeting about his new job. It served as a crushing reminder he'd be gone soon. She had heard from Delilah that things had gone well at the rodeo. Delilah had stepped in and taken her place again, something her friend had only been too happy to do. And Caro knew why: Delilah had a crush on Chance.

"What should I do next?" she asked her boss, stowing away the pitchfork she'd been using to muck stalls.

Colt glanced at the whiteboard hanging on the tack-room wall. It was Monday. No clients at the barn. That meant a quiet day, something Caro could use. Her hands hadn't stopped shaking since she'd heard James was going to court.

"Why don't you lunge Titan next?" Colt suggested, tipping his cowboy hat back. "You can use the covered arena."

She nodded and gave him a faux salute, another thing that reminded her of Chance. "Will do."

At least she got to work with horses. If she were to be a prisoner for an undetermined length of time, it helped that her job dealt with the animals she loved.

"Colt," someone called.

Caro froze. Her boss turned toward the barn entrance. Natalie stood with an amused look on her face.

"It's time," she said.

Chance dropped the lead rope he'd been holding. "Right now?"

Natalie rolled her eyes. "No. Ten minutes from now. Yes, right now."

Caro glanced between them, her mind spinning. "I'll put Inga away," she said, whistling for her dog. She'd gone off to explore the manure pile, a favorite hangout for the ranch animals. "And the horses we have in turnout." Her boss's look of bemused terror amused the heck out of her, too. "I can follow behind in a few minutes."

"No," he said. "We'll wait for you."

"I don't think that's a good idea," Natalie said, wincing. "Oh, Lord."

Colt ran for his wife, calling over his shoulder, "Okay, follow behind."

And they were gone. Caro called Inga to her side. The dog had become her constant companion. "Natalie's going to have a baby," she told her. "That means you need to stay home."

Home.

She wished the ranch were her home. She'd never felt so safe. So protected. So loved as she had staying with the Reynoldses. Chance might have been keeping his distance, but that was to be expected. They'd had a deal, she and him. She didn't blame him for honoring it. She just…missed him. She missed their practice sessions. She missed how overprotective he was. She missed being made to feel as if she were special when she nailed a routine and he smiled at her in approval.

Carolina drove to the hospital in a near daze. The only thing she made a conscious decision about was to double back in case James followed her. She didn't see him, and she was in too much of a hurry to get to the hospital to do it again.

And that's why she didn't spot him in the hospital parking lot, waiting for her to get out of the truck.

"Hello, Caro."

She pressed her back up against the vehicle. They were in a crowded parking lot. People came and went. She heard an ambulance in the distance.

He's not going to hurt you here.

She did something she would have been unable to do two months ago. She squared her shoulders and stepped forward.

"Hello, James."

Lord, what had she seen in the man?

She'd found his loosely cropped brown hair attractive when she'd first met him. Now she loathed its contrived messiness. She'd liked his gray eyes, too. Had thought them kind. Now she knew they hid the soul of an evil man.

"We need to talk," he said.

"How did you know I'd be here?" she asked, her heart rate suddenly taking off.

He glanced around. Someone parked their car a few rows away. "I followed Colt and Natalie. Once I realized where they were going, I knew you wouldn't be far behind."

"Oh." Clever. She should have taken better precautions. If she hadn't been mooning over Chance, she might have noticed James waiting for her.

"I want you to drop the charges," he said, crossing big arms over his chest. "I don't need the grief a conviction will bring me."

She almost laughed. He didn't need the grief? Had she needed the bruises he'd given her? The trip to the hospital? The succeeding weeks of pain, sadness and fear?

She stood strong. "I guess you should have thought of that when you beat the crap out of me."

He took one step toward her. They were in the middle of a parking aisle, she reminded herself. She could run if she had to. Duck behind one of the other vehicles. Call for help.

"I don't think you understand. I really need you to drop those charges."

There was menace in his eyes. She didn't care. The man was a bully. She would not allow him to bully her again.

"Is that what your graffiti at my work was all about? A pep talk? A way to woo my sympathies?" She curled her lip at him, hoping he could see her complete disdain. "Get a life, James. And get a good lawyer. You're going down."

She turned away, focusing on the two-story hospital in front of her. They had security inside. She just needed to make it to the lobby.

BOOM.

The sound made her jump and turn and scream all at the same time. James stood by her truck. He held a baseball bat, though where he'd gotten it from was anyone's guess. And her truck—it now sported a huge dent in the tailgate.

James swung the bat again, this time at her taillight.

"What are you doing?" Plastic shattered. "You're ruining my truck!"

"Drop the charges," he ordered.

"Drop dead," she said, backing away from him, the hairs on her neck standing on end. He would kill her with that bat.

She ran.

Right into a wall. Only it wasn't a wall. It was Chance, and she wanted to cry, wanted to hold him tight, wanted to take shelter in his arms and never leave his side.

Never.

"Leave her the hell alone," Chance told James, hating the man more than he'd ever hated someone or something in his life.

"Screw off, asshole," James said, waving the baseball bat in their direction.

It was all Chance could do not to thrust Caro aside. To launch at the man and use the bat to pummel some sense into him. Instead he said, "If you don't leave her alone, you'll regret it."

James cocked a brow at him, slapping the bat into the palm of his hand. "Oh, yeah? Whatcha gonna do? File a restraining order against me? Big strong Army Ranger needs a piece of paper to protect him?"

He had no idea how the man knew he was ex-military, nor did he care. "No. I paid a visit to Rose Santos and Carla Brown and told them I was with a special-victims unit. I showed them pictures of what you'd done to Caro."

The memory turned his stomach all over again. His hands shook. He clenched them to avoid wrapping them around James's throat.

"I told them what you were doing to Caro, what you would do to other women if they didn't all band together to stop you." He unclenched his hands, keeping a wary eye on the baseball bat. "And you know what, James? They agreed. They put aside their fear and their terror and their revulsion of you, and they agreed to refile charges. As we speak, Officer Connelly has a warrant out for your arrest. In fact, he's right over there—" he pointed to the right "—along with several of his officers. We all saw you pull up in front of the hospital."

Caro's eyes filled with tears, but they weren't tears of fear. They were tears of joy, relief and, yes, gratitude. He hugged her tighter before setting her aside, putting himself between her and James.

James had lost his cocky self-assurance. He glanced around him, wide-eyed. Three officers approached, guns drawn.

"Drop the weapon," one of them shouted.

Chance saw it then. Saw the fear he'd been hoping to see. The desire to run. The panic. All the things James had made his victims feel.

Chance laughed. "And here's something funny— my sister-in-law isn't having a baby right now, asshole. This was all a setup. You're going down, and I'm the man who made it happen."

Chapter 21

They put him in jail.

"But how did you know he would follow Colt and Natalie to the hospital?" Caro asked Chance. They all sat around the kitchen table: Claire, Natalie, Colt and Chance. Adam was in the family room playing video games. Inga and Natalie's new puppy kept him company.

"We didn't," Natalie answered for him. "We just knew he'd been watching the place, so we figured he'd follow us, thinking you were in the truck."

Chance nodded his agreement, which was all he'd been doing since they'd arrived home. He'd been as quiet as a possum.

"I still can't believe you didn't tell me about this," Colt said. "I thought for sure you were having that baby."

Caro glanced at Natalie in time to see her smile. "We needed to make sure Caro thought it was real."

"And I needed to draw James out," Chance said, his first words since they'd returned to the ranch. "My biggest concern was he might bring a weapon." His gaze encompassed the whole table. "A real weapon. I was glad to see all he had was a baseball bat. Even better, it's all on the hospital's security cameras. Between Carla and Rose pressing charges and the video, James will go away for a long, long time."

Caro wanted to cry. It was over. Chance had done it. He'd saved her as he'd saved so many people over the course of his life.

"Thank you," she said softly.

He glanced at her, but she couldn't read the expression in his eyes and it drove her nuts. She would have thought he'd be ecstatic, but instead he'd been quiet, almost sad.

"Well, I still think you should have told me," Colt said, getting up and filling a glass with water at the tap. "I drove like a maniac on our way to the hospital."

"You'll get to drive like a maniac again," Natalie said, standing, too.

She doubled over.

"Nat!" Colt yelled, the glass clattering in the sink.

"It's okay," she wheezed. She lifted a hand. "Just knocked the breath out of me."

"What?" Colt asked.

Natalie peeked up at him. "I think I had my first contraction."

Claire gaped. "You're in labor?"

She grunted, leaned over again, managing to gasp. "We need to get back to the hospital."

From the family room, they heard Adam say, "Again?"

Which made Natalie and Colt laugh. Caro looked at Chance, wanting to ask him what was wrong. He should be excited. He was about to become an uncle again. But as she watched, he stood without saying a word. He grabbed his hat and shoved it on his head.

"I'll drive me and Caro to the hospital."

Her relief was like a physical release. She could feel her shoulders relax. He wouldn't be able to ignore her in the truck.

"I'll put the dogs away first," she volunteered.

"We'll ride with Colt and Natalie," Claire said, turning to the family room. "Come on, Adam."

The boy sighed in resignation as Caro scooped up the puppy. It took her only a minute to lock the baby Malinois in the laundry room and another few minutes to lock up Inga.

Shortly after, she climbed into the truck beside Chance.

"Seat belt," he reminded her.

He didn't smile. Didn't comment on his sister-in-law's impending delivery. Didn't do anything other than stare straight ahead and put the truck in drive.

"Chance, what's wrong?"

She thought he would ignore her. Thought he might brush her off with a comment. Instead he shifted in his seat, glancing at her for a second.

"I'm leaving in a couple weeks."

The words were like the stab of a needle. No, a hundred needles…a thousand. She'd known it was coming. She'd never deluded herself into thinking it wasn't. Still…

"I'm sorry to hear that," she said, looking out the

passenger-side window. She didn't want him to see her eyes. If he did, he might note the tears she fought.

"I heard from my new commander over the weekend. I fly out to Germany first, then back to the Middle East."

Back to the war zone. A place where he might be killed. A place of danger.

She gulped down the lump in her throat. "What will you do there?"

He shrugged. "Mostly escorting corporate executives in and around war zones."

She nodded, her voice raspy with unshed tears as she asked, "Isn't that dangerous?"

He shrugged again. "I'm used to danger."

Yes, he was. She could not have asked for a better bodyguard. It was what he did. What he was good at. She didn't blame him for wanting to go back to it.

But was it wrong of her to wish? To dream? To wonder what might have happened had she been woman enough to capture his heart? She inhaled against more tears.

"Congratulations?" She forced a bright smile, making sure she had herself firmly in control before turning to face him. "I think."

At last their gazes met, and Caro's heart flipped over at what she saw. Sadness. Resignation. Maybe even a hint of fear. But no. Chance didn't feel fear. He was a warrior. A man who had dedicated his life to protecting people, no matter what it might cost him personally.

"No, it's good." He focused on the road again. "I'm going to break the news to Colt and Natalie once the baby is born."

Good Lord, it was getting hard to breathe. "And the rodeo business? What about that?"

He gripped the steering wheel, hard. "It's almost the end of the season. And I won't be leaving for a little while yet. I'll be able to finish it out."

Leaving. She'd known it was coming. Still…

"Take care of yourself while you're over there," she said. "Promise me you'll keep in touch."

They'd reached the end of the ranch's private road, and Chance held her gaze as he said, "I will."

It was the longest night of his life, not because his brother's wife was in labor for twelve hours before she finally gave birth to a healthy baby boy they named Weston, but because he kept catching glimpses of Caro's face while they waited all afternoon for news.

Her face was splotchy. Pinched. Dark circles rimmed her eyes.

He wasn't an idiot. He knew why she'd barely cracked a smile when the Galloping Girlz arrived at the hospital. One of them had asked her if everything was okay. He'd watched as she'd pasted on a bright smile and explained she was just tired now that everything was over with James.

Don't think about it, buddy. This was always the deal.

He knew that. Just as she'd known it, too. Didn't make it any easier to swallow, because the plain and simple truth was he cared. If things had been different, he would have asked her out. He would have wooed and wined and dined her and…

What?

No sense in dwelling on what wouldn't ever happen. "You can go in now," a nurse said, her smile aimed at the lobby of waiting people. All of Colt and Natalie's friends. Wes and Jillian. Zach and Mariah. Ethan, his sister's fiancé. "Just close family for now."

He stood. Ethan and Claire did, too, his sister holding out her hand for Adam. Caro stayed seated, but Chance motioned her up. "You're part of the family, too."

He caught the look of surprise on his sister's face, but she didn't balk. Claire was too sweet for that, and Natalie didn't seem to mind when they came in together. In fact, she smiled brightly.

"Look what the stork brought."

Adam rushed to the bed, most likely because he couldn't see the baby swaddled in blankets, but when he finally caught his first glimpse, he drew up short.

"Why is he so red?"

There was such a look of intrigued revulsion on the boy's face that Chance would have laughed if he'd been in a better frame of mind.

"He's exhausted," Natalie said, her eyes as blue as the blankets around her son. "It's a lot of work being carried by a stork all that way."

To which Adam replied, "Aunt Natalie, I know babies don't come from a stork. They come from vaginas."

Stunned silence. Colt emitted a sound reminiscent of a bird squawking. Natalie glanced at Claire. Claire shrugged. Then, as if on cue, they all started laughing. Caro just watched, and Chance realized she felt like an intruder. He scooted closer to her and whispered, "My nephew has no filter."

She glanced up at him and smiled gratefully. "So I've learned."

"What do you think, you guys?" Natalie said, holding her baby differently to give everyone a better view. "Weston, meet your family. Family, meet Weston."

Meet your family.

"I think he's adorable," his sister said.

"I think he looks like a dried-up tomato." Adam chortled.

"And I think he's perfect," his soon-to-be brother-in-law said. "I want one just like him."

Which made Claire look at Ethan with adoration. Chance averted his gaze. He knew now why he'd invited Caro into the room. He felt like an outsider, too. The brother who had always been off on another continent. The one who only saw people via video chat and conversed through text messages. It had never bothered him before, but right now it did. In a couple of weeks, he'd be leaving. Life would go on here. Ethan was talking about starting up a therapy center for veterans suffering from PTSD. He didn't have the money to do it himself, so Chance had connected him with a wealthy friend—the man he was going to work for, actually, Jaxston Stone, the owner of DTS.

"How are you feeling, Natalie?" Caro asked. Hospital lights did nothing to detract from her pretty features. Chance longed to touch her face.

Natalie smiled. "Tired. Sore. Elated. Scared."

"Scared?" Caro asked.

She glanced around the room with a bemused expression on her face. "It occurred to me a few minutes ago that this little bundle of joy is now solely my responsibility."

"And mine," Colt added.

"Yes, but still a responsibility. It's like learning you were given a monkey."

"A monkey!" Colt said. "Are you calling my son ugly?"

"He kind of looks like a monkey," Adam said.

Natalie smiled again. "No, no. I'm just saying that monkeys are cute, and I think I might know how to care for one, but until I do, it's a little scary."

"I know exactly how you feel," Claire said. "But you'll get used to it. In a few years, you'll be missing the days when he couldn't talk back."

"Can I hold him?" Adam interjected.

"Of course," Natalie said. "Just make sure you support his head."

They all watched as the two cousins were introduced to each other, and Chance found himself wanting to slip an arm about Caro and draw her closer. It must be the emotions of the day that had him feeling so out of sorts.

"You want to hold him, Chance?" Natalie asked, motioning with her chin toward Adam. "You'll be leaving us here soon. Better get your fill."

He gulped. Did he want to hold his nephew? He hadn't been around for Adam's birth. Come to think of it, he couldn't recall a single time that he'd held an infant.

"Ah, sure?"

Adam turned to him. "It's easy. Just don't break his head."

Chance almost laughed. Almost. Because in the next instant, he was holding his nephew and staring down into his eyes and he saw... Colt. And his sister. And his mother before that, and it reminded him of his mom and how much he missed her, and how he wished she were here right now. He needed to look away, because the man who didn't cry, who prided himself on never shedding tears, suddenly couldn't breathe.

Something was wrong.

The whole way home Chance said not one word. She'd tried to engage him in conversation, but he'd merely grunted a time or two. She'd given up after the first few miles.

"See you this weekend," he said as he put his truck in gear. He moved to open his door.

"Chance." She stopped him with her hand.

He reacted as if she'd hit him. It immediately prompted her to pull her hand away.

"Sorry," she said, though she didn't know why she was apologizing. "I wanted to say I don't want things to be awkward between us. We still have two more rodeos to perform together. I want them to be good times, not bad."

Night had fallen, but she could still make out his face in the light of the dashboard.

"I'm going to miss my family," he said.

She reached for him again. It was an automatic gesture, and this time he didn't pull away. This time he let her hand rest on his.

"I looked around the hospital room, and I realized I would be gone soon, but they would still be here, back at the ranch, living life without me."

Don't go.

Oh, how she wanted to say the words.

"I won't get to see Weston grow up. Not really. I'll

miss out on Adam's first prom. In a few years, they'll both be grown up and graduated and I'll be...where?"

She took a deep breath made shaky by her tears. "You'll be here," she said, her free hand lifting to her chest, "in their hearts."

He seemed so sad in that moment, so lost, that she did the unthinkable. She crossed the line, the invisible barrier that had stood between them for weeks. She kissed him. He didn't move at first, but then he kissed her back and she knew where it would lead. She didn't care.

Stay, she tried to tell him with every kiss. *Don't leave.*

He didn't seem to hear, and that was all right, too, because she was desperate enough to take what she could get. When he slipped out of his truck, she did, too. And when he held out a hand, she took it. Colt was spending the night at the hospital. They had the house to themselves. He led her to his room, his childhood bedroom, slowly undressing her, kissing her shoulder at one point.

"Did he hurt you there?" he asked.

It took her a moment to understand what he meant. "Yes."

He kissed the spot again. "I'm sorry."

It was all she could do not to cry.

I love you.

The words were right there, on the edge of her tongue, but she couldn't say them. Not when he laid her down on the bed. Not when he kissed every spot that James had bruised, including her heart. Not later, when they were done and he held her.

I love you.

If only the words would make him stay.

Chapter 22

Chance's flight departed at three on a Sunday afternoon. Caro knew that because, unbeknownst to him, she'd driven to the airport, parked at the end of the runway and watched his plane leave the ground, tears in her eyes.

"It's for the best," she kept telling herself. The military was Chance's life. No, she quickly amended, protecting people was his life. Nothing would stop him from doing that. Not his family. Not her. Not anyone.

"You look like death," Colt said when she showed up for work. Caro had burrowed beneath a heavy sweatshirt. They'd never gone back to the way it'd been before, when all she'd done was ride for Colt on the weekends. Colt had insisted she stay on, and Caro had said yes. It beat waitressing over the winter, which was how she usually supported herself. But even she was surprised when he'd offered her the apartment as part of her salary. It was a godsend, and she knew how lucky she was.

"Just tired," she said.

"Well, get ready. You're going to be even more tired. My sister's going a little crazy with this whole wedding deal. She's already done a site map. She told me she'd be over tomorrow to figure out where they're going to put everything."

The wedding. Once it had seemed distant, far in the future, but it was only weeks away. Christmas. A time for celebrating and new beginnings. For family and friendship. She should be grateful to be included as a member of the Reynolds clan, even if she wasn't. Not really.

She had hoped.

But she refused to dwell. Losing Chance had left her numb, and she needed something, anything, to keep her occupied.

"Tell me what I can do to help," she said, forcing a smile, but her boss didn't reply. He stared down at her, concern in his eyes.

"Did you tell him you loved him?"

She thought she'd misheard him. "What?"

"My brother. Does he know you're in love with him?"

She didn't know what to say. Didn't know what to do. She could deny it, but Colt and Natalie had been so kind. She couldn't lie to them. Not now. Not ever.

"I don't think so," she said softly, looking at the ground. It was hard to look at Colt. He reminded her so much of Chance.

"You should have told him."

She took a deep breath. "I did, in a way."

Colt shook his head. "Idiot."

She didn't know if he referred to her or to Chance.

"My brother's never been one for seeing what's right in front of his face."

It was Chance he talked about, then. Phew.

"In high school, Harriet Peterson had the biggest crush on him. Everyone in school knew it, but not Chance. He was too busy riding horses, hunting squirrels or riding broncs. Clueless."

"Please don't tell him."

"I won't."

She grabbed a rake. She didn't want to talk about it anymore. It was painful enough without discussing the matter with Chance's brother.

True to his word, Colt and Claire kept her busy. The wedding promised to be a big deal with several A-list celebrities attending. Of course, Chance wouldn't be there. He'd promised to try, but since he'd just started his new job, he didn't think he'd be able to make it.

"That's my brother for you," Claire said a week before the wedding. They were in Natalie's family room, putting together wedding decorations. Caro had decided she stunk at using a glue gun, but that didn't stop her from trying to stick together twigs that would hopefully look like a tree. They planned to place the tree in the center of a table and hang tiny pictures of Claire and Ethan on the branches. "You never know when he's going to show up, or *if* he'll show up."

Caro didn't know what she would do if he did. Probably run in the other direction. Since he'd left, her feelings hadn't changed one bit, especially since he'd been true to his word. He stayed in touch. She received regular updates from him, always chatty, always up-beat, never personal. That was okay. She didn't want personal. Personal caused pain, and she'd already had enough of that in her life.

"Do you think you can get me more twigs?" Claire said. "I put a pile of them on the front stoop."

Caro nodded and headed for the front door. She was looking down, which was why she didn't immediately see him.

See *him*.

Chance.

At first, she thought she was seeing things and it was really Colt standing there. They looked so much alike. But no. It wasn't Colt. It was Chance. She couldn't breathe.

"Hello, Caro."

His voice. She'd forgotten how it sounded. So deep. So masculine. So… Chance.

"You're here." Stupid thing to say, but she couldn't think, couldn't do anything but stand stiffly.

"I'm here," he echoed.

She swallowed. "Claire will be so happy."

"Claire already knows."

Once again, she felt incapable of forming a response. "She knows?" she parroted back.

"I told her I was coming."

"But she just said—"

She straightened suddenly, realizing she'd been set up. In typical Reynolds fashion they'd orchestrated Chance's homecoming so she would walk outside right as he was arriving.

Why?

"Aren't you going to give me a kiss hello?"

And she saw it then. The crooked smile, the twinkle in his green eyes.

"Well, I don't know." She headed down the steps, stopping just in front of him. "That depends."

"On what?"

He looked so good. More tan. Fitter, if that were possible. And tired. As if he'd flown thousands of miles to be there, standing in front of her. And maybe he had.

"It depends on if you're here to stay or not." She inhaled deeply before taking the plunge. "Because I can't do it again, Chance. I can't watch you leave. The first time nearly killed me."

His Adam's apple bobbed as he swallowed. "I know."

And then he was there, in front of her, and his arms were wrapping around her and she knew it wasn't a dream. Somehow he was there and he loved her. She saw it in his eyes just before he bent his head and kissed her.

"Caro," he said softly, a long while later, drawing back and resting his chin on her head. "If only you knew how much I missed this."

Her eyes burned. She still couldn't believe it was true.

"I knew the moment my plane took off that I'd made a mistake, but I couldn't bail. I had an obligation, so I stuck it out until they could find a replacement."

She started to weep softly, because it was like a dream. A really great dream where he said all the things she'd hoped he would.

"I told them I had to be back in time for my sister's wedding because there was this girl, and she would be there and I had a question to ask her."

She ducked her head, for some reason ashamed of her tears. He tipped her head back.

"Carolina Cruthers, I love you."

She tried to duck her head again, but he wouldn't let her. Her eyes blurred with tears and she sobbed, though she tried hard not to. She wanted to see him clearly, to memorize the look in his eyes.

"I've been such a fool, Caro. I was afraid to start a new life. To let go of the familiar. To be with my real family."

His lips brushed hers. She opened eyes she hadn't known she'd closed.

"You," he said softly, gently.

And then he kissed her again and she kissed him back, letting him know without words that she loved him, and when a long while later, he stepped back and pulled a ring from his pocket, she started crying again, especially when he bent down on one knee and, in front of all the people who mattered—Claire and Ethan and Adam, Natalie and Weston and Colt, even the Galloping Girlz, who materialized out of nowhere—asked her to marry him.

"Yes," she sobbed. "Of course, yes."

He slipped the ring on her finger and then pulled her to him as she murmured, "I love you," to him for the first time in her life.

The first of many times.

Epilogue

There were three rules of a Christmas wedding. One, it must snow, even if the wedding was in California at an elevation that rarely, if ever, saw snow. Two, the bridesmaids must wear red, even if one of those bridesmaids insisted she never looked good in red, although that same bridesmaid was quite pleased with her breast-feeding boobies. Three, the bride and groom needed to arrive at the wedding in a horse-drawn wagon, jingle bells clanging, red ribbons waving, wedding guests smiling.

All three rules were honored at the wedding of Claire Reynolds and Ethan McCall. The best man, a little boy named Adam, beamed the whole time. The groomsmen, of which there were two, also beamed, although Claire's brothers insisted they outshone the bride. They maintained that brothers were allowed to tease a sister, even on that sister's wedding day.

There was another, lesser known rule: engaged couples were allowed to kiss as often as they liked. This was, perhaps, Chance Reynolds's favorite rule, and one he never broke.

"You're going to make my lips fall off," Caro teased as Chance rocked her back and forth on the dance floor. "I swear you've kissed me more times tonight than you have the whole time we've been together."

Chance's eyes glittered. "That's because you look exceptionally beautiful tonight in your red stripper gown."

She laughed. She couldn't help it. "You better not let Claire hear you say that. She loves this color."

Her future husband smiled. "Yes, but my sister-in-law does not. I heard she might pretend to like it, but Natalie is sublimely self-aware of how it hugs her every curve. Colt said she's embarrassed."

Claire glanced in Colt and Natalie's direction. "But she looks so sexy in it."

Beneath the roof of the covered arena, which had been cleared of jumps and turned into a huge ballroom, Chance pulled her closer.

"Not as sexy as you." He lowered his head. "I swear I'm going to enjoy peeling every inch of this dress off your body tonight."

"Ah, ah, ah," she gently chided. "Not until we're married."

They'd set a date in the spring, before the start of rodeo season. Chance would be taking over his brother's business, at least for now, because ever since he'd quit working for DTS, job offers had been piling in. He was presently considering four different positions: head of security for a big internet firm; ranch manager of the soon-to-be-built Dark Horse Ranch, where veterans could be treated for PTSD and would be conveniently located next door; and her favorite, personal bodyguard to the stars. The latter offer had come in from family friend Rand Jefferson, the A-lister who'd married former Galloping Girl Samantha. But the one he was actually considering, Chance's favorite of the offers he'd received so far, was working for the sheriff's department alongside Officer Connelly. Who would have thought?

"You keep saying that," Chance said, "but I have high hopes to convince you otherwise." He wagged his eyebrows.

She playfully batted his arm. "Good luck with that, soldier."

"You guys, look!"

They both turned toward Adam, who skillfully navigated the crowded dance floor with Inga up on her hind legs. Or maybe it was Bella, Natalie's dog. It was hard to tell beneath an arena full of Christmas lights. Either way, the dog had a big red bow around her neck. She looked clearly puzzled by this new human ritual. When the dog looked into Caro's eyes, she knew it was Inga.

"Poor thing," Chance said.

Caro laughed. "She better get used to it. Once we have kids, all bets are off."

She glanced up to see the glint in his eyes. She knew he was thinking back to the day in the hospital when he'd held his nephew for the first time. She'd seen the same look on his face then. Longing. Happiness. Belonging.

"Soon enough," she said softly.

"Yes. Soon," he echoed, because they weren't going

to wait. Once they were married, they would try to get pregnant right away. Caro vowed that she would bring their children up in a completely different way than her own upbringing. Chance had vowed the same thing. Perhaps between the two of them, two previously damaged people could make good parents. She knew they would.

He kissed her again, and she didn't have the heart to tease him anymore. She loved him. Heart and soul. She didn't know what she'd done to deserve him, but now that she had him, she would never let him go.

"Hey, hey," said the bride as she danced by on her groom's arm, her smile bright enough to light the room. "Save it for later."

Ethan laughed gently as he whisked Claire by the two of them. Colt and Natalie twirled by next, Colt pasting a lascivious grin on his face as he pretended to gawk at his wife's magnificent cleavage. Everyone laughed. Caro and Chance. Samantha and her famous husband, Rand. Wes and Jillian. Mariah and Zach. So many friends. So much love in the room. Caro didn't think her heart could ever be as full.

Once upon a time, she'd dreamed of being part of the Reynolds family. Back then she would have never imagined that her dream could come true. So many things had gone wrong in her life, starting with her childhood and ending with James. But one thing had gone right, and it was the most important thing. She'd found the man of her dreams.

Three months later, as she and Chance said their wedding vows, Carolina knew a joy like no other. It was a day of celebration. Adam had been officially declared cancer free. Claire and Ethan had learned they were pregnant, a feat Chance vowed to replicate, soon.

And as they danced at their own wedding, this time by the pond that was really more like a lake, in the spot where Chance had declared he would build his own small family a home, Caro realized she'd been wrong.

It was possible to feel as if your heart might burst with love. That same feeling could happen again and again. And it did. Through the birth of children, more weddings, more children and all the things that life brought the two of them. And though their lives were full of the inevitable ups and downs, they loved each other.

And that was the most important rule of all.

* * * * *

Cathy Gillen Thacker is married and a mother of three. She and her husband spent eighteen years in Texas and now reside in North Carolina. Her mysteries, romantic comedies and heartwarming family stories have made numerous appearances on bestseller lists. A popular Harlequin author for many years, she loves telling passionate stories with happy endings and thinks nothing beats a good romance and a hot cup of tea! You can visit Cathy at her website, cathygillenthacker.com.

Books by Cathy Gillen Thacker

Harlequin Western Romance

Texas Legends: The McCabes

The Texas Cowboy's Baby Rescue

Texas Legacies: The Lockharts

A Texas Soldier's Family
A Texas Cowboy's Christmas
The Texas Valentine Twins
Wanted: Texas Daddy
A Texas Soldier's Christmas

Visit the Author Profile page
at Harlequin.com for more titles.

THE TEXAS LAWMAN'S WOMAN

Cathy Gillen Thacker

For Daphne and Lilah
and all the joy they've brought to our lives.

Chapter 1

Shelley Meyerson's heart leaped as she caught sight of the broad-shouldered lawman walking out of the dressing room. She blinked, so shocked she nearly fell off the pedestal. "*He's* the best man?"

Colt McCabe locked eyes with Shelley, looking about as pleased as she felt. His chiseled jaw clenched. "Don't tell me *she's* the maid of honor!"

"Now, now, you two," their mutual friend, wedding planner Patricia Wilson, scolded, checking out the fit of Shelley's yellow, silk bridesmaid dress. "Surely you can get along for a few days. After all, you're going to have to…since you're both living in Laramie County again."

Don't remind me, Shelley thought with a dramatic sigh.

Looking as handsome as ever in a black tuxedo and pleated white shirt, Colt sized Shelley up. "She's never going to forgive me."

For good reason, Shelley mused, remembering the hurt and humiliation she had suffered as if it were yesterday. She whirled toward Colt so quickly the seamstress stabbed her with a pin. But the pain in her ribs was nothing compared to the pain in her heart. She lifted up her skirt, revealing her favorite pair of cranberry-red cowgirl boots, and stomped down off the pedestal, not stopping until they were toe-to-toe. "You stood me up on prom night, you big galoot!"

Lips thinning, the big, strapping lawman rocked forward on the toes of his boots. "I got there."

Yes, he certainly had, Shelley thought, staring at the enticing contours of his broad muscular chest. And even that had been the stuff of Laramie, Texas legend. The town had talked about it for weeks and weeks. "Two hours late. Unshowered. Unshaven." Shelley threw up her hands in exasperation. "No flowers. No tuxedo…"

Because if he had looked then the way he looked now… Well, who knew what would have happened? Certainly they would have followed through on their secret, incredibly romantic plans. Instead, she'd spent the evening alone, crying her eyes out into her pillow, the gorgeous dress and silky lingerie she'd spent weeks picking out crumpled beneath her.

Colt stepped nearer, inundating her with the smell of soap and cologne and the intoxicatingly familiar essence that was him. "I told you where I'd been," he reminded quietly.

That night, and many days after.

Shelley glared up at him, crushed all over again. "With Buddy."

Colt stood, legs braced apart, hands on his waist. To

her fury, he was no more apologetic now than he had been then. "He needed me, Shelley."

I needed you.

"Right," Shelley retorted with a cool indifference that belied the emotion churning inside her. "So you said, Colt. Many times."

When was she going to get over this? Over him? Shelley had thought she was. Until the moment they came face-to-face again. Then, it was as if no time at all had passed. As if they were still as deeply in love as she'd once dreamed them to be.

But maybe it would be best if she did just forget it all and move on. Otherwise, her heart would remain broken forever. At least when it came to her sexy former boyfriend...

Colt shoved a hand through his short, dark brown hair, and turned back to the wedding planner. "This isn't going to work."

Patricia stepped between them. "The heck it isn't. Kendall and Gerry chose the two of you to be maid of honor and best man, so you're both going to suck it up and get along until the nuptials are over. Got it? The bride and groom have been through enough."

That was certainly true. Like Colt, Gerry had grown up wanting to help others. Gerry had become a navy medic and saved many lives, until he'd been injured in an accident on an aircraft carrier and spent the past six months recuperating in a series of military hospitals. Now, finally, he was well enough to return to active duty. After all they'd been through together, it had been the happiest day of both their lives when he'd asked Kendall to marry him. But a long engagement was not in the cards for them because they only had thirty days to pack up, marry and honeymoon before they headed for his next assignment in San Diego.

Hence, their wedding was being put together with lightning speed, with preparations starting before the two lovebirds even hit town.

"This isn't about you." Patricia guided Shelley back up on the pedestal, so the seamstress could continue the fitting. "It's about making the bride and groom happy. Now, I know you haven't been back in town all that long, Shelley—"

"Four days, six hours and twenty-two minutes," Colt interrupted in a bored tone, "if anyone is counting."

Shelley looked at him, not surprised he had been clocking the time, much as she had. It had been hard as heck, trying to steer clear of him during the move-in process, but she had. Until now, anyway.

He shrugged, obviously relishing the fact he could still get under her skin. "Laramie's not that big." He flexed his shoulders restlessly, then narrowed his midnight-blue eyes. "I figured we would run into each other eventually."

Another silence fell. This one even more telling.

Once more, Patricia stepped between them. "This is what we're going to do. We're going to get both of you fitted for your wedding finery, and then the two of you are going to go out somewhere." She lifted a hand to cut off their heated protests. "I don't care where. And you're going to sit down together and broker some sort of truce so that none of your past angst taints the upcoming wedding in any way."

Shelley knew the wedding planner was right. She had returned to Laramie to inhabit the house where she had grown up. Colt was living just down the street in a house he had bought. In a county of ten thousand people, Shelley knew there was no way they'd be able to avoid each other indefinitely. Maybe it was time she and Colt acted like the grown-ups they were now instead of the love struck teenagers they had once been, and buried the hatchet for good.

From the look of consternation that crossed Colt's face, she could tell that the handsome bachelor seemed similarly chastened.

Fifteen minutes later, their chores as attendants done, they walked out of the Lockhart Bridal Salon on Main Street. Just after six, the sun was sinking slowly toward the horizon in the bright blue Texas sky. The unseasonably cool June day had the temperature in the low eighties. There was very low humidity and a nice breeze. "So where do you want to go?" Colt asked Shelley.

With the clock running and her cash dwindling, there was little choice about that. "My place," she said.

Colt reacted as if she had just invited him over to see her etchings. Shelley put an end to that notion with an unsentimental glance. Their days of even thinking about hooking up were over. "I've got to go home," she said flatly. She had responsibilities to tend.

Colt lifted a brow and warned, "You should know... I've got Buddy with me."

She stopped as they reached his blue Ford pickup truck. All four windows of the extended cab were down. A beautiful brown, white and black Bernese mountain dog was sitting in the front seat. These days, there was more white on the canine's face than either brown or black. "I can see that." Shelley stared at the dog that had inadvertently crushed her dreams and been Colt's constant companion for the past twelve-plus years. The big fluffy-haired pet was still as friendly and alert as ever.

And he *still* brought a flood of resentment to her heart.

Buddy looked at Shelley as if he remembered her. And her attitude. Yet he still wanted to be her friend. She pushed her guilt away. That dog, and the nonstop chaos he had caused, was just as responsible for her breakup with Colt as Colt was. She had to remember that. The look on his face, the one that always set her heart to racing, said he surely did.

"I can take him home first," he offered.

That, Shelley knew, would just delay the inevitable, because Colt and Buddy were practically inseparable—and she might as well come to terms with that. "No," she replied with a resigned sigh. "Bring him."

"You're sure?" Colt asked.

Shelley shrugged. She could do this. She knew she could. "If we're going to be living just a few houses away, you and I are going to have to make peace with the past. And I have to make friends with your dog, too." She had to get to the point where Buddy was just another dog, instead of the love who had stolen Colt's heart.

"Then I'll see you in five," he promised.

Colt watched as Shelley got into the aging red Prius she had inherited from her parents and led the way over to Spring Street. The big yellow-and-white Victorian was the same as it had been when her parents were alive. A century old, it had a covered porch that wrapped around the entire house.

A porch swing stood sentry to the right of the front door.

It was—and had been—the perfect place to see everything that happened up and down the shady, tree-lined street. It had also been the perfect place for snuggling. Colt and Shelley had logged a lot of hours on that swing when they were dating. Just looking at it brought back a flood of memories.

Of course, she'd logged a lot of hours on it after they had broken up, too, as she'd sat there, swinging and fuming. And even more after he'd had the gall to tell her in no uncertain terms what he thought of the man she was marrying. Not that he'd been any better at picking a mate. He had yet to find the right woman.

Exhaling in frustration, Colt got out and went around to the passenger side. He opened the door, grabbed the leash on the floor and snapped it onto Buddy's collar.

Buddy was still staring at Shelley as if trying to figure her out, too. Colt petted his dog on the head. "I know she's pretty," he said softly. "But she doesn't like dogs."

The pooch looked at Colt seriously.

"Yeah, well." Colt shook his head. "I know. Hard to believe. But it's true. So you be on your best behavior, fella," he told his dog sternly. "We don't want her adding to her already gigantic grudge against us."

Buddy's days of enthusiastically jumping down from the cab were long over. Colt lifted his eighty-five-pound companion on the grass next to the curb, then waited while Buddy lifted a leg.

Meanwhile, Shelley hurried toward the front door. "You can wait on the porch," she said over her shoulder.

A minute and a half later, a high school girl came

out, pocketing cash. Shelley followed, a good-looking toddler in her arms.

Colt couldn't help but stare. He had always been attracted to Shelley, even when they were at war with each other. It would have been impossible not to be, given her cloud of soft shoulder-length auburn hair and her fathomless pine-green eyes. But seeing Shelley hold the child so tenderly put her in a whole new light. This was a maternal side of her that he hadn't anticipated. And found just as appealing as her inherent femininity and lithe dancer's body. She was, and always had been, the woman he most wanted to bed. That hadn't changed, either.

Oblivious to the direction of his thoughts, Shelley smiled for the first time since they'd set eyes on each other again. "Colt, meet my son, Austin. He's two."

Colt noted her little boy had the same auburn hair, appealing face and dark green eyes as his mother. Able to see why Shelley was so proud—the little tyke was as cute as could be, and intelligent, too—Colt extended his hand to the little boy.

Austin clasped the hand-carved red wooden truck in his hand that Colt knew was three generations old. He recalled seeing it when he had been dating Shelley years ago. The antique toy had been saved for her first child. At the time, because he and Shelley had been in the grip of a fierce teenage romance, everyone thought that Colt might be the daddy to that baby.

It hadn't turned out that way, however.

Shelley's son turned his head and buried it in Shelley's shoulder. The action shifted the scooped neckline of her T-shirt, baring a hint of lace and silky smooth skin. Noticing, Colt felt himself stir.

Not good. Not good at all. The last thing they needed was their former chemistry sparking to life. The two of them were just too different. He hadn't ever completely thawed her in the past.

He sure wasn't going to do it now.

Her son was much more welcoming. The little boy proudly showed Colt his truck and said, "Mine. My truck."

"It sure is your truck," he agreed.

Satisfied that Colt understood the import of what he was holding, Austin turned back to Shelley. "Down, Momma. Want down."

Shelley looked at Buddy, who was sitting next to where Colt was standing in a perfect sit-stay.

Although it wasn't necessary, Colt took his dog over to a cushioned wicker chair that had also been there for years. He pointed to the section of the porch beside it, and Buddy obediently lay down. Paws stretched out in front of them, he waited.

Colt sat down next to Buddy, and then Shelley set her son on the other end of the wide front porch.

Oblivious to the tension between the adults, Austin walked over to a wicker basket full of toys. He pulled a wooden cube from the pile, opened the lid and dumped the shaped blocks out onto the painted floor. Grinning, he plopped down beside it, shut the lid and began fitting a piece into the similarly shaped slots, while Shelley looked on happily.

"I hear you are going to be teaching dance classes at the community center full-time now," Colt said.

Shelley smiled. "Classes start tomorrow afternoon."

Colt recalled her on the dance line for the marching band, in that short skirt, skimpier top and boots. She'd been the captain of the group, and man, she had been able to move—to the point that no one could take their eyes off her. Especially him. Not that he needed to be remembering that.

"I hear you're in law enforcement."

Colt nodded. "I'm a deputy with the sheriff's department."

Shelley shook her head, clearly perplexed. "I never thought you'd go through with that."

"Why not?" Colt returned, holding her gaze.

She lifted her slender shoulder in an elegant shrug. "You were never the hall monitor type."

The truth was, he did have the softest heart in the department. But not about to admit that, Colt pointed out instead, "You said you always wanted to be rich and live in the big city...yet here you are, back in Laramie, moving into the house you grew up in."

A mixture of regret and disappointment flickered across her face. "I guess that's what the saying 'Life happens while you are making other plans' means."

Abruptly, she looked so sad and disillusioned Colt's heart went out to her. "What happened to you?" he asked gently.

She didn't take her eyes off his. "I got divorced."

There it was. Another link between them. Something else they unexpectedly had in common. "Me, too," he said quietly.

She looked at him with understanding. "When?"

He cleared his throat. "Five years ago."

Suddenly, Colt wanted to know the facts he hadn't let anyone else tell him. Not that Shelley had ever been particularly forthcoming about the failures in her life. Appreciating the way her auburn hair fell softly over her shoulders, he pinned her with a glance and asked, "You?"

"My marriage officially ended two years ago, although we were separated for nine months before that."

Colt's glance slid to her son.

Shelley answered the question before he could ask.

"Yes, Austin is Tully Laffer's son. We separated right after I learned I was pregnant." She emitted a rueful sigh that let him know she was as disappointed in the turns her romantic life had taken as he was in his. "Anyway, our divorce became final shortly after Austin was born. I stayed in Dallas for a while, then finally decided to come back home. I figured it would be easier to raise my son here."

There seemed to be a lot she was leaving out—and he wanted to know what. Which was odd. He usually wasn't this nosy. "Your ex doesn't mind?"

Shelley turned a fond glance to her son and sat back in her chair. She crossed her legs at the knee. Her khaki skirt rose higher on her thigh, giving him a glimpse of taut, tan skin. "Turns out Tully's not interested in the whole parenting thing."

That was no surprise to Colt. He'd only had to meet the guy once to know the spoiled rich kid was all wrong for Shelley. Not that she'd listened to him, or anyone else in Laramie for that matter.

"What about his family?"

Shelley grimaced. "His parents were barely there when he was growing up. They have a jet-setting lifestyle that has them constantly on the go. The last thing they want is any demands from grandchildren."

"I'm sorry."

"So am I." She linked her hands around her knee. "I think they're all really missing out."

No kidding, Colt thought, his glance moving briefly back to Austin, who was still playing contentedly.

Her son certainly deserved better. As did Shelley. Aware he had an apology of his own to give that was long overdue, Colt leaned toward her and cleared his throat. "So…about prom."

Pink color flooded Shelley's cheeks. "I'm sorry." She lifted a staying hand and continued gazing deep into his eyes, as serious now about burying the hatchet between them as he was. "I shouldn't still be upset about that."

Colt winced. "Yeah, you should."

She lifted her brow. He felt the pull of attraction and knew it was time for him to set the record straight. "I should have called you that night to let you know what was going on."

Her expression gentled. "In your defense, you were a little busy helping to comfort a lost puppy who'd gotten his leg stuck between a rock and a fallen tree. A puppy who likely would have died had you not spotted him and stopped to help."

Colt reached over and patted Buddy's head, taking comfort in the way his pet leaned into him affectionately. "Once the fire and rescue team arrived, I should have taken the time to call and tell you what was going on."

Looking as if she appreciated his honesty, she asked in return, "Why didn't you?"

"I told myself it was because this guy needed me with him in order to stay calm while the firefighters sawed that tree."

Their gazes met. "And in reality?" she asked even more softly.

And here was the hell of it. "I think you're right. I didn't want to go to prom."

"Because you hated dancing," she guessed.

Because I didn't want to fall any harder for you than I already had. "Because I knew if we followed through on the plans that we had for that night—" *and we slept together for the first time* "—it would kill me when you broke up with me."

"If we had followed through on our plans, I wouldn't have broken up with you."

Colt wanted to believe that. Life had taught him otherwise. "Come on, Shelley. At least be honest about this. We didn't want the same things for our futures. You were headed to Dallas to study dance at SMU. I was going to San Angelo State to get a degree in law enforcement."

"That was then."

"And now?" he prompted.

"I find myself wanting a quiet life, filled with the familiar, too."

Colt knew she had convinced herself she would be happy in Laramie. He also knew you couldn't really go back again. That sometimes the past was meant to be just that. Which was why he shouldn't be entertaining the notion of becoming anything other than the most casual of friends with her.

Still, he was curious. "What about marriage?" Was she looking for husband number two?

Shelley made a face, shook her head. "Been there, done that."

"Well, see, that's where we're different." He rubbed

a hand across his jaw. "I do want to get married again someday. If I can find the right woman..."

"Then I hope you get that."

They were quiet as they watched the little boy play.

Austin pushed his wooden box away and walked toward Colt.

Shelley tensed, ready to leap into action. "Is it okay?" she asked nervously, eyeing Colt's large companion.

Colt nodded, as relaxed as Shelley was wary. "Buddy's been trained as a therapy dog. He's great with kids."

Seeming to know he was safe with the big animal, Austin bent down to look Buddy in the face. The Bernese mountain dog lay with his head flat on the ground, the only sign he knew of the child's interest was the shifting of eyebrows on his face.

"Do you want to pet the doggie?" Colt asked Austin, hunkering down beside the two. "You can do it like this." He demonstrated.

Austin gently patted Buddy on the top of his head. Buddy remained perfectly still except for his tail, which thumped gently on the wooden porch floor.

"Doggie!" the little boy said.

"Doggie," Colt repeated, petting Buddy, too.

The get-to-know-each-other session continued for several more minutes. Finally, Austin straightened and toddled back to the wicker toy basket. He picked up his little red truck and took it to Buddy. Instead of handing it over to his new friend, he held it just out of reach. "Mine," he announced, clutching it tight in his hand. "My toy."

"It's okay," Colt soothed. "Buddy isn't going to take it from you."

Austin held tight to his belonging, and then moved away. All the while Buddy remained calm and content.

Watching, Shelley smiled. "I'm glad you kept him," she said finally, looking Colt in the eye. "The two of you belong together."

No, he thought, *the two of us belong together.* Always did, always would. If only we didn't have such different outlooks on damn near everything. Pushing that unwanted thought away, he rose. "Well, apologies made, Buddy and I better be on our way."

Shelley rose, too. "I'm sorry about all the bad feelings, all these years."

Relief sifted through him. "Me, too."

She lifted a palm. "Friends?"

Colt returned the amiable high five, glad the two of them were finally beginning to put the past behind them. "Friends," he said.

Nothing more. Nothing less.

Chapter 2

"Yeah, well, I don't believe it," Rio Vasquez said in the locker room as he changed into his tan uniform. "No woman ever forgives a man for standing her up on one of the most important nights of her life."

Colt fastened his holster around his waist. "We're adults now. We were kids when all that went down."

"Doesn't matter." Rio sat down to put on his boots. "The heart is still the heart."

"Yeah, yeah, yeah." Colt checked his flashlight and his gun. "You hot-blooded Latinos think you know everything there is to know about passion."

"We do." Rio stood and slapped his pal amicably on the shoulder. "And what my romantic radar says is that no grudge held that long is ever going to be set aside that easily."

"Meaning what?" Colt joked back, studying Rio's

circumspect expression. "You think Shelley's just *pretending* to forgive me?"

His friend shrugged. "I'm sure in her rational mind she thinks she ought to let the past be just that. Whether or not she can ever really trust you not to hurt her again is another matter entirely."

Rio had a point, Colt conceded, as he walked out to his squad car to begin his nightly patrol. His truce with Shelley had come about a lot more quickly than he ever would have guessed possible. Partly because they both had a lot more life experience and hence were now able to sort out what was important and what wasn't. Another factor was the pressure of the wedding, and their mutual desire to do right by their friends. But there were lingering feelings, of that he was sure.

He'd have liked to stay longer on her porch. Get caught up on more than just the basics. Forge new bonds.

But it had been clear, despite her deeply ingrained Texas charm and hospitality, that as soon as the olive branch was extended, she'd wanted him and Buddy out and on their way.

And that had to mean something. He just wasn't sure what.

At bedtime, Shelley opened up the drawer in Austin's changing table and got her second big surprise of the day. "Oh, no. Tell me we're not out of diapers!" She rushed to the closet, then the diaper bag, Austin toddling along right behind her. Nothing. Which meant she was going to have to put Austin in the car and run out to get another box of disposables.

Not that Austin, who'd had an unusually long and

late nap, seemed to mind being carried out to her Prius shortly after 9:00 p.m. "We go bye-bye," he announced cheerfully.

"One of these days we'll be completely unpacked and then it will be a lot easier to get organized," Shelley promised as she strapped Austin into his car seat.

"Diapers!" Austin shouted, waving his arms.

Well, Shelley thought wearily, at least her son knew what they were after. Unfortunately, the only store open that late was on the outskirts of town, near the entrance to the Lake Laramie State Park grounds. For once, the Mega-Mart was not crowded with summer campers, so Shelley and Austin were able to zip in and out.

The problem appeared en route home as dusk was falling. Shelley had just turned onto the two-lane highway toward town and gone about a half mile when a pair of headlights coming the opposite direction wove into her lane, then out again, then back toward her.

Terrified, she hit her horn and brake simultaneously, steering her car as far onto the shoulder as she could go without actually swerving off the road. And still the oncoming vehicle kept heading right for her, weaving back and forth. Knowing she had no choice if she wanted to avoid a collision, Shelley swung the steering wheel farther right and veered off the highway to get out of the way of the wildly careening vehicle.

Her car shot forward as it completely cleared the shoulder and the low ditch beside it, then slammed down on the rough sagebrush-covered ground, bumping hard once, with teeth-clenching force, and then, to a lesser degree, again and again and again.

Finally, the Prius ground to a halt while the big sedan that had almost crashed into her continued on its way, not slowing down in the slightest as it swerved into the wrong lane yet again.

Only this time, she noted in slow-motion horror, the SUV coming toward it was not able to react fast enough. Despite the squealing brakes and blaring horn, the two vehicles collided with a huge boom. A dark-colored SUV went airborne before crash-landing onto its side. The instigating white sedan was thrust into a field one hundred yards south of Shelley's Prius. And then all fell horribly silent.

Hands shaking, Shelley turned off her ignition but kept the headlights on. She hit the emergency flashers and swung around to look at Austin. He was still strapped safely into his car seat, but looked as stunned and shell-shocked by their unexpected leap off the road and near miss as she felt.

Her heart pounding, Shelley scrambled out of the car, opened the back door and removed her son from his car seat, clutching him fiercely.

My heaven, that had been close!

"You okay, li'l fella?" Shelley asked, stroking his back.

Austin nodded. He put his head on her chest. She could feel him trembling. Poor thing. Still cuddling her son in her arms, Shelley reached for her phone and dialed 9-1-1. The operator came on the line. Shelley quickly described what had happened.

"Is anyone hurt?"

"I don't know." She looked at the crash scene, which was eerily still. "I can't tell from here."

"Can you get a visual for us? So we'll have an idea how many ambulances to send?"

Her whole body quaking with a mixture of adrenaline and nerves, Shelley strapped Austin in his seat, got back in the car, and did as required. Emergency lights flashing the entire way, she drove slowly through the field to the scene of the accident. The SUV that had taken the hit had flipped and was still on its side in a nearby field. It had a New York license plate and two passengers inside.

The sedan that had caused the crash bore Texas plates. The man who'd been driving was sitting behind a deployed airbag that looked like it had deflated. He was shouting belligerently in a slurred voice.

Shelley got back on the line and told the operator what she knew.

Fortunately, by the time she had finished, several other motorists were on the scene. One immediately set out flares to stop oncoming traffic. Another went over to the SUV. Everyone left their own vehicles' lights on to better illuminate the scene.

Moments later, Shelley couldn't help noticing that Austin, who normally chattered nonstop while they were in the car, was still ominously silent. She pivoted around in her seat to face him. Her toddler was staring at the scene uncomprehendingly. "Austin?" she asked, aware she was trapped now by all the vehicles, too. "Are you okay?"

He didn't respond. Just continued to stare in that same dazed, emotionless way.

Panicked, Shelley shut down her ignition and jumped out of the car. She reached in to release Austin from his safety harness. He had seemed fine a moment ago, but was it possible he'd somehow gotten hurt without her knowledge? Shelley checked her son over but found nothing—no cuts, bruises or any outward sign of injury.

A Laramie County Sheriff's Department car drove up, siren blaring, lights flashing. The officer parked horizontally across the road, further blocking off the scene. Deputy Colt McCabe stepped out wearing a tan uniform.

As he strode toward her, Shelley had never been so glad to see anyone in her life.

Handsome brow furrowed in concern, he asked, "Were you involved?"

She nodded. "I was run off the road by that white sedan, just before those two vehicles crashed."

A siren blared in the distance.

"Is Austin okay?"

"I'm not sure. I—" Austin rested limply in her arms, and he looked awfully pale in the bright yellow headlights. He still wasn't reacting much. She'd half expected him to be crying by now; there was so much chaos and confusion. The fact he wasn't alarmed her.

"He might be going into shock." Colt went back to his squad car, got a blanket out of the trunk. He brought it back to her. "Here. Put this around him. Keep him warm. We'll get him to the E.R., too."

The siren grew louder, then fell silent as another squad car arrived and parked horizontally to block off the opposite direction. Deputy Rio Vasquez stepped out. And still no paramedics, ambulances or fire trucks, Shelley noted in frustration, although to her relief she hadn't yet noticed smoke or leaking gasoline.

"It's going to be okay," Colt told Shelley firmly, wrapping a reassuring arm around her.

Rio headed for the sedan to assess injuries. Colt took the SUV. While they did their jobs, Shelley paced, Austin cradled in her arms, turning him so he could no longer see the crash site. In the background she heard the blur of angry voices, apportioning blame. All the airbags had gone off, and had since deflated, but there were still possible injuries, so everyone was advised to stay put until the paramedics arrived. Unfortunately, the driver of the sedan got out of his car anyway. He pushed past Rio and the people trying to help him and wove toward Shelley drunkenly.

"What the heck is going on here?" he slurred, a cut streaming blood from his scalp.

Colt moved to assist. "Mr. Zellecky?"

The elderly man lurched unsteadily. "No need for alarm. Everything's fine."

"What's the ETA on the paramedics?" Colt asked into the radio on his shoulder.

"Another five minutes."

That was a lifetime! Shelley thought in despair.

Colt turned to Rio. "I'm getting Mr. Zellecky to the hospital."

Colt took another look at her subdued, pale son and told Shelley, "You and Austin should come, too."

Seconds later, they were all strapped in and on their way.

He drove them to Laramie Community Hospital. Shelley sat in back with Austin. Mr. Zellecky rode shotgun. He seemed roaring drunk when they started out. By the time they'd gone two miles, he was slumped over in his seat, unconscious.

Colt was on the speakerphone with the E.R. "Got a

shocky two-year-old and a seventy-something diabetic coming in. Terrence Zellecky."

A pause. "Mr. Zellecky whose wife just had a stroke?"

"That's him," Colt confirmed. "He was apparently driving erratically and got in a car accident. He was belligerent at the scene, but is now unconscious in the front seat of my squad car."

"We'll greet you at the door."

And a crew did.

Faster than Shelley could have imagined possible, they had loaded the diabetic on a stretcher and were rushing him into the E.R.

Colt followed with Shelley. When her legs proved too wobbly to move quickly, he took Austin from her and led her through the pneumatic doors. From there a triage nurse took over. The next thing Shelley knew she was in a treatment room with Austin.

An oxygen mask was placed on Austin's face, while he sat on her lap, blanket still wrapped around him, keeping him warm. The triage nurse took his vitals. A pediatrician entered soon after and checked for injuries. To Shelley's relief, none were found. His stunned demeanor had been due to the shock of being in an accident, and the resulting rush of cortisol and adrenaline flooding his tiny system.

"We'll continue to keep him warm, make sure he's breathing well, give him some juice to drink and he'll feel better in no time," the pediatrician pronounced, looking as happy as Shelley that Austin was going to be just fine.

The doctor and nurse slipped out, and Shelley concentrated on soothing Austin. As her baby boy breathed in the oxygen rich air, his color returned—and so did his usual high spirits. Eventually, he had recovered enough to try to pull off his mask and say, "Sirens, Momma, sirens! Police car!"

"Yes," Shelley acknowledged softly, replacing the mask, "we saw sirens and a police car."

"Eeeee!" Austin reenacted the screeching and squealing, then gasped the way Shelley had gasped. He flailed his arms. "Boom!"

"Like I said—" Colt appeared in the doorway to the exam room, still resplendent in his tan uniform, his hat slanted across his brow "—a lot to take in for a little guy." He smiled over at Austin. "Everything okay here?" he asked gently.

Shelley had never imagined Colt could be so tender. Heart in her throat, she nodded.

Sirens sounded in the distance.

Behind Colt, another doc appeared in the hallway. "Good thing you brought Mr. Zellecky in when you did, Colt. Another ten minutes with his blood sugar that low and he'd have been in a diabetic coma. That coupled with his heart condition could have been fatal."

"Is he going to be okay?" Colt turned to the doctor, concerned.

"Yeah. But we're going to have to do something about him driving."

"I know." Colt stepped out into the hallway, his expression grim.

"And good work for getting the toddler here quickly, too...."

The murmur of voices moved off.

A nurse came back in with a container of juice. "How about we move you two up to Pediatrics? You'll be a lot more comfortable there until we get the discharge paperwork together."

More sirens sounded. Austin put his hands over his ears, suddenly looking completely stressed out again.

"Good idea," Shelley said. She'd no sooner gotten settled upstairs than Colt reappeared. "I'm headed back to the scene. Obviously, we're going to need a witness statement from you, but it doesn't have to be done now."

"Thank you. I'd prefer not to talk about it in front of Austin."

He met her eyes. "How about I come by your house tomorrow morning? Say around eight?"

Shelley nodded.

"And then there's the matter of your car..."

Shelley bit down in frustration. She'd been so concerned about her son, she hadn't even thought about that.

"Would you like help with that, too?" Colt offered.

She swallowed hard, realizing it would be so easy to lean on him, now that she was back in town. "You can get it to me?" she asked, trying hard not to think about what had happened the last time she had let herself count on a man.

He smiled as he locked eyes with her son, and then turned back to her. "In a strictly unofficial capacity, yeah, I can."

Despite herself, Shelley found herself really appreciating his propensity for going above and beyond the call of duty. "That would be great, Colt. Thank you."

"Then I'll see you tomorrow morning." He paused to bestow another tender smile on Austin, tipped his hat at her and strode out the door.

* * *

"A word with you, Colt?" Sheriff Ben Shepherd said late the following morning.

Colt pushed back from his computer and followed his boss into his private office.

Ben shut the door. A humorless brunette in her mid-forties was already there, waiting. "You remember Investigator Adams?"

Hard not to. Ilyse Adams was the internal affairs officer for the department. Colt sat down in the chair indicated.

Ben took a seat behind his desk. Ilyse, already sitting, opened up a notepad on her lap. A veteran of the Chicago police force, she had been hired after a traffic ticket and bribery scandal erupted the previous year in an adjacent county. Her job was to keep corruption at bay and ensure protocol was followed at every level.

"What's going on?" Colt asked, afraid he already knew.

Ben steepled his hands in front of him. "There's been a complaint you acted unprofessionally at the accident scene last night in not citing Mr. Zellecky for reckless driving."

Colt exhaled. He'd known, after talking to the others in the E.R., that there was going to be trouble. "It didn't seem appropriate, given Mr. Zellecky's medical condition."

Ben sighed. "The New York couple Mr. Zellecky hit feel otherwise. They allege deference was paid to the local resident who caused the accident over them."

Aware the complaint mirrored what actually had been going on in Spring County the previous year, Colt protested, "That's not true. Rio and I tended to both of them on a priority basis." They'd been nothing but helpful and accommodating.

"I'd agree if you had cited Mr. Zellecky for causing the accident, but you didn't." Ben fixed Colt with a somber glance. "You will now."

Colt pressed his lips together. "Yes, sir."

"Do you have a problem with that, Deputy McCabe?" Investigator Adams asked coyly.

"Yeah, now that you ask," Colt drawled, "as a matter of fact, I do."

"Go on," Ilyse encouraged with her usual can't-wait-to-gut-you smile. Although, to date, she had yet to actually charge anyone in the department with illegal or unethical behavior. Some were questioning the value of such a high-salaried employee when there was no corruption to be found.

Colt looked the IA officer in the eye. "Taking Mr. Zellecky to court is a waste of time and resources."

As protective of his officers as he was determined to run a clean department, Ben Shepherd intervened sternly, "That's not for you to decide, Colt."

Wasn't it? "I beg to differ." Colt leaned forward to make his point. "These kinds of decisions are what set us apart from big-city police forces. We know our residents. And this accident, as unfortunate as it was, wasn't caused by deliberate carelessness—it was illness-related."

Although his boss listened intently, the internal affairs officer looked skeptical. Undeterred, Colt continued, "It's no secret Mr. Zellecky's recently been under an enormous amount of stress. Consequently, his blood glucose levels have been all over the map. Very low blood sugar levels cause acute disorientation, to the point the diabetic both acts and appears drunk."

"Exactly why he shouldn't have been driving," the IA officer said.

Colt interjected, "I talked to Mr. Zellecky last night after he was stabilized. He said he felt fine when he started out on his errand. So there was no point in citing him with reckless driving since I did not think the charges would stick."

"So you're judge *and* jury, is that it?" Ilyse Adams asked coolly.

"I used my judgment and my common sense," Colt affirmed.

The IA officer consulted her notes. "Well, that judgment is suspect. We're going to be confidentially reviewing every case you've handled in the last six months. Should this prove to be a pattern with you, you'll suffer the appropriate sanctions."

Sheriff Ben Shepherd said nothing to counter the IA officer's assertion.

The knowledge he could face disciplinary action hit Colt like a blow to the gut.

"And if it proves I've done nothing wrong?" he asked, taken aback that an outsider might hold the keys to his future. "Last night or at any other time?"

"Then no one but the three of us and the department attorney will ever know there was an investigation," the sheriff promised. "In the meantime…" Sheriff Shepherd retrieved a thick envelope from his desk and handed it to Colt. "You have a chance to prove you can do your job, no matter whom or what is involved."

Colt looked at the name and address on the papers due to be served. He swore inwardly.

"Got a problem?" Sheriff Shepherd queried.

They wanted to see him do his job no matter what? Then that's exactly what he'd do.

"No, sir," Colt said crisply. "I do not."

Shelley opened the door to find a uniformed Colt McCabe on the other side of it. A faint hint of beard shadowed his face, a hint of weariness in his midnight-blue eyes, but otherwise, he was as handsome as ever. Which was a true testament to his stamina after what had to be—if her calculations were correct—nearly fourteen hours on the job.

"Thanks for getting my car back to me last night." It had been in the hospital parking lot when she'd come out with her son.

"The tow service delivered it. I figured you'd need it when Austin was released."

"I did." She moved to usher him inside. "Here to take the accident report?"

"That's right." He gestured toward the wicker furniture that stood opposite the porch swing and said, "Okay if we do it out here?"

As grateful as she was feeling, maybe it was best he didn't come in. Shelley nodded and brought Austin with her. He sat down to play with his toys.

Colt got out his laptop computer. His eyes were calmly intense, his lips grim. "If you could start from the beginning…"

Slipping into business mode, too, Shelley told him everything she remembered. When they finished, he stood, put his laptop back in the carrying case and then pulled out a thick envelope and a clipboard. "If you could just sign here indicating you've received this," he said.

Puzzled by the extraofficial sound of his voice and the coolness of his manner, Shelley did as requested.

Colt took the clipboard back and looked her right in the eye. "Shelley Meyerson, you've just been served."

Chapter 3

Shelley stared at Colt in confusion. "Is this a joke?"

"No, ma'am, it's not." Colt took another paper with the words Notice of Eviction across the top and pasted it to the front door.

Shelley ripped it right back off and stared down at the order demanding she vacate the property ten days from now. "And stop calling me *ma'am!*" she said, fuming.

Austin toddled over to where Colt stood. He hooked both his arms around Colt's legs and tilted his head back. "Up!" Austin commanded, giving Colt a toothy grin.

For the first time since the police business started, Colt's demeanor became more guy next door than lawman. He smiled down at Austin, then looked at Shelley.

"Up!" Austin repeated, even more insistently.

"If you don't mind, I'd appreciate it if you could hold him for a moment," Shelley murmured, trying to retain her composure.

His manner as gentle as always, Colt complied.

Anxious to read the papers, she sat down on the wicker chair and fumbled with the clasp on the envelope. Heart pounding, she scanned the legal documents. "This can't be right! How can I possibly be evicted or my home foreclosed on? There's no mortgage. That was paid off with the money I inherited. I've been paying the taxes and the insurance from the trust. Not that there's much left in that." Just enough to serve as a nest egg, until she started getting paychecks for her dance classes at the community center.

Austin patted Colt's shoulders and chest with the flat of his palms, testing the solid muscle beneath. Despite her distress, she couldn't help but behold the sight of Colt standing there in his uniform, her toddler cradled in his arms.

"What this?" Austin tugged on the laminated plate above the badge.

Colt gently stayed the tiny fingers, explaining, "It's my name pin. It says Deputy Colt McCabe."

"Deppity," Austin repeated. He grinned at Colt. "Deppity! Deppity!"

Returning to the business at hand, Shelley quickly went through the rest of the papers. "My house is being put up for auction in ten days? On the county courthouse steps? How can they do that when I never even heard of this collection agency?" She threw up her hands in frustration, stood and put the papers aside momentarily.

She met Colt's implacable gaze. To her disappointment, she found not an ounce of sympathy or emotion, just cool professionalism.

Then again, given the fact he was here to do a job, maybe she shouldn't expect any. "None of this makes any sense." Sighing, Shelley held out her arms to Austin. He slid into them happily.

Colt straightened the brim of his Stetson. "Sounds like you need to see a lawyer."

Shelley shook her head. There was no need for that. "I'm sure I can clear this up," she stated confidently. Clearly, a pretty big mistake had been made. "All I have to do is make a few phone calls,"

Briefly, his expression betrayed skepticism. "Well... good luck with that." Colt tipped his hat at her and headed off.

Shelley went back inside the house, into the kitchen she had just unpacked. She settled Austin in the high chair with a bowl of his favorite dry cereal and a sippy cup of milk, and reached for the phone.

Unfortunately, the bank that had made the claim against Shelley's childhood home wouldn't talk to her—the matter had already been turned over to collections. The collection company wouldn't speak to her, either, as the matter had already been settled in court via the claim against her home, and the foreclosure proceedings. As far as they were concerned, it was too little too late.

But as far as Shelley was concerned, it was just the beginning.

She called her attorney friend, Liz Cartwright-Anderson. Liz had a few minutes between appointments and asked Shelley to come in with the paperwork immediately.

Shelley slid the papers into her carryall, scooped up Austin and headed out to her car. And just that quickly, the morning went from bad to worse. Her right front tire was flat as a pancake.

Shelley sighed and clapped her hand against her forehead.

Austin, who was still in her arms, looked over at her, cocked his head seriously and slapped his palm on his forehead, too.

Shelley laughed through her tears.

And that was when Colt McCabe happened to drive by again.

All Colt wanted as he headed down Spring Street toward his home was a quick bite and a good six hours' sleep. After being on duty all night and most of the morning, he was dragging.

He perked up the moment he saw Shelley walk out of her house, her little boy cradled in her arms.

Damn, but she was beautiful with her auburn hair upswept, her lithe dancer's body clad in a delicate blouse, knee-length khaki skirt and sandals. But... hold on a second. Was she crying? Or laughing? Or a little bit of both?

His glance followed the direction of her gaze. He saw the deflated tire and knew the gentlemanly thing to do was to stop and offer aid. So he steered over to the curb, just short of her driveway, parked and got out. Shirttail of his rumpled Oxford hanging over a pair of old jeans, he ambled toward her. "Car trouble?"

A jerky nod as more tears flowed.

Austin leaned forward and patted Shelley on the cheeks. "Momma crying..." the little boy pronounced to Colt as if that were the most curious thing in the whole world.

"I can see that." Seeing her tears, it was all Colt could do not to pull Shelley into his arms to offer her the comfort she so desperately needed. He smiled down at her son, and then looked back at her. "Got a spare?"

"Yes." Shelley sniffed. "In the trunk. But there's no time." She sucked in a deep breath that lifted her breasts against the soft cotton of her pale yellow blouse. "I've got to get these papers to Liz Cartwright-Anderson's office now or she's not going to have time to look at them today."

The fatigue Colt had been feeling faded. He steered her toward his pickup. "Then let's go. I'll drive you."

Shelley hesitated for a moment and looked as if she wanted to argue, then was forced to give in. "Thanks. I would really appreciate it."

Colt got the car seat from her Prius and installed it in the rear seat of his pickup truck. She sent him an admiring glance, reminiscent of their high school days. "That was quick. It always takes me forever."

Colt slid behind the wheel, glad to see Shelley had regained her composure. Trying not to think how comfortable this all felt, he started his truck and headed out. "I teach a class on the proper installation of safety seats over at the community center. It's part of my duties as a sheriff's deputy."

Which was, as it turned out, the wrong thing to say since it quickly reminded her he'd been the one to serve her with the foreclosure and eviction notice that very morning. Lips pursed, she kept her attention focused on the scenery until they reached their destination five minutes later. Shelley leaped out and opened the rear door. "Well, thanks for the ride."

Reluctant for their time together to end, Colt moved to assist her with her son. "If you want, I could hang out with Austin while you talk to Liz."

Again, she seemed ready to refuse.

Austin gave her reason to rethink that decision as he glanced up at a nearby tree. "Bird, Momma!" he shouted enthusiastically, after being lifted from his car seat. "Look!" He grabbed his mother's face. "Look, Momma, look!"

Shelley mollified her son, then gazed over at Colt in resignation. "Okay, but seriously, this is the last favor I'm taking from you."

Colt respected her independence even as he doubted the viability of her declaration. He favored her with an accepting nod, and joined her in the office that housed the law practice of Liz Cartwright-Anderson and her husband, Travis Anderson.

Shelley plucked the hand-carved little red truck from her bag and handed it to her son. "You're going to stay with Colt while I go talk to Liz," she explained to her son.

Austin scowled. "No!" He shouted at the top of his lungs when his mother attempted to leave. "I. Go. Momma!" He vaulted out of the chair she'd set him in and wrapped himself around Shelley's leg, refusing to let go. Sighing, she sent Colt another apologetic glance and picked Austin up.

"Yell if you need me." Colt sat down in the waiting room and opened a magazine.

Mother and son disappeared down a hall.

More shouting followed, at earsplitting levels. "I. Want. My. Deppity!"

Shelley appeared again. She looked at her wit's end with her irascible toddler. "Do you mind coming back?" she asked in desperation. "Maybe Austin will sit on your lap."

"Sure thing." Colt rose casually and joined her in the hallway.

The little boy grabbed a handful of Colt's shirt and latched on to Shelley's delicate cotton blouse with his other. "Deppity and Momma!" he said with a satisfied grin.

His mother was not amused. "Someone needs an *N-A-P*," Shelley muttered beneath her breath.

Austin shook his head, then fixed his gaze toward the ceiling. His head fell sideways, until it rested on Colt's shoulder. "No nap," Austin declared just as feistily, clearly able to spell at least one word. He turned, and with both hands suddenly reached for Colt again. "I want my deppity."

"Looks like you have your hands full," Colt murmured to Shelley.

She sighed with the fatigue of a single mom. "You have no idea…"

Still, he couldn't help but think, she handled it all well.

Their old friend appeared in a stylish suit and heels, her hair cut in the short, practical style common to working mothers. Liz smiled, understanding as only another mom to a toddler could. A wicker basket of toys in hand, sheaf of papers tucked beneath her arm, she ushered everyone into the conference room and motioned for them to take a seat.

While Austin sat on Colt's lap and dug into the toys, Liz explained to Shelley, "I just looked up the court documents. The debt in question was run up by your ex-husband, Tully Laffer. He apparently took out a line of credit against the property you inherited from your parents, at 903 Spring Street, here in Laramie."

A look of panic crossed Shelley's pretty face. "Whoa, whoa, whoa." She held up both palms. "Tully doesn't have any ownership in that property. Although we initially inherited it jointly, it was given to me in the divorce settlement, free and clear."

"His name is still on the deed," her attorney retorted.

"Which means what?" Shelley asked, appearing even more frantic.

Liz sobered. "As far as the law is concerned, your ex is still part-owner. Which is why the liens were placed on the property."

Shelley wrung her hands. Austin mimicked his mom and did the same. "Why didn't anyone tell me any of this?"

"Letters were sent—" Liz shifted a paper Shelley's way "—to this townhome in Dallas."

Shelley looked at the address and then her shoulders slumped. "That's where we lived when we were married. Where Tully still lives."

Liz continued, "When Tully didn't respond to the notices from the bank or the collection agency they hired to enforce the debt, the bank took him to court. He did not appear and a default judgment was made in the bank's favor." She paused. "The property was foreclosed on last week, and you now have ten days to vacate the premises. Meanwhile, arrangements have already been made to sell the property at auction."

"On the courthouse steps of the county that it is in, on the first Tuesday of each month." Shelley recited the facts she had already committed to memory.

Liz nodded. "Right. Which means you have ten days before the eviction takes place, sixteen before it's actually auctioned."

Shelley sat back in her chair, her expression sober. "All right. What's next? How do I stop this?"

"I can take the case to court and ask that the lien be reversed at least temporarily since you were not given proper notice."

"And if the judge agrees?" Shelley asked, seeming not to breathe, as Austin cuddled against Colt's chest.

"It will buy us some time but that's all." The noted attorney paused briefly to let her words sink in. "You are still going to have to deal with Tully's one hundred and fifty thousand dollar debt."

Colt drove Shelley and her son home. He offered to stay around long enough for her to make a few calls. It wasn't much of a sacrifice. Little Austin was adorable and so well behaved. The boy unearthed Colt's yearning to have a son and a woman to come home to. It sure beat his lonely house down the street.

Unfortunately, judging by the demoralized expression on her face, the latter part of Shelley's morning went no better than the first. "No luck?" Colt asked when she joined them on the front porch, where he and Austin sat on the chain-hung swing.

"Momma!" Austin said, reaching for her.

Shelley caught him before he lost his balance and fell off the seat of the swing. Because he still had a hold of Colt, too, she sat down beside them, her baby boy wedging distance between them.

"None." Her slender shoulders slumped. "I've left messages for Tully everywhere. He hasn't responded."

Colt turned his glance away from the sexy glimpse of soft, silky thigh peeking out from beneath the hem of her khaki skirt. He focused on the pretty contours of her oval face. "Is this typical?"

She went still for one telling beat. "When it comes to financial matters? Oh, yes. He's as irresponsible as the day is long."

He stared at her, wanting like hell to understand. "And you married him anyway." When she had to have known…

Shelley turned and met his searching gaze with a bravado strictly her own. "When I first met him, he was a heck of a lot of fun. I wanted to go everywhere and see everything and break out of the small-town Texas mold. Thanks to Tully's trust fund, he and I had the means to go just about everywhere. Or so I thought," she finished darkly.

"Go on," he said gruffly, having an unsettling feeling that he knew where this was headed.

"Turns out he'd blown through much of his money by the time he met me. Credit cards and cash advances were footing a lot of our travels. Until it all caught up with us anyway, on our fifth wedding anniversary. Suddenly—" Shelley drew in a jerky breath "—we not only did not have a dime to our names, we couldn't charge anything, either. It was then I found out that instead of three credit cards charged to the max, we had twenty-five."

Colt blinked. "You're kidding."

"Nope. His entire trust fund was gone. Our debt went well into the six figures." Her shame and anger was palpable. "His parents bailed us out. That time. They insisted we both get regular jobs and live within our means. And for a time, we did. Or at least I did."

Colt braced for the rest, suspecting by the regret in her voice that it had been bad.

"Unable to live on a budget, Tully secretly got a couple of cards with predatory lenders. You know, ones with thirty percent interest rates. When he maxed those out, the credit card companies sent us to collections."

"Which is when you found out."

Shelley's chin took on the stubborn tilt he knew so well. "Tully still didn't think it was a big deal. But I couldn't live that way. And coupled with the fact that I was pregnant, well…it was clear we were definitely not meant to be together."

"So you ended it?" he asked in a soft voice.

She nodded. "To my relief, Tully agreed to a divorce. He didn't like my 'uptight' attitude any more than I liked his irresponsibility. My attorney managed to get Tully's new debts assigned only to him. Rather than see him go to the poorhouse, his parents bailed him out *again.* And I got the house I had inherited from my folks, free and clear. It's in the divorce papers. I just verified that much."

"But the title to this house wasn't changed at the time of your divorce," Colt guessed as Austin climbed out of his arms and off the seat of the swing.

Shelley sighed. "No. It wasn't," she said, watching her son toddle over to get his little red truck. "And it should have been."

"So now what?"

Austin wedged between Colt's legs and ran the wooden vehicle up and down his jean-clad thigh.

She cast a worried look at him, wondering if Colt minded his leg being used as a racetrack, complete with a lot of vrooming noises. She spoke above her rowdy son. "We cross our fingers and hope that Liz is able to talk a judge into throwing out the default judgment against me. So I can keep my house."

Colt let her know with a slight lift of his hand he didn't mind her son's playfulness. "And then?"

"I'm going to get the title changed and make sure the one hundred and fifty thousand dollar debt Tully incurred with the credit line against my house is assigned only to him. In the meantime—" she reached over and resituated Austin up on her lap, the action pulling the hem of her skirt several inches higher on her thigh "—I've got my first set of dance lessons to teach this afternoon, and let's not forget that the bride and groom are supposed to be in Laramie this evening."

Acutely aware her legs were sexier than ever, Colt said, "Ah, yes, the wedding."

Looking more sweetly maternal than ever, Shelley ruffled her baby boy's hair and hugged him close. "Right now, that's about the only thing, save this little guy, that can make me smile."

"Turns out I'm going to need more help with this wedding than I thought," Kendall told Shelley over the phone, later that afternoon.

Shelley walked toward the community center drop-off day care, where her son would stay while she taught dance classes. "I'm maid of honor," she told her long-time best friend. Although the two of them had lived thousands of miles apart the past few years, they were still like sisters. Sensing this was going to take a minute, Shelley ducked outside and found her way to one of the benches on the property. "That's my job."

Kendall paused. "How are you at tasting and selecting a wedding cake?"

"Sounds like a fun job." Shelley rummaged through her bag for her notepad and pen. "No question there. But isn't that done by the bride and groom?" She got ready to write.

Kendall inhaled deeply. "It was supposed to be. We have an appointment with the Sugar Love bakery in Laramie at seven this evening. The only problem is, Gerry and I are still in Bethesda."

Maryland? Shelley thought in shock, momentarily putting down her pen. "Why? What happened?"

"Gerry started running a little fever this morning, so we went by the naval hospital to have him checked out by his doc there, and it turns out he has a mild pneumonia."

"Oh, no!"

"The staff treated and released him, but they don't want him to fly right now. We're going to have to drive to Texas when he's given the all clear to travel, and that won't be for a few days. The good news is—" Kendall's voice cracked "—the movers hadn't actually packed up any of our stuff yet, so we still have a place to stay, although there are boxes everywhere."

"Oh, hon…."

"Now, don't start," Kendall ordered in a low, quavering voice, "or you really will make me cry."

Right. Deep breath. Shelley focused on the practical and asked calmly, "What can I do to help?"

"Keep my appointment at the bakery and pick out a cake. We've been best friends forever. You know what I like."

Shelley made a few notes. "Anything with coconut, butter cream frosting and strawberries."

"Pretty much. Although Gerry's favorites are dark chocolate and pecans, so whatever you can come up with that will look wedding-ish and still fit our budget, which the bakery already has, would be great."

"Don't you worry." Shelley wrote some more. "I'm on it."

"You're sure? I know you just moved in, too."

"It's not a problem. Honestly. You just take care of Gerry. I'll manage everything here."

Luckily, Shelley's sitter was available to watch Austin, and would stay until she got back from the bakery. By the time she got her son in his stroller and walked the short distance from the community center to her home, the sitter was already there.

With the two of them already playing happily, Shelley went upstairs to change out of her leotard and skirt, into a spaghetti-strapped sundress and flats. It was only when she walked out to the driveway that she realized she hadn't taken care of the Prius's flat tire yet.

But someone had.

She stared down at her car, perfect as could be.

And there was only one knight in shining armor who would have had the audacity to ignore her instructions to leave the flat tire be and fix it anyway. Steam practically coming out of her ears, Shelley drove her car halfway down the block, parked and got out. Sure enough, Colt McCabe's pickup truck was sitting in the driveway, and his dog, Buddy, was lounging on the porch of his Craftsman-style charcoal-and-white home.

Aware she had just enough time to handle this without being late for her appointment at the bakery, she marched up to his front door. Buddy rose, tail wagging, as she rang the bell.

Colt answered. Decked out in a dark blue button-up shirt, neatly pressed jeans and brown dress boots, he looked ready for a date. He smelled incredible, too. Like sandalwood, soap and leather.

His gaze roved the floral fabric of her formfitting dress. Smile deepening, he returned his attention to her eyes. "Well, isn't this a nice surprise," he drawled, holding open the storm door. "Come on in."

Figuring it would be best not to have this conversation on the porch, where any of the neighbors could witness it, Shelley walked on in, Buddy on her heels. He brushed against her, clearly wanting to be petted.

Colt snapped his fingers and pointed at a thick corduroy pillow lying in front of the field stone fireplace. "Buddy. Cushion."

Inside, his house was neat and clean. In the living room, a coordinating multicolored braided rug covered the wide plank floor. The upholstered sofa and comfortable club chairs were covered in a masculine dove-gray tweed fabric. Table lamps were formed out of a heavy dark bronze. A burnished mahogany coffee table, captain's desk and end tables completed the decor.

Shelley supposed the casual elegance and pulled-together decorating scheme shouldn't surprise her. Though Colt did his best to ignore it, he came from money, too. Lots of it.

Word was, his multimillionaire investor father and wildcatter mother had set up substantial trusts for all five of their sons that were, for the most part, ignored by their fiercely proud offspring.

He lifted his eyebrows and waited for her gaze to meet his. "What's up?"

"Did you fix my flat tire?" Shelley demanded, indignation flushing her cheeks.

Colt's eyes twinkled. "Why do I think if I say yes I'll be shot at dawn?"

"Just answer the question."

He rubbed the flat of his hand across his newly shaven jaw. "I *might* know something about that."

"I told you not to do that."

"Yeah, I know." Heat emanating from his big, rugged frame, he shrugged and offered, "But I figured you had enough on your plate right now and took matters into my own hands…"

Shelley hung on to her patience by a thread. "What do I owe you then?"

"Nothing." He gave her another long, slow once-over before returning his gaze ever so deliberately to her face. "I was being neighborly."

Finding him too close for comfort, Shelley stepped back, bumping into an end table in the process. "Well, I can't just accept it without giving you anything in return."

"Because that would make you beholden to me."

"Yes." Shelley propped her hands on her hips. "And I don't want to be."

Colt's expression changed. "You really want to help me out, too?"

Wasn't that what she had just been saying? "Yes!"

He hooked a hand around her waist and tugged her forward so they were standing toe-to-toe. "Then do me one little favor," he encouraged softly, his head slanting slowly downward, "and return this."

Chapter 4

It was, Shelley realized, their first kiss in years. And yet it felt as if no time at all had elapsed. Colt still took command with no effort at all. He still tasted and felt the same, so strong and sure and masculine. He still turned her world upside down.

She had dreamed of this moment forever, even as she had warned herself that it would never happen. And the fact of the matter was, she thought, as she abruptly came to her senses and pushed him away, it shouldn't be happening now. "Whoa there, Deputy!"

The look Colt gave her reminded her of the way he had always liked to end a fight—with a slow, hot kiss that left her barely able to stand on two feet, never mind recall what they had been disagreeing about.

He grinned at her, the way he had then, too—all lazy, confident male. "And here we were just getting to know each other again," he teased, reaching out to caress her cheek.

Shelley moved away from him and released an indignant breath. "When it comes to the two of us, *someone* has to put on the brakes."

Buddy lifted his head, curious.

"We're not kids anymore, Shelley," Colt reminded her.

"That's right." She ignored the dark, soulful eyes of his dog, the expression relaying to Shelley that his owner was a good guy.

"And as adults we should both know better," she snapped, irked to find herself so vulnerable again.

She shouldn't want Colt. Shouldn't still be tingling from head to toe....

He gave her a once-over that left her all the more aroused. "You said you forgave me."

Shelley drew in a long, bracing breath. "I said I wanted us to be friends."

His blue eyes filled with merriment. "I can be friendly."

His low sexy tone made her think of kisses that rocked her world. It was all Shelley could do not to groan out loud. "Not that kind of pal."

"No bed buddies?"

Great, now she was thinking of him naked beneath the sheets. "No bed buddies. And," she added emphatically, before he could go there, too, "no boyfriend-girlfriend, either."

He chuckled. "I don't recall asking you out on a date."

She slid him a long look. "You did something even worse."

He folded his arms and rocked back on his heels. "I can't wait to hear what that might be."

Shelley harrumphed. "You have inserted yourself in my life."

He flashed a smile that sent another low, throbbing beat of anticipation rushing through her. "By fixing your tire."

Shelley swallowed. "And making friends with my son, and having me make peace with Buddy...and heaven only knows what else."

Hearing his name, Buddy rose and lumbered arthritically over to stand next to Shelley. He looked up, waiting to be petted.

Unable to resist the dog's dark, liquid eyes, Shelley knelt beside him to stroke his head, taking comfort in Buddy's soft, silky fur. "We can't go back, Colt." Briefly, she buried her face in the dog's neck, and could have sworn that she almost felt Buddy "hug" her in return.

Colt ambled over. He petted Buddy, too, then took Shelley by the hand and brought her around to face him. "I don't want to go back." He stepped closer, his eyes heavy-lidded and sexy.

Shelley hitched in a breath as Buddy moseyed off again. "We can't pretend we want the same things."

A low, wry laugh rumbled out of him. "When I was kissing you just now, it felt like we did."

Shelley flushed. Struggling to hold on to her equilibrium, she said, "Obviously, we're going to see each other. We live in the same town, on the same street. I'm fine with saying hello and being polite to each other."

His smile reminded her that he knew things about her that no one else did. Like how she most wanted to be kissed...

"But then you want us to keep right on going," Colt guessed.

Part of Shelley wanted to spend just one night making love with him, so she'd know what it felt like. The other half knew once would never ever be enough. And that in turn could lead to another breakup, which her heart really couldn't bear. She sensed, despite his bravado, that another ending would be just as tough on him, if only in regard to his pride.

"Intimacy of any kind just isn't in the cards for us," she told him. "Never has been. Never will be."

Shelley had just arrived at the Sugar Love bakery when the door opened and closed behind her. She turned to see Colt stride in and head straight for her side. "What are *you* doing here?" Shelley demanded before she could stop herself. Every time she turned around, he was there again!

He grinned at her prickly manner. "Gerry asked me to pick out the groom's cake. Make sure it wasn't too girly."

Shock turned to annoyance. "You could have warned me when we were at your place." Instead, as always, he left her feeling slightly off-kilter.

He shrugged in all innocence. "I tried, but we were too busy…"

Betty, the pastry chef, quirked a brow at the low note of innuendo in Colt's voice, prompting Shelley to jump in to lamely finish his sentence. "Talking about everything that happened, and getting caught up on things."

His hot gaze skimmed her face. "We made a start… that's for sure."

No, Shelley thought. "We're already there."

Colt just smiled. Tingling everywhere his eyes had touched and everywhere they hadn't, she turned back to Betty.

"Kendall and Gerry want six round layers, all different flavors," the baker told them. "They are leaving it to you two to taste and select the cake."

"How about a plain vanilla one on the bottom?" Shelley suggested, anxious to get this over with.

Looking as if he was enjoying this way too much, Colt offered, "Followed by dark chocolate."

Which he knew was Shelley's absolute favorite. Darn the man, he just wouldn't quit.

Betty offered up individual bites of each. Colt and Shelley simultaneously savored the deep, delicious flavors and voted yes on both. "Maybe a layer of strawberry cake on top of that," Shelley said, after tasting the next most popular menu item.

"And then carrot raisin," Colt chimed in.

Shelley wrinkled her nose. "After strawberry?" she echoed, incredulous.

He nodded, his impish eyes at odds with the solemn expression on his face. "This way they'd have their fruits and veggies in one cake."

A notion that went, Shelley acknowledged, right along with Gerry's wicked sense of humor. It was why he and Colt had been such good friends growing up. When they'd all stopped chuckling, Betty suggested, "How about a toasted almond layer in between the strawberry and the carrot, for aesthetic sake?"

"I could go with that," Colt demurred.

And on they went. By the time they had finished choosing everything from the exact shade of buttercream frosting, and the bride and groom figurines for the top of the cake, an hour had passed. The order placed, Colt and Shelley walked out of the bakery. They weren't hand in hand, but by that point, it almost felt as if they were.

"Funny, I always thought if we ever got to this point, it'd be our wedding cake we were picking out," Colt blurted out.

His surprisingly sentimental words mirrored her wistful feelings. Which was why, Shelley told herself, she had to be practical. Pushing aside her own wish that everything had turned out differently for the two of them, Shelley countered, "*If* and *didn't happen* being the operative words." She slanted him a warning glance.

He didn't back down. "If it matters..." he confessed gruffly. "Standing you up on prom night was the single biggest mistake of my life."

Not forgiving his tardiness and going with him, hours late, had been hers. Knowing she could easily fall for him all over again made her cautious. The urge to slip her hand into his even stronger, she met the intensity of his gaze. "And why is that, Deputy?"

"Because if I'd kept that commitment, you and I might still be together now."

Nostalgia, regret and longing combined to give her a passionate punch to the gut. She turned away. "You already said you knew we weren't right for each other then." Just as she did now.

He put his hands on her shoulders and brought her right back. "Maybe I was wrong about that." Colt gazed soberly down at her. "Maybe what wasn't right were the plans we had for that night. The truth is, I didn't want to take your virginity that way. Even as young as I was, I knew you deserved so much more than a clandestine hookup on an air mattress in a borrowed tent at Lake Laramie campgrounds."

Like it or not, Shelley knew this stuff had to be said. She took his arm and propelled him into the nearby alley, well out of earshot, so they could have this out in private. She looked deep into his eyes, wishing she didn't want so badly to kiss and hold him and spend every waking second with him again. Because she well knew giving into temptation would only bring heartache. The two of them were just too different for the outcome to be otherwise.

She leaned up against the warmth of the historic brick building, protected from the passing cars and steady stream of pedestrian traffic on the adjacent Main Street. "First of all, it's not like we had a lot of options, since concerned parents were staking out local hotels to make sure high school students didn't end up there. So if we wanted to be together and avoid detection, we had to go with the more rustic Plan B."

She took a deep, bolstering breath. "Second of all, I was very much on board with what was going down. I knew the risks…yet still wanted the rewards." *Wanted you.* "And you did, too."

His memory clearly jarred, he favored her with a half smile that sent tingles soaring through her.

"What happened back then was mutual," Shelley continued softly. "You and I both enlisted the help of all our friends to cover for us. We *both* planned that rendezvous down to the last detail."

"I remember," he said thickly.

"Then you should also remember that in the weeks leading up to that night, I didn't feel in the least bit shortchanged by the rustic setting of the campground. On the contrary, I was certain that making love to each other for the very first time on senior prom night was going to make it all that more special."

It would have bonded them together for an eternity. Just as the abrupt cancellation of their highly romantic plans had flung them apart for what felt like forever.

Shelley swallowed a lump in her throat. "But for a lot of reasons we chose not to go down that path." Her heart had been trampled on, and she had been humiliated in front of all their friends. "So you have to quit talking about prom night," Shelley insisted. "It does neither of us any good."

"Can't help it," Colt returned just as stubbornly. "I'm a guy who likes to rectify his mistakes."

"Or see what it would have been like on the road not taken?" Shelley retorted.

Colt shook his head, refusing to be dissuaded from his trip down memory lane. "Seeing you again, being with you, has brought it all back."

For her, too.

He sifted a hand through her hair and continued huskily, "Wishing I had followed through on all my promises to you—"

And made love to me, Shelley guessed.

"—is all I can think about."

She couldn't help it: she'd been fantasizing, too. And although they were both single again now, she was also a mom with parental responsibilities to fulfill—and a myriad of personal financial problems to sort out. She could not afford to be an impetuous romantic anymore. Nor could she take the kind of emotional gamble he proposed. Especially knowing he could shut her out again at any time.

"Then think about something different, Colt." Shelley put her hands on his chest and pushed him away. "Because what we planned for that evening is never going to happen. All we can be from this point forward is friends. Good friends, but…" She stopped in midsentence, blinked, sure her eyes were playing tricks on her.

But there he was at the other end of the alley. The exact person she'd been trying to find.

"Tully."

Shelley's gasp rang in the alley as her ex-husband, the man Colt had loathed from the first moment he'd set eyes on him, strode toward them.

"I heard you were looking for me," Tully Laffer said.

Several inches shorter than Colt, clad in plaid shorts, coordinating polo shirt and deck shoes, expensive sunglasses shading his eyes, he looked more ready for a party on his parents' yacht than an evening in a small West Texas town.

Colt knew the polite thing to do would be to excuse himself and let the two exes talk in private. However, he wasn't feeling particularly well mannered. He never did when Tully was around.

Fortunately, Colt noted, Shelley was focused totally on her ex—and not his dubious attitude. She stormed toward Tully, hands knotted at her sides. "Did you take out a line of credit against my parents' house?"

Tully took off his sunglasses and hooked them in the front of his shirt. "I needed collateral to get the loan to start my adventure-tours business."

Shelley looked as though she wanted to punch him. "Then your business better pay me back. Pronto."

Tully shoved a hand through his thinning, sun-streaked hair. "I'd like to. Really, I would, Shel."

"But?" Shelley continued to stare down her ex.

Colt couldn't say he blamed her. It appeared her ex-husband was just as much an irresponsible party boy now as he had been when she had met him.

Tully gestured impotently. "I never quite got the biz off the ground. I mean, I went to a lot of the places I was going to offer packages on, like Belize, Aruba and Tibet, but it's a lot more work getting things arranged than I bargained on."

Shelley stepped backward, her body nudging Colt's in the process. "You knew what the property settlement was at the time of our divorce, that you had no claim to that house I inherited."

"Technically, yeah. But when I went to apply for the loan and the property turned up in my name, too, they said I could use it."

"So you decided to commit fraud?" Colt asked, feeling bereft when Shelley moved slightly to the left so she was no longer touching him.

Tully squinted at Colt. "I figured it wouldn't hurt to use it. Temporarily."

And if that wasn't an out-and-out confession of a crime, Colt thought grimly, he didn't know what was.

Shelley trembled with rage. "And the foreclosure notices? All those certified letters you signed for, saying I was going to lose my childhood home because you defaulted on your one hundred and fifty thousand dollar bank loan?"

"I was sorry about that. But you weren't even liv-

ing there. You hadn't for years." A mixture of resentment and greed colored Tully's low tone. "You just
held on to it."

"Except now I am living in it again, Tully, with
my son."

Her ex spread his arms dramatically. "Well, I didn't
know that! Last I heard, you were still living in Dallas and teaching classes at that big studio in the Park
Cities. I had no idea you intended to come back here
of all places. I thought you hated life in a small town!"

Shelley tensed. "That was then. This is now."

Tully narrowed his gaze. "Then you really have
changed, because the Shelley I married never would
have come back here."

Who was the "Shelley" that Tully Laffer had married? Colt wondered.

"The Shelley you married no longer exists. She had
the stardust stamped out of her eyes a long time ago."

Well, that was true, Colt conceded. There was a
cold practicality in her now, when it came to romance
anyway, that had certainly not been there when she
was a teenager.

Tully scowled. "Look, I tried to get the money to
stop the foreclosure. I just couldn't. Times are tight,
you know? So do us both a favor and stop being so
damn cynical and acting like I did any of this to hurt
you!"

"I have every right to be cynical!" Shelley countered bitterly, tears shimmering in her pretty eyes. "Because of what you did, Austin and I are about to lose
our home!"

Tully shrugged. "Well, there's nothing anyone can
do about that now."

"Actually, there *are* remedies for this," Colt interjected. "All Shelley has to do is file a criminal complaint with the sheriff's department. The district attorney will take it from there."

For the first time, Tully began to appear nervous. Although, he had to know he was in big-time trouble, Colt reasoned. Otherwise, why else would the loser have driven all the way out to Laramie to talk to Shelley face-to-face? Unless Tully was hoping to charm and finagle his way out of this?

"Now, now, there's no need for that," Tully huffed.

Colt clenched his jaw. "I disagree."

Tully turned his attention back to Shelley. "Look," he cajoled, beseeching her with puppy dog eyes, "I know I did wrong and I want to fix it. I just need a little more time."

Like hell he did, Colt thought furiously.

"Yeah, well, I need a hundred and fifty thousand dollars to pay back the bank, Tully, before they evict me out of my home!"

Tully scoffed. "They're not really going to do that."

"The property is set to be surrendered nine days from now," Colt pointed out. "It'll be auctioned seven days after that."

"How do you know?" Tully demanded.

"I served her the eviction papers."

Her ex looked affronted. "Well, then, that just shows what kind of friend you are," he scolded Colt. "You should have misplaced them."

Colt shook his head disapprovingly. "That's not the way the world works, Tully."

The other man flashed a smug grin. "It can be."

Refusing to be charmed into taking an easier stance,

Shelley shot daggers at Tully. "Do whatever you need to do. But I expect repayment, Tully—in full. Or I promise you're going to be facing more than just me in court."

"Okay, okay." He raised his hands in self-defense. "I'll track down my parents…and see what I can do." Then he walked away.

Shelley leaned back against the brick alley wall. She looked exhausted, which was no surprise, given all she had been through.

"You're wasting your time, putting any faith in him," Colt warned.

She slanted Colt an unhappy look. "Normally, I would agree with you, but right now I don't have a choice. I need this resolved and his parents have money. Lots of it."

Colt's parents had lots of money, too. But it didn't mean they bailed out their children when their offspring should be standing on their own two feet. "Didn't you say the Laffers had cut Tully off?" Colt leaned a shoulder against the wall, facing her, his back to Main Street.

"Well, what would you have me do?" Silky auburn hair tumbled across her shoulders as she swiveled to face him. "Actually go to the D.A. and file criminal charges against Tully for fraud?"

"That is what happened, isn't it?" Colt challenged.

Shelley sucked in an indignant breath. "Look, Colt, I wouldn't expect you to understand…"

"Oh, I understand," Colt retorted, bitterness knotting his gut as an onslaught of unwelcome memories assailed him. "Better than you know."

Shelley came closer. "What are you talking about?"

Now that she was living back in Laramie, Colt figured Shelley would hear bits and pieces of the story anyway. "Yvette came close to marrying someone else before we got together. They broke up because he was cheating on her with another woman. I never imagined she would want the guy back."

"But she did," Shelley guessed.

Colt nodded slowly.

"How long were the two of you married?" she asked, searching his face.

"Three years." The compassion in Shelley's gaze helped him go on. "And in all that time, they never totally stopped having contact with each other. At first, they were arguing about possessions, and who got what, and who was supposed to pay the final light bill on the place they had rented together. Stuff like that."

"But eventually that kind of thing has to end…"

"You would think," Colt agreed. "But it didn't. Her ex would accuse her of anonymously saying something bad about him on Facebook. She was sure she had left a pair of her earrings in the glove compartment of his car and wanted him to look for them." Colt exhaled wearily. "It was always something. Anything to keep them communicating on one level or another."

Shelley watched him with an expectant air. "When did Yvette realize she still loved her ex?"

Colt grimaced. "About the same time I found them in bed together."

"Oh, my God. Colt." Sympathy radiated in her soft eyes. "What did you do?"

The only thing he could at that point and keep his self-respect. "I moved out, hired a lawyer and got a divorce." Colt shook his head in remonstration, recalling,

"The irony of it was, once they had their reunion, they decided they weren't meant to be after all, so Yvette asked me to take her back."

Shelley's expression turned stormy. "Tell me you didn't!"

He hadn't even been tempted. "You either love someone or you don't…and I had no interest in going down that road again." The question was, did Shelley?

She touched his arm lightly. Her fingers felt gentle and delicate on his skin. "Your situation was horrible."

It sure as hell had been.

"Mine is different."

Colt lifted a skeptical brow. "Really?"

"Tully and I haven't had any contact with each other in over two years," Shelley explained. "Since our divorce was finalized, there has been zero communication—and there was very little in the months before that."

Colt wanted to trust her on this, but past experience made him wary. "And yet the moment you reach out to Tully, he shows up in Laramie. Even though it was, what? Probably a two-hundred-mile drive for him?"

"Tully probably thought he'd have better luck charming me in person than on the phone. It did not work." She glared at Colt. "I meant what I said to him. I'm going to tell the bank the truth about what happened, and I'm going to get my money back."

"Then why not go to the district attorney now? Especially since you and I both just heard Tully admit that he knew full well the property was not his to use as collateral and hence was being erroneously foreclosed on?"

"Because I don't want Tully to go to jail. I don't want

to have to one day tell my son that I filed the complaint that put his biological father in prison." She sighed heavily. "My son is too young and innocent to realize it now…but one of these days, he's going to start asking questions about why he doesn't have a daddy. And that's going to be tough enough without me making things even uglier."

"So you'll do what?" Colt asked in frustration. "Just let the two of you be thrown out of your home?"

Shelley folded her arms in front of her. "It's not going to come to that."

"Now who is fooling themselves?"

Shelley's jaw set. "With Liz's help, I'll make everyone involved understand how unfair all this is."

Colt bit down on an oath, then warned, "Fairness and legality are two different things, Shelley." A fact that was hammered home to him in the course of his job every single day.

She thrust out her soft, kissable lower lip. "In this case, they *are* going to have to be the same." Colt certainly hoped her assertion was correct. Otherwise, she had a world of hurt ahead of her.

Chapter 5

"Honestly, Colt McCabe!" Charlene Zellecky fumed as she and Colt walked out of the courtroom, right behind the New York couple whose SUV had been totaled in the wreck. "What in the world has gotten into you?"

Privately admitting he *felt* like a heartless bastard at the moment, Colt cut a glance toward Charlene's elderly father. His head bowed in shame, tears of humiliation still streaming from his eyes at the tongue-lashing he had received from the judge, Mr. Zellecky disappeared into the men's room to compose himself.

In contrast, the New York couple who had escaped physical—if not financial—injury, seemed happy with the result. They had insisted to the judge that the instigating driver be taken off the streets. The prosecutor had concurred. Eventually, so had the judge.

Charlene continued furiously, "There was absolutely

no need to haul my father into court and have his driver's license suspended! You could have just asked my dad to bring his license to the station and surrender it, and he would have done it. And darn it all, Colt, you know that!"

Out of the corner of his eye, Colt caught internal affairs officer Ilyse Adams watching the exchange. Since the complaint against Colt had been filed, it seemed the investigator had been dogging his every move, including his appearance in traffic court that morning.

Colt turned his attention back to Mr. Zellecky's daughter. Although he privately agreed with her, publicly he had a job to do. "The law applies to everyone, no matter what the circumstances," he stated calmly. "Like the prosecutor said, your dad is lucky he didn't kill himself or someone else that night…"

Charlene drew a breath and ran a hand through her short silver-streaked hair. "I'm not disputing what happened was absolutely horrible, Colt. But to bring my father up on criminal charges, when you know how bad he already feels, and that he's already apologized—in person—to everyone involved in the accident, even if they won't ever accept his mea culpa."

She cast a scathing look at the New York couple leaving the courthouse, then turned back to Colt. Tears glimmered in her eyes. "The fact is, you publicly humiliated my dad, and you didn't need to. And I can't forgive you for that! Softest heart in the department, indeed!" Charlene caught up with her dad. Together, they headed for the exit. The older man's head remained bowed in shame. Watching them depart, Colt felt all the worse.

Ilyse Adams approached Colt. The staid brunette

inclined her head toward the closed courtroom doors. "Good job testifying in there."

"I stated the facts." It didn't mean he felt good about putting an aging diabetic with a sick wife through the wringer. Especially when Mr. Zellecky was known to be a pillar of the community. So the guy had made an error in judgment by getting behind the wheel when he knew he was having problems regulating his blood sugar and medication. He hadn't set out to behave in an irresponsible fashion. In fact, it was just the opposite.

Investigator Adams studied Colt as if he were a specimen under a microscope. "Just so you know. We've decided to extend the investigation to every case you've handled for the last year."

Because they found something, or because they didn't? Colt wondered.

There was no clue in Investigator Adams's expression as she continued, "We're looking for any other places where you might have skirted procedure to reach a speedy—if ill-gotten—conclusion that unwarrantedly favors local residents."

Still sure he'd done nothing wrong, Colt nodded tersely. "Let me know if you have any questions."

"I'm sure I will."

That was the hell of it. Colt was sure Investigator Adams would, too. Especially since her job also seemed to be on the line. With more people questioning her worth to the department by the day.

Out of the corner of his eye, Colt saw Shelley and attorney Liz Cartwright-Anderson walk through the metal detectors near the entrance. Colt dismissed the investigator with a glance. He'd seen little of Shelley the past five days and wanted to catch up. "Excuse me. I have to talk to a friend."

Colt intercepted Shelley before she could go inside the courtroom.

Before he could ask her about her hearing with the judge—slated for that very morning—Shelley regarded him with a mixture of sympathy and wary surprise. "I just ran into the Zelleckys. Is it true Mr. Zellecky was charged with vehicular assault? A felony?"

Colt nodded. That had been, as Shelley seemed to realize, the district attorney's call. "It was pleaded down to reckless driving, a misdemeanor."

"With a one year loss of license, a two hundred dollar fine and fifty hours of community service!" Shelley looked distraught.

Colt knew how she felt. It did seem harsh under the circumstances. He had no doubt others would think so, too.

Luckily, with the exception of Charlene, people weren't blaming him for the situation's outcome.

Before he could comment, however, three teenagers walked out of traffic court. Colt had dealings with the high school seniors before, earlier in the spring.

"It wasn't your fault you blew through that stop sign." Hector patted his friend Jasper on the back. "You just didn't see it."

"Good thing you're eighteen and had the money to pay the fine on your own," their friend Ryan continued. "Otherwise, your parents would have found out, because they would have had to go to court with you."

Hector frowned. "Won't they still know when Jasper's insurance goes up?"

"Yeah, but by then I'll be off at college. Oh, hi there,

Deputy McCabe." His troubles momentarily forgotten, Jasper winked, amending, "I mean *Officer Cool*."

Shelley shot Colt a curious look.

He shrugged, not wanting to get into it.

Still grinning, the boys mock-saluted Colt and sauntered off, still talking about their recent misadventure.

Liz tugged on Shelley's arm. "Our case is up next. Let's go."

Hating to see Shelley face such an ordeal alone, Colt offered, "I was officially off duty as soon as my appearance ended. So… I'm here if you want moral support."

Shelley shot him a grateful glance. Friendship was so much safer than what they had been heading toward. Still, she felt a jolt of electricity course through her when she reached over and squeezed his hand. "Thanks, Colt. At this point, I'll take all I can get."

Together, the three of them walked into the courtroom. Liz and Shelley settled at the plaintiff's table. Colt took a seat in the back.

Judge Atticus Warfield listened intently as Liz presented the petition that the foreclosure of 903 Spring Street be vacated. "As you can see, Your Honor, according to the divorce settlement, my client owns the Meyerson home she inherited from her parents, free and clear. The title should have been changed to her name only at the time of the divorce. Unfortunately, it wasn't, and that legal snafu allowed Tully Laffer to improperly use the property as collateral for a one hundred and fifty thousand dollar business loan he took out, and later defaulted on."

"Please continue," the judge directed when the lawyer took a moment too long to catch her breath.

"Certainly, Your Honor." Liz delicately cleared her

throat. "Subsequent notifications went to my client's former marital address, and were signed for by her ex-husband on their mutual behalf. She had no knowledge of any of this until the eviction notice was served at the property where she and her two-year-old son are currently residing. Had she known about any of this, she would have taken steps to rectify the situation immediately."

The judge removed his glasses. "That's really the point, isn't it, Counselor?" Judge Warfield turned to Shelley. "That you didn't perform your own due diligence."

Uh-oh, Colt thought. *The tough as nails jurist was at it again.*

"From what I can discern here in the documents you and your attorney have presented to me, your ex-husband's financial shenanigans have been going on for some time. Hence, you should have checked to make sure all the paperwork was in order at the time your marriage ended. Certainly, it was your duty to know what was happening with your property at all times, whether you were living in Laramie or not."

Shelley blanched. She, too, could see the way this was going, Colt thought, his heart going out to her.

"I know that, Your Honor," Shelley stammered.

"But you did not act as a conscientious property owner. So, now you have to take responsibility." Judge Warfield put his glasses back on. "Your argument is with your ex-husband, Ms. Meyerson. Not the bank that foreclosed on the property to collect on the substantial debt he racked up. So I suggest you take the matter up with Tully Laffer." The judge banged his gavel. "Case dismissed!"

Shelley walked out into the hallway, and Colt was right behind her. She looked white as a ghost. "I thought for sure Judge Warfield would order an injunction and stop the eviction!" she lamented to her attorney.

Liz shook her head, clearly disappointed, too, although she had made it clear from the get-go that stopping anything at this late stage of the game was not likely to happen.

"What can we do now?" Shelley asked as they walked out into the marble floored hallway. She sank down on a bench and then gestured to Colt, indicating he should be privy to this conversation, too.

Liz sat down beside Shelley and went over the options while Colt stood sentry next to the bench. "We could appeal Judge Warfield's decision, of course," the lawyer said, "but that would require waiting six to nine months for a hearing."

"Then that's out," Shelley decided.

Liz offered up another suggestion. "You could go ahead and let them evict you and forfeit the property and then repurchase it at auction. Sue your ex in civil court and try to recover the money he owes you as well as additional damages."

Shelley shook her head, tearing up slightly. "I don't have the money for all of that." She wiped the moisture beneath her eyes with her fingertips.

"Or you could press criminal charges for fraud, since Tully did all this without your permission. And attempt to use that action to try and get an injunction placed on the eviction order."

Shelley bit her lip. "What are the chances of us being able to accomplish that in the next five days?"

Liz frowned. "Not good."

Shelley fell silent. "I know what the judge said, but I still think my quarrel is with the bank. They notified Tully but they didn't notify me, and they had a duty to check and see that we were no longer legally married."

Liz—who had a reputation for wanting to right all wrongs—lit up. "You want to sue the bank?"

Shelley grinned back. "I want you to write a demand letter *threatening* to sue the bank if they don't put a stay on the eviction and auction, which would hopefully give us the time to sort this all out."

Liz paused. "You understand this is a big bank. It's going to be like trying to knock off a spaceship with a peashooter."

"It's also a public relations nightmare for them," Shelley scoffed. "A single mom being kicked out of her home versus a big bank that's just not interested in finding out the truth behind an unwarranted foreclosure…."

"I thought you wanted to keep this situation with your ex-husband from going public and getting ugly," Colt interjected.

Shelley sobered, her concern for her son intact. "I still want to settle this quietly, as should the bank. But the powers that be don't know that."

"So you'll bluff…" Colt surmised.

She nodded. "And hope Tully's creditors realize the error of their ways and go after Tully and any property he still has as recompense for his debt, instead of foreclosing on mine."

When Liz told Shelley what it would cost to have her put that strategy into motion, Shelley flinched slightly but didn't deter from her path. She stood and slung her handbag over her shoulder, all positive energy once again. "I know it looks impossible now," she stated resolutely, "but I'm not going to let them evict us."

Colt watched her saunter off, unsure whether to admire her courage or worry over her continued naiveté.

"Are you sure you can handle all this?" Kendall asked Shelley over the phone two days later.

Trying not to worry about the fact she'd not yet heard anything from the bank regarding Liz's demand letter, Shelley carried her phone out onto the front porch. Finished with teaching for the day, and still waiting for her son to wake up from his afternoon nap, she sank down on the porch swing.

"I promised you a dance for the procession," Shelley told Kendall, "and I'll deliver one." She had been working on the choreography between classes of budding ballerinas and hip hop dancers.

"But that plus all the other little things—like making the ribbons for the pews and cutting up little squares of netting for the birdseed—is an awful lot."

Not, Shelley rationalized, compared to what Kendall and her fiancé had been through since he'd been injured. "How is Gerry?" she asked gently.

"Responding to the antibiotics, but still running a low-grade fever."

"And as long as he has fever…"

Kendall's voice quavered. "His doctors won't give him permission to travel, so we can't finish our move from the naval station in Bethesda to the naval station in San Diego."

"But your families are there to help you, aren't they?"

"Yes, thank heavens. But with the ceremony only fifteen days away…"

"Tell your moms not to worry. With Colt and I both on the job, it's all going to get done," she promised her friend. "Speaking of whom…"

"He's there?"

"It figures. Right on schedule."

The two women ended the call just as he drove up. Buddy was sitting beside him, looking out the window.

Colt got out of his pickup truck. Dressed in faded jeans and a rumpled short-sleeved button up, his dark hair gleaming in the afternoon sun, he strode around the back of the truck. He always looked good in uniform. In street clothes, he was even more sexy, and as she watched him move in his easy, purposeful way, Shelley felt her heart leap in her chest. She hadn't realized until now how much she had missed seeing him, since moving away from Laramie. Grinning, Colt paused to open the tailgate. He hefted two fifty-pound bags of birdseed onto his broad shoulders and ambled toward her. "Where do you want these?"

Still clad in the black leotard, matching tie-on skirt and red ballet slippers she'd worn to class, Shelley held the door open. "Upstairs." She led the way, with Colt right behind her. As she reached the landing, she put her finger to her lips. "We have to be quiet," she whispered. "Austin's still napping."

"No problem," Colt whispered back.

Damn, but he smelled good, too. Like soap and a very brisk, masculine cologne.

Shelley led the way up the stairs, past the master

suite and the nursery—where Austin still slept—to the last room. Her old bedroom was embarrassingly intact from her high school days. One look at Colt's face as he took in the white provincial twin bed with the pink-and-white gingham bedspread, told her he remembered, too. A mixture of mischief and nostalgia glimmered in his eyes as he looked over at the window, which overlooked the side of the wraparound front porch.

He had climbed up the trellis to the roof more than once, while—unbeknownst to her parents—Shelley waited to let him in.

Once inside her bedroom, they had spent many a night with moonlight falling over them, making out on her bed. The sentimental curve of Colt's lips told her he was remembering, too.

Shelley shook her head and met Colt's glance. "I can't believe we used to do that," she whispered.

He nodded. "If we'd been caught…"

Her tummy tightened with an aching need that had gone unmet for way too long. "Life as we knew it would have been over for both of us."

"Grounded for life. Definitely."

But they hadn't been. And now, Shelley thought wistfully, being here with him like this brought only white-hot memories. It was a good thing they had agreed to be just friends.

It was no secret to Colt that the residents of Laramie loved to shower newlyweds as they ran down the community church steps to the waiting limo. Hence, there were three more bags of birdseed in the back of his truck. By the time he had carried them all up to

Shelley's room, where the rolls of ribbon and white netting awaited, Austin was standing up in his crib. Bright green eyes still rimmed with sleep, cheeks flushed pink, his auburn curls damp and standing on end, he was pounding on the crib railing with the flat of both hands.

"Mom-ma!" Austin yelled at the top of his lungs. "I up!" Spying Colt in the hallway, his grin widened merrily. "My deppity!" Holding out both arms, the little tyke gestured to Colt to pick him up. "Mine!" he declared, even more possessively. "My deppity!"

Colt was just as happy to see the little boy. Shelley was luckier than she knew. The longing to have a family of his own swelled in his chest. If only she could see him that way, as a potentially loving husband and father instead of as the inconsiderate heartbreaker he had once been....

"Hold on there! Not so fast, fella," Shelley intercepted Austin before he could try and vault out of the bed and launch himself into Colt's arms. "We have a wet diaper that needs tending to."

Austin plopped down obediently and stretched out on his crib mattress to await changing. When Shelley reached for the elastic of his shorts, her son pushed her hand away. "No!" he insisted. "Deppity do it."

Shelley flushed, clearly embarrassed. "Sweetheart, we can't ask Colt to do that. It's not his job. It's mine."

"Want Deppity!" Austin demanded, his lower lip quavering.

Here was his chance to let Shelley see him in a new light. "I don't mind," Colt volunteered.

Shelley paused. "Have you ever even changed a diaper?"

Colt's mouth twitched. "Try me and find out."

Still looking skeptical, Shelley handed him a pull-up diaper and packet of wipes. "By all means, have at it."

Colt stepped forward. Actually, he hadn't ever done this. But he'd watched it done many times. How hard could it be? Plenty, as it turned out. First of all, he couldn't seem to get the taped sides on the soggy pull-up diaper to separate. He tugged once. The tape held. Tugged again. Still, nothing. Austin giggled as if they were playing a game.

Colt hoped he didn't appear as befuddled as he felt. "Hmm." He stroked the underside of his jaw with his knuckles. "Maybe we should try the other side."

Unfortunately, it had the same problem. Glued together elastic that just wouldn't part.

Sympathetic to his plight, Austin pushed Colt's hand away. "I do it," he said. He stood, and grabbing one part of the diaper in each tiny fist, he gave a mighty tug. Just like that, the sides split apart, easy as could be.

"You must have loosened it for him," Shelley mocked.

"Very funny," Colt groused, unable to help chuckling, too.

With a rebel yell and a giggle, Austin kicked free of his damp pull-up. Shelley stepped in long enough to clean the diaper area with a wipe, then handed Colt a clean pull-up diaper. "Back to you…."

The good news was that the sides of the disposable diaper were already together. The bad news was Colt could not figure out which side was the front and which was the back. There were animal characters printed on both.

Shelley watched in bemusement, as if wondering if he would ask for help. The answer was no. Austin stood, hands clasped on the railing, waiting for Colt to continue.

He turned it every which way, then finally decided to put the donkey and the elephant on the front, the tiger and the bear on the back.

Austin shook his head, before Colt could follow through. "Nuh-uh," he said firmly.

Colt turned the diaper around. Austin stepped in and Colt slid the pull-up on. Followed it with the clean pair of cotton shorts Shelley produced.

"All done!" Austin exclaimed. Clamoring to get out, he jumped up and down on the crib mattress, still holding on to the railing.

"Say thank you to Colt for helping," Shelley said.

"Thank you!" Austin beamed, just as the doorbell rang.

"Expecting someone?" Colt asked Shelley.

"No." Shelley picked up Austin and handed him over to Colt. "But then I wasn't expecting you, either."

Moving past him in an intoxicating drift of perfume, she led the way down the stairs. Colt followed, Austin cradled comfortably in his arms. Shelley opened the door. To both their surprise, on the other side of the threshold stood Colt's parents.

Shelley hadn't seen Josie and Wade McCabe for years, but she had always liked Colt's folks. His father, a tall handsome man with silver threading his dark hair, was a multimillionaire investor. His mother, a youthful looking woman with glossy brown hair and azure eyes, was a famous lady wildcatter, known for finding oil where no one else could. They'd fallen in love when Josie went to work for Wade, and their love story was the stuff of Laramie County legend. Together, they'd nurtured successful careers and raised five sons.

"Hi, Shelley. Good to see you again," Josie said. She eyed Shelley speculatively, as if she were wondering if something was going on with the high school sweethearts again. "Hate to stop by without calling first, but we're about to leave town and we need to speak with Colt before we go."

His brow furrowed in concern, he stepped out onto the porch with his parents.

"I'll let you-all talk privately," Shelley said. She took Austin from Colt and went inside.

To her embarrassment, her son was none too happy about being separated from Colt. "My deppity!" he bellowed, trying to wiggle out of Shelley's arms to run back to Colt. "Mine! Mine!"

"You can see him in a minute," Shelley soothed, moving politely away from the trio conversing quietly on her front porch. She soothed her son by gently rubbing his back. "Right now we need to fix a snack for our deppity. Would you like to help me do that?"

The only thing Austin liked more than eating food was messing with it. "I can cook?" he asked, his protest momentarily forgotten.

"You sure can," Shelley promised, relieved he was no longer acting like a little heathen. She strapped him into his wheeled booster chair, pulled it up to the table and got to work.

Five minutes later, he was happily ensconced, finger painting dabs of cream cheese and jelly onto wheat crackers, then stuffing them into his mouth.

Colt suddenly appeared in the doorway. He looked ticked off.

"So what's going on with your parents?" Shelley asked, before she could stop herself.

Colt evaded her gaze. "My folks ran into someone I know who was asking a lot of questions about me. They wanted to know why."

"And the answer to that was…?"

Simultaneously mulling over her question and responding to the attempt to get his attention, Colt bent down to take the cracker Austin held out to him. The two locked eyes with such affection Shelley felt her heart expand.

"Thanks, sport," Colt said.

Austin grinned and set about making another. Shelley waited while Colt munched on his cracker as if it were the best thing in the entire world, even though Shelley was pretty sure the handsome lawman wouldn't have mixed cream cheese and grape jelly on his own.

Finally, Colt turned back to her. "I don't really know why the officer was asking my folks those particular questions."

"You think the person was out of line, though, in their inquiry."

Colt grimaced. "Yes."

This was a side of him she'd never seen. "So what are you going to do about it?"

Colt shrugged his broad shoulders. "Nothing much I can do. In case you haven't heard," he quipped, "free speech is a cornerstone of our constitution. Not just allowed, but encouraged."

Frustrated he was trying to use wry humor to deflect attention from himself, Shelley edged closer. "You could tell the person doing the talking out of turn that you didn't appreciate their curiosity."

Colt's jaw tautened. Again, he averted his attention right back to her son. He hunkered down with a smile to accept another cracker. "It wouldn't help," he said, more pensive than ever.

"Really?" Shelley prodded, hoping to get Colt to confide in her instead of shutting her out like he'd been known to do in the past. "Because I can't imagine anyone wanting to hurt you."

Colt flashed a brooding smile and didn't respond. He patted Austin on the shoulder, then rose. "I've got to go," he told her gently. "So...rain check on helping you fill those birdseed bags?"

Shelley ached to be there for him, the way he had recently been there for her. But his barriers were firmly in place and it seemed all he wanted now was his privacy.

She swallowed. "No problem. We still have almost two weeks till the wedding." Then she squared her shoulders and walked him as far as the kitchen doorway.

Maybe it was having him here in this house, in the intimacy of the kitchen, and seeing his parents again. Suddenly it felt as if they were somehow sliding back in time to the days when they had been not just friends, but had their lives intimately entwined.

Which in turn made her regret having stated unequivocally that they would be just friends. Nothing more.

"In the meantime," Shelley reminded pleasantly, "don't forget that at eight o'clock Monday evening the entire wedding party is meeting up at the Laramie Community Chapel."

He came toward her with easy grace, his eyes darkening with heat and something more. He reached up to gently touch her cheek and promised with a tenderness that threatened to completely undo her, "I'll be there."

Chapter 6

Two evenings later, Colt parked down the street from the community chapel. He had just put his truck in park, when fellow groomsman and coworker Deputy Rio Vasquez approached his vehicle. Like Colt, Rio had worked the day shift and was now in casual attire. Unlike Colt, Rio looked as if he had the weight of the world on his shoulders.

"Got a minute to talk before we go to the wedding party meeting?" Rio asked.

Always ready to help a friend, Colt nodded. He left the engine and AC running as the other deputy slid in out of the 105-degree summer heat.

"You want to tell me what's going on with you?" Rio bit out gruffly.

Aware his friend was beginning to sound like his parents when they'd stopped by to talk to him the other day, Colt asked carefully, "What do you mean?"

Rio made no effort to contain his exasperation. "You spent the entire shift in an interview room with Ilyse Adams."

Colt had also complained to Sheriff Ben Shepherd about the IA officer "unofficially" interviewing his parents while commenting on how well he seemed to be doing. Financially. Which in turn had led them to explain that he had a trust fund to draw on any time he pleased.

Not that he did.

He'd achieved success the old-fashioned way, by scrimping and saving, and putting his money toward things that counted—like his dog, his house and his truck.

"Does this have anything to do with the complaint that New York couple lodged against you?" Rio asked. "For rushing Mr. Zellecky to the hospital instead of hauling him off to jail?"

Yes, Colt thought, and no.

Aware he had also promised his boss he would continue to keep the internal affairs investigation quiet in exchange for Ben Shepherd instructing Investigator Adams to keep Colt's family and friends out of any ensuing ugliness, he wasn't at liberty to confide in Rio.

Unfortunately, that meant continuing to keep Shelley in the dark, too. Hence, Colt had found it easier to avoid her the past couple of days, rather than face any more questions—or be put in a situation where he had to edit his every word to her. Bad enough he was having to do it now to Rio.

"Investigator Adams is going through old files and incident reports, looking for any signs of procedural irregularity. You know that."

Rio grimaced. "I also know they were all cases you were personally or peripherally involved in."

"Hence, the interrogation. She's assured me she'll eventually get around to looking into the actions of everyone else on staff, too."

Rio went silent. "In the six months she's been here, she's never focused on just one officer. It's been more of a daily, procedural review of the department at large."

Colt waved at the wedding planner walking into the community chapel, indicating he and Rio would be there momentarily. "And she's yet to find anything."

"Exactly the point. You know how tight the county's budget has been in recent years. The word is if Investigator Adams doesn't find something soon, she and her large paycheck will be shown the door."

"Maybe that's what needs to happen." Maybe they needed to go back to the sheriff supervising the ethics of the department.

Rio frowned in a way that reminded Colt that the other officer had once had his own problems in this regard, when he'd been too soft on a local resident who'd been going through a hard time. "You sure you don't need a lawyer helping you with this?"

Colt saw no reason to hire someone to defend him when he'd done nothing wrong. "I'm sure," he said firmly.

Patricia Wilson emerged from the chapel. She glared at Colt and Rio and pointed at her watch.

Colt turned off the engine and pulled the keys from the ignition. "Looks like they're waiting on us," he said, gesturing toward the wedding planner. "We better go before Shelley comes out to read us the riot act, too."

Not that he would mind seeing the spark of indignation in her pretty green eyes and the flush on her cheeks. Not that he would mind having a moment alone with her at all.

"What do you mean we have to dance?" he asked when they came face-to-face inside the chapel.

Shelley had expected the news she had just delivered would be met with mixed reviews. Not surprisingly, the lawman with two left feet had taken it worst of all.

Trying not to think about the fact that Colt had been avoiding her since his parents' unexpected visit, Shelley explained, "Kendall and Gerry have decided they want to do a nontraditional procession to the altar. Or, in other words, they want to record everyone dancing down the aisle, like in that YouTube video. And I promised them I would choreograph it for them."

Shelley's pulse raced under the intensity of Colt's gaze. You would think by the way he was drinking her in with his eyes that he had really missed her. But how could that be the case? When he lived right down the street and could have just stopped by and said hello to her when he'd been out walking Buddy each evening after work.

Not that she should be surprised, Shelley thought, since it wasn't the first time he had found better things to do with his time than hang out with her.

Aware everyone was waiting for her to continue, Shelley pointed to the aisle they would be using for the processional during the actual ceremony. "So, I thought it would be the best way to rehearse it here." She plucked a stack of papers off a pew and began handing them out. "I've also typed up the basic steps we'll be using, with diagrams outlining the moves, and made copies of the song on CD, so you-all can practice at home. And of course we'll go over it one more time with Kendall and Gerry the night of the actual wedding rehearsal."

A murmur of assent went through the assembled group.

Shelley smiled. "Also, the bride and groom really want this to be a surprise to all their guests, so mum is the word. Okay, everyone?"

Thankfully, everyone picked up the simple dance quickly except for one person. Not surprisingly, Colt was still stressed out about it when the session concluded. She walked out to the parking lot with him.

"It really isn't all that hard," Shelley told him.

He lifted an eyebrow at her. "Says the professional dancer."

"All you need is a little more practice. Maybe a private lesson or two?" She shrugged, then took a risk, telling herself she was doing this for Kendall and Gerry. "I've got time tonight if we do it back at my house."

To Shelley's frustration, her offer seemed to rouse his ire even more. "I appreciate the extra effort, but it's not going to help. I can't dance. And after what just went down in there—" he stabbed a finger in the direction of the chapel interior "—I would think you'd know that."

Shelley had heard the same complaint from virtually every man who had been dragged to group lessons with his wife. "Everyone can dance."

His jaw clenched. "Not me."

"Yes, you."

They stared at each other, silently waging battle.

Eventually, she won. "Fine," Colt said, stalking over to his pickup truck. "I'll prove it to you."

Shelley shook her head ruefully as she headed for her Prius. "My house in five."

When they arrived, the babysitter was waiting for them. Shelley paid her, and the high school senior headed out. Shelley took the CD over to the stereo in the living room. She gestured for him to help her move the coffee table and ottoman out of the way.

"Will this wake Austin?"

Shelley went over to the armoire and rummaged through the shelves, finally emerging with what she needed. "No. We had really noisy neighbors at our previous apartment, so once he's down for the night, he sleeps through everything. He won't be awake until seven tomorrow morning."

Shelley marked off the center of the room with two rolls of bright blue painter's tape. "We'll pretend this is the aisle. So we'll start back here." She took Colt by the hand and led him to the starting point. Then, remote in hand, started the stereo.

The first four steps were a simple boogie.

As he had at the church, Colt tripped all over himself trying to approximate the movements. "The problem is you're not feeling the beat," Shelley explained.

"No surprise there, since I can never figure out where it is."

"Of course you can." She stepped beside him and laced her arm around his waist. Hands on his hips, she attempted to move his body to the bass. Twice to the left, twice to the right.

He was all over the place.

Shelley frowned. His stiffness had him moving clumsily between and on the beats. "Stop resisting me."

A muscle ticked in his jaw. "I'm not trying to fight you."

"Yes, you are. Look into my eyes, Colt. Put your hands on me." She shifted his palms over her hips. "Feel this. Feel how the music is one with my body. See the pulsing…"

"Yeah…"

"Now you do it, too."

He tried to imitate her and promptly went off the beat again.

Shelley had an idea. One she never would have used on an ordinary client. But something that probably would work with him. Or at least get him in a more cooperative frame of mind. "Pretend we're um… you know…"

He didn't.

She cleared her throat. "Getting it on."

Laughter rumbled from his chest. "Excuse me?"

Shelley decided showing was better than telling in this instance.

"Instead of moving side to side, move front to back."

"Don't you mean up and in?"

"Wiseguy."

"Hey," he chided softly, letting her know with a smoldering look that making love was something he not only clearly knew how to do, but excelled at.

"That's it," Shelley encouraged, her hands still on his hips, and his intimately clasping hers. "Pretend you and I are making love. And this is the way I want you." She rocked gently back and forth, keeping to the beat of the music. "And to be with me, you have to move the way I am."

Presto. He was right on target. Right on the beat. So was she.

And that was the moment when everything changed for the better. Colt's arms moved up to encircle her spine, his head lowered, and their lips met in a fiery kiss that had been a long, long time coming. A kiss that wouldn't mean anything tomorrow, but meant everything to her now.

Shelley caught her breath and opened her mouth to the plundering pressure of his lips and tongue. A thrill soared through her, sending whispers of pleasure through her entire body. Yearning spiraled, need flourished and passion won out.

Suddenly, it didn't matter what they were trying to accomplish here. All she cared about was the touch and taste and feel of him as he clasped her to him in one long demanding line. Held against him this way, she felt all woman to his man.

She felt as if her future was spread out before her like an invitation to happiness unlike any she had ever experienced.

And, sensible or not, she wanted that contentment, wanted to feel cared for, to be touched and held and yes, physically loved and wanted, more than she could say. She wanted what she'd always felt they were destined to have....

Colt hadn't come over here tonight expecting either of them to end up in each other's arms. Then again, maybe he should have known it wouldn't take much for the considerable sparks between them to ignite again. The truth was, he'd always wanted Shelley. Had from the very first second he had ever laid eyes on her. And, for long after they had broken up, she had remained the woman he most wanted to have in his life, in his heart, in his bed.

And now here they were again, wrapped in each other's arms, kissing as though there was no tomorrow. Only tonight. Only this moment in time. And damned if he wasn't determined to put aside all past hurts and make the most of the opportunity to get close to her again, to let her know she was safe with him and always would be.

He'd hurt her once. He never would again.

The muscles in his body banded tight, he lifted his head. Giving her the out he felt duty bound to offer. "Maybe we should stop…"

She smiled in a way that made his heart soften around the edges a little more. "And maybe we shouldn't.…" she whispered back.

She went up on tiptoe, mouth open, her tongue as avid as the rest of her supple form. He felt her nipples pressing through the soft fabric of her blouse while her hips rocked forward, and he was acutely aware that her knees were parting slightly, even now.

His body hardened all the more, proof of how much he wanted to be buried deep inside her.

She nipped at his neck. "Come upstairs with me, Colt."

He grinned devilishly. "If you insist…"

The old Shelley had been determined, stubborn, and…when it came to love…reckless to a fault.

The new Shelley was even more so…

Colt couldn't say he minded. She brought out the rebel in him, too. Her breath fast yet surprisingly steady, she took him by the hand. Bypassing the master suite where she now clearly bunked, to her old room. The one with the white provincial twin bed that would barely fit one of them, never mind both.

Heart pounding, he lifted a curious brow.

She smiled. "If we're finally going to fulfill our teenage fantasies after all these years—" she looked at him wantonly "—we have to do it here, Colt."

Colt couldn't say he hadn't wanted the same. Many nights he had lain awake, imagining taking the ultimate step to oneness with her, right here. Imagining the heat, the passion of making love with her.

A dancer, who was so aware and so at ease with her body, she didn't disappoint. Pirouetting gracefully away from him, Shelley shut the door gently behind them, switched on a lamp. Soft light spilling from atop the dresser, she came toward him, toeing off her shoes as she went.

Her fingers found the buttons.

He let her do her shirt, because it was just so electrifying watching her do a slow striptease just for him, then took over when it came to her bra. Finding her breasts as luscious and round and full, her nipples the same delicate rose as he recalled, he bent his head. She tasted every bit as good as he remembered, too, and the soft sound of longing that escaped her throat went through him like fire. It reminded him of all the hours they'd spent in the throes of teenage passion, all the days and nights they'd done everything short of actually make love. And the night they hadn't followed their plans and taken it to the next level. He owed it to her to make all her dreams come true. Which was why, he knew, they couldn't do this. Not here. Not now. Not, he swore vehemently to himself, like this.

Shelley blinked and grabbed the gingham bedspread. She sank down on the blanket and pressed it over her chest, barring most of her soft, silken skin from view. Which was a good thing, Colt noted. Otherwise he might change his mind. His body was lobbying for that even now.

"What do you mean, you've changed your mind?"

Colt sat down beside her. If ever there had been a time for strength of character, this was it, unquenched desire or no. "I can't take advantage of you this way," he told her gruffly.

She bit her lip, looking as though she didn't know whether to kiss him or punch him. "Has it escaped your memory that I invited you up here?" Her cheeks flushed a delectable pink. "That I gave you every indication I wanted this?" To demonstrate, she ran a silken finger down his chest, past his waist.

He caught her wandering hand in his before it could reach his fly. "Only to prove a point," he countered, glad he hadn't undressed, 'cause if he had…

Her mouth dropped open, as if she couldn't possibly have heard him right. "Wh-what?"

He tightened his grip on her, and kept her there when she would have moved away. "I get that you're trying to confirm you're desirable," he told her gently. "And heaven only knows, Shelley, you are."

As always, she took what he was trying to say all wrong. Her breasts lifted in righteous indignation. "Well, it's nice to know you want me even if you don't want me," she sputtered.

"What I want is for you to want more for yourself,"

Colt told her, impatient as ever when she acted on emotion instead of common sense. "What I want is for you to *stop* settling for less than you deserve."

The tension between them was palpable. She wrested her hand from his grip and ran her fingers playfully over top of his jean-clad thigh. She sent him a sidelong glance that could have persuaded him to do damn near anything, if he weren't so set on protecting her, that was.

She goaded him with a soft, sexy smile. "I thought I was going to get that. Right now. Right here. With you."

If only he could follow his baser notions.

Colt lifted her hand to his lips and kissed the back of it, then the inside of her wrist. He savored the fragrance of her perfume and the silken warmth of her skin. And told himself, for tonight anyway, it would have to be enough.

"You were only going to get a portion of what you deserve tonight, Shelley." And much as he was reluctant to admit it, the physical would only go so far toward satisfying her, heart and soul. That, Colt knew beyond a shadow of a doubt.

Surprised she didn't seem to require more from him—from whatever this rekindled relationship of theirs was now turning into—he gruffly continued. "Don't you want what Kendall and Gerry have?" *Didn't everyone—deep down?*

Skepticism curled the corners of her lips. "An incredibly deep, everlasting love that will carry me and my 'beloved' through whatever life throws at us? Sure, *in theory,* I want that."

So he wasn't the only one who was bitter, deep

down, post divorce. "And in practicality?" Colt pressed, more enamored of her than ever.

The veil of seductiveness slowly fell away from her eyes. "In practicality, Colt, I don't believe a love like that exists. Not for me, anyway, and certainly not for me and you as a couple. Which is why I want to enjoy a passionate fling with you."

"And the reason being…?" he asked, desperately trying to grasp her logic.

"Because I haven't had sex in God only knows how long and being around you makes me want to have sex. And since everything else in my life is going all to heck, I just figure…" She paused long enough to look him straight in the eye, honest now, honest and sad. "Why shouldn't I do something that will at least make me feel good on some level?"

Aha, now they were getting to the heart of the matter.

Understanding dawning on him, Colt drawled, "I'm guessing you haven't heard from the bank that foreclosed on the house."

Shelley threaded a weary hand through her silky auburn hair. Her shoulders slumped and she sat back against the headboard. "No. I did. Right before I went to the church."

"I'm guessing it wasn't good news," he said.

She winced. "You guessed right. Bank officials apparently talked to Tully to get his side of things. And he said that obviously there was some confusion. Of course I knew what was going on. That I was all for him using the house as collateral so he could start his own business." She released an angry breath. "That I was just having second thoughts now that we'd actually *lost* the property."

Bastard. "So he lied." No wonder Shelley was so reluctant to get involved with any man again.

"Yes, Tully lied." Shelley continued clutching the bedspread to her breasts. "In addition to forging my signature on the power of attorney for the loan documents."

Colt studied her. "So now what? Do you still want to sue the bank for wrongful foreclosure?"

"Liz thinks my best chance for success is in going after Tully, since he is really the culprit here, not the bank. Their loan officials were deceived as surely as I was."

Aware the clock was running out faster than she seemed to realize, he warned, "You've only got two days before the eviction happens."

Shelley stiffened at the reminder. Turning her back to him, she began to put on her blouse. "I know that, Colt." Her mouth took on that stubborn line Colt knew so well. "Which is why I called Tully again and made it clear that I will take him to civil court over this, if I have to."

"You know…it's not too late to file criminal charges for fraud," he reminded her.

Shelley whirled around. "Weren't you listening the first time? I want Tully to make amends, not go to jail."

Pushing aside his disappointment, Colt didn't know what else he could possibly say on the matter.

"But you don't agree with me," Shelley guessed, propping her hands on her hips.

He shrugged, thinking of another woman in his life

who had refused to emotionally let go of her ex. "It's not my place to disagree or agree."

"On that, we do concur." As another tense silence fell, she instinctively knew that something else seemed to be weighing on his mind. "So what else are you thinking?"

She wasn't going to let it go. Colt knew that he probably should shrug it off, but he couldn't. "That I wish you had wanted to hook up with me tonight for some other reason than just needing an escape."

Shelley's eyes narrowed. Although she didn't outwardly disagree with his assessment, she strode forward to show him out. "And you know what I wish?" she huffed when they had reached the front door. "I wish you didn't always want everything to be so darn perfect."

Chapter 7

Colt was on his way to Ben Shepherd's office for what seemed like the millionth time in the past week and a half when he caught sight of Shelley standing in the hallway outside Ilyse Adams's office. Clad in a flowery knee-length skirt, flats and scoop-necked pink T-shirt, her auburn hair in a graceful ponytail at the nape of her neck, she looked absolutely gorgeous. The little boy she had perched on her hip looked pretty cute, too.

"I just wish you would stop calling and emailing me," Shelley was saying to Ilyse, as Colt approached.

Austin lit up when Colt neared. "My deppity!" the toddler exclaimed, launching himself at Colt so swiftly that Shelley nearly lost her hold on him.

"Mine! My deppity!" Austin twisted toward Colt, little arms outstretched.

Colt grinned at Shelley. "May I?"

Looking as if she might just have forgiven Colt for rebuffing her the other evening, she returned with a grateful glance. "Please." She transferred her little boy to Colt.

"And while you're at it, Colt," Shelley continued, as Austin immediately snuggled up to Colt's chest, laying his head happily on Colt's shoulder, "maybe you can explain to Investigator Adams that I've already told you everything there was to tell about the accident, week before last." She turned and shot him a beseeching look. "I really have nothing else to add."

Ilyse Adams interjected pleasantly, "We just want to make sure all our paperwork is in order."

What the internal affairs officer really wanted, Colt mused, was for Shelley to somehow implicate him for wrongdoing.

"Well, if you have questions about the report I gave, then you need to talk to Colt since he's the officer who took my statement. The only thing I'm interested in right now is stopping the eviction that is set to happen tomorrow morning, unless someone around here—" Shelley's glance encompassed the sheriff's station "—comes to their senses and reverses the order."

"That's not our job," Ilyse Adams returned with measured calm.

"Yeah, I'm getting that." Shelley held out her arms to Austin. He took one look at the distressed expression on his mother's face and went right back to her. "Momma not happy," he pronounced.

"Isn't that the truth," Shelley muttered under her breath. "Anyway, unless you happen to have some sway with Sheriff Shepherd and can talk him out of carrying out the orders set for tomorrow morning, then please stop harassing me!" she told Adams.

Then she turned on her heel and sauntered off, skirt swaying.

Not about to let the chance to rescue Shelley go by, Colt lengthened his steps to catch up. "Let me get that door for you."

He reached her just in time and stepped with Shelley out into the sunlight. She looked so distraught his heart ached for her. "Are you okay?"

"Yes. No. I don't know." She paused to peer up at him. "Unless *you* happen to know a way I can stop the eviction."

Which, Colt knew, was set for the following morning. He exhaled, as powerless as she in this instance. "Save a court order, reversing it seems like a long shot at this point...."

Silence fell as she sat down on the stone ledge surrounding the courthouse, and settled Austin more comfortably on her lap. Picking up on her low mood, the toddler frowned and cuddled closer to his mother. Colt wished he could take Shelley in his arms and comfort her, too. The fact he was in uniform and still on duty kept him firmly in place. "I get off in a few hours. If you want me to come over and help pack..."

"To go where?" Shelley rose and squared her shoulders. "I'm not giving up, Colt. Not now. Not ever."

Minutes later, Colt found out why his boss had wanted to see him. He studied the orders, set to be enforced at ten the next morning. "For obvious reasons, I am tasking you to do this," Ben Shepherd said.

The brass wanted to see just how impartial he could

be? "No problem," Colt said. Although he wasn't looking forward to it. Not one bit.

As expected, Shelley did not make it easy on him.

She answered her front door, the following morning, a mutinous look on her face. For once her son was nowhere in sight. "Ma'am." Tipping the brim of his hat at Shelley, Colt adapted an extremely official tone. "I'm here to enforce the order of eviction."

Shelley cast a disparaging look at the moving truck coming slowly down Spring Street, then turned back to him. "Of course you are," she drawled, her eyes a fiery green.

Colt stood, clipboard in hand, methodically going through the procedure. "Have you removed all personal items from the property?"

She folded her arms in front of her and sent him a withering glare. "You know darn well I haven't."

"You have until 5:00 p.m. today to do so."

Shelley frowned as the truck turned into her driveway, and two off-duty deputies—both in street clothes—got out. Beginning to look a little nervous, Shelley turned back to him. "What happens if I don't comply?"

Wary of letting his personal feelings intrude, Colt kept a hard edge to his voice. "Then the sheriff's department will do it for you, and all your belongings will be turned over for auction."

Shelley looked as if she wanted to smack someone. Namely, him.

Colt did his best to be sensitive. "You can take your porch swing, too." He knew how much that meant to her.

She rolled her eyes. "Well, now I'm grateful."

"Fortunately," Rio Vasquez said as he and Kyle McCabe walked up to join them, "you've got friends to help you." The deputy paused, able to convey the sympathy that Colt could not, a fact for which he was extremely grateful. "Where do you want to start?" Rio asked.

For the first time, Shelley's lip trembled. She blinked furiously. Then she stiffened her shoulders and turned her back to Colt. "That's the least of my problems, guys." She sniffed. "Even if we get all the furniture out in time, I don't have anywhere to store the stuff. Never mind stay…"

"Actually…" Kyle smiled with an affable wink, letting her know, thanks to the cooperation of Colt's buddies, it had all been worked out. "You do."

Hours later, everything Shelley owned and/or had inherited was on the premises of Colt McCabe's home. His two-story Craftsman-style house was packed to the gills with boxes and belongings. Her furniture filled his garage to overflowing.

Colt was still up the street, finishing the job by putting a lockbox on all the doors to her home. The eviction and foreclosure notices that she had removed were also back up for everyone to see.

Shelley had never felt so humiliated.

Her only solace at the moment was that Austin had not been here to see any of it.

Instead, her son was at his babysitter's house, hanging out with her and her family. Shelley was inside Colt's house, trying to shift the hastily packed boxes in a way that would clear a path, while Colt's dog watched patiently from his cushion by the fireplace.

Shelley glanced at Buddy. "I bet you're wondering what the heck is going on here," she said.

The dog tilted his head to one side.

In need of solace herself, Shelley kneeled down next to him. Was this why people had dogs? Because they looked at you with such innate understanding? All she knew for certain was that she was in need of a good confessional.

She petted the soft fur on the very top of his head. "I don't know why I wasn't more prepared for what occurred this morning." Buddy rolled over on his side so she could rub his belly. "I mean, I certainly should have been... But I just kept thinking that a miracle was going to happen, that Colt would be able to pull some strings with the sheriff's department, or that Tully would come forward with the money to repay the bank."

Only none of that had happened.

And now, thanks to her refusal to face reality, she and her son were homeless.

"You have to know," a low voice said from the open doorway, "I would have stopped it if I could."

"Colt." Shelley got slowly to her feet, embarrassed at the way she had treated him. She drew a deep, enervating breath and walked toward him. "I'm so sorry I was rude to you this morning."

"Hey. Under the circumstances..." His eyes crinkled at the corners. "I've seen a lot worse."

Still in his uniform, he closed the distance between them and wrapped her in his arms. Hugging her close, he stroked a hand through her hair. "It had to be gut-wrenching to have to leave your home."

Too weary to resist, even if it was in their mutual

best interest to do so, she asked, "Is that why you offered to let me store all my stuff here and handled the actual eviction yourself? Because you felt sorry for me?"

He kissed her temple and moved back far enough to look into her eyes again as he confided in a low, tender tone, "I supervised the removal because I was assigned the task." He paused a moment to let her digest that.

Then continued huskily, "I made sure you had a rental van and help packing up because I know this whole situation sucks big-time, and I wanted to make it as easy on you and Austin as I could."

His compassion melted the rest of her defenses. More than anything, she wanted to be friends with him again. Close friends. "Still the softest heart in the department, I see."

He groaned as if that were the last thing he wanted to hear.

Eager to get their relationship back on an even keel, she teased, "You know it's true."

His eyes grazed hers before he turned away. "I do. I just wish it wasn't."

"Don't say that!" She moved close enough to take him in her arms and offer the kind of comfort he had just offered her. "Your kindness is what I love most about you."

He glanced down at the hand she had placed on his biceps. "Love?"

Flushing, Shelley withdrew her palm. "You know what I mean."

He nodded and stepped back.

Aware she'd touched a nerve without meaning to, Shelley hitched in a breath. Suddenly, she and Colt were a million miles apart again—at least emotionally. That disappointed her as much as the events of the morning. She hated the fact that their relationship had always been so complicated. Never more so, it seemed, than right now.

She slowly withdrew. "Well, I guess I better find a place for Austin and me to sleep tonight. And then I have to go pick him up from the sitter."

Colt cut her off as she reached the door. "Why not here?"

"You can't be serious," Shelley said, pivoting around to face him.

He shrugged, his broad shoulders straining the tan fabric of his uniform. "I admit it's a little crowded with all the boxes. But I've got room." He gave her a long beseeching look, then gestured toward the second floor. "There are four bedrooms upstairs. Only two of them have beds in them. We could easily set up Austin's crib in one of them. Maybe make a play area on the sun porch, off the kitchen."

Shelley was so tempted. Yet she knew it was a big risk to take. "You know what people will think if I move in here..." she said, her gaze moving in the direction of the bedrooms.

"Exactly what we're worried about," two voices said in unison.

"Mom. Dad," Colt announced as he and Shelley turned to greet his parents.

Wade nodded in acknowledgment. "Colt. Shelley."

Josie rushed forward to embrace her, much as her own mother would have done. "Shelley, honey, we heard what happened to you. And we're so very sorry."

Aware of how much she needed a mother in her life

again, especially now, Shelley managed a wan smile. "Thank you."

Wade hugged Shelley, too. As tender as his son, he groused, "I don't know why Colt didn't come to me if you needed help. He knows that I own a company that buys up distressed properties and resells them at a profit. Although in your case, because you are a friend of the family, I could see that margin was vastly reduced."

Colt looked away, his mouth tight. Shelley knew his family's money had always embarrassed him. Made him feel apart from his peers. She lifted a delicate palm before Wade could say anything else. "Colt knows I wouldn't feel right making my problem someone else's."

Josie stepped forward, all maternal concern. "You've obviously accepted our son's help."

"Just temporarily," Shelley allowed, her discomfort increasing. She faced both of Colt's parents. Their visit would have been insulting had she not known their offer came from love. In fact, Colt's innate generosity was very much a family trait for all the McCabes. "Colt knows I'll be out of his way in a day or two." Colt blinked, as if this was news to him.

His reaction confirmed Shelley's hunch that he had been hoping she and her son would stay until everything was sorted out and she was back on solid financial ground again.

But he had to know that if she did stay for a longer period of time, she would end up leaning on him in a way neither of them were prepared for. Josie smiled. "It could be even sooner, if you accept our offer of hospitality and come stay at our ranch. Now that the kids are all grown and out, Wade and I have plenty of room. You and Austin could have the run of the place for as long as you needed."

Colt's face grew thunderous. "Mom, Dad...a word?"

Josie and Wade exchanged glances. Clearly, they were not surprised by their hopelessly gallant son's reaction. The three McCabes stepped outside. Not wanting to hear what was said, Shelley went to the rear of the house. Eventually, doors opened and shut, and she heard a pickup driving away.

Colt came out to the sun porch to find her.

Her body stiff with tension, Shelley turned to face him. "So? What happened...?"

"I told them they were out of line."

Shelley sat on the edge of an Adirondack chair with a dark plaid cushion. "They're worried about you. They know how kind you are, and how needy I am at the moment."

"I wouldn't call you that."

Times like this, she really missed the soothing sway of her porch swing, which was now stored along with many other precious items in Colt's garage. She curved her fingers over the arms of the chair.

"Why didn't you tell me about the companies your father owned?"

He pulled up a chair opposite her and sat so they were knee to knee. He took her hand in his. "Because if anyone loaned you the money to buy yourself out of this mess you're in, it was going to be me," he told her stubbornly.

Did he even realize what he was saying? It seemed so...*territorial.*

Shelley drew in a sharp breath. "Colt..." Accepting

the Southern hospitality of a friend was one thing, accepting money quite another.

Money, and the fights over it, had destroyed her marriage to Tully. She didn't want financial matters destroying her friendship with Colt. A friendship that was just beginning to bloom again. Even if he had wisely nixed the idea of an affair.

"I have a trust fund, Shelley. One that runs well into seven figures. I could easily buy your house at auction, and I have every intention of doing so, too."

He was moving from simply assisting to taking over. She knew, even if he didn't end up purchasing her house, that a move like that would change the relationship between them irrevocably. Deep down, she didn't want to be with someone who felt he had to bail her out.

She withdrew her hands from his. "Not if you want to stay in my life, you won't."

Colt stared at her in shock. Clearly, he hadn't expected her to turn him down. And maybe the old Shelley wouldn't have. But if she was going to be the kind of mom Austin would be proud of, she was going to have to do things differently.

She shifted back in her chair so their knees were no longer touching. "I got into this mess because I didn't accept full responsibility for my own financial situation, Colt. I didn't insist Tully and I both work regular jobs, and I turned a blind eye to our credit card debt and Tully's lavish spending. And there I was today, doing it again." Shelley rose and began to pace. "Acting as if things were magically going to work out when all the other indications were telling me otherwise."

She whirled back to face Colt. "I have to stop pretending that I am not responsible, because as much as I don't want to admit it, the judge was right. I should have known that Tully would pull the rug out from under me like this after our divorce."

Colt rose and followed her to the screened window that overlooked the small, well-maintained backyard. "For what it's worth, I was hoping a miracle would happen, too. The point is—" he paused emphatically "—it still could."

Shelley resisted the urge to launch herself into his arms and hold on tight. "Only if it's one of my making," she stated firmly. Walking back inside, she found her purse and her car keys. "I meant what I told your parents. My son and I will be out of here in a few days. And so will my stuff."

Colt would have liked to argue with Shelley, but he was summoned back to work to be interviewed—again—by the internal affairs investigator.

"Is it true that Shelley Meyerson has moved in with you?" Ilyse Adams asked the moment Colt walked into her office.

A stone-faced Colt stalked right back out and went to the vending machine area, the IA official hot on his heels. "You are free to question me about whatever you want at work, but my personal life is my own."

Ilyse leaned against the machine. Because the area was empty at the moment, she continued her interrogation. "Not always. Not if you're involved in any sort of exchange of favors."

She made it sound really sordid. Colt fished in his pocket for change. "Now you're really reaching."

"Am I? Because of all the people involved in the accident that night, Shelley Meyerson is the only one who won't consent to a second or third interview."

Colt fed quarters into the machine and hit the button for a Diet Dr Pepper. "She shouldn't have to waste her time on that."

The can thunked against the bottom of the dispenser. "Is that what you told her?"

Colt retrieved his drink, and then popped the lid. He sipped his drink languidly. "We didn't discuss it."

Ilyse paused to get herself a soda, too. "What did you discuss when you were helping her move into your place?"

Seeing a few other officers headed their way, Colt headed back to Ilyse's office. "The fact that it's going to be a temporary setup and she hopes to be out in a few days."

Ilyse regarded him with skepticism. "Is she paying rent?"

Maybe Rio was right: maybe he *did* need a lawyer. Colt settled down in a chair in front of her desk. "I don't charge my friends rent when they opt to bunk at my place for a few days."

Another imperious lift of the brow prodded him to go on. "I know you're not from Texas, Investigator Adams, but we have something called hospitality here that says it's rude to charge your friends when they stay over."

Ilyse took her time opening her own soft drink. "Are the two of you intimately involved?"

Does wishing we were count? Colt wondered. He hadn't been able to stop thinking about making love to Shelley since he had come to his senses and called a halt to their make-out session in her old bedroom.

But that was none of the department's business. Colt flashed a warning smile. "You are crossing a line here, Investigator."

Ilyse Adams sipped her drink. "No, Deputy Mc-Cabe, it's *you* who are crossing a line. And the sooner you realize that and do something to rectify the situation, the better."

Unfortunately, Investigator Adams had a half dozen other cases she had dug up out of the files that she wanted to question him on, so it was nearly midnight by the time Colt got back to his house.

Shelley and Austin were long asleep by then, and he did not disturb them as he tiptoed past the guest bedroom. He showered and headed for his own bed, figuring he would see his two houseguests in the morning.

Given how long his day had been, sleep should have come easily.

It didn't. All he could think about was Ilyse Adams's dogged determination to find something to nail him with. The last thing he wanted was for Shelley to be dragged into this mess, and now, given Adams's focus on his *friendship* with Shelley, that could well happen.

So, the first thing the next morning, while Shelley and Austin were sleeping in, Colt did what his friend Rio had been urging him to do, and he called a lawyer and finagled an appointment for that afternoon at four o'clock.

Colt had just hung up the phone and walked back inside the house when he ran into Shelley. She was clad in old-fashioned cotton pajamas—the kind that were made of pink-and-white-striped cotton and buttoned up the front. Her red hair tumbling in loose sexy waves over her shoulders, cheeks pink with sleep, she looked incredibly beautiful. And sexy. Sexy enough to make him really regret his decision not to have a fling with her.

Austin was walking along behind her. The tyke stopped to crouch down next to Buddy, look into his eyes and pet him gently on the head.

Smiling at the heartwarming picture her toddler and his dog made, Shelley turned back to Colt. "You don't have to go outside to talk on the phone, you know. We're not that light of sleepers."

Actually, he kind of did. Not just because the sheriff and Investigator Adams had told him to keep the investigation quiet, and hence, somewhat unofficial, for now. But because Shelley was inadvertently becoming a target of Ilyse Adams, too. And she had enough to deal with without worrying about the thinly veiled assumptions of the internal affairs officer.

Colt smiled, resisting the urge to take Shelley in his arms and do something far from G-rated. He swallowed, and ignoring the quickening of his pulse, looked her over with casual affection. "How did you sleep?"

"Fine." Shelley rolled her eyes. "Once we went to sleep. It took a while, though. Buddy wanted that *R-E-D T-R-U-C-K* you saw him playing with the other day. The wooden one."

"The one your grandfather made for your dad—and that your father kept for his first grandchild?" Her dad had been showing it off, even when Shelley and Colt were an item back in high school.

"That would be it. Don't mention it, but somewhere in all the chaos yesterday, it went missing. I'm pretty sure I packed it in some box and will eventually find it. But in the meantime, if you wouldn't mind keeping an eye out for it...?"

"Will do," he promised.

Shelley's eyes swept his uniform. "Headed for work?"

Colt nodded. "I should be home around six or so," he said, aware how cozy and domestic this all suddenly felt. How conducive for getting intimately involved, just as his parents had alleged. He cleared his throat. "Please, make yourself at home."

"Not for long—" Shelley rose on tiptoe to give him a quick, platonic peck on the cheek "—but thanks... we will."

Chapter 8

Travis Anderson, who'd had his own brush with an unlawful firing several years before, listened intently while Colt explained what had happened in the aftermath of Mr. Zellecky's car accident.

When Colt had finished, the attorney stated bluntly, "I had a chance to look at the county sheriff department's employee guidelines. I don't think your actions are a fireable offense, given the fact you may well have saved two lives with your actions."

Colt relaxed in relief.

"However, the scope of the internal affairs investigation concerns me." Travis frowned. "What else do they have?"

Wishing this weren't such a big deal, Colt settled more comfortably in his chair. "Last spring, I intercepted three seniors outside the high school. They were contemplating breaking into the principal's office to toilet paper his office. I talked them out of it, and because they hadn't actually done anything when I caught them, except be on school property after hours, I didn't cite them with anything or file any paperwork."

"Why do I have a feeling there's more to this story?" Travis asked with lawyerly calm.

Wincing, Colt continued his account of what happened. "Their close call was mentioned on Facebook. One of the teachers heard about it and complained. She said I should have thrown the book at the kids. I disagreed. I didn't want to saddle them with criminal records for the rest of their lives."

"What happened after that?"

"The superintendent suspended them for three days," he replied.

"Were you reprimanded?"

Colt cleared his throat. "Unofficially."

"Anything else?"

He went through half a dozen similar incidents. All involved judgment calls on his part.

Travis made another notation on the pad in front of him. "Sounds like they may be building a case that you have a tendency to be soft on crime."

Colt clenched his jaw. "What do I have to do to protect myself and my job?"

"They'll be looking for patterns of behavior, so my advice is don't give them any more ammunition. Follow procedure to the letter, down to the smallest detail. Be every bit as tough on crime as they want you to be. And hopefully this will blow over."

Unable to imagine what it would feel like to be

kicked out of law enforcement, Colt muttered, "And if it doesn't?"

Travis shook his head, his expression grim. "That's a bridge we never want to have to cross. But in the meantime, you might want to help Shelley and her son find somewhere else to live."

Exactly what his parents had said. "I'm not kicking them out." Even though she had said they would be going anyway, in a few days.

"You might want to reconsider that," Travis advised. "Since, from a legal perspective, distancing yourself from Shelley and any of her current problems would substantially weaken the case they are building against you."

Upset, Colt left Travis's office, only to run into the person he least expected to see at that particular moment, walking into the office building.

Shelley blinked and stopped just short of the door as he closed the distance between them.

Colt felt his mouth water just looking at her. Damn, but she was pretty in the early-evening light. She wore a pretty blue print sundress and coordinating sandals. The corset-style bodice hugged her torso, while the wide straps showed off her feminine shoulders and beautiful dancer's arms. The flirty skirt flared out over her hips and swirled around her spectacularly sexy legs. His heart hammering in his chest, he couldn't keep his eyes off of her.

"Colt?" Shelley ran a hand through the loose waves of her auburn hair. She looked at the Cartwright & Anderson, Attorneys At Law sign. "What are you doing here?"

Forced to fib, Colt replied offhandedly, "Just taking care of some personal business." Stuff he hoped would never become public. "You?"

"I have an appointment with Liz. I have an idea how to better handle my situation, and I want to get her opinion on it."

Colt wondered if that meant Shelley was finally ready to hold her ex accountable and file criminal charges. Aware, though, that this was a decision only she could make, he held his tongue and merely said, "Good luck."

"Thanks." Shelley paused and bit her lip, as if she didn't know quite where to start. "Listen, if you're headed home…"

"I am."

She leaned in close enough for him to get a whiff of her perfume. "Then you'll be happy to know your place is all yours again. Well," she amended with a hasty lift of her delicate hand, "except for the stuff I had to leave stacked in your garage. Everything inside the house, as well as my sofa and chairs, kitchen table and bed, I was able to move over to Main Street."

Colt did a double take.

"Jenna Lockhart Remington agreed to let me rent the one-bedroom apartment above her bridal salon until I get everything straightened out," Shelley explained.

That was a lot of change for her son. "Is Austin okay with all this?"

Her face became pinched with stress. "Except for the fact we still can't find his little red truck. Luckily, I've been able to keep distracting him." She paused. "At least he has the rest of his toys and his own crib to sleep in, his stroller and booster chair to sit in."

Colt nodded, trying not to show how disappointed he felt. Although this would certainly make his lawyer happy. He forced a smile. "Hopefully, the toy truck will turn up."

Shelley smiled back, looking as reluctant to part ways with him as he was with her. "I'm sure it will. I'm sure it's right in front of my eyes. I've just been so busy and distracted I can't see it." She glanced at her watch. "Well, I better go in. I don't want to be late." She touched his hand briefly before moving away. "Thanks again for putting us up last night."

"It was my pleasure," Colt said. Although it would have been a lot better had they stayed.

The feeling intensified when he actually got home.

His house, always such a haven of peace and solitude, echoed with silence. With the wistful feeling of what might have been, if only Shelley hadn't been so intent on solving her own problems. Buddy noticed, too. He stayed close by Colt's side while they had dinner and got ready for bed. Fortunately, the last few days had left Colt exhausted, and he fell asleep swiftly.

At two o'clock, the phone rang, jarring them both awake.

Groggily, Colt picked it up. Beside him, Buddy lifted his head, too.

"Colt?" Shelley's voice was distraught. He could barely hear her over the sound of Austin's sobbing. "I'm so s-sorry to wake you."

Colt sat up, wide-awake. "What is it?"

"The little red truck. Austin woke up, clamoring for it, and there's nothing I can say or do…" Hearing the way her son was crying, as if his little heart was breaking, damn near had Colt tearing up, too. Shelley was right. Her son had been through so much in the past couple of weeks. They both had.

"What can I do?" Colt asked, already reaching for his jeans.

"It's got to be at the house. He was carrying it around with him, before we left, the day we were evicted. The only thing is I don't have a key anymore. The sheriff's department changed the locks at the time I surrendered the property."

Colt remembered. It was standard procedure in evictions on foreclosed properties.

"Can you get in? Have a look around?"

That *wasn't* standard procedure.

"I hate to ask," Shelley had to shout to be heard above her son's heart-wrenching sobs, "but I think everything that's happened has finally caught up with him. Austin really needs his favorite toy."

"I'm on it," he said.

"Thank you, Colt. Thank you so much!"

Colt headed briskly down the stairs. Located his truck keys and his wallet. "I'll call you when I find it," he promised.

"What are you doing here?" the watch commander asked when Colt strolled into the station ten minutes later.

The less others knew, the better. Colt was about to go off protocol again, and he didn't want anyone else catching grief about it. The only good thing was that the internal affairs officer was nowhere around this time of night. Colt casually waved off the commander's question. "Long story."

"Aren't you on duty first thing tomorrow morning?" a female officer said.

"Yep." He kept right on going, past the bull pen of desks and computers, where reports were typed up, to the locker room. "Which is why I have to get the electric bill out of the jacket in my locker and pay the darn thing before my lights and air-conditioning are turned off."

"We don't want you sweating too much," the female officer said with a wink.

Colt chuckled at the flirtatious joke, as he was meant to, and slipped into the locker room. He grabbed the spare jacket from his metal cubicle, along with the actual bill—which wasn't actually due for another week. From there, he went to the room where the keys to foreclosed properties were kept.

A quick run-through of the files netted him the key he needed.

He slipped it into the pocket of his pants and headed out again.

He waved the bill at the watch commander as he passed. "Got it."

"Get some sleep, will you, Colt?"

"Just as soon as I take care of business," he promised.

Short minutes later, he was at Shelley's foreclosed house. The neighborhood was as quiet as the middle of the night dictated, and Colt had no problem slipping in the back door and surveying the rooms with his flashlight, until at last he saw what he had been looking for and hunkered down. "Bingo!"

In the center of town, Shelley walked the floors with her wailing toddler in her arms. "Oh, sweetheart, please stop crying," she urged while rubbing his back.

Austin cried all the harder, in a way that just broke her heart. "Truck, Momma. Want truck...." He dissolved into fresh sobs.

A knock sounded on the apartment door.

Hoping it was Colt, and that he'd located the only thing that would calm her hopelessly distraught child, Shelley rushed to answer it.

Colt stood on the other side. Clad in jeans and a rumpled cotton shirt, his handsome face covered with a day's growth of beard, his short, dark hair standing on end, he looked sexy as all get-out, and most important of all, he was holding the much wanted toy aloft like a trophy.

"Mine!" Austin squealed. He lurched for the miniature vehicle so suddenly Shelley would have lost her grip on him had Colt not been there to step in and take her son in his strong arms.

"Mine! My truck!" Austin said, showing Colt.

"And what a fine truck it is," Colt soothed in his low, reassuring baritone.

Austin hugged Colt fiercely. "My deppity," he exclaimed. And it was then, when her son finally stopped sobbing his heart out and actually smiled, that Shelley burst into tears herself.

Colt didn't have much experience rocking a baby to sleep, but he'd seen it done plenty of times, and as it happened, it was pretty easy when a tyke was as absolutely exhausted as Austin.

Ten minutes after Colt sat down in the rocking chair, Austin and his truck snuggled in a blanket and tucked against his chest, he had a soundly sleeping toddler in his arms.

Which was good, because Colt was more than a little clumsy as he put Austin back into his crib. Not that it mattered. The little guy was so fast asleep, he didn't stir in the least. Very aware of the bed where Shelley had been sleeping next to the crib, Colt shut the door and went in search of her.

She was curled up on the sofa, a wad of damp tissues in her hand.

Colt sat down beside her, and unable to help himself, sifted a hand through the mussed silk of her auburn hair. "Are you going to be okay?"

She nodded. However, her red, swollen eyes and trembling lower lip said otherwise.

He scooted closer. "What else is going on?" he asked gently.

Shelley shifted toward him. The open V of her pajama top revealed the delectably smooth skin over her collarbone. Lower still, the uppermost curves of her breasts. "You mean beside a distraught baby boy, and a lost toy, an unwanted eviction, two residential moves in three days, and a house that is going to be auctioned off in less than a week?"

Put that way.... Tenderness welling from deep within him, Colt ran his thumb over the curve of her cheek. "You might just have a little too much on your plate for any one person to deal with."

Her expression turned even more vulnerable. "You think?"

He wrapped his arm about her shoulders, tucking her snugly into the curve of his body. "How did your meeting with Liz go?"

Cuddling close, she said in a low, muffled voice, "What do you think? It was a disaster."

"Because?" He pressed a kiss on her temple. Her head fell wearily back to rest against his biceps.

She drew a quavering breath. "I had this bright idea that I could place a lien on Tully's personal property until he paid the money he owed me."

"Does he have one hundred and fifty thousand dollars in assets?" Colt asked, curious.

Shelley raked her teeth across her soft lower lip. "Not since he blew through all the money in his trust fund, but he has a lot of very expensive toys. A Jet Ski and a speed boat, a motorcycle and a sports car. At least he did, when we divorced." She sighed. "Anyway, I thought maybe if he was forced to surrender some of his toys to pay off the debt that he might suddenly be a lot more motivated to help me find a way to keep the house out of auction."

There she was…depending yet again on her ex to come through for her, when they all knew it was a pipe dream.

Frustration knotted Colt's gut. "But Liz didn't think it was a good idea?" he guessed.

Shelley scrubbed the tears from her face. "Nope. I'd need a court order to do that, and first there would have to be a civil lawsuit filed against Tully, settled in my favor. And that's not at all feasible because it would cost a minimum of ten thousand dollars just to get the ball rolling. So—" she pressed her fingers beneath her eyes, struggling not to cry again "—I'm back where I started."

Colt shifted her over onto his lap, much the way he had, years ago, when they'd been dating. "I could still help you, you know. I could bid on the house for you on Tuesday, and make sure I end up with it." His attorney wouldn't like it. Neither would the department. But so what? He'd be helping her.

Shelley shifted around so she could look into his eyes. She stared at him a long, careful moment. "I appreciate the thought," she said finally, biting her lip again.

"But...?" Colt tried his best to figure out what kind of assistance she needed.

Shelley slowly wrapped her arms around his shoulders. "This is the only kind of help I need..."

Shelley hadn't expected the night to end with her kissing Colt. But it was what she wanted. *He* was what she wanted. Right now, she'd take any way to find release and forget the difficulties going on in the rest of her life.

And Colt, with his strong body and even stronger heart, beckoned like a lighthouse on stormy seas. She reveled in the feel of him, so hard and hot and masculine. She reveled in the spirit of him, so generous and giving and practical, so unafraid to face whatever came his way.

Shelley needed to lose herself in his strength and find a way to duplicate it in herself during this very difficult time. She needed to make up for the mistakes of the past and find a way to segue into the future.

Being with Colt, the way they had always been destined to be together, seemed the perfect way. She traced the contours of his face with her fingertips, reveling in the abrasion of his evening beard. "Don't turn me down tonight," she whispered, inhaling the sandalwood and leather scent of his cologne.

His mouth was on her neck, tracing her racing pulse. "Not planning to."

His low, smoldering voice made her heart skitter. She sat back to gaze intimately into his beautiful blue eyes. "Really?"

He smiled. "Really." He cupped her head in his hands and kissed her deeply, his mouth claiming hers in the way she'd been dreaming about. "You're all I've been able to think about."

She let out a breath, ready to let herself need, just for a little bit, wanting this more than she had ever wanted anything in her life. "In that case…" She gave herself up to him, tangling her tongue with his, absorbing the fact he was so big and strong and hard. Everywhere. Processing the fact that this was about to change everything, irrevocably. She broke off the kiss. "This isn't just because I need rescuing, is it?"

And kissing and holding and loving….

His eyes opened, dark and intense. He pulled her all the way onto his lap, rocking her against him, making her quiver. He rubbed his thumb across her lower lip, absorbing the dewy moisture from their kiss. "It may be part of the appeal."

She smiled, loving that he was so direct about his desire. Knowing he wanted her as much as she wanted him warmed her from the inside out. She pressed her lips to his again, reveling in the hot, male taste of him. "And the other…?"

His hand ran down her spine to rest at the small of her back. The other slipped inside her pajama top, to rest atop her racing heart. He looked down at her, his expression suddenly unbearably tender. "Is the fact I've always been crazy about you." His hand slipped lower, across the top of her bare breast. "And curious about you." He found her nipple, caressing it so gently she moaned. "About what it would be like to finally…"

Shelley trembled with need. "Make love."

He met her gaze. "Yes."

She liked the way he said that, too. So open and honest. Liked the way he shifted her again, so they were prone on the sofa, his body braced against the back cushions, hers lying flat. Head propped on his hand, one leg cozily inserted between the two of hers, he leaned down to kiss her. Long and hard and deep. Soft and sweet. Over and over, pulling her in, the same way he had years before in their long, sexy make-out sessions. Held against him that way, it was impossible not to respond. Button by button, he opened up her pajama top. Paused to look his fill. "You are so beautiful."

He made her feel beautiful whenever he looked at her like that. Made her feel that they were destined to be together. His lips blazed a path where his hands had been, creating a firestorm of sensation and pressing need. Throbbing deep inside, Shelley moaned and brought him close. She knew, from experience, how easily he could… "Colt…" She wanted him inside her.

"I know."

She groaned again, not sure she could wait. "I want…"

"This?" Easing a hand inside her pajama pants, he swept his palm across her lower abdomen, stroking, seeking, discovering, and in the next moment she found the release she sought. He held her, still stroking, still kissing her, until her shudders finally dissipated, and then he shifted again to stretch out over top of her.

"I still want you," she whispered. More than ever.

He smiled. "I know." He kissed her again, even more thoroughly and lovingly this time. "I want you, too."

Colt just wasn't sure this was the time or place. Not when she was still so distraught about everything. He buried his face in her hair and took a deep bolstering breath, then levered his body off the sofa and stood.

Shelley rose on her elbows, her pajama top falling open, her pajama pants and silky underwear riding just below her bikini line. She looked aghast. "You're not leaving."

As much as he wanted to make love to her, he wanted to protect her more. Lower body aching, he ran his hands through his hair. "I want you to think about this."

"Oh, no." Shelley scrambled to her feet, her top still falling open, revealing the pale roundness of her breasts and her taut, rosy nipples. She caught his wrist. "We're not leaving this uneven! With you making love to me and me *not* making love to you."

As much as he did want to make love to her, he wanted to build something solid and long lasting even more. "Shelley…"

The one thing he did *not* want was for her to think he took advantage of the situation—and her—by enticing her into something uncharacteristically reckless. Doing so would be worse than standing her up for prom. Far worse. Colt didn't think he could live with her not wanting to ever see or speak to him again.

"You don't have to do this," Colt rasped.

But it seemed, as she led him back to the sofa and knelt between his knees, that she did. She lifted her head and looked at him, then pressed a string of kisses from his knee, across the inside of his thigh. The feel of her mouth, so soft and sweet, even through the fabric of his jeans, sent heat soaring through him.

Smiling at his reaction, Shelley kissed her way past his navel, over his ribs, to his nipples. "Let me adore you," she whispered again, her nimble fingers already unfastening his belt, then his jeans.

He groaned as her hand slipped inside. Found what she was looking for and stroked, slow and sure. And suddenly, Colt knew if he didn't do something soon, another opportunity would be lost. He wasn't giving up the chance to be close to her again, the way they both wanted. Not when they'd wanted this for so long.

Hands beneath her shoulders, he lifted her and guided her into a prone position. By the time he had stripped off his clothes, she was naked, too. The sight of her, her eyes misty with longing, breasts swollen and peaking, smooth legs open and waiting, sent him over the edge. He draped her with his body, their hearts pounding in unison. With a cry of surrender, she arched up to meet him, cupping him with impatient hands and guiding him all the way home. Colt caught his breath as hot, wet silk closed around him, her thighs pressed against him, and her lips met his once again.

Aware this was just the beginning, Colt lifted her legs so they were wrapped tightly around his waist. He dove even deeper, filling her completely, kissing and possessing her with everything he had. White-hot, she kissed and stroked, giving him everything he'd ever wanted in return. Until he no longer knew where she ended and he began. And then, just that quickly, they tumbled into ecstasy…and beyond.

When it was over, Shelley was the first to move away. She flashed him a wobbly smile. And Colt knew then, without her even uttering a word, that in her view, this was just a temporary hookup in her very temporary world.

Chapter 9

Shelley was in the apartment kitchen Friday morning, slicing bananas, when her cell phone rang. Caller ID let her known it was the bride. "How are things in Maryland?" she asked.

"Gerry's temperature finally returned to normal and he's almost done with his antibiotics," Kendall announced happily.

Shelley spooned warm oatmeal over the fruit and sprinkled the top with a little brown sugar. "That's great!"

Kendall sighed. "But he still can't fly and the doctors want him to wait a few more days before he sets off cross-country in a car."

Shelley's heart went out to her friend. "That's not so great."

"Luckily, we've still got eight days till the wedding, seven till the rehearsal dinner, so we should easily be able to make it," Kendall responded with her customary optimism. "Even if we will be arriving at the last minute since the doctors have advised us to split the traveling over three days."

Shelley set the bowl on the table and motioned to her son, who was playing nearby with his beloved little red truck. Austin toddled over, and with her help, climbed up into his booster seat. "Well, that is good news." Shelley scooted her son's chair closer to the table.

"Yes, it is. Thankfully, we have a lot of help in addition to what you and the rest of the wedding party are doing for us back in Laramie." She cleared her throat. "Our dads and a couple of Gerry's navy pals are loading up a van and driving all our furniture and one of our cars out to California. Our moms will be staying to help us clean our apartment and will drive back with us to Texas."

Shelley got Austin started on his cereal and then went back to pour him a sippy cup of milk. "Sounds like you have everything under control."

Unlike me.

"What isn't so wonderful is that the ring bearer has the chicken pox. So, he's not going to be able to be in the wedding. I was hoping you'd let Austin do it in his place."

The sentiment was sweet—and heartfelt. But... "I don't know, Kendall. He's only two and a half. And going through that everything-is-mine stage."

"But he's so smart and so cute. And we could even have you and Colt bring him up the aisle together. Please? It would mean so much to Gerry and me to have Austin be part of the ceremony. We'll have him hand off the ring pillow as soon as he gets up the aisle."

Austin was extremely cooperative with Colt, Shelley

knew. Unable to deny her dear friends anything when they had been through so much, Shelley relented with a smile. "Okay. You've convinced me."

"Fabulous! I can't wait to tell Gerry. Now, about the rest of the wedding details..."

When Colt took Buddy for a walk after work, he was still brooding over the abrupt way Shelley had shown him the door following their lovemaking the previous night. He was halfway down Spring Street when he noticed Shelley's red Prius parked in front of the Meyerson home. Clad in a pair of white cotton shorts, a dark green T-shirt, and sneakers, she was sitting on the porch of her childhood residence, Austin playing beside her.

The first thing that went through his mind was that she was trespassing. Now that she had been officially evicted, no one—except county and bank officials involved in the auction and transfer of the property to new owners—was allowed to be there.

And that included him. Although he had disregarded that fact the evening before when he'd hijacked the key from the sheriff's department and let himself in to look for Austin's toy truck. At the time he'd told himself it was a necessary action if he wanted to help Shelley and comfort her inconsolable son.

When he'd had to use a few stealth moves to get the key back to its rightful place this morning, he realized it had been a colossally stupid move.

He should have gone through the proper channels, explained the situation and somehow gotten permission, even if it was the middle of the night.

But he hadn't.

Now it was up to him to get back on the right path. And make sure Shelley didn't get in trouble, too, as a result of his recklessness.

Aware the first order of business, however, was getting her off the property—without actually *throwing* her off—he and Buddy headed up the front walk to the front steps.

"Hey," he said to her.

Shelley met his eyes. "Hi," she returned.

Austin rose from his place on the wide wooden porch, his cherished red truck in hand. "My deppity!" he yelled. "My doggy!"

Colt released his hold on Buddy's leash.

The aging canine lumbered slowly up the steps, his arthritic hips moving slowly. He went straight to Austin and lay down in front of him, tail thumping.

Austin ran over to hug Colt, then returned to Buddy. He knelt down and hugged him, too. Buddy wagged all the harder.

Colt looked at the piles of netting, ribbon and birdseed on the porch floor next to Shelley. Behind her, attached to the porch ceiling, were the heavy metal hooks that had once held her beloved porch swing.

"What's going on?" he asked, able to tell from her pensive look that it was something.

Shelley sighed. "I talked to Kendall today and realized I am way behind on filling these bags."

Guilt flooded through him. "I was going to help with that..."

She wrinkled her nose. With a wave of her hand, she invited him to have a seat next to her. "Not to worry. There are still plenty left to do."

"Want to move the operation down to my house?

It'd be more comfortable." It would also be within the law. And since he needed to firmly adhere to all the rules and regulations…

She flashed him a too-bright smile. "I'd prefer to stay here. Austin needs a place to play while I do this and he's happy here. And I have some hard thinking to do."

Figuring it wouldn't hurt to sit there for just a minute, even if they were technically trespassing, Colt sank down on the steps beside her. "What about?" He held out an eight-inch square of netting.

Shelley poured in a quarter cup of birdseed. "This house. The situation. My next move." She reached for a ribbon as he gathered the edges together and held it that way while she deftly tied it shut.

Colt tossed the filled bundle into a box, along with the others, then reached for another square of white netting. "Any idea what that will be?"

Shelley turned to sit cross-legged on the porch floor, facing him. "You really want to hear all this? 'Cause it involves my ex."

Colt tried not to look at the sleek, soft insides of her thighs below the hem of her shorts. He lifted his gaze. "I want to hear about anything that is bothering you." To his surprise, it was true. He wanted to be involved with every aspect of her life. This house, what she did, was at the heart of it.

"Okay." Shelley shook her head in dismay. "Well, I'm a mess." The soft curves of her breasts lifted and fell as she sighed. "My emotions are all over the map. One minute, I think I should just let the property go and move on."

She paused to tie on another ribbon and then met his

eyes. "At other times, like now, the mere idea of that is unbearable." Abruptly, she looked as if she was struggling not to cry. "I wonder," she continued thickly, "how can I not fight this? How can I just let this house go? Especially given all it means to me and could mean to Austin in the future?"

On the street, a car full of teenagers drove by slowly. Colt saw them staring at the eviction and foreclosure paperwork pasted to the front of the house. Uncomfortably aware they shouldn't be there, especially with his ethics under review, but unwilling to move Shelley along until she was ready to go, Colt asked, "And on the other hand?"

Shelley gave a desultory wave at the three boys. Though Colt was pretty sure she didn't know Jasper, Hector or Ryan.

He turned to look at them again. They waved at him and drove off.

Shelley bit her lip, looking sadder and more conflicted than ever. "I worry about the ugliness of going after Tully for fraud, how that could affect Austin one day."

He brushed her cheek with the pad of his thumb. "The truth is, it will affect him either way."

"I know." Shelley ran a hand over her eyes. "Believe me, I know."

He waited, sensing there was more.

She stopped working on the bags, sat back. "When I was a kid, as an only child to two doting parents, I worried about pleasing everyone and not making any waves, when all I really wanted was to be free."

How he remembered that. "Your secret wild child," he said with a wide grin.

"Right." A mixture of ruefulness and mischief lit her pretty green eyes. "There I was, diligently following all the rules by day—and not irritating anyone—and there I was at night, sneaking you into my bedroom after curfew for forbidden make-out sessions."

"Hey. You had a little help with that misbehaving." Probably because there was no accounting for the fierceness of teenage lust and love.

She wrinkled her nose playfully. "I guess I do."

Colt angled a thumb at his chest. "I've got a maverick streak, too."

She blushed and nodded, admitting, "It's what drew us together initially."

And still did, Colt thought. Because beneath her identities of responsible teacher and protective mother, her wild streak was still there. She'd shown it to him the night before when they made love without regard to anything but the exquisite pleasure they could give each other.

"My inability to directly go after what I really wanted is what also made me leave Laramie and run off with my ex. It was easier to just let Tully lead me astray than be solely responsible for my own future happiness."

Colt understood that, too. He hadn't cared where he found solace after he and Shelley broke up, which was how he'd ended up marrying too young, as well. "But that changed when Austin came along."

Shelley sobered. "And it has to change even more now." She tucked a strand of her auburn hair behind her ear. "I came back to Laramie so I could reconnect with my roots and give Austin the kind of stability I had growing up. I wanted him to feel as connected to his family's past legacy as I was to mine. Because there is comfort in that, Colt, in knowing who you are and where you come from."

"I agree." Colt squeezed her hand.

"Which is what makes everything I've done the past few days, or more specifically, not done, so crazy." Grimacing, Shelley got to her feet and began to pace in agitation. "Here I was worried about whether or not Austin would have a dad who was a criminal, when what I really should have been worried about was keeping this house." She paused, her chin taking on that stubborn tilt he knew so well. "And like it or not, there is only one way I'm going to be able to do that."

Hope rising within him, Colt pushed to his feet. "You want to file a criminal complaint?"

"Yes." Shelley came even closer, letting him know with a look that she was finally ready to let go of her ex-husband, and all the baggage that came with him. "I want to do it now. Tonight. Before any more time elapses. And, Colt?" she said even more resolutely. "I'd really like it if you would go with me."

Rio took the report while Colt walked Austin around the sheriff's station. The little fella was definitely the center of attention amongst his fellow officers. Especially when he snuggled in Colt's arms and patted him on the face, then looked lovingly into Colt's eyes and exclaimed, "My deppity! Mine!" repeatedly, making everyone laugh.

Except one person. Investigator Ilyse Adams was neither touched nor amused.

The internal affairs officer motioned for Colt to step into her office. "Got a minute?"

"As long as my pal can come, too."

Shooting him a disdainful look, she slipped behind her desk. "What were you doing in the building last night?"

Not something I'm proud of, especially in retrospect, Colt thought warily.

It wasn't the first time he had bypassed protocol to get the job done. However, it was the first time he'd second-guessed his own actions and felt guilty about it. But not about to tell the internal affairs officer that, he looked her in the eye. "It was a test. I wanted to see how closely you were watching me. Now I know."

"We are watching you," she warned quietly.

Colt resented the scrutiny even as he pushed aside his remorse. "Oh, believe me, I know."

"Did you get your electric bill paid?"

Colt swore silently to himself. So she'd looked at the security tapes and talked to the watch commander. "Not yet."

"Hmm." A wealth of accusation in a single word. "Hope your lights and air-conditioning don't go off." She gestured toward a chair. "Have a seat." Austin sat on his lap, snuggling close, his beloved truck clutched in his little hands.

"I wanted to talk to you about the first incident with Mr. Zellecky last January, the one you didn't report. You know, the one where he ran into a stop sign with his car?"

"There was no damage to the pole."

"He had to go up over the curb to hit it, and his fender was damaged. That qualifies as reckless driving, no? And yet you did not write up the incident."

Here we go again.… Colt exhaled. "I know how important it is for senior citizens to keep their licenses, how much they want to be able to keep driving in order to remain independent and lead full, productive lives."

Adams tapped her pen on the desktop. "What if that had been a kid on a bike instead of a stop sign?"

"Then it would have been a different situation. As it was, Mr. Zellecky was sweaty and pale. I knew he was a diabetic and could see he was having a sugar low."

"Just like the night he had a much more severe accident."

With a major difference. No one else had been hurt that time. There had been no real damage except a slight dent in Mr. Zellecky's car's fender.

Colt continued relating events. "I called his daughter. She came right over and took him to the doctor, and that's when they changed his medication."

"None of that is your concern. Your job is to uphold the law. At the very least, a warning citation *should have been written.*"

Colt was beginning to see that. "And it will be in the future," he promised.

Ilyse Adams remained skeptical. "You're not going to disagree with me? Plead your case?"

There had been a time, a few weeks ago, when Colt would have. He looked down at the little boy on his lap, exhaled wearily and said, "Much as any of us might want to, we can't go back and revise the past." It was what it was. He couldn't erase his mistakes, much as he might want to. All he could do—here and with Shelley—was apologize and move on.

And hope he'd be cut some slack.

Shelley came out of an interview room the same time Colt came out of Investigator Adams's office,

Austin once again perched in his arms. "What was going on in there?" she asked, looking both curious and completely worn-out.

Colt gave Shelley as much information as he was permitted, which wasn't much. "We were talking law enforcement business." *Or, in other words, Adams insinuated all sorts of things and read me the riot act.* But not wanting to discuss any of that with Shelley, Colt asked, "Did you get your report made?"

She nodded. "It's not going to stop the auction, though. They're going to have to do their own investigation and verify everything I told them. That will take a few days." They paused to wait for the elevator.

Colt noticed Ilyse Adams was right behind them. Eavesdropping? Aware Shelley was waiting for him to reply, he comforted her as best he could. "The property may not sell the first go-round. A lot of time foreclosures don't."

She flashed a wan smile, first at him, then at Investigator Adams. "I keep hoping that." Shelley sighed. "I also know it's probably wishful thinking on my part."

The elevator doors opened, and they stepped inside. To his relief, the IA officer decided to wait for the next car. "Have you eaten dinner?" Colt asked. He knew she'd clearly had a very long, tiring day and could use some TLC.

A soft smile curved her lips. "I fed Austin at five."

"That wasn't my question."

She shrugged and shifted Austin in her arms. Tuckered out from the show he'd put on, he yawned and rested his head on her shoulder. "I wasn't really hungry," Shelley said.

Colt bent and kissed her temple, feeling very connected to her in a very fundamental way. "Want to share a pizza?"

A wealth of consideration came and went in her bemused expression. "I have to put Austin to bed..."

Wishing he could follow his instincts and make love with her again—tonight—he volunteered casually, "I'll go pick one up while you do that."

Laughter bubbled up from her throat. "You're persistent." She would hand him that.

He smiled. "I take it that is a yes."

It wasn't a *date*. Shelley told herself that over and over as she got the sleepy Austin ready for bed and put him down for the night. To her relief, her son had barely stretched out in his crib when he was snoozing away.

Hence, there was really no need for her to run in and brush her teeth and run a comb through her hair. Never mind spritz on a little perfume. Even less of a reason to tidy up before Colt walked in the door twenty minutes later, box of pizza and a couple of Diet Dr Peppers in hand.

As they sat down at the café-style table, Shelley couldn't help but think how intimate this all was. Would it continue once Kendall and Gerry tied the knot? She glanced at the calendar posted on her fridge. "Just think...one week from tomorrow is the wedding."

Colt opened a packet and sprinkled extra red pepper on his slice. "Did you miss having a big wedding?"

Shelley recalled they had both eloped, to the shock and dismay of their friends. "I didn't want one at the time."

He studied her over the rim of his glass. "I thought you wanted the big fairy-tale wedding."

She had, when she had been dating him. That had changed when they broke up. "Not me."

He watched as she blissfully savored her first bite of her favorite pie, pizza with everything, then smiled over at her. "Why not?"

Shelley sighed. "A couple of reasons." Finding she could use a little extra heat, too, she reached for the red pepper flakes. "My parents weren't too keen on Tully. They thought he was too reckless. His parents were just ticked off at him in general. So the idea of trying to get everyone together to plan something…"

"Horrendous."

"And then some."

He helped himself to another slice brimming with meat and veggies and a light sprinkling of cheese. "Any other reason?"

"I think I knew even then if I waited and thought about it I'd never go through with it, and besides I wanted adventure. And eloping was adventurous."

"What do you want now—if not marriage?"

"Security and stability."

He met her eyes. "Do you want a relationship?"

She hadn't—until Colt had come back in her life. Shelley shrugged. "If I could find someone I can trust not to lie to me—or keep me in the dark about what's really going on with him." *Like Tully did.* She studied Colt's inscrutable look, concluding he hadn't been totally satisfied with her answer. Yet this was something they needed to talk about if they were going to be friends, or more than friends. "What do *you* want in a potential life mate?"

Colt flashed a sexy smile. "A family. A woman who puts our relationship above all else. Someone who will be there for me, not just for the moment, but for the rest of my life."

Shelley searched his face, looking for clues that would help her gain more insight into the inner workings of his heart. "Would you have to be married again, to make it work?"

Colt sobered. "I'd like to be. And I think, if children are involved, that we—"

Shelley raised an eyebrow in surprise.

"—my woman and I," Colt corrected, "should be."

As much as Shelley hated to admit it, she knew there was really no other option. She had only to look at her son, who was already wildly emotionally attached to Colt, to confirm this.

So, for the sake of her little boy, if she ever got seriously involved with someone to the point they were a fixture in her life, she would have to consider marriage.

She just wasn't sure she could be happily tethered to someone over the long haul, without the kind of fierce romantic love Kendall and Gerry shared as the foundation.

On the other hand, she and Colt were certainly enjoying being together now. However, it had just been a few weeks. She had so much going on with the house and the new job, not to mention helping her son adjust to all the changes.

Colt leaned closer and asked huskily, "Want to take it one day at a time?"

Shelley smiled her relief. Colt to the rescue once again. "Deputy McCabe, you read my mind."

Chapter 10

Colt was outside, getting ready to mow his lawn early Sunday evening, when social worker Mitzy Martin stopped by. He pushed the mower onto the driveway, parking it as she approached.

Mitzy got straight to the point. "I heard the Meyerson home is going up for auction next Tuesday, but I'm a little leery of buying anything sight unseen."

His heart lurched. Shelley had been hoping no one would show any interest, and he knew she'd be less than pleased to hear about Mitzy's inquiry.

"Purchasing a property at auction is definitely a risk," Colt said carefully.

Mitzy gave him a beseeching look. "Is there any way I can get in the house to have a look around before Tuesday?"

Colt shook his head. "The county does not open up

the foreclosed homes to prospective buyers." It wasn't part of the process.

"Can I walk the perimeter?"

Remembering he was supposed to be enforcing the law to the letter no matter what, Colt squinted warily. "You're not supposed to."

"Which isn't quite the same thing as telling me not to do it," the social worker teased. Known as somewhat of a maverick herself for her habit of bucking the system when too many rules and regulations got in the way of the greater good, she shrugged. "Besides, I already did, and I couldn't see a darn thing. All the blinds are closed. You can see the exterior and that is it." She frowned, looking more conflicted than ever.

Colt poured fuel into the mower. "Sorry."

Mitzy watched him screw both caps on tight, then set the gasoline container safely aside. "Well, since there's no getting the key from the sheriff's department...."

"There isn't." Bad enough that he had done it to get Austin's red truck.

Mitzy peered up at him. "You've been in the house recently, though, haven't you?"

Too recently, Colt thought, remembering the key he had barely been able to return. Maybe the sheriff and the internal affairs investigator were right...and he had started to cross the line in his attempt to swiftly right all wrongs.

"A few times," he acknowledged, wiping his hands with a rag.

"And you are good friends with Shelley," Mitzy observed.

Although Shelley hadn't kicked him out last night, right after they'd made love—instead, he'd been the one who'd had to leave to take the early shift on patrol—Colt wished he and Shelley were a lot more than a temporary hookup to each other. He wanted to know they had a future together.

Returning his attention to the conversation, Colt turned to Mitzy. "What do you want to know about the property?"

Her lips pursed thoughtfully. "Is there any reason why I *shouldn't* bid on the Meyerson house that you know about? Anything major wrong with the plumbing or electrical or anything we can't see from the outside?"

Colt hesitated, not sure how to answer that. Yes, the house seemed to be in good shape, structurally and cosmetically. But beyond that he didn't really know. So he couldn't in all good conscience answer.

"I mean, would *you* bid on the place, personally, if you didn't already have a house?"

That was easy to answer with absolute honesty. "No," Colt said firmly. "I wouldn't." *Because I would never do that to Shelley. Unless, of course, she asked.*

Mitzy took a different tack. "Would you advise *me* to bid on the house?"

Colt shrugged. "It depends on how you feel about bank-owned properties, I guess."

Her brow furrowed. "What do you mean?"

More confident now that he was on solid intellectual ground, Colt related what he knew about foreclosed homes in general. "Some people think, because of how the owners came to be evicted, that the properties have bad karma or worry that the residence could be in bad shape. Others look at the repossessed dwellings and just see a bargain, pure and simple. They're not concerned about whatever the circumstances were that led to the place being abandoned, and just want a home at rock-bottom price."

Mitzy narrowed her eyes at him. "So is this your roundabout way of telling me not to bid on the house?"

"No." Colt exhaled wearily. "Not at all." Although if that was what Mitzy took away from the conversation, who was he to say her instincts were wrong?

"But you won't tell me it's a great opportunity and advise me to bid on it, either...will you?"

How could he? Colt wondered, feeling even more conflicted. Truth was, the house on Spring Street was still Shelley's home at heart, and the place where she wanted to put down roots and raise her son.

"Never mind," Mitzy said hastily, lifting a palm. "You don't have to answer that, Colt. I probably shouldn't have asked it anyway. It's really not ethical, given the fact you personally oversaw the eviction. We're both employees of the county, and the county has been tasked with the sale for the bank."

He cleared his throat. "Thanks for understanding."

Unfortunately, Mitzy wasn't the only one inquiring. Colt had four more phone calls that afternoon, two more that evening. Everyone phrased the same questions. He told them all the same thing. He couldn't recommend they buy it. He couldn't recommend they *not* make a bid. He couldn't recommend anything. Period.

The one thing he did know was that this much interest in a house up for auction was not good. Not where Shelley and her son were concerned.

"How is Shelley doing?" Rio asked Colt Monday morning as the two of them headed into the briefing room for the preshift report.

Colt hadn't actually seen her since they'd made love Saturday night. Not that he hadn't tried. Between his work and hers, and the prewedding stuff she had to do to get ready for Kendall and Gerry's nuptials, she just hadn't had time to spend with him. Or maybe she hadn't wanted to for fear they were getting too close?

"She's okay," Colt told Rio as they sat down, "considering everything that's gone on with her lately."

"Yeah, I heard about the horrendous plumbing problems," another deputy sympathized, sinking into the chair in front of Colt.

"I thought it was the electrical work." A third deputy joined the conversation.

"No. It was the furnace," argued a fourth.

A red-haired female deputy threw in, "She has an HVAC, fellas, which means the air-conditioning and the heat are *both* on the blink, too."

Colt shoved a hand through his hair. Since when had Shelley's financial difficulties become the concern of the entire sheriff's department? "Where did you hear all this?" he asked with a frown.

Another female deputy shrugged. "It's all over town. A lot of people were thinking about bidding on the property, until they heard the truth. That Shelley let her house go under foreclosure because she just wasn't going to be able to afford the massive repairs it needed."

"And it's a shame," another said, "because on the exterior, anyway, that is one beautiful home."

A contemplative silence fell.

Colt considered correcting the misinformation. But knew if he did, that the bidding would begin in earnest the next morning…and Shelley would lose her house for sure. So as much as the ethical part of him wanted to set the record straight, the part of him that was close to her couldn't be responsible for that. Eventually someone asked, "Is it possible she can buy it back for herself at a reduced price—at auction—and afford all the repairs that way?"

"I'm pretty sure that's illegal." Rio frowned. "Otherwise, people whose homes were valued less than the loan would let them go, and then just go back and rebuy them at auction for a much lower price."

"Not many people would have the cash to do that," Colt felt compelled to point out.

"But some could," Rio persisted, "and an unethical action like that with just one property could subsequently devalue all nearby homes. Which wouldn't be fair to the people who were conscientiously paying their mortgage, underwater or not."

"Still," another officer speculated compassionately, "that house has been in Shelley's family for three generations. I can't see her letting it go without a fight."

She wasn't, Colt thought, but leery of letting what he knew of Shelley's private business become public until the district attorney made a decision whether or not to file charges against her ex-husband, he kept silent.

Oblivious to his dilemma, the red-haired deputy couldn't help wondering, "So if Shelley's not going to buy her family home back herself because she can't do so legally…just what is her plan, Colt? How's she going to make sure the property doesn't sell tomorrow? And earn herself another month before it goes up on the block again…?"

* * *

Shelley had been getting odd looks all day. It started with her morning introduction to ballet class for pre-schoolers, continued through the noon session of swing dance for seniors, and was still going on as she finished up a Zumba class for new moms.

Conversations were started in whispers, and abruptly stopped when she neared. And on top of that everyone was super nice to her when they did say hello.

Nice, in a pitying sort of way.

So it was really no surprise when just after her jazz-tap class for high school girls concluded that Colt walked in. Clad in his khaki uniform, holster on his hip, hat slanted low across his brow, he looked masculine and sexy. To the point all the high school girls gathering up their things nearly swooned. He swaggered toward her, his midnight-blue eyes locked unwaveringly on hers. "Got a minute?"

Her pulse jumped. Acutely aware of him, as well as all the curious eyes upon them, she nodded. "Two, maybe. I've got another class starting shortly."

A muscle ticked in his jaw. "About tomorrow? You can't go to the auction."

Shelley didn't know what was more annoying—the steel in his voice, or the presumption he could tell her what to do. "Refresh my memory. At what point did you become my social secretary?"

He remained implacable, despite her sarcasm. "It's just not a good idea."

Why? Did he think she was going to make a scene?

Colt continued. "Your presence there could be perceived as an attempt to be influential."

"And may prevent people from bidding," Shelley guessed.

Colt gave a slight shrug and kept his gaze meshed with hers. "It's possible."

Unsure whether he was trying to protect her or warn her, Shelley retorted, "Then that would be a good thing. Wouldn't it? Since I don't want the property to sell."

He grimaced. "I've been tasked with helping to oversee the proceedings. My job there will be to keep law and order."

What was it with this lawman? Always showing up at the worst possible time for her? "And you couldn't have refused this particular assignment?" she queried drily.

For a second, she thought he wouldn't answer her. Finally, he clenched his jaw and said, "No."

"Like you couldn't avoid the actual eviction of me from the property, either."

Colt looked as though he wanted to be anywhere but there. "It's complicated, Shelley."

Just like her feelings for him.... One minute she thought she was falling in love with him, the next, she was as wary of him as ever. "I guess so."

Since I can't stop wanting you, even when I don't want to desire you.

Colt looked pained. "I'm not doing this to make you angry with me," he said, folding his arms across his brawny chest.

"Really?" Shelley shot back, suddenly feeling close to tears. "Because you're doing a pretty good job of it, Deputy McCabe."

A palpable tension filled the air. Colt turned and briefly surveyed the watching crowd. He seemed to be weighing what to do and say next. Finally, his eyes cut back to hers, and his tone was considerably softer. "I think your house might not sell, in any case...."

"Then from your lips to God's ear," she murmured back, needing his tenderness as much as she needed his steady, reassuring presence in her life. Because she really needed more time to work things out on her end. And auctions of foreclosed properties were only held once a month, on the courthouse steps. So if her house didn't sell tomorrow, she'd have four more weeks to come up with something. And wouldn't that be a bonus.

Colt stepped closer, his gaze a lot less *official*. "Any further word from the D.A.?" he asked.

Across the room, the parents and kids from the previous class streamed out, while the next class streamed in. Keeping one eye on the clock, Shelley nodded. "The prosecutor's office will file formal charges once they verify everything I've told them. Unfortunately, it won't be in advance of the auction."

"What about your ex?" he asked gruffly. "Have you heard from Tully?"

"No. He seems to have gone into hiding."

Colt snorted in contempt. "After what he told the bank, I'm not surprised."

"Me, either." Tully had to know he was in deep trouble, the kind that smooth talking and good old boy charm would not get him out of.

Colt continued watching her. "Do you have plans for tonight?"

Shelley wasn't sure if he was offering as a friend or a lover.

Not that it mattered, since, when it came to Colt and

the upcoming wedding, she had much more important things to worry about.

"Actually… I was hoping you'd come over to my place," she said, keeping her real agenda under wraps.

"Want me to bring anything?"

Glad he hadn't suspected what she had planned, Shelley murmured, "Just yourself."

Box of Shelley's favorite Godiva chocolates in hand, Colt took the stairs two at a time up to her apartment. She'd asked him to arrive after Austin was asleep—and that could only mean one thing.

She was ready to pick up where they'd left off.

Which was true, it turned out. Just not the way he thought.

Colt blinked as she ushered him toward the center of the room, which had been taped off to resemble an aisle, similar to the one at the church. The portable stereo was set up. She was clad in what he had come to recognize as her workout clothes—a white spandex tank top, sexy black stretch pants and high-heeled red shoes with a strap across the arch. "You asked me over for a private dance lesson?"

Shelley wrinkled her nose. "You can't deny you need it." She popped the lid off the chocolates and helped herself to one shaped like a seashell. "We didn't get very far in our last lesson…"

Wondering how he was going to get out of this, he ate one, too. "That I remember." As well as what followed.

Shelley read his mind with her usual ease. "Just so you're aware? *That* is not going to happen again. We're here to *work* tonight." She slapped the lid on the box of chocolates.

A fierce hunger tugged at him. Damned if she wasn't pretty when she was holding him at arm's length. Shrugging matter-of-factly, he sauntered close enough to inhale the intoxicating fragrance of her perfume. "You never know. When I'm holding you close…"

She harrumphed, all business. Pine-green eyes locked with his, her hand to the center of his chest, she shoved him a safe distance away. "That's not going to happen tonight because I'm going to make you dance your booty off."

And work it she did. For the next three hours, Shelley made him listen to the two songs they were using for the processional and the recessional over and over again. Back and forth they went, across her apartment living room, her hands all over him in a strictly professional way that, while instructional, still drove him mad.

"Finally—" Shelley beamed as the clock approached midnight, and they moved together in perfect rhythm "—you're getting the hang of it."

About time, Colt thought. He was aching all over, and not just from the exertion. He spun her around, caught her against him, and then eased her off her feet into a slow, sultry dip. He winked. "I'm nothing if not a slow learner." Gradually, he brought her back to a standing position beside him.

Shelley shot him a sassy look. "In some things."

Deciding he'd had more than enough fancy footwork for one night, Colt gathered her close once again. This time, he didn't let go. "And in other things," he teased her provocatively, "I've never needed any lessons at all." Nor, had she....

Shelley replied hoarsely, "This wasn't in the plan for tonight."

He threaded a hand through her hair, tilting her head up to his. "Maybe not yours..." But it had certainly been in his.

Her sudden air of vulnerability told him she thought he was moving way too fast. Problem was, trying to contain his feelings for her had never worked in the past. It wasn't working now.

He brought her against him, determined to prove to her that this time they couldn't just walk away. They owed it to themselves to explore the fierce pull of their attraction that was truly beyond their control. Because if there was one thing Colt knew for certain, it was that only Shelley could make him feel this way.

Shelley knew she should say no. Ask Colt to slow down. Give them time to sort everything out before they jumped into lovemaking again. However, her heart propelled her in the opposite direction. The truth was she needed to lean on him tonight and lose herself in pleasure as surely as they had lost themselves in the dancing. And if the way he was kissing and caressing her through her clothes was any indication, he needed her, too.

"You are so bad for me," she scolded, guiding him over to the sofa.

When he fell back onto the cushions, she sprawled on top of him.

He threaded his hands through her hair. "And you,"

he told her huskily, diving into yet another kiss, "are so good for me."

Shelley couldn't dispute the seriousness of his claim, any more than she could dispute the raw honesty in his kiss. She opened her mouth to his, letting his tongue sweep her mouth, caressing his in return, finding solace...finding strength.

She knew they were moving too fast. She didn't care. She wanted him. Still kissing him ardently, she undid the buttons. With his help, she got it all the way off and tossed it onto the floor. He did the same with her spandex tank top and soft, stretchy bra. Smiling at him tenderly, both of them naked from the waist up, Shelley settled more fully on his lap and wrapped her legs around his waist. Her arms wreathed his neck, and still they kissed, her breasts nestled in the hard, hair-covered surface of his chest.

Until even that wasn't enough.

He shifted her again, pulled her to a standing position with him and gave her the once-over that let her know how very beautiful she was in his eyes.

"You're perfect. You know that, don't you?" he murmured.

Shelley grinned. Gripping his hand, she did a little pirouette. "You certainly make me feel that way."

He kissed her shoulder, the nape of her neck, the curve of her breast. He made his way to the hollow, then the erect tips, suckling gently. "And I want you naked."

With the rest of her aching to be touched, too, Shelley whispered back, "Sounds good to me."

Excitement roaring through her, Shelley tugged at his jeans. He peeled off her pants. They kicked free of the rest of their clothes. His eyes filled with a combination of possession, lust and something very close to love, Colt danced her backward to the wall. Shelley made a soft, involuntary sound in the back of her throat, her body as compliant and ready as her knees were weak. Her wrists in his hands, he pinned her hands on either side of her head, the hardness of his sex dipping down to press against the softness of hers.

The erotic friction of his body slowly, rhythmically teasing hers drove her wild. As did his long, hot, openmouthed kisses, the hard press of his muscular chest against her bare breasts. And she still wanted more.

Shelley writhed against him, loving the friction, erotically enticing him, too. Until it wasn't enough for him, either. He hissed in a breath. "Shelley." And let go of her wrists. She took advantage of the freedom to wrap her hands around him, intimately caressing, tempting, loving. With another urgent groan, he gripped her hips and lifted her. Aware he was her every male fantasy come true, she gasped and guided him home.

He surged inside, their kisses navigating them into the rhythm they'd been craving. The heat of their bodies combined with the river of pleasure pouring forth. Again and again they moved, rocking together, giving, seeking, finding more, until at last the dam burst and Shelley found the solace she needed. Colt was right after her, his shudders of release only adding to the sharp, joyous pleasure she felt.

Affirming that however this started, whyever it had continued, it was a hell of a lot more than simple sex.

It was friendship.

It was lust.

It was needs expressed and met.

It was, simply put, everything she wanted and needed to give her a more fulfilled life.

"I take it back," Shelley said a short time later, when their shudders had finally stopped, and they'd moved from the wall to the sofa. She curled against him, replete with a satisfaction as deep and enthralling as his. She pressed a kiss into his neck. "That was exactly what I needed."

Colt knew it was what he had needed, too.

Perhaps this was the only way they could communicate without all sorts of other stuff getting in the way. He reached for her, ready to go again.

Her cell phone rang.

They frowned in tandem, both of their glances moving to the clock. It was one-thirty in the morning.

Shelley extricated herself from his arms and, mindful of her son sleeping in the next room, rushed to pick up. "Who would be calling at this hour?" she murmured, sending him a distressed look over her shoulder. "I hope it's not bad news!"

But, Colt soon discovered from the look on her face as she listened, it was. "You have some nerve," Shelley said angrily. "I can't do that. Because I don't have that kind of money, that's why. No! I've got to go." Shelley ended the call and turned off her phone.

Tamping down his own resentment, Colt guessed, "Your ex?"

"Who else?" Shelley fumed. Her face pinched with stress, she slipped into the bathroom and returned, belting a knee-length, pale yellow robe. She sank down on the sofa and ran a hand through the mussed strands of her auburn hair. "He wanted me to buy back my own house at auction. So that he could repay me later when he has the money, which of course he claims he is close to getting, in full. Can you believe that?"

Yes, Colt thought, he could.

But wary another I-told-you-so was not what she needed right now, he took her hand in his and said, "There are still other options."

Chapter 11

"If you're talking about loaning me the money to make a bid...." Shelley cautioned.

Colt reached for his boxer-briefs. "Given we're involved—and I'm part of the sheriff's department, which managed the actual eviction and is now providing security for the auction—it's too close to the ethical line. Whether it would be actual fraud for me to give you the money to buy it back at a greatly reduced price or not, I don't know."

"But it would look like fraud."

Colt stood and tugged on his jeans. "And if it looks bad and smells bad..."

"It is bad."

"However, there are still my dad's companies." Colt zipped, snapped and buckled, then reached for his shirt. "Their sole purpose is to purchase distressed properties, turn them around, and resell or rent them. All I'd have to do is make the call and he'd have someone there in the morning."

Shelley didn't doubt that for a moment. The McCabes were known far and wide for their kindness and generosity. Extricating her hand from Colt's protective grip, she stood and looked him square in the eye. "As much as I appreciate that…it's not his problem."

Looking disappointed, Colt buttoned his shirt. "It would be a business arrangement, Shelley. Best of all, you wouldn't have to purchase the house back immediately. You could rent it from his management company and take all the time you need to sort everything out with your ex."

For a moment, Shelley was tempted. Fortunately, she came to her senses and levelheadedness returned. She sat back down beside him on the bed. "Accepting such a huge favor would also leave me beholden to your father—and you—in a distinctively uncomfortable way. I told you," she reminded gently, "friends and money don't mix. I want to count you…and your family…as friends."

"So we're back to just crossing our fingers and hoping it doesn't sell tomorrow?"

She nodded slowly.

"At least tell me you're not planning to attend the auction," Colt urged.

Shelley rested her head on his shoulder. "I admit part of me really wants to go. But I also know that you're right—it's not something I should try to handle emotionally. Besides—" she shrugged, as they both got to their feet "—you'll be there. You can tell me what happens, right?"

All business, he looked down at her. "I'll make sure to let you know as soon as the auction is over."

"Great." Shelley sighed in relief. "Thank you." Resisting the urge to draw him back down onto the bed with her, she leaned up and brushed her lips across his. "In the meantime, I really have to get some sleep. I've got five classes to teach tomorrow."

He gave her a brief, heartfelt hug and kissed the top of her head. "I can take a hint. But one of these days, when life settles down, you and I are going to have to find a way to spend an entire night together."

Shelley smiled. "That sounds good." *Better, in fact, than you know.*

Shortly after midnight, Spring Street should have been utterly peaceful when Colt turned onto it. And it was, with the exception of one residence.

Frowning, he watched as the arcing yellow beam of a flashlight and a trio of shadowy figures disappeared behind 903 Spring Street.

Figuring it was an interested party attempting to get a look inside prior to the auction, Colt steered his car to the curb and got out.

As he walked across the lawn and rounded the house, he heard the voices that pretty much confirmed it. "Come on, just break the window."

"No. That would make too much noise!"

"Then jimmy the lock!"

"Here! Give me that crowbar!"

Colt eased nearer, and came upon the graduating class's three rowdiest high school students. He stood, legs braced apart, arms folded in front of him, and drawled, "You fellows need a hand?"

The crowbar hit the porch with a clatter. The beam

of the flashlight arced through the air and hit Colt in the face. "Oh, thank God!" Hector said, in obvious relief. "It's only Colt McCabe."

Only? Colt thought, rubbing his jaw. He was a deputy. It was his job to enforce the law, on duty or not.

"Yeah. You scared us, man," Ryan said, holding tight to the twelve-pack of Budweiser in his arms. "We thought it was someone who was going to turn us in. Not the coolest deputy on the force."

Was that how he was perceived? Colt wondered. Not as an understanding potential mentor, but as a conscienceless wimp?

"Want to join us for a brew?" Jasper offered, popping open a can.

Colt pointed out sternly, "You need to be twenty-one to drink alcohol in Texas."

"So, what's a little lawbreaking among amigos?" Hector shrugged, accepting the can from his friend and taking a swig. "I'm sure it's nothing you and your friends didn't do after you graduated high school."

Colt picked up his cell phone, dialed. "Yeah. McCabe. I need backup immediately." Colt gave the details.

Jasper scoffed. "He didn't really call anyone."

Hector nodded. "He's just trying to scare us into giving him our beer."

"Besides, it's not like we did anything…" Ryan said.

With a reproving look, Colt reminded them, "You're underage, in possession, trespassing—"

Hector interrupted, "Hey! We were trespassing at Laramie High. You didn't take us in then."

"My mistake," Colt muttered.

Two sheriff cars pulled up at the curb, lights whirling, sirens off. Ryan blinked at the sight of the two deputies getting out of the squad cars. "Holy...frijoles! You're not joking around? You're really going to arrest us?" Hector gasped as the beer was confiscated and all three boys were swiftly turned, frisked and read their Miranda rights.

Realizing he should have thrown the book at the kids the first time around, Colt told the kids, "You really are under arrest."

Maybe this time, he ascertained privately, the kids would learn their lesson and knock off the juvenile hijinks.

Colt gave the other two officers on scene the full report of what he'd witnessed, with the newly handcuffed kids cussing him out and glaring at him all the while, then headed home.

He took his dog for a brief walk in the moonlight, and then settled down to sleep, Buddy sprawled out on his cushion next to Colt's bed.

It seemed just minutes later, Colt's alarm went off.

He showered, dressed and then headed for the station.

He was accosted the moment he walked in by the parents of Ryan, Jasper and Hector. "How could you do this?" Hector's mother screeched. "This arrest will put Hector's football scholarship in jeopardy!"

"If you wanted to see our boys arrested," Jasper's mother said, "you should have done it last April, when it would only have been a trespassing charge."

Ryan's dad added resentfully, "Now they have three charges to defend themselves against! Trespassing, attempted breaking and entering, and minors in possession of alcohol!"

Hector walked out to rejoin his parents. "We thought you were the cool deputy," he said bitterly. His friends nodded in agreement as they, too, joined their parents. "Now we know better. You just pretended to be our friend. You're worse than the rest of them!"

Ilyse Adams appeared before Colt could begin to respond. "Deputy McCabe?" the internal affairs officer interjected crisply. "A word?" Moments later, Colt found himself in Sheriff Ben Shepherd's office. "What happened last night?" Investigator Adams asked.

Colt sat down and filled them both in.

"Obviously, the parents are irate," Ben concluded with a sigh.

Colt had gathered that, and then some. "They've been here all night, along with their sons?"

The sheriff shook his head. "The three teens were so belligerent when they were brought in, so sure this was some sort of cruel joke, that a decision was made to let the boys cool their heels in lockup. Their parents weren't notified until an hour ago. Naturally, they all rushed down here to post bond immediately."

"I think you should know the boys are blaming this on you," Ilyse informed Colt archly. "They said they got the idea to party there when they saw you sneaking into the house a couple of nights ago."

Colt winced.

"Is it true?" the sheriff asked.

Colt reluctantly explained, "Shelley's son, Austin, left his little red car there, and he was inconsolable."

"So rather than go through the proper channels," Investigator Adams said implacably, "or at the very least notify officials of what you proposed to do, you smuggled the key out of the station in the middle of the night, retrieved the item for Ms. Meyerson and her little boy and then snuck the key back the next day."

Colt swallowed. Put that way, it did sound highly unethical, as well as illegal. "That about covers it, yeah."

A grave silence fell, rife with the many mistakes Colt had made. He was just beginning to see how many.

Ilyse Adams exhaled heavily, stood. "I'll add this to the report, Sheriff." She gave Colt a long, debilitating look and exited the room.

The indicting silence continued. "You understand what a very thin line you are walking, don't you?" Ben Shepherd asked, steepling his hands together on his desk. "That if it weren't for the years of fine service you've given to Laramie County, you would've already been let go. And, in all honesty, that still may happen when this investigation is concluded."

Completely off balance, Colt nodded.

Sheriff Shepherd rose and ushered Colt out. "Better get a move on. With the auction starting in an hour, you should already be on the courthouse steps. And, Colt?" Ben clapped a warning hand on his shoulder. "No more mistakes. Not a one."

"Any word from Colt yet?" Liz Cartwright-Anderson asked at the end of the noon-hour Zumba Class for New Moms.

Shelley shook her head. Her attorney, more than anyone, knew how much she was hoping her family home would not sell this morning. But with thirty-six distressed properties set to be auctioned on the courthouse steps, and a reported three hundred people there to bid on them, it might be a while longer before she knew anything. "What about Tully? Anything there?"

Liz blotted her face with the ends of the towel she had looped around her neck. "Actually, I was going to call you in a little bit, but since we have a moment…" The attorney pulled Shelley aside and told her in a low, confidential tone, "The D.A.'s office found evidence of fraud—they're going to prosecute. They've talked to a judge, who agrees because of Tully's family money and connections that your ex could be a flight risk. She issued a bench warrant for Tully. The police in Dallas are searching for him as we speak."

Shelley sighed, the relief she felt overriding any residual guilt. "Oh, Liz, that's great." Now if she could only hold on to her house long enough to see justice done. "And speaking of the most dedicated lawman around…or at least the one you're crazy about…." Liz elbowed Shelley.

Was it that obvious? Shelley turned to see Colt striding through the wave of women gathering up their belongings, and the kindergarten dance class streaming in.

As he neared her, her heart swelled. Darn it all, if he wasn't everything she could hope for, after all! The smile on his face told her everything. "It didn't sell?" she croaked.

He stopped just short of her. "Not a single bid."

Joy bubbled up inside her, and she did a little happy dance. "So that means I've got an entire month before the property will be on the auction block again!"

"That's right. You've got until the first Tuesday of next month."

Dizzy with relief, Shelley threw herself into his arms and held on tight. "Oh, Colt, thank you!" she cried, pressing up against his hard chest and inhaling the clean, masculine scent of him. "Thank you so much!"

Although he was still in uniform, ostensibly still on duty, with dozens of females surrounding them, Colt hugged her back. He buried his face in her hair. "I didn't really do anything," he whispered back.

Her stomach quivered. "Yes, you did. You and I both know it." Belatedly aware others were looking—and listening in—Shelley withdrew. "I really want to celebrate. What time do you get off tonight?"

He straightened with easy grace. "I should be done around six."

"Then it's a date. Austin and I will meet you at your place to give you a proper thank-you for everything you've done for us."

His eyes were warm, his smile enticing, but Shelley sensed that something was off. She paused, nerves jumping, hoping she hadn't presumed too much. "That's okay, isn't it?"

Colt nodded. He stepped back, all uniformed deputy on duty now. "More than okay," he said quietly. With a friendly wave for all those around them, he strode off.

"You *are* crazy about him," Liz observed at Shelley's elbow.

Needing to keep her feelings to herself until she had sorted them out, Shelley countered archly, "You just think everyone's in love, since you fell so hard for Travis."

Liz smiled, confident as ever. "I don't deny that having felt it myself, I can spot true love in a heartbeat now. And where I'm seeing it now is in you, and that hunky lawman walking out of here."

* * *

Was she in love with Colt? Did he feel that way about her? Shelley thought about that all afternoon, and she was still mulling it over when she walked Austin up to the handsome deputy's front door at six that evening.

On the other side of the front door, Buddy let out a single woof. Colt answered the door seconds later. Shelley's heart cartwheeled at the sight of him. He was always strikingly handsome in uniform, but off duty, he was incredibly masculine and sexy, too.

Never more so than right now. He'd obviously shaved when he had gotten home. Fresh out of the shower, his short dark brown hair was damp and mussed. Knee-length olive-green cargo shorts gave a distracting view of muscular legs, adorned with the perfect amount of crisp dark hair. A short-sleeved navy V-neck T-shirt molded to his broad shoulders and brawny chest. Comfortable-looking leather moccasins covered his feet. As he leaned in to give her a brief, one-armed hug hello, Shelley breathed in the intoxicatingly good scent of him. He smelled of soap and cologne, and looked as happy to see her as she was to see him.

"Right on time," he teased.

It had been hard not to be early, she'd been so eager to see him. "I'm nothing if not punctual," she teased right back.

He smiled again, then hunkered down.

At eye level, Austin grinned. "My deppity!" he said, stretching out his arms to be picked up.

Colt obliged, cradling him close. "My Austin!"

Austin chortled, and while holding on to Colt's neck, pointed at the dog beside him. "My Bud-dy…"

Hearing his name, Buddy wagged his tail, waiting

to be petted. Still crouched down to toddler level, Colt shifted around so Austin could pat the top of Buddy's head. "Hi, doggy," Austin said.

Buddy thumped his tail harder.

Colt and Shelley laughed. "Momma, my red truck," Austin commanded.

Shelley pulled it out of her bag and handed it over.

Austin scooted off Colt's thigh. Car in hand, he led the way inside the house, talking to Buddy all the while. "We play now..." he said.

Buddy lumbered after him obediently.

"If you'll keep an eye on Austin, I'll get the rest of my things," Shelley said.

Colt straightened, slow and lazy. Holding her gaze, he brushed his lips across hers. "No problem."

Longing for the moment they could spend some quality time alone, Shelley headed for the car. Fifteen minutes later, she was cozily ensconced in his kitchen. The salad was made. Their potatoes were baking in the oven. Austin's kid-friendly macaroni and cheese was cooking on the stove.

"You know, I could have cooked for you tonight," Colt observed.

Shelley rubbed olive oil, fresh ground pepper and sea salt into the rib-eye steaks she'd brought, then turned them over and did the same to the other side. She slanted Colt a playful glance. "I asked you out. Remember?"

He lounged against the counter as she washed her hands. "So this is a date."

Knowing if she gave in to her whim and started kissing him, she wouldn't want to stop, Shelley moved past him. "A thank-you."

"I keep telling you…" He watched her place her favorite cast-iron skillet on the stove and turn on the flame beneath it. "I didn't do or say anything at the auction. The reality is that the house just didn't sell."

"That's exactly my point." Shelley added butter and sliced mushrooms to the pan. Leaving them to cook, she closed the distance between her and Colt once again. "Despite the fact you really wanted to help me, you didn't go behind my back and try to have your dad's company purchase the property, which we both know you could have done. You just supported me emotionally, which was what I really wanted and needed from you."

An indecipherable emotion flickered in Colt's eyes. For a moment, he looked surprisingly ill at ease. "I'm not the faultless hero you think I am," he said in a low, gruff tone.

Shelley could see she'd made him uncomfortable with her praise. Which was no surprise, since she'd never known Colt to brag about his accomplishments. "And modest, too," she teased, going up on tiptoe to kiss his cheek, knowing full well how gallant he was deep inside. "I like that."

He studied her.

"All I'm trying to say is…you've given me everything I needed these last few weeks, and I appreciate it. More than I can say."

His conflicted expression intensified. He inhaled deeply, still brooding, and the phone rang. Whatever he'd been about to say to her cut short by the numbers on the caller ID screen, Colt said, "I have to get it—it's work," and answered the call.

"Yeah, McCabe." He fell silent. "I…" Frowning,

he listened even more intently. "Roger that," he said brusquely. "Thanks for calling." He hung up.

Shelley studied his furrowed brow. "Bad news?"

His lips tightened. "Work schedule change."

Oh, no.... "Tell me you don't have to work this weekend during any of the wedding activities."

He looked away, then strode over to check on Austin, who was playing trucks next to a contentedly watching Buddy. "I don't have to work at all until Monday." Colt gave Austin's shoulder a companionable pat. Her son rewarded Colt with a smile.

"You've got the next five days off? Really?"

Colt came back to Shelley's side, still looking a little stunned. "I don't go back until nine o'clock Monday morning."

Shelley failed to see what the problem was. She, for one, would love a little unexpected time off. "Well, that's great, isn't it?"

He seemed even more distant. Shrugged. "Yeah. Sure."

She studied him, concern welling deep inside her. "You could say it a little more convincingly."

He remained silent, as if his thoughts were a million miles away. Which left Shelley to guess what the real problem was. She gave the mushrooms a stir. "How often do you take time off?"

"Lately?" A bemused edge of his normal good humor crept back into Colt's expression. He paced the kitchen restlessly. "Not all that often."

If she didn't know better, she would think he was holding something back. Something important. "Do you use up all your vacation time every year?"

"Not so far, no."

Wondering if she would ever get him to totally open up so they could move forward with their relationship, she probed, "What happens to it?"

"It used to accrue. Now department policy is use it or lose it."

"What do the other deputies do?"

"Depends on the person," he said quietly. "If they're married or not."

"So if you were married...?"

He met her gaze and held it. "I'd probably take it."

"Did you when you were married before?"

He let out a breath, looking pained. "No, but... Yvette and I weren't getting along all that well, because of all the stuff with her ex."

"So you hid at work?" Shelley assumed, struggling not to push too hard.

"Maybe."

She lifted a brow. Waited.

"Okay. Yeah. I did. Plus, I really like being a member of the sheriff's department."

She checked on the potatoes, which still had a ways to go, and moved closer. She lounged by the counter next to him. "Even all the hall monitor stuff?"

He slanted her a sideways glance. "Obviously, I didn't enjoy evicting you."

"Glad to hear it."

"However—" he caught her by the waist and brought her against him "—I wouldn't have wanted to turn the task over to anyone else."

Heat spiraled through her middle, settling low. "Because you thought you could be more humane about it?"

He shrugged, beginning to struggle with his own

mounting desire. "I just knew I would watch out for you." He shifted her away from his hardness.

"And you did," Shelley concurred, aching for the time when they could be together the way she truly wanted. "Arranging people to help move my stuff, letting me store it here, even putting me up for a night."

"That, I would have liked to do longer."

It certainly would have made lovemaking a lot easier. "So I gathered," she concluded softly.

They exchanged smiles, clearly on the same page there.

"Why did you want to be in law enforcement?" Shelley removed the sautéed mushrooms, turned the burner up to high, added a little more butter and olive oil. When it was bubbling, she added the steaks and was rewarded with a sizzling sound.

"I like helping people."

More specifically... "Rescuing them."

He nodded.

"What about the rest of it? Arresting people you know?"

He plucked a carrot slice out of the salad. "Not so much fun."

Shelley munched on a radish. "Have you ever thought about doing anything else?"

Colt took three plates out of the cupboard and set them on the table. "I don't know what I'd be if I wasn't a cop."

"That's not really an answer to the question."

He grimaced. "No. I guess it isn't. Truth of the matter is, I like helping people, and law enforcement allows me to do that." He added cutlery to the table and then reached past her for the napkins. "What about you? Have you ever thought about being anything but a dance teacher?"

Shelley moved to accommodate him, lightly brushing his taut biceps in the process. "All the time."

He remained at her side. "Then what keeps you at it?"

Shelley cocked her head. "I guess I like helping people, too, and generally speaking—unless it's an unwilling child being dragged to class by a stage parent—"

"Or a clumsy best man in a wedding," Colt said with a wink.

"—dancing *does* make people happy."

Austin appeared at her feet and tugged on the hem of her skirt. "I happy, Momma."

So was she. More than she had been in a very long time. She lifted Austin up in her arms. "I know you are, sweetie."

Austin wiggled to get down, and went right back over to his canine pal. "Buddy happy."

Colt and Shelley shared a smile. "He sure seems to be," he said.

Austin crossed over to Colt. He looked up and raised his arms, wanting to be picked up. "Deppity happy?" Austin asked.

That, Shelley thought, studying the sudden, brooding expression back in Colt's eyes, was the question of the evening.

Colt knew Shelley deserved an explanation. However, the last thing he wanted to do was involve her in his problems when she had so much trouble of her own right now.

"Of course I'm happy," Colt told Austin as he obligingly lifted her son into his arms, and cuddled her little boy close. "I'm always happy when you and your mom and Buddy are around."

"Buddy nice."

"Yes, he is," Colt agreed.

"Buddy mine," Austin stated emphatically.

Colt paused, not sure how to explain, especially when one day in the near future that might well be true. Finally, he said, "Buddy and I have been together a long time, since he was a very tiny puppy."

Austin's lower lip thrust out. "No. My doggie. Mine!"

Colt couldn't help but grin. The little tyke was tenacious; he'd give him that.

Shelley frowned. "Don't encourage him, Colt. I'm trying to end this phase. Not extend it."

Colt sobered. "Sorry. You're right."

For the rest of the evening, Colt tried to explain that while Buddy was actually his dog, Buddy could be Austin's *friend.* "You can visit whenever you want. Buddy loves to see you, but the thing is, Austin, Buddy is part of my family. Buddy and I are a team. We belong together."

"My team!" Austin insisted, petting Buddy's head.

"I don't think he gets it," Shelley said with a sigh.

The funny thing was, Colt didn't really want the little tyke to get it. Not if it meant Austin distanced himself from either Buddy or Colt. He shrugged, able to envision the day when they would all live under one roof. "Maybe we should all be a team," he suggested mildly.

Shelley paused to consider that, her green eyes intent. "A friends and family type thing?"

Ultimately, he wanted a lot more than that. But

until he and Shelley both got their personal situations straightened out, this would have to do. "Sounds great to me." Colt grinned and encompassed them all in a hug.

Chapter 12

"Well, it's definitely not a good sign," Travis Anderson told Colt the next morning, after being informed of the latest developments in Colt's situation. "Being told to take vacation never is. On the other hand—" Travis shrugged and poured his client a cup of coffee "—the sheriff easily could have suspended or even fired you for removing that key and entering Shelley's former residence without following proper protocol."

No joke. Colt drank deeply of the strong, aromatic brew. "I really screwed up."

Travis topped off his own mug, then led the way from the break room back to his office. "Take it easy. You haven't been let go yet." The attorney sat down behind his desk. Colt took a client chair.

Travis studied him. "When do you return to work?"

"Monday morning. For a meeting in Ben Shepherd's office."

"Do you want me there?"

What he wanted, Colt thought, was to be able to tell Shelley everything. How he'd been playing fast and loose with the regulations for years. How up until now only the end result had mattered. How everything looked different now that she and her son had come into his life.

He wanted a more solid underpinning. He wanted to be able to lean on her the way she'd been leaning on him. But he couldn't do that. For starters, he had been instructed by his superiors to keep this entire situation out of the public realm. The only reason he could talk to Travis about it was because he was his attorney.

Second, Shelley had enough on her shoulders. Dealing with her louse of an ex-husband, losing her home, trying to get the inherited property back. He wasn't going to saddle her with his troubles, too.

"Because if you think it would help ward off any ill-advised action on the part of your employer," Travis continued, "I'd be happy to accompany you."

Pulled back into the conversation, as abruptly as he'd left it, Colt shook his head. "That would look like I'm expecting to be terminated."

"And you're not."

Colt exhaled wearily and shoved his hands through his hair. "At this point, I think it could go either way." The real question was, would Shelley stand by him if he did get fired? Or would she put him in the same category as her irresponsible, untrustworthy ex-husband…and kick him to the curb, too?

"Do you ever get the feeling that if it weren't for bad luck, we'd have no luck at all?" Kendall asked Shelley over the phone the next morning.

Unfortunately, Shelley knew exactly what the bride-to-be meant. Things sure seemed to have gone south lately. Aside from the exceptionally intense heat wave predicted to blanket the area over the next five days—thus insuring an absolutely blistering hot wedding weekend for Kendall and her groom—Shelley's newly blossoming romance with Colt had suddenly and unexpectedly hit a roadblock.

Why, Shelley didn't know.

Everything had seemed fine two days ago. In fact, when Colt had made love to her on the eve of the auction, it had felt as if she could count on him for absolutely everything.

After the auction, however, there'd been a change.

It was nothing she could put her finger on, exactly. They'd had a wonderful dinner. They'd played with Austin and Buddy until both fell asleep, then snuck up to Colt's bedroom and succumbed to the passion simmering between them. Truth was, she'd never felt such a searing physical connection to another man.

Emotionally, well, that was something else entirely. Last night there'd been something different. A peculiar quietness on Colt's part, as he'd held her close, then brought her to him to make love to her all over again. And though she'd had all of his body, she hadn't had all of his soul.

There was a tiny part of him that, when they weren't driving each other wild with pleasure, was a million miles away. And that indecipherable barrier between them had left her feeling a little out of the loop. Which was how she had used to feel when her ex was up to something he didn't want her to know about. Not that

Colt would be hiding anything financial or otherwise from her. Would he?

She shouldn't be thinking about any of this, Shelley informed herself sternly.

"I don't know." Kendall sounded near tears. "Sometimes I think Gerry and I should have shelved our dream of getting married in our hometown and just eloped."

Uh-oh. Pulled swiftly back to the present, Shelley asked, "What's wrong now?"

Kendall sighed. "You're not going to believe it. Or maybe you will. The moving van with all of our stuff in it broke down in the mountains of Tennessee. We just heard from our dads. They're waiting on a tow truck now to try to get the van off the highway, but there's a huge traffic jam. Apparently, it's a real mess."

Shelley could imagine. Ready to help in any way she could, she asked, "Where are you and Gerry now?"

"Arkansas. But we're going to have to double back to help them out because all of our belongings are going to have to be moved from the broken down truck into a new moving van. As soon as we get one, anyway."

It was Thursday morning. Kendall and Gerry were supposed to arrive with their moms late that evening.

"What is this going to do to your arrival time?"

"I have no idea. I mean, I know we'll make it to the rehearsal dinner on Friday…"

But, as it happened, Kendall and Gerry didn't make it to the rehearsal dinner. They weren't in Laramie County at all when everyone gathered at the church Friday evening.

The minister smiled at the bridesmaids and grooms-men surrounding him at the rear of the church. "Good news, everyone. The bride and groom and their families will be in Laramie at midnight tonight."

An exultant cheer went up. Austin and little Bethany, the flower girl, clapped, too, although Austin had to set his little red truck aside to do it.

"The more challenging news is, they've asked that we do the rehearsal without them."

"How are we going to do that?" the wedding planner, Patricia, asked.

The minister smiled. "We'll have everyone in the wedding party do their part, and then use stand-ins for the happy couple. I'm sure Shelley and Colt won't mind filling in for the bride and groom."

Did she mind?

Shelley couldn't say. All she knew for sure was that she was extremely nervous about Austin fulfilling *his* role. She was beginning to think he had another two-year molar coming in; he had been cranky and uncooperative all day.

Shelley set Austin down on the red carpet runner just inside the entrance to the historic chapel and knelt beside her son. "See what Bethany's doing?" Shelley pointed at the flower girl, walking slowly up the aisle, tossing petals in her wake. "You are going to follow her. And you're going to hold this wonderful blue pillow, just like I showed you, while you walk up the aisle."

Austin scowled at the pillow.

Colt knelt on the other side of her son. "It's a very important job," he told Austin, while surreptitiously easing the little red truck from her son's hands and sliding it into his pocket, then replacing it with the blue velvet ring pillow. "It's pretty big, too," Colt continued solemnly, "but I think you're big enough to carry it. What do you think?"

To Shelley's relief, Austin puffed out his little chest. "I can do it!" he said.

Colt encouraged him with a broad smile. "Great."

Austin took two steps forward, the pillow with the attached rings tilting precariously in his hands. A moment later, he turned and, oblivious to the music and the waiting minister, came back to Colt. "You come," he demanded.

"Honey you're supposed to do this by yourself," Shelley whispered.

"I. Want. My. Deppity!" Austin shouted at the top of his lungs.

Everyone chuckled.

Shelley shut her eyes and said a silent prayer for co-operation. "Austin. Honey…"

Austin dropped the pillow and latched on to Colt's hand. "Mine! My deppity!"

"Tell you what." Colt bent down to replace the pillow in Austin's hands. "How about you and I walk down the aisle and we'll carry the pillow together."

"That's not precedent," Patricia sputtered.

The reverend stepped in. "It's a joyous occasion, so, I say, whatever works."

Sensing he had just gotten his way, Austin beamed. The music continued. Colt escorted Austin up the aisle then turned back to Shelley. "It might look more scripted if you were on the other side," he said.

Everyone, including the wedding planner, nodded.

Shelley hurried to catch up. Together the three of them continued up the aisle, as if they were indeed a cohesive unit. Austin grinned widely. He looked from Shelley to Colt and back again. "You hold pillow, too, Momma."

Figuring the minister was right—whatever worked—Shelley did as her little boy suggested.

When they reached the altar, the wedding planner explained to Shelley, "Because Austin is so young, we're going to have him give the pillow to the minister, who will set it and the rings aside until the proper time." Patricia Wilson paused. "And then Austin will walk off into the wings, where his babysitter will be waiting to take him back to the nursery for the duration of the ceremony." This had also been explained, in depth, to Austin.

There was only one problem with that.

He refused to surrender the ring pillow. "No!" he yelled when the minister attempted to take it from him. Austin clasped the pillow tightly to his chest. "Mine!"

Less amused laughter followed.

Shelley knew that the last thing everyone needed was a recalcitrant toddler messing up the ceremony for Kendall and Gerry.

She lifted a staying hand. "Austin. Honey…"

Once again, Colt came to the rescue. He knelt in front of Austin, deftly removed the rings from the fastening and replaced them with the little red truck. Colt pointed in the direction of the babysitter. "Can you carry your truck on that pillow, all the way over there, all by yourself?"

Again, Austin puffed out his little chest. "Yes," he told his deppity. "I. Can."

And just like that, Shelley noted, another crisis was averted.

* * *

Shelley knew that Colt had been on edge about the prospect of dancing up the aisle. Fortunately, the choreography went smoothly for the entire wedding party. It was the rehearsal of the actual wedding ceremony that gave them both trouble. The moment the minister asked them to fill in for the bride and the groom, everything got fuzzy.

It felt surreal to be standing next to Colt, as if they were actually getting married, as the minister began. Colt looked similarly dazed.

Was that what it would feel like, Shelley wondered, looking deep into Colt's eyes, if she and he ever did wed?

And was he thinking the same thing?

It seemed so as the two of them went to the altar together. Candles in hand, they lit the unity candle, symbolizing the merging of two hearts and souls into one. And it seemed even more real when they returned to their places in front of the minister and began to recite the vows.

"Will you live together, as friend and mate? Will you love him as a person, respect him as an equal, sharing joy as well as sorrow, triumph as well as defeat? And keep him beside you as long as you both shall live?" the minister asked her.

Shelley choked up. "I do," she whispered, and could have sworn she saw Colt's eyes shimmer, too.

The minister turned to Colt, his expression as sober as the situation demanded. "Will you listen to her innermost thoughts, be considerate and tender in your care of her, stand by her faithfully, and accept full responsibility for her every necessity as long as you both shall live?"

Looking more serious than she had ever seen him, Colt said, "I do." And the way he looked at her then, Shelley could almost believe it.

The chapel was hushed. The minister brought forward the rings. "There are two rings because there are two people. They are a symbol of their commitment to each other, and the new life these two people are beginning."

Hands trembling, Shelley slid the drugstore ring on Colt's finger. "I give you this ring as I give you myself, with love and affection."

Colt placed the ring on Shelley's finger. Huskily, he repeated the same vow.

Tears brimmed in Shelley's eyes.

"And here's where the 'groom' will kiss the 'bride,'" the minister announced.

And then, to everyone's surprise, Colt did just that.

Shelley saw the kiss coming. She could have avoided it. Like she could have avoided so much else in her life. But the truth was, she wanted Colt. Wanted to feel his chest pressed up against hers, and his arms around her. She wanted to feel the warm, sure pressure of his lips on hers. Boy, did she ever!

It was only an instant, but it was the kind of instant that changed everything. That made them go from two old flames who were just messing around, to two people who just might be on the verge of something long-lasting and truly meaningful. It was the kind of kiss that opened up a lifetime of possibilities and made dreams come true. It was the kind of kiss that grabbed you by the heart and soul...and never let go.

Even when the laughter rose, and they moved apart, something was different. Something was wonderful and special, and oh, so romantic.

And that feeling intensified as the evening progressed, and the group went on to the rehearsal dinner, where, to their delight, the real bride and groom and their respective families eventually did show up. Where laughter and hugs and tears were given all around. Toasts made. Promises given. Wishes fulfilled.

And it was on that note that the prewedding celebration ended, and Colt and Shelley took their leave. They walked out of the restaurant together, into the warm starlit night. It was barely ten o'clock.

"What time is the babysitter expecting you?" Colt asked gruffly.

There was no mistaking the ardent light in his eyes. Or the fierce longing in Shelley's heart. "I told her midnight."

"Want to go to my place?"

Shelley smiled. "I do."

Buddy was asleep on his cushion next to the fireplace when they walked in the front door. He lifted his head, thumped his tail, then sighed and lay back down again.

"Is he all right?" Shelley asked, going over to check. Buddy thumped his tail again, stretched, but did not get up.

She looked into his dark liquid eyes and petted him. He leaned into her touch affectionately, and let out another sigh.

Colt squatted down to join them.

"He's just tired," Colt said. "And knows that when I come in this late, I usually just head on to bed."

"You don't have to take him out?" she asked.

"He handles that himself, via the dog door that leads into the backyard."

"Ah," she said with an understanding nod.

"Right now, I think he wants to go back to sleep."

Shelley rose along with Colt. He took her hand and led the way to the kitchen. "Want to get something to drink?" he asked.

Hand to his wrist, she stopped him before he could hit the lights. "No," she said softly, "I don't."

He backed her up against the counter, his large body trapping hers. "Then what do you want?" he murmured seductively.

She reached for the knot of his tie, undid that and the first few buttons of his shirt. "What I've wanted all evening. You."

Hands beneath her hips, he lifted her so she was sitting on the counter. Hands circling her back, he stepped between her legs. "You know what I want?" He strung kisses across the top of her head, the shell of her ear, the nape of her neck.

She shook her head, willing him to open up and be vulnerable, too.

"I wished it were us tonight, getting married," he whispered. His arms tightened around her as he buried his face in her hair.

Her heart ached with happiness. Moisture welled in her eyes. "Oh, Colt…"

He drew back, locked eyes and rubbed his thumb along the curve of her cheekbone. "I wish I'd never stood you up, and that we had never split up. Or married other people...."

Shelley sighed. As much as she wanted to go back in time.... Hands on his shoulders, she looked at him soberly. "We weren't ready to get married then."

"Things are different now."

"I know," Shelley concurred. "More so than I ever would have expected, even a few weeks ago."

He clasped her hands in his. "Do you want to get married again?"

He'd been honest. She needed to be forthright, too. Her lower lip trembled. "I'm beginning to see how it might be possible."

He smiled tenderly. "Me, too."

He captured her lips, kissing her deeply, and she kissed him back with just as much passion. Hungering for more, he gripped her hips, stepping even more fully into the apex of her legs. Pressed up against all that hard, male muscle, sent heat soaring through her. And him.

His hands glided upward, over her ribs. One palm cupped her breast. The fingers on the other hand inched down the back zipper of her dress. Before she knew it, her shoulders were bare, her bra was unhooked. And still they kissed, even as he pushed away the cloth, and his thumbs found the tender crests. His lips followed his hands. His fingers found their way inside her bikini panties, adoring anew, and she sucked in a breath, shockingly turned on. Reduced to a quivering, aching mass, she heard herself making sounds she'd never made before.

He laughed in satisfaction and returned his lips to hers, kissing her more deeply still. "Colt. I want..."

"I know."

She flattened her hands against the solid wall of his chest, gasped softly. "Now."

He touched her again, his fingers gently paving the way.

And then they were sliding off her confining silk panties, undoing his pants, and still he kept right on stroking her thighs until something shattered inside her...and she climaxed with an intensity that stunned them both.

His control snapped, and soon he was doing some demanding of his own. Bringing her all the way to the edge of the counter, he slid into her with one smooth, hard thrust. She lost her breath as she moved to meet him, clamping down around him, the pleasure so intense they both cried out with it. And still they kissed, their bodies moving in perfect union, laying claim to the need, to the night, to each other, until ecstasy reigned and passion won out once again.

Basking in the sweet afterglow, Shelley knew, at long last, what she'd been trying so hard to deny. This relationship was different from any she'd ever had. It was real. It was true. It was the heart and soul of her future.

More important still, if the way Colt had just made love to her was any indication, he felt that way, too.

Chapter 13

"If I didn't know better, I'd think you and Colt were the ones getting married today," the wedding planner teased, as she and Shelley unpacked the boxes of white satin bows that would decorate the sanctuary of the chapel.

Colt came in from the outside, bringing with him a blast of sweltering Texas heat. "If this is about Shelley and I stepping in for the bride and groom at the rehearsal last night—"

"It is," another bridesmaid teased.

A groomsman said, "Those vows sure looked real to me."

They'd felt real, Colt thought. To him, and unless he missed his guess, to Shelley, too.

But wary of embarrassing her in front of the wedding party, Colt quipped, "Those vows are real—to

Kendall and Gerry." He set down the boxes of flowers next to the ones he'd already carried in. "And how come the lucky couple isn't here helping us decorate the chapel, anyway? I thought that was part of the original plan." His deliberately clueless comments created the uproar he expected.

"Oh, for heaven's sake!" Patricia exclaimed. "Everyone knows the bride and groom can't see each other on their wedding day until the ceremony begins. Otherwise, it's bad luck."

Colt slipped Shelley a wink only she could see, and pretended to be even more obtuse. "And here I thought that was just insurance, to keep the two from kissing. You know, so the bride wouldn't mess up her makeup or hair."

"Well, it's easy to see where your mind is," one of the bridesmaids joshed.

Shelley and Colt exchanged bemused glances.

"Same place it was last night when you planted one on Shelley..." a groomsman added.

Still holding Shelley's gaze, Colt smiled and continued with comically exaggerated seriousness, "I was just trying to get us all in the right mind-set for the romantic goings-on today."

Guffaws abounded. "Mmm-hmm," the wedding planner interjected, clearly not believing his fib for one second. "I know passion when I see it." Patricia wagged her finger at Colt and Shelley. "And you two lovebirds have something very intense going on between the two of you, whether you want to admit it or not."

Shelley rolled her eyes, her cheeks flushing self-consciously. "As gratifying as it is to have you-all defining our relationship for us," she drawled to everyone listening, "we really need to get back to work…"

"Agreed," the wedding planner added. She started barking out orders right and left for the attendants to decorate the pews with white satin ribbons and bows, and bouquets of baby's breath and pink roses. Unfortunately, the constant activity did nothing to halt the speculation.

By the time the work was done, and Colt and Shelley left the church, she could barely look him in the eye.

Colt caressed her with a glance. "They're just teasing us, you know."

Shelley released a pent-up sigh. "I was hoping to keep this all private."

That was hard to do, Colt mused, when they could not seem to stay away from each other. He led Shelley through the shimmering noon heat to his pickup truck. They didn't have a lot of time, since both of them had to shower and change and get back to the church by 2:00 p.m. for formal preceremony photos. He opened the passenger door to his truck and let the accumulated heat pour out. Wishing he could kiss her, he consoled, "It is private."

"Not when you two look at each other like you're the answer to each other's prayers!" a bridesmaid called out, moving past.

Shelley pressed the flat of her hand to her forehead. "Will you-all stop?" she shouted back.

"Just admit you two are an item again and we'll stop," another bridesmaid teased, climbing into her car.

Colt took one look at Shelley's face and knew she'd had enough. "Let's get out of here," he said gruffly. Hand beneath her elbow, he lifted her up into the cab, watched as she folded her lithe body into the leather seat of his pickup.

He circled around behind the wheel and then started the engine.

"Maybe we should admit something," he suggested mildly.

Shelley bit her lip as warm air poured out of the AC vents. "We will," she promised, still looking a little distracted and conflicted, "but right now it's Gerry and Kendall's day. And the focus should be entirely on them."

Colt hadn't considered that. "You're right." He pulled out of the parking lot and headed down Main Street, waiting at the red light before turning onto Oak. Intending to take the back way to Shelley's apartment, he turned again onto the less traveled Crockett Avenue. And that was when they both saw him—the silver-haired man weaving uncertainly in the scorching midday heat, before lurching forward and collapsing facedown on the cement sidewalk.

Colt knew who it was, even before he steered over to the curb, and he and Shelley jumped out of the truck. They both raced to help.

"Mr. Zellecky!" Shelley knelt beside him. "Are you all right?"

The older gentleman merely groaned. Turned slightly. Blood oozed from a cut on his forehead. His right wrist was tilted crookedly. Broken, Colt thought.

Mr. Zellecky moaned again, in obvious pain.

Colt pulled out his cell phone, dialed 9-1-1 and reported the situation. Assured paramedics were on the way, he turned back to Mr. Zellecky. "Don't move. The ambulance will be here shortly."

"I gotta get up," Mr. Zellecky said in a slurred voice that denoted precariously low blood sugar levels. "I have to get to Nellie. She needs me..."

"You'll see Mrs. Zellecky," Colt promised, patting the older gentleman's hand. "But first we have to take care of you."

Shelley knew by the conflicted look on Colt's face when he arrived to take her and Austin to the church several hours later, that all was still not well. "How are things with Mr. Zellecky?"

With the tenderness borne of a real father, Colt stepped in to help finish what Shelley had been attempting to do—secure her son's clip-on bowtie. "They were taking him to surgery to repair his broken wrist when I left the E.R."

Shelley stepped back to give Colt room to work. "Oh, dear."

Colt lifted Austin into his arms so her son could check out Colt's neckwear and "adjust it," too. Colt's sober look turned to a grin as Austin patted him affectionately on the cheeks. "They're going to keep him in the hospital for a few days, try and figure out what is going on with his diabetes."

Shelley stepped closer when Austin made a lunge for her, too, then wrapped an arm about both of them, her heart brimming with joy and contentment.

Aware she'd never felt more like a family, Shelley paused to drink in the poignancy of the moment. "Does anyone know what Mr. Zellecky was doing out in this heat?"

Colt shook his head. He turned to her, the minty warmth of his breath brushing her upturned face. "His daughter was on the way, though, so I'm sure she'll figure it out."

Austin squirmed. Colt set him down and watched him toddle off to find his red truck.

Shelley studied Colt. "This isn't your fault. It may have happened even if Mr. Zellecky still had his driver's license."

Colt nodded, an indistinguishable emotion flickering in his eyes. Intellectually, he seemed to know she was right. Emotionally was a different matter. It was also clear he didn't want to discuss it further.

Shelley knew they were going to have to put that aside and concentrate on the happy day ahead.

Luckily, at the church, everything went exactly as planned.

Kendall was a radiant bride. Gerry, the beaming groom. The flower girl looked adorable spreading petals across the satin runner that draped the center aisle, and Austin not only carried the real wedding rings with the dignity required, but surrendered them in exchange for his little red truck, which he promptly carried off on the blue velvet ring pillow to the babysitter waiting in the wings.

Shelley breathed a sigh of relief. Colt reached over and squeezed her hand. And the procession began.

The hopelessly romantic rock ballad followed. The dancing down the aisle elicited a joyous reaction from the guests.

"You definitely earned a gold star today," Colt told Shelley hours later when the father-daughter dance had ended and the rest of the wedding party took the floor at the reception. Enjoying the soft, sweet essence of her, he caught her against him. "That dance was truly something."

"Thanks…and you really did look good today," Shelley praised, gazing up into his eyes.

So had she. "And it's all due to you." *And all the time the two of us have spent making love recently.* The physical and emotional intimacy had left them in synch in a way he had never dreamed possible. "It's turned out to be a really great wedding, hasn't it?"

Shelley nodded. "I don't think there's a person here who doesn't believe Kendall and Gerry are really meant for each other."

Colt had never liked weddings, but he was enjoying this one, maybe because she was here beside him.

"All you have to do is look at them to know they're really going to be happy. Not just for now, but the rest of their lives." Her expression wistful, she studied the bride and groom and then turned back to him. "My parents had that."

Colt felt his heart clench. "So do mine."

Her eyes filled with longing. "I want that." She just didn't seem to know if she would ever have it.

Knowing now wasn't the time to talk about what their relationship was—or could be—Colt brushed his lips across her temple. He brought her closer still, reveling in her intoxicating allure. "I do, too."

And one day, he thought, as the reception continued to unfold, they would both realize all their hopes and dreams.

Shortly after midnight, the DJ played the last song of the night. The bride and groom departed via limo to their honeymoon suite in nearby San Angelo. Colt, Shelley and the rest of the wedding party were left with the task of carrying the gifts out to the cars for transport to Kendall's parents' home.

Once that had been completed, Colt drove Shelley back to her apartment. Wondering just how tired she was, reluctant for the evening to end, he cut the engine. A comfortable silence fell. "I imagine Austin is long asleep."

Shelley answered his smile with a sultry grin. "I called a little while ago. The babysitter said he was so tired he fell asleep before she could even get him in his crib."

"Poor little tyke."

The mood shifted, became more intimate still. "Want to come up?"

"For a nightcap?" he teased.

She held his eyes a long, telling moment. "Or... whatever."

He caught her hand and lifted it to his lips. "Sounds good to me."

Before that could happen, a chime sounded. Shelley removed the cell phone from her purse, stared at the screen. "Why would the Laramie County Jail be calling me? Never mind at this time of night!" The phone went silent after the second chime. Frowning, Shelley accessed her voice mail.

Colt watched her face go pale. "What did the message say?"

Grimly, Shelley turned on the speaker and hit the replay button.

Her ex-husband's noxious voice filled the cab of his truck. "Darn it all, Shelley, have you lost your mind... accusing me of fraud, and letting them issue a bench warrant for my arrest!"

Shelley tensed as Tully continued his tirade. "The jail gave me one phone call, Shelley, and you're it. So, if you ever want to get your house back, you better drop those charges and get me out of here! Tonight!" *Click.*

Shelley slumped against the seat, looking as miserable as Colt had ever seen her. She rubbed at her temples. "I can't believe Tully called me instead of his parents."

Colt could.

Realizing she hadn't thought it through to what it would feel like to have her ex hauled off to jail as a result of her criminal complaint, Colt stated matter-of-factly, "What Tully did or did not do with his one phone call is not your problem."

Unfortunately, he could see that the tenderhearted Shelley didn't quite believe that. "What if he got the money together he owed me?" she asked, biting her lip.

"Then he would have come right out and said so," Colt countered, sure Tully was still playing her for a sucker.

Still clearly wanting to avoid any ugliness if at all possible, Shelley fell silent.

Frustration churned through him. Much as he didn't want to insert himself into the middle of this, he would do anything to protect her and Austin from further harm. "You want someone to talk to Tully?"

Shelley turned to Colt in obvious relief, the color coming back into her cheeks. "Would you?"

Glad Shelley hadn't insisted on coming down to the county jail herself—for that would have intimated that she was never going to be able to separate herself from her irresponsible ex-husband—Colt left Shelley at her apartment and drove to lockup.

There, his problems really started.

"I don't think it's a good idea," the desk sergeant said.

Normally, it wouldn't have been. But these were extenuating circumstances. "I only need a minute."

"To do what?" the sergeant countered.

"Let Laffer know that Shelley isn't bailing him out of this mess."

"And?"

"Get the name and number of an attorney or other friend I can call who will help Laffer post bail, since he squandered his first call on Shelley."

The sergeant stood. "That's real sweet of you, McCabe, but why not just let him sit in jail?"

That definitely was Colt's inclination. Not to mention he was bending the rules—again. "Because I want this wrapped up as swiftly as possible," he confessed. "And the sooner Laffer gets a lawyer and gets out of here, the sooner we can *all* go on with our lives."

"Well, can't fault you for that," the desk sergeant concurred with a long-suffering sigh. "'Cause he is one entitled fellow who has a way of spreading misery wherever he goes."

"Tell me about it," Colt grumbled.

Minutes later, he was in the conference room with Tully. Gone were the usual expensive clothes and sunglasses—in their place an ill-fitting orange jumpsuit and handcuffs. He looked unkempt, angry and defiant.

"I wanted Shelley."

Very aware of the two guards standing sentry on opposite sides of the small room, Colt settled in the chair opposite Tully. "She's not coming. She's not doing anything for you. So if you have someone else you want me to call on your behalf…?" Colt waited, pen and paper in hand.

"Just her."

Colt rose with a dismissive shrug. "I tried."

Shock turned to hatred. "You're not going to get her back, you know."

I already have.

"She's always going to be sweet on me," Tully taunted.

Colt tried to keep his temper in check. "And you know this because…?"

"We have a connection."

He pushed the chair toward the table with a decisive thud. "That ended when you divorced."

Tully slouched. "It'll never end. She'll always care about me because she's the mother of my child. And she'll always forgive me no matter what I do, because that's the kind of woman she is—loving and loyal, sweet and tender—"

Seething, Colt stormed out of the conference room.

And saw Shelley standing at the end of the hall. In a pair of faded jeans, boots and a dark blue T-shirt, she looked pretty as could be.

His first thought was: she shouldn't be here. His second: Why *was* she here?

Aware all eyes were on them, Colt strode toward her. Of course she hadn't done as he asked. Of course she wouldn't trust this to him. Or anyone else, for that matter. Not that he had.

Anxiously, she asked, "Did you get a number or a name?"

He drew a deep breath. Hand to her elbow, he guided

her out through the double doors to the steps at the front of the building. "He wasn't interested."

Shelley's shoulders slumped. "He still wants to talk to me."

Colt shrugged. "A lot of people want a lot of different things. It doesn't mean it's going to happen."

Shelley sighed, ran a hand through her hair. "I'll notify his parents."

"You don't have to do that."

She looked at him, more miserable than ever. "I know I don't, Colt," she told him in a low voice, firm with resolve, "but it's the decent thing to do."

He needed to understand why, find out where this was all leading. He narrowed his eyes. "Because you were once married?"

She leaned back against the limestone and crossed her arms in front of her. "And because," she said very quietly, "whether I am able to save my house from being sold to another buyer or not, I want justice done…and I want this to be over. And letting Tully's parents know—through neutral channels—that he is in jail on charges of fraud is the fastest way to accomplish that."

Shelley knew Colt didn't agree with her plan, but to his credit, he backed her anyway. He returned to the apartment with her, waited while she paid her sitter, then walked the teenager out and made sure she got safely into her car for her short drive home.

Colt returned to the apartment. He brewed a pot of coffee and made himself at home while Shelley pulled out her laptop computer and got to work.

Half an hour later, she had written emails to both her

attorney, Liz Cartwright-Anderson, and the law firm that represented Mr. and Mrs. Laffer, stating where Tully was, and why, and that he had come to her for help, which she refused to give. Hence, she was turning it over to the lawyers to sort things out in whatever way they saw fit.

Finished, she let Colt see the letters she'd sent, then the two of them settled on the sofa in her apartment.

In the bedroom nearby, Austin slept on.

It was nearly three in the morning. The wedding and reception seemed light-years away. Yet Shelley was no more willing to let Colt go now than she had been earlier in the evening.

Aware she was much more comfortable in jeans and a scoop-necked T-shirt than he was in his tuxedo shirt and pants, Shelley let her eyes drift over him. He looked so sexy, with his sleeves rolled up and the first few buttons of his shirt undone. She reached over and took his hand in hers. "I'm sorry I asked you to speak to Tully on my behalf."

He stared at her. "Why did you come to the jail when you knew I was already down there, handling it?"

Guilt rushed through her. She drew a deep, enervating breath. "Because I realized I was doing it again, running from responsibility and just letting things happen without being actively involved in the resolution. I don't want to ever do that again, Colt. I want to know that I'm capable of solving my problems myself."

He studied her, his eyes inscrutable. "And you think going down to the jail was a step in the right direction?"

"Yes. Just as filing charges was the right thing to do."

"Sure it wasn't a step in Tully's direction?"

The knowledge he might be feeling a little jealous sent a rush of affection rushing through her, as well as the need to reassure him frankly and honestly. "I don't love Tully, Colt. In retrospect, I'm not sure I ever did, because to love someone you have to first know them, and Tully was never truly up-front with me about anything.

"I mean, he was great, at least in the beginning, at showing me a good time. But when our relationship was put to the test—" Shelley paused and shook her head ruefully "—he was *never* completely honest with me. He *never* told me everything that was going on with him. It was a lousy way to live. I can't ever do it again."

Which meant, Colt thought, he was in a heap of trouble, given all he had been keeping from Shelley. Some by choice. Some not.

Mistaking his silence for something other than guilt, Shelley slid over onto his lap. Gazing at him affectionately, she threaded her fingers through his hair. "You, on the other hand, always tell me what you're thinking and feeling." She wrinkled her nose playfully. "Even at times like tonight when you know it's not what I want to hear...."

If only it were that simple. Aware he felt content and remorseful at the same time, Colt shifted her even closer and buried his face in her hair. "Don't make me out to be a saint. I'm not even close."

"You're closer than you know, Colt McCabe," she said softly, undoing another button, and then another, on his starched white shirt. Her hands slid inside to caress his chest. "Which is why," she murmured, kissing him tenderly, "I've fallen so hard and fast for you."

And why, Colt thought, she could easily stop falling so hard for him. The good thing was, she wasn't going to know. Not tonight. Maybe not ever, if he had his way.

In the meantime, he could do his best to continue to protect her and give her everything she needed. And what she needed right now was him, Colt thought as he drew her down to a bed of pillows on the floor.

Heart pounding, he rolled her onto her side and stretched out beside her. Damned, if, in the soft light of the apartment, she wasn't the prettiest she'd been all night. Although she'd been gorgeous in that yellow silk bridesmaid dress, it was nothing compared to how she looked now, with her auburn hair down and mussed, navy T-shirt pushed up above her ribs, the waistband of her jeans riding low on her hips.

Her lips were as pink as her cheeks. Her eyes hot with desire. Her skin as soft and smooth as satin.

She reached for the button on his pants. "Let's get these off."

He obliged, even as he did a little handiwork of his own.

Naked, they stretched out again. "Come on, lawman," she coaxed. "Time's awastin'."

The spark that had been evident all night ignited. He kissed her again, giving and taking, angling his head until she arched her back, lifting herself to him. Stroking her with his hands and branding her with his lips, he claimed her as surely as she claimed him. Until she was shifting overtop of him, doing some demanding of her own.

Her eyes met his. Their mouths collided as surely as their bodies in a deep, soul-shattering kiss. When she surrounded him with her sweet warmth, he went as deep as he could go…and still they couldn't get enough. Couldn't give enough. Couldn't stop the fierce kaleidoscope of passion. Until there was nothing but the two of them…nothing but this moment in time.

Chapter 14

"What doing, Momma?" Austin asked Shelley early Sunday afternoon.

Shelley paused to pick up her son. She showed him the potato salad she was packing in ice. "I'm making food for a picnic supper."

Austin looked over the portable containers of Southern-style green beans, sliced melon and berries. "Deppity?"

"Yes. Colt and Buddy are both going with us to Lake Laramie."

Austin considered that. "Soon?" he asked.

Shelley consulted her watch. "Probably in fifteen minutes."

Or, knowing Colt, who had a tendency to be early for their dates, even sooner.

His little red truck in hand, Austin went back over to the basket of toys next to the sofa. Happily awaiting their guests, he sat down and pulled out several more vehicles.

The doorbell rang. Austin beamed and stood. "Deppity?"

Sharing her son's excitement, Shelley placed the last of the fried chicken onto paper towels to drain. She turned off the stove and hurried to get the door. Instead of the man she expected to see, a woman stood there, leather notepad in one hand, a badge in the other.

"Shelley Meyerson? Ilyse Adams—we've met before. I'd like to talk to you about Colt McCabe, if I may."

All sorts of scenarios raced through Shelley's mind, none of them good. "He's all right, isn't he?"

Another official-looking smile. The kind that prefaced serious business. "I'm here about something else."

Stymied, Shelley ushered her in.

Austin toddled over. "Not Deppity," he announced unhappily.

"No. Not Deppity." Shelley resituated her son with his toys, and then asked Investigator Adams, "Can I get you something to drink?"

She opened her notebook. "I'd prefer to get right down to business."

This was starting to sound scary, Shelley thought as she sat opposite her at the kitchen table.

Ms. Adams turned on a tape recorder and set it on the table between them. "What is your relationship with Colt McCabe?"

Wasn't that the question of the day? Shelley mused. "We're friends," she offered casually.

"Just friends?"

Shelley's gut tightened. "Close friends."

Her guest's glance narrowed. "Are the two of you romantically involved?"

Uneasiness sifted through Shelley. "That is none of your business."

"So you prefer not to answer that?" Ilyse Adams pressed.

Shelley sat back. Determined to remain calm in the face of rising anxiety, she folded her hands in front of her. "What's this all about?" She paused, letting her resistance to this line of questioning be known. "Why do you care who Colt is seeing in his private life?"

Investigator Adams raised her brow. "Did you know he has a reputation for bending the rules to help people, in sometimes unorthodox ways, particularly when he feels he is rescuing someone?"

Shelley shrugged. "That's no secret. He's always been a bit of a maverick."

A brief pause. "Why is that, do you think?"

Shelley let out a long breath. "He's not really the hall-monitor type. He doesn't get a charge out of getting anyone else in trouble."

"So he has trouble arresting people, even when they do wrong. Is that what you're saying?"

Shelley shook her head. "He likes to let people off with a warning. Give them a second chance."

A tight smile. "Yet Deputy McCabe didn't do that when it came to the attempted break-in of your former home."

Shelley blinked. This was really getting surreal. "What break-in?"

It was the investigator's turn to look surprised. "You didn't know about the three teenagers who tried to use the residence for an underage drinking party?"

Shock rendered Shelley momentarily speechless. "No."

"Or that Deputy McCabe caught them in the act, and called it in?"

"No. He never said anything." Which led Shelley to wonder what else Colt hadn't told her.

Ilyse Adams picked up on Shelley's unease. "Can you tell me what happened with the auction of your home at 903 Spring Street?"

"The house didn't sell."

Investigator Adams studied her. "How did you feel about that?"

Shelley glanced at her son, who was still playing quietly. Relieved he had no idea what was going on, she turned back. "How do you think I felt?" Her tone was a little curt. "Relieved."

"Did you have anything to do with the rumors about the purported condition of the house, started by Colt McCabe?"

What rumors? "I have no idea what you're talking about."

"Did you ask Colt McCabe to infer there was something wrong with the property prior to the auction?"

"No!" Shelley quickly denied. "Why would I do that when it's clearly not the case?"

A telltale silence fell.

"Oh," Shelley said heavily, feeling even more distressed. "You're asserting that Colt did that."

The heavy silence confirmed that was so.

Adams continued, "Did you offer Deputy McCabe anything in return for such activities?"

"Like what?"

Ilyse Adams shrugged, waited.

"Money?" Shelley guessed finally.

"Or something more personal," Adams offered, her words rife with meaning.

More personal. Shelley guessed where this was going. "Like sex," she stated bluntly, glad Austin was way too young and innocent to understand what was being inferred here.

Looking as if she believed that was indeed the situation, Investigator Adams gave Shelley a chance to expand on that statement.

An angry flush climbed from Shelley's neck into her cheeks. "No. I did not offer myself up in exchange for anything else. With Colt or any other law enforcement officer! I would never do that!"

Investigator Adams tilted her head. "It's common knowledge that you were pretty upset when Deputy McCabe posted the eviction notice and supervised the actual move-out."

This was getting ridiculous! "Well, duh! Of course I was."

"With him, specifically."

Embarrassed by her highly emotional reaction at that time, Shelley blew out a weary breath. "When I thought about it, I realized Colt was just doing his job."

"Yet, immediately after that, the two of you became...close."

The way the internal affairs officer said it made her liaison with Colt sound sordid and ugly when it hadn't been. Shelley stood, went to the front door, and opened it wide. "I don't know what you're trying to do here, but you are way off target. Colt would never do any of the things you've insinuated."

Taking the hint, Adams stood and politely gathered her belongings.

Shelley noted the tape recorder was still on.

"Are you sure about that?"

That was the hell of it. Right now, given all she had just learned, Shelley honestly didn't know what to think. She did know, however, that Colt McCabe had a lot of explaining to do. And it wouldn't be done in front of her son.

Mystified, Colt put down the phone and looked at his canine companion. "Change of plans, fella. Shelley wants to meet us here."

Five minutes later, Shelley parked her Prius at the curb. Colt had only to look at the way she carried herself to know she was really upset. But then, he had gathered that on the phone, although she hadn't given him a clue why. Her face a blotchy pink, she marched to the door. Unable to mistake the boiling fury and resentment in her eyes, Colt stepped out to greet her. "Where's Austin?"

"With his babysitter. I didn't want him to hear what I had to say."

Colt moved to usher her inside. She remained on the porch, arms crossed in front of her. "Ilyse Adams, from the Laramie County Sheriff's Department, visited me this afternoon."

Like lightning, the guilt that had been weighing on him since the inquiry began came back to haunt him.

"Are you under investigation?" Shelley snapped.

Knowing nothing would be gained by becoming overemotional, Colt took her by the hand and led her into his home. "Yes."

Shelley got as far as the foyer, then sank down on the steps, leading to the second floor. "Why?"

Colt sat beside her. "It appears I've broken too many rules," he confided.

She grew even more distraught. "Regarding me?"

Colt knew she was going to put the pieces together eventually. "Sort of."

She waited.

Exhaling deeply, Colt continued. "The night of the wreck I didn't follow procedure when I rushed you and Austin and Mr. Zellecky to the hospital. A complaint was lodged against me by the out-of-towners—they said I gave preferential treatment to the town residents over them."

Shelley leaped to her feet, fists at her sides. "That's not true."

Colt stood, too. "It doesn't matter." He followed at a distance as she paced to the fireplace. "It was enough to spark an internal affairs investigation into my behavior that has since been expanded."

Misery turned the corners of her lips down. "To me, too. Ilyse Adams thinks I slept with you so you'd spread rumors about my house to keep it from selling at auction."

Colt swore heatedly.

"Naturally, I told her it wasn't true. That I hadn't offered you a quid pro quo for anything."

Colt worked to contain his own temper. "I can't believe this."

Shelley edged closer, studying him with a critical eye. "But you did start the rumors, didn't you?"

Colt winced. "Not on purpose." Reluctantly, he pushed on. "Mitzy Martin stopped by to inquire about the house.

She wanted to see it so she could decide whether or not to make a bid. But the rules governing property set for auction by Laramie County wouldn't allow anyone to set foot inside the home once the foreclosure and eviction were complete, so I had to refuse her request."

Shelley's brow furrowed. "But you did bend the rules the night Austin lost his little red truck!"

Colt shifted uncomfortably. "That was different."

Shocked and dismayed, she concluded, "Because it was for me and Austin. Not Mitzy…right?"

What could Colt say to that? It was true. He hadn't been applying the rules fairly. Still, Shelley deserved to know how the rest of the situation had come about.

"That day, Mitzy also asked me a ton of questions about the condition of the interior of your home. For the same procedure-related reasons, I couldn't answer any of them. As a result, she jumped to all sorts of conclusions, which I again could not correct." He cleared his throat. "Next thing I hear, her version has hit the local rumor mill. Everyone is speculating you let the house go because it required so many expensive repairs, it just wasn't going to be worth it."

Shelley sighed. "Which was why no one bid on it."

"Probably, yeah."

"And now the Internal Affairs of Laramie County Sheriff's Department thinks I had something to do with that, too!" Shelley cried. "That I may have acted improperly in collusion with you to prevent the auction of my house!"

Colt swore again. What a mess. "I'll set them straight. I promise, you won't get in trouble over any of this."

She scoffed and stalked away from him, even more indignant. "That's not really the problem here, Colt."

This was not the way he'd seen the day going. "Then what is?"

Shelley swung around again. "Why didn't you—or anyone else in Laramie, for that matter—tell me my house was nearly broken into?"

Colt returned her scowl. "Several reasons. The property wasn't yours anymore—you'd been evicted, so technically it was no longer any of your business. And probably no one else mentioned it because they didn't want to upset you."

But the hell of it was, Colt realized in retrospect, she was upset. More so now, probably, than she would have been then.

"And the internal affairs investigation?" Shelley asserted tightly. "I assume this is a pretty big deal."

Enough to cost me my career. Enough to prompt me to go to an attorney for advice.

Unfortunately, he hadn't followed the counsel he had received from Travis Anderson. Instead, he had listened to his heart. And his heart had taken him right back to Shelley, and her son, and his need to protect them both.

Shelley fixed him with a coolly assessing look. "Why didn't you tell me about that?"

"First, I was told by the department to keep it quiet. They didn't want it hitting the press or becoming public knowledge. Second, I was trying to protect you. You already had so much to deal with... I didn't want to burden you with my problems."

Hurt overrode her resentment. "It didn't occur to you that I might have wanted to know something like that? That I'd want to support you?" Her voice quavered. "Because that's what people do, you know, people who are close. They turn to each other. Or is our relationship always going to be one-sided?"

He hadn't seen her look so vulnerable since the first time they had broken up. He took her into his arms. "You're being unfair."

Tears glistening in her eyes, she whirled away from him. "I'm being forthright," she countered. "Something you obviously know very little about!"

Her accusation stung, but he didn't argue the point.

With a moan of frustration, Shelley threaded her hands through her hair. "I can't believe I'm in the same situation all over again!" She shook her head, looking even more flummoxed. "Just with a different man."

Colt grimaced. Now he was the one getting really ticked off. "Tell me you're not comparing me to Tully." Because, by heaven, if she was...

Shelley advanced on him, not stopping until they were nose to nose. "He used to say the reason he didn't tell me things was because he didn't want to worry me, either."

Colt folded his arms in front of him. "We're not the same," he reminded her flatly.

She stabbed a finger at his chest. "Aren't you?" She shook her head in wordless remonstration, bitterness and hurt tightening the contours of her soft lips. "I'm not going to be with someone who deliberately deceives me, no matter what the excuse!"

Gut tightening, Colt recognized the walls around her heart. "What are you saying?" he asked.

"Exactly what you think." Her tone steely with resolve, she slayed him with a glance. "You and I are finished, Colt. I don't ever want to see or speak to you again."

Chapter 15

"I thought you'd be happier," Liz told Shelley Tuesday afternoon. "The bank not only accepted Mr. and Mrs. Laffer's prompt reimbursement of their son's debt and all associated fees, they've deeded the house back to you, effective immediately." She handed over the key. "You can move back in today if you like."

Except that would mean getting the stuff out of Colt's garage. And that, in turn, would mean talking to him without breaking down in tears.

Misunderstanding the reason for her melancholy, Liz continued, "Charges against Tully were dropped, and he has been released. So you no longer have that weighing on you."

Shelley nodded. Maybe it was foolish, but she had never wanted to see her ex-husband in jail. She had just wanted the wrong corrected, and that had happened, thanks to the quick private settlement Liz and the other attorneys had worked out.

"And, last but not least, in exchange for you voluntarily dropping the charges and waiving all rights to future litigation on the matter, a cashier's check arrived today from your ex-in-laws to help with all your moving and legal expenses." Liz rocked back in her chair. "So you can take that right over to the bank and deposit it. And call it a day on the whole matter."

Shelley smiled in relief. "I am happy about all of that." It had been the best possible solution to a very messy situation.

The attorney continued to study her. "Then…?"

Liz and Shelley had been friends long before Liz had become Shelley's attorney. Which made it easier for Shelley to confide, "Colt and I broke up. Again." And it hurt worse this time than the last, which was saying a lot.

A mixture of surprise and heartfelt compassion glimmered in Liz's eyes. "Why? You two looked so happy at Kendall and Gerry's wedding!"

"We were." Shelley slid the check into her purse, then fit the house key onto her key ring. "Until I found out everything that had been going on, anyway." Briefly, she explained about Investigator Adams's visit on Sunday afternoon.

Liz shook her head as if unable to believe it. "Ilyse Adams actually thought you slept with Colt in exchange for his help?"

Shelley nodded miserably. And that line of questioning had sparked an onslaught of uncertainty within her.

The only thing she knew for certain was that real lasting romantic love had never entered their conversation. Turning back to her friend, she reflected on a soft exhalation of breath. "It's all such a mess. I think all the drama lately may have just clouded our thinking and magnified our feelings into something that wasn't quite real..."

Liz made a skeptical face. She came around her desk, sat down in the other client chair and took Shelley's hand in hers. "I understand why you're hurt. Colt should have confided at least part of what was going on with you."

Shelley's throat felt tight. "I felt like such a fool." Here she'd thought they were so close. Only to find out...they weren't. Otherwise, Colt would have told her something.

"As for the rest..." Liz continued briskly. "Professionally, Colt really couldn't discuss the actual internal affairs investigation, without getting into more hot water than he was already in."

Shelley nodded, agreeing in retrospect about that much. She couldn't really blame him for trying to save his job.

Liz's brows knit together. "How did that investigation turn out, by the way?"

An answering worry spiraled through Shelley. "I don't know." Yet perversely she wished she did.

"He's still on mandatory 'vacation'?"

"Until tomorrow. Then he meets with the sheriff and Ilyse Adams to discuss Internal Affairs' findings."

Silence fell.

Eventually, Liz blew out a breath and raked a hand through her hair. "You really compared him to Tully?"

Misery engulfed her anew. "I really did."

"Do you still think that way?"

Not sure what she felt—except happy to be back in her Laramie home again, Shelley shrugged. It was odd how much Colt had become part of her big picture in such a short time. Even more curious, how reluctant she was to actually let him go emotionally. And yet…there were some very heavy issues still standing in their way.

"I don't like being blindsided." She'd had enough of that in the past. "And Colt is so good at putting on a poker face."

"That's part of his job as a cop, keeping his feelings to himself."

Her melancholy deepened. "I know."

Liz arched a brow. "Then what else is bothering you?"

Helplessness sweeping over her, Shelley lifted her hands in frustration. "That's just it. I don't know exactly why I can't find it in my heart to forgive him."

Never one to suffer fools, Liz stood. "Then I expect you better figure it out before you and Colt lose the best thing that's ever happened to either of you."

"You sure it's okay that we do this without you being around?" Rio asked.

Colt nodded at the three off-duty deputies who had volunteered to help Shelley move her stuff out of his garage and back down the street. "I think she'd prefer it that way, given the fact she never wants to see or speak to me again."

"She didn't mean it."

Colt grimaced, recalling the look she'd given him before she left. "Oh, I think she did."

Rio slapped him on the back. "You're missing a great opportunity."

"Yeah, you could show her your rippling muscles," Sam teased. "Remind her how much her little boy adores you. Could thaw the ice a little."

Given how much he still wanted Shelley, Colt hoped the ice would remain intact. It was the only thing that would alleviate his heartache. He held up a silencing palm. "Look, it was never going to work. I should have known all along that she was going to dump me at the first misstep, and the fact is, I make a lot of missteps." Colt concluded grimly, "So it's for the best."

Rio scoffed. "If that were the case, you wouldn't be looking so brokenhearted."

Colt fished his keys out of his pocket. "I got over losing her once. I'll get over it again. The difference is, this time I won't give her another chance to show me the door." *And stomp all over my heart.*

His three friends sighed. Exchanged looks. Said nothing more.

"And don't blame her," Colt warned over his shoulder as he bypassed the U-Haul van sitting in the driveway, and headed for his pickup truck at the curb. "It's not her fault. It's mine." *I'm the one who can't get my life together. I'm the one who can't stop thinking about a woman who wants nothing to do with me.*

Fortunately, Colt had a lot of things to do that morning to keep from obsessing over Shelley.

His first stop was a meeting in Ben Shepherd's office with the sheriff and Investigator Ilyse Adams, where Colt quickly learned the consequences of his actions of late—a ten-day suspension without pay, and a red flag in his file.

"We're counting the seven vacation days you've already taken as part of the suspension," the sheriff told

Colt, "so you'll be getting that time off back. Meanwhile, your salary will be docked accordingly."

Colt nodded. Given what he'd done, it all seemed more than fair.

"The larger question is," Ben continued, "what do you want to do next?"

Besides find a way to turn back the clock and permanently mend things with Shelley? To reverse the hurt he'd laid on her?

Ilyse Adams warned, "If you go back on patrol, you'll be expected to follow every rule and regulation, and administer the law with an evenhandedness and lack of sentimentality that has been lacking in your previous law enforcement service."

Colt had no doubt they'd both be watching his every move. Although even that wasn't as disturbing a prospect as he had expected it to be.

"On the other hand, if you're willing to try something a little different, something more suited to your personality," his boss continued, "we think we might have just the role for you…"

Colt talked with the sheriff and Investigator Adams about the pros and cons of their proposal. He then promised to give them an answer the following day, but in his heart, he already knew what he was going to do.

From the sheriff's station, Colt went to check in on Mr. Zellecky, who had been released from the hospital a few days earlier. The older gentleman ushered Colt into his home. A quick look around proved that Mr. Zellecky wasn't anywhere near the homemaker his ailing wife had been. The house showed weeks of neglect—and Mr. Zellecky didn't seem to be faring much better. His face and arms remained bruised from the fall. Stitches lined his forehead. "How are you feeling?" Colt asked, empathy welling within him. "Is there anything you need? Anything I can do for you?"

Mr. Zellecky removed a stack of newspapers and magazines from the sofa, and indicated Colt should take a seat. "Can you reverse the hands of time? Wipe out all my recent tomfoolery and Nellie's stroke?"

Colt shook his head. "But I can arrange to give you a ride to the hospital whenever you need one."

"Don't want me walking there in the summer heat?"

Colt squinted. "Our EMS crews are busy enough, don't you think?"

Mr. Zellecky smiled ruefully. "Yeah, I suppose that wasn't such a good idea."

"Why did you set off like that?" Prior to the last month or so, the older gentleman had always seemed like such a sensible guy.

"Nellie called me from the rehab unit over at the hospital. She was crying and she said she needed to see me." He shrugged his thin shoulders offhandedly. "And I can't drive anymore, so..."

"You could have called your daughter," Colt reminded him. "Or one of the neighbors."

"They all have jobs. Besides, I've leaned on them enough. And since the closest taxi service is in San Angelo..."

Which was, Colt knew, a good forty-five minutes away.

"Walking that day seemed like the best option. Until I collapsed in the heat, anyway."

A stubborn silence followed. Mr. Zellecky settled heavily in his worn recliner. "Let me tell you something, son. Getting older really sucks."

Colt refused the invitation to the pity party. "A lot of things suck," he returned evenly. *Like losing Shelley...* It didn't mean Mr. Zellecky had to be careless with his life. It didn't mean either of them should just give up.

The older gentleman eyed him. "Do you know what it is to be so in love with a woman you can't imagine a life without her?"

Colt was so damn lovesick he was beginning to think he might.

Mr. Zellecky rushed on, not giving Colt a chance to respond. "Well, that's how I feel about my Nellie. All I've ever really wanted in life was to keep her and my daughter safe and happy, and now I can't even get to the hospital when my wife says she needs to see me. Unless I'm in an ambulance...which probably isn't the right way to go about it."

Colt chuckled at Mr. Zellecky's wry, self-deprecating joke, then said seriously, "I understand you wanting to do what you want and need to do, when and how you see fit."

Mr. Zellecky's eyes narrowed. "I figured you would, a maverick like you."

"I also understand there has to be a better way to solve all our problems than what you or I have demonstrated thus far."

Interest lit his faded eyes. "You think?"

"I do." Colt leaned forward, hands clasped between his knees. "And I'll find it."

"Up, Momma! Swing! Up!"

"I know, honey, I'm working on it," Shelley told her son. Unfortunately, the wooden swing and the chains that supported it were too heavy for her to lift on her own—and the ceiling hooks too high for her to reach—so she'd had to get out the ladder and try to attach one side at a time.

"Want. Swing! Now!" Austin stamped his little foot, from his vantage point ten feet away.

"We'll get there," Shelley promised, sighing as she unhooked the unevenly hung swing yet again and set about counting links. More carefully this time.

From behind her, she heard footsteps, then a low, achingly familiar voice. "Need a hand?"

Tears stung her eyes. Deliberately, she pushed them back. "Colt."

He trod slowly closer. In worn jeans and an untucked pale blue button-up that brought out the intense dark blue of his eyes, he looked sexy and ready for action. Bedroom action.

A shimmer of desire swept through her, more intense than any longing she had ever felt. Followed swiftly by an even more potent joy. And on top of all that, palpable tension.

Oblivious to the welter of confused feelings roaring through her, he hooked his hands in the pockets of his jeans and rocked back on his heels. "It's the neighborly thing to do. Then again—" his eyes latched on hers, held, almost imploring this time "—if you'd prefer not to ever speak to or see me again…"

Shelley flushed as her words came back to haunt her. She swallowed before he could go on. "I might have been a little hasty, given we live on the same street, and all…."

Colt nodded. "That, we do," he drawled.

The question was, Shelley thought, what else was going to be possible? Would it be as much as she had begun to privately hope? Before she could find out, her son dropped his toy truck where he stood, ran to Colt and held out his arms, begging to be picked up.

"Deppity!" Austin cried.

Colt picked him up and cradled him as tenderly as any father. "Hey there, little fella."

Shelley's heart melted.

"Buddy!" Austin shouted happily again.

Buddy loped arthritically up the steps to stand behind Colt. Tail wagging, he looked up at Shelley's son, who squirmed to be put down.

Colt complied. "Buddy!" Austin said again, wrapping his arms about the dog's neck. Buddy wagged all the more. "See truck!" Small hand on the pet's shoulder, Austin ushered him over to his basket of toys.

Colt returned his attention to the task she'd been attempting. Two minutes later, the swing was up, sturdy as ever. "Test it out. Make sure it's the right height for you."

Shelley sat down. Found it to be just a tad high. Her feet barely touched the floor. She stood again, moved so he could adjust it. "Actually, I'm glad you came by." Acutely aware of how good he smelled and looked, she watched him lower it by two links. "I've been wanting to talk to you. I'm sorry about everything I said the other day…"

He motioned for her to test it again. "You had a right to be hurt and angry."

Shelley sat and found the height to be absolutely perfect. "But no right to break up with you again."

He stood with his back to the post, arms folded. "Why did you?"

It was so complicated she barely knew where to

begin. Determined to try, Shelley drew a deep breath. "You know, I said that I had forgiven you for everything that happened in the past. And I really thought I had."

He studied her thoughtfully. "But that wasn't true."

"I think there was a part of me that kept waiting for you to hurt me again."

"So when it happened—"

Shelley moved to stand beside him. "I told myself it was over."

He looked down at her, his expression implacable. "And is it?"

Shelley's pulse raced. She knew she was going to have to risk everything in order to get the only thing that would make her truly happy. "The truth is, in all this time, my feelings for you have never changed. You've always had my heart."

To her disappointment, Colt looked unconvinced. "And yet you married someone else," he said very softly.

"On the rebound. Hoping he would help me forget you. And while he distracted me plenty with his love of adventure and his incessant problems, he was never able to make me forget about you."

Aware he was listening intently, she drew another deep breath. "My feelings for you are the reason why my marriage never worked, why I never wanted to look too hard at my life—or face up to my responsibilities. Because I knew if I did that," she finished brokenly, "my heart would eventually lead me back home, to Laramie, where you still were."

Colt's expression gentled. He took her hand in his and tugged her toward him. "I really regretted the way things ended, too. Although you were right to be angry with me." He sighed as he tightened his fingers on hers. "I should have told you everything that was going on."

Shelley's heart pounded. "Why didn't you?"

Colt sobered. He drew her toward the swing and sat beside her. "At the time, I thought I had good reason. You wouldn't let me help you outright by buying the house, so I helped you *unofficially* by keeping my mouth shut and letting the rumors about the property stand."

Shelley could see how difficult this had been for him to admit.

Colt stretched his arm along the back of the swing. His muscular thigh pressed against hers. "I told myself I was helping everyone, that no one was going to be happy if they bought your home while you were still trying to get it back."

"Well, that is true." Shelley settled into the curve of his body. "It would have been a real mess if someone else had bought it before Tully's parents came in and remedied the situation."

Colt nodded, his expression rueful. "But on another level, what I did still wasn't right. I didn't feel any better standing down in that situation than I did when I was unable to help you directly."

Another silence fell. "What about the Internal Affairs inquiry? Aside from the fact you were forbidden to make it public knowledge, why didn't you tell me at least some of that?" She was pretty sure he could have, if he'd wanted to.

Colt squinted. "I told myself I didn't want you to feel bad—even inadvertently—because my attempts to help you and Austin were at the center of my difficulty."

"And what do you know now?" Shelley asked, warming to his honesty.

"That it was really because I was trying to control the outcome of whatever happened in my sphere. The same way I thought if I didn't arrest the three teenagers I'd keep them from tarnishing their permanent records. Or by not citing Mr. Zellecky for his first fender bender with the stop sign, he'd be able to keep his license." Colt sighed, his frustration and regret evident. "I realize now that in addition to enforcing the laws, I was trying to keep people safe from all harm. But curtailing other people's recklessness or covering up their mistakes is not my responsibility as a law officer."

Because that, Shelley knew, was like playing God. "That's a pretty big admission."

He nodded, acknowledging that he'd needed to search his soul as much as she had needed to search hers—if they were ever to become better people. He took her hand in his. "As much as I have always liked helping others, it's always bothered me to have to arrest someone I know if there are extenuating circumstances. Or, as you put it, I'm really not the hall monitor type."

She winced at the words she previously used.

She needn't have worried; he'd taken no offense. Instead, he seemed almost happy about it.

"The truth is," he continued, "it wasn't until you came back that I began to understand why everything has been so wrong for so long." He paused, shook his head in obvious regret. "I've lived in the moment all my life. And not really allowed myself to really consider the consequences of my actions."

Shelley searched his face. "And everything that has

happened the past few weeks has forced you to look at that." Just as her circumstances had forced her to take a hard look at her own shortcomings and the responsibility she bore.

Colt nodded in acknowledgment."Ultimately, I realized that as much as I love being a cop, I love helping people more. Which is why I'm taking on a new position with the sheriff's department as director of Community Outreach. My task will be to help citizens who are in trouble, or headed there, find solutions that will keep them from further harm." He smiled with pride. "The first two initiatives are going to involve wayward teens and senior citizens who have lost their driving privileges."

"Oh, Colt. That's really wonderful!" It was the perfect fit for his generosity and gallantry.

Beaming, he looked deep into her eyes. "But that's only a small part of the changes I'm making to my life."

Shelley's heart leaped.

"It's not just my professional life that needs work," he told her in a low, rusty-sounding voice. "I've got to repair the damage I've done in my personal life, too. And I'm going to start by admitting the mistakes I've made where you're concerned."

This sounded promising, Shelley thought as Colt shifted her onto his lap. "Because the truth is," he continued softly, "it was wrong of me to assume you needed me to rescue you. And even more wrong encouraging you to pick up where we left off and jump into bed with me. Without considering how not working out our past problems would affect our ability to forge a strong, enduring relationship."

Shelley snuggled closer, her spirits soaring. "Because if we had done that...."

"If we'd been really honest with each other, and I'd told you how much you really mean to me," he said thickly.

She met his eyes, knowing she had come home, at long last, to him. "Or you to me."

"Then I would have known you would stick with me, despite all my shortcomings."

"You're right about that." There would have been no misunderstandings, no separation. Tears misted in her eyes. "And I do love you, Colt, so very much. I think I always have."

"I love you, too, Shelley," he told her huskily, his happiness mirroring her own. "So very much." He paused to kiss her again, and then looked deeply into her eyes. "Which is why I want us to take a step back and take our time getting to know each other again. Because this time, Shelley, I don't want to make any mistakes." He wrapped his arms around her and kissed her until she kissed him back with all her heart.

"This time," he promised her tenderly, "I want us to build something that will last the rest of our lives."

Epilogue

One year later...

"Are you sure you know what to do?" Patricia Wilson asked Colt as he and his groomsmen stood in the anteroom of the Laramie Community Chapel.

Colt winked at the wedding planner, aware he'd never been more sure of anything in his life. He drawled, "After two rehearsals, I think Shelley and I've both got it down pat."

Patricia frowned at his boutonniere. "You only had one rehearsal as bride and groom. In the other you were standing in for Kendall and Gerry." Her eyes narrowed in disapproval. "And your bow tie is crooked."

"I've got it," a soft, feminine voice insisted.

Everyone turned to see Shelley gliding in the door. Patricia gasped in dismay. "Shelley! For heaven's sake!" She threw up her hands so suddenly she nearly dropped her clipboard. "What are you *doing* here?"

Shelley sashayed toward Colt, a vision in white satin and lace, a tiara perched on her upswept auburn hair. "I want a word with my groom."

Patricia appeared ready to faint. "But Colt's not supposed to see you until you walk down the aisle!"

Shelley beamed up at Colt, an alluring glint of mischief sparkling in her pretty eyes. "I think we'll both survive the faux pas." Determined as ever, Shelley turned him in the direction she wanted him to go. "We'll be right back." Slipping her hand in his, she tugged him into the choir room across the hall.

"Where are Austin and Buddy?" Colt asked.

Shelley shut the door firmly, a dazzling smile on her face. "With Liz and the other bridesmaids." She glided toward him again, in a drift of silk and incredibly feminine perfume, not stopping until she was just short of him. "And your bow tie really is crooked, Colt." Her hands came up to adjust it. "I think your boutonniere could use a little straightening, too."

Loving the way she took care of him, he waited until she had finished, then caught her hand and pressed it against his heart. "Damned if you aren't the most beautiful bride I've ever seen," he murmured reverently. To the point, he couldn't stop gazing at her. Couldn't stop wanting her. Would never ever stop cherishing her with all his heart and soul. He linked his arms about her waist, drew her as close as her poufy skirt would allow. "You take my breath away. You know that?"

Happiness sparkled in her smile. "I have an inkling." She rose on tiptoe, wreathed her arms about his neck, and pressed her lips to his. "Because you do the exact same thing to me, Colt McCabe."

Their lips met in the tenderest of kisses. "So what's this about?" he asked when they finally drew apart.

Her eyes turned misty with emotion. "I just wanted to make sure you knew how very much I love you."

Colt never tired of hearing her confess what was in her heart. "I do. And for the record, I love you like crazy, too."

They gazed into each other's eyes.

"This day has been a long time coming," Shelley whispered.

Colt caressed her cheek with his thumb. "With good reason. This time I wanted to do everything right."

"And we have."

They'd had a proper courtship, with tons of romance. And lots of time to plan for their big day.

Her dance classes were filled to capacity. Austin had grown into a fiercely affectionate and independent three-and-a-half-year-old. At thirteen, Buddy was defying the statistics and still going strong.

Even Colt's house had sold the first week on the market. There was literally nothing standing in their way of setting up housekeeping together, at long last.

Except one thing.

Colt kissed the top of her head. As reluctant as he was to let her go, he knew he had no choice. "You better head back to your place, otherwise we'll never get married today."

Shelley sighed, looking as contented as he felt. "You promise you'll be waiting for me when I come up the aisle?"

"I'll do you one better. I promise I'll be there the rest

of our lives." He bent his head and kissed her again, passionately this time.

Shelley slipped out of the room and circled around to the entrance of the church.

Colt and the groomsmen walked out to stand beside the minister. The music started.

Buddy and Austin marched up the aisle, side by side, looking adorable as all get-out.

The bridesmaids followed, one at a time.

Finally, it was Shelley's turn.

Just like a princess out of a fairy tale, she floated up the aisle, bouquet in hand, looking more radiant than he had ever seen her. As she came toward him, Colt took her hand. They stood in front of the minister, joyously said their vows. And stepped into the future as their life as husband and wife began.

* * * * *

SPECIAL EXCERPT FROM

An NYPD officer's widow becomes the target of
her husband's killer. Can her husband's best friend
and his K-9 partner keep her safe and take the
murderer down once and for all?

Read on for a sneak preview of
Sworn to Protect by Shirlee McCoy,
the exciting conclusion to the
True Blue K-9 Unit series, available
November 2019 from Love Inspired Suspense.

"Come in," Katie Jameson called, bracing herself for the
meeting with Dr. Ritter.

The door swung open and a man in a white lab coat
stepped in, holding her chart close to his face.

Only, he was not the doctor she was expecting.

Dr. Ritter was in his early sixties with salt-and-pepper
hair and enough extra weight to fill out his lab coat. The
doctor who was moving toward her had dark hair and a
muscular build. His scuffed shoes and baggy lab coat made
her wonder if he were a resident at the hospital where she
would be giving birth.

"Good morning," she said. She had been meeting
with Dr. Ritter since the beginning of the pregnancy. He
understood her feelings about the birth. Talking about the
fact that Jordan wouldn't be around for his daughter's birth,

her childhood, her life always brought her close to the tears she despised.

"Morning," he mumbled.

"Is Dr. Ritter running late?" she asked, uneasiness joining the unsettled feeling in the pit of her stomach.

"He won't be able to make it," the man said, lowering the charts and grinning.

She went cold with terror.

She knew the hazel eyes, the lopsided grin, the high forehead. "Martin," she stammered.

"Sorry it took me so long to get to you, sweetheart. I had to watch from a distance until I was certain we could be alone."

"Watch?"

"They wanted to keep me in the hospital, but our love is too strong to be denied. I escaped for you. For us." He lifted a hand, and if she had not jerked back, his fingers would have brushed her cheek.

He scowled. "Have they brainwashed you? Have they turned you against me?"

"You did that yourself when you murdered my husband," she responded.

Don't miss
Sworn to Protect *by Shirlee McCoy,*
available November 2019 wherever
Love Inspired® *Suspense books and ebooks are sold.*

www.LoveInspired.com

Looking for more satisfying love stories
with community and family at their core?

Check out **Harlequin® Special Edition**
and **Love Inspired®** books!

New books available every month!

CONNECT WITH US AT:

Facebook.com/groups/HarlequinConnection

**ROMANCE WHEN
YOU NEED IT**

HFGENRE2018

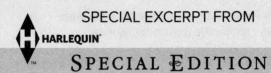
"Three weeks?" she repeated. "I might not remember
anything about myself for three weeks?"

Dr. Addison gave her a reassuring smile. "Could be
sooner. But we'll run some tests, and based on how well
you're doing now, I don't see any reason why you can't
be discharged later today."

Discharged where? Where did she live?

With your husband, she reminded herself.

She bolted upright again, her gaze moving to Sawyer,
who pocketed his phone and came back over, sitting
down and taking her hand in both of his. "Do I—do we—
have children?" she asked him. She couldn't forget her
own children. She couldn't.

"No," he said, glancing away for a moment. "Your
parents and Jenna will be here in fifteen minutes," he

said. "They're ecstatic you're awake. I let them know you might not remember them straightaway."

"Jenna?" she asked.

"Your twin sister. You're very close. To your parents, too. Your family is incredible—very warm and loving."

That was good.

She took a deep breath and looked at her hand in his. Her left hand. She wasn't wearing a wedding ring. He wore one, though—a gold band. So where was hers?

"Why aren't I wearing a wedding ring?" she asked.

His expression changed on a dime. He looked at her, then down at his feet. Dark brown cowboy boots.

Uh-oh, she thought. *He doesn't want to tell me. What is that about?*

Two orderlies came in just then, and Dr. Addison let Maddie know it was time for her CT scan, and that by the time she was done, her family would probably be here.

"I'll be waiting right here," Sawyer said, gently cupping his hand to her cheek.

As the orderlies wheeled her toward the door, she realized she missed Sawyer—looking at him, talking to him, her hand in his, his hand on her face. That had to be a good sign, right?

Even if she wasn't wearing her ring.

Don't miss
A Wyoming Christmas to Remember
by Melissa Senate,
available November 2019 wherever
Harlequin® Special Edition books and ebooks are sold.

www.Harlequin.com

Love Harlequin romance?

DISCOVER.

Be the first to find out about promotions, news and exclusive content!

Facebook.com/HarlequinBooks

Twitter.com/HarlequinBooks

Instagram.com/HarlequinBooks

Pinterest.com/HarlequinBooks

ReaderService.com

EXPLORE.

Sign up for the Harlequin e-newsletter and download a free book from any series at **TryHarlequin.com.**

CONNECT.

Join our Harlequin community to share your thoughts and connect with other romance readers!
Facebook.com/groups/HarlequinConnection

HARLEQUIN®

**ROMANCE WHEN
YOU NEED IT**

HSOCIAL2018